Mary

Such for seeing you this year! —

Enjoy!

Patty

A NOVEL

Patty Dickson

A FINE HOW DO YOU DO
A NOVEL

Copyright © 2016 Patricia Dickson Tappan.

Front cover photo of Ambleside Harbour by Richard Greenstein
Photos of Ambleside and the author by Michelle Lavergne-Colberg
Illustrations used by permission of the artist, Sharon Hardy.
Automobile photo used by permission of exoticclassics.com.
All the characters in this book and their circumstances are fictional creations.

All rights reserved. No part of this book may be used or reproduced by any means, graphic, electronic, or mechanical, including photocopying, recording, taping or by any information storage retrieval system without the written permission of the author except in the case of brief quotations embodied in critical articles and reviews.

iUniverse books may be ordered through booksellers or by contacting:

iUniverse
1663 Liberty Drive
Bloomington, IN 47403
www.iuniverse.com
1-800-Authors (1-800-288-4677)

Because of the dynamic nature of the Internet, any web addresses or links contained in this book may have changed since publication and may no longer be valid. The views expressed in this work are solely those of the author and do not necessarily reflect the views of the publisher, and the publisher hereby disclaims any responsibility for them.

ISBN: 978-1-4917-9822-5 (sc)
ISBN: 978-1-4917-9821-8 (e)

Library of Congress Control Number: 2016908297

Print information available on the last page.

iUniverse rev. date: 06/06/2016

Contents

Acknowledgments xi
Cast of Major Characters.. xiii
Chapter One 1
Chapter Two 5
Chapter Three 8
Chapter Four... 13
Chapter Five.. 16
Chapter Six 18
Chapter Seven 23
Chapter Eight 27
Chapter Nine 30
Chapter Ten 32
Chapter Eleven.. 36
Chapter Twelve 41
Chapter Thirteen 46
Chapter Fourteen 49
Chapter Fifteen 52
Chapter Sixteen... 57
Chapter Seventeen... 61
Chapter Eighteen 68
Chapter Nineteen... 73
Chapter Twenty... 75

Chapter Twenty-One.. 78
Chapter Twenty-Two... 86
Chapter Twenty-Three 89
Chapter Twenty-Four 93
Chapter Twenty-Five 99
Chapter Twenty-Six.. 102
Chapter Twenty-Seven.. 107
Chapter Twenty-Eight 112
Chapter Twenty-Nine.. 118
Chapter Thirty 123
Chapter Thirty-One.. 127
Chapter Thirty-Two 129
Chapter Thirty-Three.. 135
Chapter Thirty-Four 138
Chapter Thirty- Five 143
Chapter Thirty-Six.. 148
Chapter Thirty-Seven.. 152
Chapter Thirty-Eight 157
Chapter Thirty-Nine... 162
Chapter Forty.. 171
Chapter Forty-One 176
Chapter Forty-Two... 185
Chapter Forty-Three 191
Chapter Forty-Four 199
Chapter Forty-Five 204
Chapter Forty-Six... 207
Chapter Forty-Seven 212
Chapter Forty-Eight 215
Chapter Forty-Nine.. 223
Chapter Fifty... 226

Chapter Fifty-One	229
Chapter Fifty-Two	234
Chapter Fifty-Three	238
Chapter Fifty-Four	245
Chapter Fifty-Five	249
Chapter Fifty-Six	254
Chapter Fifty-Seven	259
Chapter Fifty-Eight	267
Chapter Fifty-Nine	277
Chapter Sixty	282
Chapter Sixty-One	286
Chapter Sixty-Two	290
Chapter Sixty-Three	298
Chapter Sixty-Four	305
Chapter Sixty-Five	309
Chapter Sixty-Six	314
Chapter Sixty-Seven	322
Chapter Sixty-Eight	330
Chapter Sixty-Nine	337
Chapter Seventy	346

"A FINE HOW DO YOU DO"
IS
LOVINGLY DEDICATED
TO
MISS ELSIE STOUGAARD
OF
BOSTON,
MY FIRST CAREGIVER,
MY LIFELONG AUNT ELSIE

"AUNT ELSIE, YOU ONLY HAVE ONE EARRING ON,"
SAID PATTY AT AGE 11

"MY DEAREST PATTY, IT DOES NOT MATTER. I HAVE
A HAT ON
AND ONE IS NOT PROPERLY DRESSED
UNLESS WEARING A HAT.
THE EARRING WILL TURN UP OR NOT."

Acknowledgments

My appreciation goes to all my wonderful new friends on Hilton Head Island and to all my dear old buddies scattered here and there, for their support and enthusiasm for "A FINE HOW DO YOU DO."

- Thank you to my son, Thomas Dickson Edgar, for your support and critiques.
- Thank you to our dearest family friend, Michelle Lavergne-Colberg, for so many wonderful memories and outrageous giggles together over the past 30 years! I greatly appreciate all your support and encouragement with the book.
- Thank you to Rosanne Ball for your computer expertise.
- Thank you to Alex Cruden, my editor, who brought the book to its final form.
- Thank you to Sharon Hardy for the hat sketches throughout the book.
- Thank you to Richard and Irene Greenstein for the cover photo of Ambleside, England.
- Thank you to all the fictitious characters in "A FINE HOW DO YOU DO" who took it upon themselves to come alive and tell their stories. I hope we all meet again.

* * *

Cast of Major Characters

Alma Boeld	Lady of the house in Ambleside, England
Alfred Boeld	(Freddie), brother of Alma
Margaret Boeld	Alfred's wife
Eric Sanders	Weatherman for the newspaper in Altoona, Pa.
Martha Sanders	Eric's wife
Gail	Daughter of Eric and Martha
Norman	Husband of Gail
Norma	Daughter of Gail and Norman
George	Eric's boss at the newspaper
Louise Smythe	Ex-wife of Tony; mother of Millicent and Suzanne
Millicent Smythe	Elder daughter of Louise and Tony
Suzanne Smythe	Younger daughter of Louise and Tony
Tony Smythe	Ex-husband of Louise; father of Millicent and Suzanne
Nelson	(Pinky), Alma's chauffeur
Bessie and Bertha	Maids at Alma's home
Elizabeth	Old friend of Alma
Bernard	Old friend of Alma

All the world's a stage,
And all the men and women merely players;
They have their exits and their entrances,
And one man in his time plays many parts,
His acts being seven ages.
--William Shakespeare

Chapter One

Eric settled into his comfortable seat on the coach train to England's Lake District, content to be alone in the compartment. He'd written a week's worth of daily weather forecasts in advance for *The Altoona Daily News* and mailed them to his boss, George, from the airport in Pittsburgh. He had withdrawn all his available cash and purchased a one-way airline ticket to Heathrow. Upon arrival in London he bought a tweed cap, which immediately gave him a newfound sense of identity. He was quite pleased with his accomplishments. Now, feeling tired, he pulled his new cap down over his eyes and drifted off.

Eric was awakened by a large hatbox tumbling down upon him. He heard the words "Pardon, Monsieur," spoken by an elderly woman with a very deep voice. Eric adjusted his cap and gazed into the most beautiful blue eyes he had ever seen. His reverie was then disturbed as a lady with two children entered the compartment. They were followed by the conductor saying, "Tickets please." Eric sat upright and presented his ticket. After some fumbling, the elderly lady, who was wearing an extraordinary large blue hat, found her ticket and became settled with her small dog on her lap. The lady with the two children presented her tickets. Eric pulled his cap down over his eyes and pretended to be asleep. The train departed from the station and was on a smooth track and all was calm in the coach car. Eric raised his cap a bit to look out the window. The shadows were creeping in, which made the scenery look like a lovely painting.

The elderly lady with the beautiful eyes was going through her carrying bag and presented a bottle of Dubonnet. "It is well past tea time, shall we share a little of my Dubonnet and get to know one another? I am Madame Alma Boeld and I live in Ambleside." She poured herself a traveling cup of Dubonnet and one for Eric. She did not include the lady with two children in conversation nor offer her any Dubonnet. "Now, my dear man, what is your name and are you a tourist visiting our lovely Lake District?"

"Well, you could say that. My name is Eric and I am from Altoona."

"And what do you do in Atlanta?"

"No, not Atlanta, Altoona. I am a newspaper weatherman," explained Eric.

"Oh, how dreadfully dreary. Cheers to you my dear fellow and may your visit here be more interesting than reporting the weather," said Alma as she lifted her cup, toasting Eric. "Where are staying once you get where you are going, and where ARE you going?"

"I'm getting off at Oxenholme and hope to find a little inn."

"Nonsense, Edward, this is the tourist season and every place is booked for months ahead."

"My name is Eric not Edward."

"Of course it is, you silly fellow," said Alma as she poured a bit more Dubonnet into her traveling cup and refilled Eric's. The lady with the two children was napping and the two girls were quietly giggling with their hands over their faces. The older child decided to speak up. "I had my twelfth birthday party in London today with my Daddy who lives there now. He used to live with us. He has a maid who needs new clothes and I told Daddy that her clothes were too small for her. We had a super party with a huge cake and a clown who did magic tricks."

"How exciting. And how old are you now?" asked Eric.

"I just told you that I am twelve now. And how old are you?"

"I was 65 last week, but I did not have a party," replied Eric.

"Oh my, this is such a cumbersome conversation," sighed Alma. "Edward, my dear fellow, would you care to come with me and my driver, Nelson? You are most welcome to stay at my home in Ambleside until you move on."

"My name is Eric, and I think I might like to do that if I won't be an inconvenience."

"Oh, for the sake of heaven, life can be one big inconvenience from time to time. That is why new experiences are always so welcome. It is all settled then," announced Alma.

Eric was overwhelmed and a bit nervous, but smiled and thought his adventure was going particularly well. He was concerned about his clothes, as he had packed only three sporty shirts and two pair of old trousers. He had brought his father's gold pocket watch and the gold cufflinks left to him in the will, which he planned on selling if his money ran out. He thought that Alma might have a fancy house and he would need some nicer clothes. However, he wanted to hang on to the watch and cufflinks in case he needed the money later on. Well, he thought, he would just spend the night and then move on and get a little job. Eric had read that now, after the recession of 1992, employment was picking up in England.

"Oh look at the dog!" screeched the younger girl. "She has wee'd all over the floor and my Mary-Janes are getting all wet." The older girl laughed and said, "Look, it is like a dancing puddle, back and forthing." Alma, who had been catnapping, was awakened by the girls' voices and dropped her handkerchief in the puddle. "Oh, Edward dear," she said, "do scramble quickly and fetch a mop. Sophie dear, come back to Mummy's lap." Eric and the dog complied. The older girl leaned over to pick up Alma's hankie from the puddle but Alma raised her hand and said, "No, no. There are many more where that one came from, so please, dear child, do not disturb it."

A few minutes later the train pulled into the Oxenholme station, which served Ambleside and other Lake Windermere towns. Passengers descended the steps, landing safely on the platform, except for Eric, who was nowhere in sight. "Well, this is a fine how do you do," muttered Alma while gathering up her hatbox.

Chapter Two

Nelson and Alma were looking for Eric when they saw two porters holding him upright. Apparently Eric had tripped over the mop and stumbled again while stepping off the coach train. "Please get in the car, Edward. We will take care of all this at home," Alma said with authority. Nelson helped Eric into the car. Eric was not seriously injured but was thoroughly uncomfortable.

As Nelson slowly drove up the darkened driveway, Eric could surmise that this was a most presentable home. There were beautiful old trees, shadows everywhere and a soothing tranquility about the surroundings. Eric was helped upstairs by Nelson and two nice ladies, Bessie and Bertha, who were wearing starched uniforms. Eric thought they were nurses. He was settled into a beautiful bedroom with a large bed and several open windows. He thought to himself that he must be dreaming, except his right knee was most painful now. The nice ladies brought ice for his knee and some aspirin and, before he knew it, he was asleep.

Eric awoke in the night and realized that he had left his suitcase on the train along with his new tweed cap and, more importantly, the cufflinks and gold watch that were in his suitcase. He screamed for help and the nice ladies appeared in their nightdresses and tried to soothe him. Eric was gasping for breath and trying to get out of bed, but the two nice ladies told him that they had noticed he had no luggage and had immediately called the next station and all his belongings would be on the return train. Nelson was already on his way to collect everything at the station. Eric gave a sigh of relief and felt sure that Martha was watching over him.

Alma appeared at Eric's bedside the next morning and tapped him on his shoulder. "How do you spell Eric, with a 'c' or a 'k'?" she asked. "I am Eric with a 'c'," he replied. "Very good. Your luggage has been retrieved, dear boy, and rests right here," said Alma, pointing to a luggage stand. Eric jumped out of bed and checked that all was in order. He gave a sigh of relief and returned to the comfortable bed. His knee felt much better.

The kind ladies with the starched uniforms appeared at noon with a plate of greens, soft-boiled eggs, a slice of ham on a biscuit, and a large cup of tea. Eric would have preferred coffee. He gobbled it all up and could not believe how comforting the fresh air was as it blew in the windows. He inhaled the lovely air, returned to the bed, fell asleep, and awoke hours later when he heard the clock striking in the hallway. He counted six strikes. Alma knocked on the door and asked, "Eric dear, are you ready for our little supper party?"

Eric was stunned and could not answer. "Eric are you there?" asked Alma as she burst through the doorway and ran over to the bed. She gave him a big hug and told him that Nelson had gone to the local haberdashery and purchased a proper outfit for supper. Alma told him that a few guests were expected at seven sharp and it would be a simple supper gathering.

Eric showered, dressed, and went downstairs to join the guests. He tried to communicate with the beautifully attired couples and felt very elegant in the trousers and blazer, but was ill at ease as everything was so strange and quite different from his life in Altoona. He wondered if Martha would know what to do. He glanced admiringly at the gold links on his shirt cuffs but was at a loss as to what to say to these elegant people.

Finally a lady came up to him and asked where he was from and if he liked it here. He told her that he was from Altoona and was just visiting for a few days. She said she was from Philadelphia and here on holiday with her niece. They smiled at each other, but did not exchange another word. Eric decided to wander into the hall and investigate the house.

When dinner was announced, he found himself seated next to a pretty woman who was an artist and painted in oils. Her husband painted also. She disclosed that they each had their own style and did not get along well. She asked Eric if he was married and he told her that he was very happily married to Martha who had remained in Altoona.

Ambleside, England

Chapter Three

Eric slept a good part of the next day and awoke in time for afternoon tea with Alma on the back terrace. The shadows on the lake were breathtaking and everything seemed to sparkle. Eric felt quite content. He thought about writing some more weather forecasts and wiring them to his boss, George. He anticipated no trouble in making them up, as he had lived in Altoona all his life and had predicted the daily weather easily for years.

Alma put down her teacup with a clink and said, "Eric dear, you seem to be deep in thoughts. I know nothing about you except that you reside in Atlanta. Is it in the southern part of your country where that dreadful Civil War took place?"

"No, Altoona is nothing like Atlanta. Atlanta is in Georgia and Altoona is in Pennsylvania. Nothing exciting happens in Altoona, but Martha and I have always been happy there. All our friends are there and we were all born in Altoona and no one has ever moved away. Even the weather is the same year after year. Oh, our daughter, Gail, married and moved away after the wedding."

"My, oh my, enough of this dreary news. I do get so weary of those who ramble on about unpleasantries. Now, my dear chap, when Nelson returns from the shop with a proper wardrobe, you must scamper upstairs. We will greet the guests this evening in the sitting room. I have invited a few close friends for your 'better than never' 65th surprise birthday celebration!" Alma smiled and stared her blue eyes directly at him. Eric almost fell off the wicker chair and immediately began to hiccup, which was his usual reaction to excitement.

"Oh, how wonderful to have a party," he managed. "Is it [hic] really just for me?"

"Of course it is, you silly goose. Do not imagine for a moment that any of us would announce our real age and then celebrate it. Oh, no, no, no," said Alma with a deep laugh.

"But how did you know my [hic] 65th birthday was last week?" asked Eric.

"My dear chap, you will find that absolutely nothing escapes me," Alma said as she rose from her chair and swept across the terrace with little Sophie at her heels.

Eric saw Nelson driving up and went out to meet him. He opened the car door to greet him and help with the packages. "This is most kind of you, Mr. Eric, but do not do this when Madame is here or any of her guests. You see, Mr. Eric, this is my job and I am paid for it, but thank you for the kind gesture."

"Oh, I am so sorry, I will never do it again. Please forgive me." Eric struggled to suppress his hiccups.

Nelson gathered large boxes from the car and motioned Eric to follow. They went up to Eric's bedroom and began unwrapping the boxes, revealing the most handsome jackets, trousers, shirts and ties. "Do I need all these [hic] handkerchiefs?" asked Eric. "They go in your breast pocket, not up your nose!" said Nelson. They both laughed and Eric felt they were becoming friends. His inner turmoil receded.

Eric appeared promptly at seven o'clock in the sitting room. He noticed a pretty woman sitting on the large footstool in front of the fire chatting with a rather plump woman and her husband. Eric walked over to them. "Greetings," said the gentleman. "You must be the birthday boy. Congrats, as we say here when we jump over the 80 mark," the gentleman said.

"How do you do, I am Eric and am sixty-five."

"Good for you, my lad. What brings you to our Lake District?" asked the gentleman.

"Well, it all happened so fast. I do not really know. I met Madame Alma Boeld on the coach train and I am her guest for a short while until my knee recovers." Another gentleman walked over and put his hand on Eric's shoulder. "I am Alfred, Alma's brother. She is always picking up strays, so we must keep an eye on her! Do you hunt, by chance?"

"No, I like the scenery here and the lake and all the twinklings in the water," said Eric. A bit of silence followed. The doorbell rang and four people arrived. Nelson took the summer shawls from the ladies and the men put their caps over the umbrellas in the stand. Everyone started talking at once and Eric wanted to disappear. Sophie came in and scouted for dropped pieces of hors d'oeuvre on the rugs. Eric began to pet her so as to appear busy. Alma glanced over and immediately summoned Eric to come and sit by her side. She put her arm around him and announced to the guests that they were new friends, and it was just pure fate that their paths should cross on the coach train and how lovely it was that the stars were in the right place in the sky, at the right time, to make the most of each passing day and never know what the next day will bring. Everyone clapped and declared "Yes! Yes!"

"Let us lift our glasses to our visiting American on his belated 65th birthday and wish him well on his journey," Alma toasted. Bertha came out, curtsied and announced that supper was ready to be served. Eric found his place card at the table and immediately put it in his pocket for a souvenir. Alma had seated Eric between herself and Elizabeth, who (Alma told him earlier) had lost her husband three years ago, gained at least fifty pounds and let her hair grow down her back. Eric noticed that she was sitting on her hair and offered to fix it but she smiled and shook her finger at him. They both began to giggle. A woman across from them stood and declared, "Alma neglected to introduce me, so my welcome to you, Eric. I am Margaret, Alfred's wife."

Eric stood up and saluted Margaret and said how nice it was to meet her. "Where are you from, Eric?" asked Margaret.

"I am from Altoona."

"Is that one of those countries near old Russia?" she asked.

"No, no. We are Americans and we like the English people," said Eric.

"Is it a long trip from Altoona to Ambleside?" Margaret inquired. Eric laughed, as he was reminded of a story he heard from his grandmother who heard it from her mother. "I will tell you a little story about Altoona," said Eric. "It goes like this. Many years ago a Chinese missionary came to Altoona from China to visit and one of our relatives asked him 'How did you get here? On the Pennsy?'"

No one laughed except the pastor whom Eric had met briefly. The pastor explained to the others: "You see, Eric's family lived in Altoona in America and the missionary was from China and there are a couple of oceans to cross. The people who live in Altoona call the Pennsylvania Railroad 'the Pennsy,' so that is the joke." Everyone looked bewildered. "That is a good one, Eric. I will remember that one!" said Alfred.

"Lovely fish, and such a nice summer wine," Elizabeth said as strings of her hair dangled in the pear salad. Bertha started to clear the table and Nelson, who was doubling as butler, came in with the birthday cake. Nelson tripped on the rug and the cake went flying. Eric jumped up and caught the plate with the cake still in place before it hit the floor. Everyone applauded and sang Happy Birthday to Eric. After the celebration, Eric started to help Nelson clear the table, but Nelson whacked him one with his apron and told him to stop.

Eric went into the hall where the guests were gathering their shawls and caps and thanking Alma for a lovely evening and wishing Eric a very prosperous year. Alma gave Eric a kiss on his cheek and retired to her bedroom. Eric went into the kitchen and sat down. Bessie and Bertha were busy washing the dishes. Nelson came in and sat down also. "Pinky, more coffee, m'lad?" asked Bertha. Nelson responded, "Yes, please." Eric was most confused as to why Bertha would address Nelson as Pinky, but he said nothing about it. They chatted a bit longer and Eric asked Nelson if he could ride with him into the village in the morning. Nelson nodded his head, excused himself and went to his apartment over the garage.

Chapter Four

"Does it often rain here?" asked Eric, as he and Alma were enjoying breakfast on the back terrace. "Not often, but often enough. I never keep watch over things I cannot control. Why do you ask?" said Alma.

"I am a weatherman, you know, at the daily newspaper in Altoona, and it is of some interest to me."

"Ah yes, of course it would be. Well, is there something special you would like to do today?" asked Alma.

"If you do not mind, I would like to go into the village and to the library."

"Very well, dear boy. There is a bicycle in the garage if you wish to use it, so ta-ta for now," said Alma with a deep laugh as she swept off into the drawing room with her silk dressing gown flowing behind her. Eric was becoming accustomed to Alma's deep laugh and theatrics and found it all most entertaining. They waved at each other and smiled.

Eric did not use the bicycle, as Nelson had agreed to drive him into the village. Eric would use the library's wire machine while Nelson picked up the vegetables and fruit. Eric had already drafted the Altoona daily forecasts for the coming week, which warned of highs around 87 degrees and suggested an umbrella in case of showers. *The Altoona Daily News* and George had been good to him over the years as he carried on the family tradition of being the weatherman for the paper. Altoona folks trusted him completely and liked the little puns he added from time to time.

Eric saw Nelson going toward the garage and went over to meet him. "Good morning, Nelson," he said. Nelson smiled and told Eric to get in the back seat. Nelson asked where he would like to go. They drove in silence and Nelson dropped Eric off at the library entrance. Eric turned and waved to Nelson but Nelson was looking at the road toward the open market.

Eric entered the library and was asked if he had a library card. He thought quickly and said that he was doing some business for Madame Alma Boeld and did not have a card of his own as yet. He was directed to the wire machine. He had never used such a machine before and found it quite intriguing. He succeeded in sending the weather report off to George.

Since Nelson was not to pick him up for another half hour he wandered among the book alleys. He noticed a fine-figured young woman with pretty legs and light brown hair stacking the shelves. He walked up to her and she turned. "Oh my, the vagabond from the train. Wonders never cease!" she said with surprise. Eric recognized her as well, smiled and said, "What a coincidence!"

"You are limping. Whatever happened to you?" she asked.

"Oh, I hurt my knee and stumbled a bit but feel just fine now. How are your girls?" Eric enquired.

"Oh, all is going as well as can be expected under the circumstances. They go to a sailing camp on the lake in the summer and I work here. It isn't proper the way it all turned out, but I am happy to be rid of him and the girls will survive. Money talks, so that is that!" she said with tears in her eyes.

Eric was shocked at all this sudden information and wondered how a young man could leave such a nice lady and two lovely daughters. "How shameful. Perhaps we could have tea or coffee one day when you are off work?" asked Eric.

"Well, not today, but tomorrow is my day off," she said, looking closely at him. "Perhaps you would enjoy a boat ride around the lake? I always feel serene and relaxed when I am on the water," she said with a sigh. "I should not have spouted off like that as I hardly know you. Please forgive me," she said with a weak smile. He looked at her face and could read her sadness and loss. "Yes, of course, I would enjoy being on a boat with you," he responded.

"There is a short Lake Windermere tour every 45 minutes or we can enjoy a full day out on the beautiful water starting at 10 o'clock. Have you been to Cumbria before?" she asked. "No, of course you haven't. So let's make a day of it and I will get tickets for the day cruise, and meet you here at the library at half past nine tomorrow."

Eric found his excitement growing. "By the way, what is your name?" he asked. "I am Louise Smythe and I know you are Eric, not Edward." They both laughed. Parting, they looked back at each other, waving. Nelson was parked in the car around the corner from the library and was most annoyed that Eric had kept him waiting.

Chapter Five

It was a humid afternoon in Altoona when Martha arrived home from visiting her daughter Gail, son-in-law Norman, and their daughter Norma in Akron, Ohio. She pulled the car into the carport and used her key to open the front door to her pleasant but modest home. She and Eric had lived here comfortably all their married life. "Hello, dear, I am home!" There was no answer, except from their old cat Stormie, who was meowing. "Eric, I am home. Where are you?" The house was totally silent except for Stormie, who continued meowing.

Martha put down her suitcase, looked around and let Stormie out the back door. The house was exactly as she left it. Eric had not watered the plants and they were very droopy and needed a drink. Martha decided to call *The Altoona Daily News* to see if Eric was still at work. "Oh, hello, George, this is Martha. May I speak to Eric please?"

"Where the hell have you two been for the past week? No one has been able to reach either of you. Did you go on vacation without telling anyone? We have all been sick with worry and pretty damn mad too! Eric mailed me his weather reports – from Pittsburgh! – but no personal message. What the hell is going on, Martha?" Martha sat still with her mouth hanging open, unable to speak. "Martha are you there?"

"Yes, I am here," she said, and hung up the phone.

Martha began to check around the house. All seemed normal except that Eric's small suitcase was missing. Then she almost fell to the floor in a faint when she noticed that his gold cufflinks and gold watch were not in his bureau. She called Gail and told her the situation and wondered if she had heard from Eric that day.

"Don't worry, Mom, Dad never goes anywhere. Surely he will turn up. He knows you were coming home today, right?" Martha could not speak or think what to do. She said good-bye and sat down in Eric's chair and began to weep.

The phone rang and Martha jumped up to answer. "Eric, is this you?"

"For God's sake, Martha, this is George again. What the hell is going on?" Martha knew what was going on and slammed down the phone. Eric had left her after 40 years of marriage. She just knew it and did not know what to do next. She didn't want anyone to know and she did not know what to say. Surely, if he had been in an accident someone would have notified her as she had left Gail's telephone number with the neighbors and on the fridge. She poured herself a tiny glass of brandy and started crying uncontrollably. She took the phone off the hook and screamed as loudly as she could. She began waving her arms all around and knocked Eric's picture off the mantle. She poured herself another glass of brandy and began to laugh hysterically. She turned on the old radio they purchased 28 years ago. It was the first purchase they made after they bought the house. She heard Uncle Bernie saying, "Have a nice evening and remember that God loves you. Keep your Bible handy and know that Uncle Bernie is always with you at 99.1 on your radio dial."

Martha threw her glass of brandy at the radio. "Shut up Uncle Bernie. Go fly a kite." She collapsed on the couch. The cat was out and so was Eric.

Chapter Six

Eric thanked Nelson for the ride back to Alma's house, but Nelson did not respond. As Eric entered the vestibule, he noticed Alma standing on a very high stool in the drawing room with two people under her skirts. Eric thought this was very odd and started to laugh, then suppressed that and ran up to Alma and asked if everything was alright and mentioning how wonderfully she was balancing herself.

"Of course everything is alright. I have always had excellent balance. The seamstresses are fitting my dresses for the summer parties where I must twirl properly, so do not annoy me right now." Eric giggled and went up to his room. He felt most comfortable here and liked Alma and wondered how long he could stay. Now that he had met Louise, all seemed to be going particularly well.

A knock on Eric's bedroom door at 6 p.m. awakened him. "Who is there?" asked Eric. It was Nelson. "Your dinner clothes are ready and Madame is expecting you for dinner at 7."

"Oh, thank you, Nelson." Eric opened his door to greet him, but Nelson had casually left the clothes on a hanger on the doorknob. Eric was confused why Nelson was not being more friendly. He liked Nelson and had thought he was a new friend. Eric brought the clothes into the bedroom. He remembered that the handkerchief belonged in the outside breast pocket of his jacket

A Fine How Do You Do

and that he should not blow his nose with it. A blue and white striped shirt was hanging under a blue jacket. He dressed himself with a new regard for his appearance and renewed confidence about himself. He decided to comb his hair forward a bit to hide his balding spot. He looked at himself in the mirror and wondered how this had all happened. It all seemed like a dream.

Alma was waiting at the table. "Good evening, Eric, sit down and tell me about your day."

"Just fine, thank you, and how was your day?" asked Eric, noticing that the table was set for two. Eric became nervous and wiped his nose with his dinner napkin. Alma's back straightened. "My days are numbered so I make the best of each one," she announced. "And what are your plans for tomorrow?"

Eric responded with pride, "I have no plans except that I met Louise at the library today and we will be spending her day off tomorrow together."

"And who is this Louise, Eric dear?"

"She is the lady from the train."

"What train?" asked Alma.

"From the train we all took together from London," Eric explained.

"Are you referring to the nursemaid with the two little girls?"

"Yes, but she is their mother. Her name is Louise Smythe," said Eric, still trying to cut the chicken leg loose. He knew he could not pick it up as he and Martha always did at their kitchen table in Altoona.

"Oh for the sake of heaven, Eric dear, that little brown wren will never amount to anything. Why would you want to be bothered with her?"

"I am not bothered, I am just going to meet her tomorrow and we shall take the boat ride around the lake," explained Eric. While he sawed at the chicken leg Alma had already connected the dots and realized exactly who this Louise Smythe must be. Working at the library with her ex-husband, Tony Smythe, living in London. It all fit together. She felt her heart stop for a moment as her napkin dropped to the floor. She called for Bessie and said, "Please tell Nelson that I shall skip dessert and go straight to my brother's house. I will meet Nelson at the car." Alma excused herself from the table as Eric was still trying to disconnect the meat of the chicken. He looked up and surprisingly found himself alone at the table.

Alma burst into Alfred's new country home and the front door slammed abruptly, almost catching her fingers. "Alfred, where are you? Your ridiculous door just about broke my fingers."

Alfred came running. "We have had a little trouble with that door. You know how it is with these bloody houses, it takes a bit for all to work properly. What is on your mind, Alma, you burst in like a typhoon!"

"I must speak with you privately," Alma whispered as Margaret came rushing into the vestibule. "What on earth is going on? One would think the sky was falling. Alma. You don't even have a shawl. What is this all about?" Margaret asked.

"Margaret dear, I must speak with my brother about some family matters. Will you please excuse us for a moment?" Alma took Alfred's arm, turning her back to Margaret.

Alma and Alfred went into the sitting room and Alma closed the door. "Freddie, Eric has met Louise and they are going on the boat ride around the lake tomorrow."

Alfred, attempting to light a pipe, looked totally confused and asked "How did they meet?"

"On the train from London. We all shared the compartment, just by chance."

"Whatever was she doing in London? Certainly not shopping. Did she have a meeting with Tony?" asked Alfred, still adjusting his pipe.

A Fine How Do You Do

"No, she brought the girls to his townhouse for the older girl's, whatever her name is, birthday celebration," said Alma. Alfred pondered for a moment. "How did Eric and Louise get together?" he asked.

"Apparently Eric bumped into her at the library, they became acquainted and now they have made plans to go on the Windermere boat ride tomorrow. What shall we do?" asked Alma, pounding her hand on the side table so sharply that the small lamp tipped over.

"Perhaps they will have a Titanic experience and both will be done in," said Alfred, with the unlit pipe in his mouth and picking up the lamp.

"Oh be serious, Freddie, and think of something,"

"Well, Alma dear," said Alfred, puffing on his unlit pipe. "Louise knows nothing about our financial association with Tony and so will not suspect anything out of the ordinary." He put down the pipe and patted the little canary in the cage.

"But what if Louise tells Eric that Tony has his own business in London with a partner from here and is making a lot of money and the partnership is called Smythe and Boeld?"

"Well, Eric may know that Louise's name is Smythe but he does not know that my last name is Boeld," said Alfred, resuming the attempt to light his pipe. Alma rolled her eyes and knocked over the lamp again, this time on purpose. "Oh, Freddie, you are so naive and stupid. Eric is staying in my home and he knows you are my brother and that our name is Boeld. What shall I do about you? You are too stupid to come in out of the rain."

Fruitlessly puffing on his empty pipe, Alfred ignored his sister's insults and her finger pointing at him and looked out the window. "Tony is quite brilliant and we all are receiving checks and all appears on the up and up, so do not worry. Tell Eric to move on," Alfred concluded.

"Yes, of course," said Alma. She kissed Alfred on the cheek, collected her gloves and went out the door. She thought to herself that Alfred had become totally helpless and useless. Margaret was a complete bother as well.

Nelson had parked in the circular driveway right under the open window of the sitting room. It was clear that he had heard the entire conversation between Alma and Alfred and was trying to fathom it all. He managed to keep his posture when Alma appeared and opened the car door for her. "I do hope all is well and that no one is ill, Madame," said Nelson. "Oh heavens no, Nelson, all is just fine, just a minor matter to straighten out," said Alma with assurance. "Of course, Madame. Homeward now?"

"Yes, thank you," said Alma as she put her head back against the seat. Nelson could see in the mirror that her blue eyes were wide open and darting around like a crazed bee. He could hear her whisper to herself "What a fine how do you do" as she began to weep into her handkerchief.

Chapter Seven

Eric and little Sophie were playing on the dining room rug when Alma returned from Alfred's home. Eric was giving little pieces of the chicken to Sophie and scratching her tummy. "I see you have not retired as yet, Eric," said Alma. "No, but I will go up now that you are home. I was worried about you as you left so very abruptly," explained Eric.

"Good night, Eric. I will not expect you for dinner tomorrow, as I have a previous invitation. Enjoy your boat trip with Louise and do take a swim at the first stop. The water is so very clear and blue there."

Alma had a frightful headache and was shaking all over. She drew a warm bath and tried to relax. She called for Bessie and asked for some warm milk and chocolates. She sat in her tub watching the lace curtains swirl as the night air blew around them. She was filled with anger and fear. She refused the warm milk and chocolates when Bessie knocked and asked that she not be disturbed again. She climbed out of the tub and into her comfortable bed totally naked. She began thinking how lovely her life had been these past years and how pleasing it was that Alfred had stepped up in society and no one seemed to sense or care that he was somewhat mentally challenged from the war. Both were now well respected and enjoying the luxury of freedom they had missed for years. Now, this terrible threat of discovery loomed and she feared that her life would fall apart and her reputation would be ruined. Perhaps she might even be picked up by the police.

Alma admitted to herself that she had suspected Tony Smythe might not be totally aboveboard but she had chanced the ride with him. He was charming and seemed well respected at his club. Alfred went along with anything Alma suggested. Tony's reputation as a brilliant investor was well known in London's financial circle, though he was a gambler and several times came close to losing all the money he had acquired. He was famous for his instant financial recoveries and was courted by a number of large financial institutions in London. He turned them all down, as he preferred to work alone.

Some time ago he had purchased a modest home in Ambleside for his family and was eager to climb the social ladder and become immensely wealthy. But he found his wife, Louise, to be a bore and divorced her. He was, however, rather fond of the two girls he had fathered.

Alfred and Alma invested in Tony's scheme and all seemed to be doing well as they had more of a return on their investment than expected in a very short time. The more money they invested the more the money came pouring in. Now all might be severely threatened because of a buffoon from Altoona whom she had stupidly befriended on the train. She slapped herself on the cheek and burst into tears, and pulled her soft linen sheets over her head once again.

Her mind began to wander back to the lovely days in Oberammergau in the beautiful Bavarian Alps when the Boelds were the finest family in town. Their father was the Bergemeister and they had a lovely pensione with flowers all around. The gate on the little white fence was always open to friends and neighbors. The Passion Play was put on every ten years and a Boeld family member always had a leading part. Her father was Jesus twice. Life was simple but rewarding until the war started. Alfred and their younger brother, William, were recruited by the Nazis and forced to fight under the German flag. Alma was a young, tall, and very pretty girl with tantalizing blue eyes. She joined the Resistance and mingled, as a spy, with the German soldiers who came to Garmisch and Munich. They found her alluring and vulnerable in her innocent country way. She would go to their parties and pick up any information she could for the Resistance. It was an exciting life for the young Alma and she enjoyed the intrigue. She became involved with a Nazi general who then discovered she was associating with the British and Americans and ordered her arrest. She was imprisoned along with other spies and prostitutes until the war ended. She returned to Oberammergau but no one would acknowledge her other than to spit at her. She learned that William had been shot down in a plane and killed and that Alfred had been taken prisoner and was in hospital in England.

A knock at the door interrupted her memories. "Who is it?" Alma asked. "'Tis Bessie and Bertha, Madame, with some warm milk."

"Go away, go away, leave me alone!" cried out Alma.

"Madame, I regret that we have some very sad news for you," said Bessie.

"What now?" asked Alma as she pulled herself up to a sitting position and asked Bessie to come in. Bessie curtsied as she entered Alma's bedroom. Bertha stayed in the hall. "Little Sophie died so quickly this evening. She apparently choked on a little chicken bone. Pinky has wrapped her in one of your lovely initialed linen towels and put her in a little wooden box. Bertha was weeping as she washed and pressed the towel. Pinky was also weeping as he was fixing the box. We will bury her in your garden in the morning. She will always be close by," explained Bessie, choking back her tears. Bertha stood close to the bedroom door; Alma could hear her weeping. Also in tears, Alma thought to herself that a sour wind was approaching and she was anxious to get back under the covers.

Bessie and Bertha retired to their room, saying a prayer for little Sophie. They had shared the same bed and quilt since they were wee babes in Ireland. As children they used to argue as to which one of them owned the quilt, but they knew it was a game. The colors on the patches were barely visible after all these years.

Chapter Eight

Eric woke early and was excited about being properly attired for the boat cruise. He put on the white linen trousers, blue striped shirt and navy blue jacket. He put the handkerchief in the breast pocket, but also one in his trouser pocket in case he needed to blow his nose. He did not wish to bother anyone, so he crept quietly out of the house and started his walk to town to meet Louise at the library. Nelson saw him depart and envied his casual and attractive outfit and watched him walk down the driveway. It was time for Nelson to go to the fresh market in town to pick up fruit and vegetables, so he decided to collect Eric on the way. Eric heard the car coming from behind and rushed into the bushes.

"Eric, how about a lift?"

"Oh, it is you, thanks, I am going to the library."

"Hop on in, my friend!" Nelson felt in control, as he now knew more about everything than he did 24 hours ago. "And what is going on at the library so early?"

"I am meeting Louise and we are going on a boat trip around the lake."

"How pleasant. It will be full of tourists, so watch your wallet." Eric realized that he had neglected to bring his wallet and also his passport. "Oh, Nelson, could we turn around? I have forgotten my wallet and passport." Nelson laughed to himself, as he was not surprised that this was the case. "I have plenty of time," said Nelson. Eric went back to the house and gathered his wallet and passport. All was quiet and he wondered why he did not hear a bark from little Sophie.

Nelson delivered Eric to the library and went on his way to the open market.

Eric and Louise arrived at the same time and greeted each other. "We are so fortunate to have such a lovely day. It so often rains here in the Lake District," remarked Louise. "Yes, a beautiful day," agreed Eric. They walked over to the dock. Eric had never been on a boat of any sort and suddenly felt very awkward and a bit frightened when he saw the large craft. "I don't swim," he exclaimed. Louise could see that Eric was a bit nervous and told him he did not need to swim and anyway they provided life preservers. Eric turned very pale and stood very close to Louise and grabbed her hand. Louise tried to calm him by telling him that in Cumbria, the lakes are the star of the show and that you can enjoy them without even getting your feet wet and the scenery is spectacular. Eric said he really didn't want to get on the boat and perhaps they could drive around instead. Louise began to think that any sort of romance with Eric was not in the stars.

She suggested that they get her car and they could drive to some interesting spots. Eric squeezed her hand, smiled, and gave her a little kiss on her cheek. Louise thought that Eric was really a very sweet man, so unlike Tony, who never held her hand or gave her a loving smile or a kiss on her cheek.

They picked up Louise's old car and went off on the land tour. They went to the Grizedale Forest and looked at all the wonderful sculptures, but Eric did not want to see the little monkeys. They visited Dove Cottage, the home of William Wordsworth. Eric did not know about Wordsworth and said he wanted to get Wordsworth's books of poems from Louise's library. They picked up sandwiches for a picnic on the lawn at Dove Cottage. Crows were hovering above, and Eric threw his sandwich as far away from him as possible. Louise sensed that Eric was most uncomfortable so she said they must not dally because she had to pick up her girls at the camp.

Nelson was busy burying little Sophie in the back garden when Alma came out with a cigarette in her mouth. "Smoking again, are you now, Madame?" asked Nelson.

"No, just having a couple of puffs. Are you putting Sophie there with the roses? That is a fine spot. Let us hope she does not bump into any underground skeletons."

"No, Madame, this a lovely resting spot for the dear girl. She was such a scampy little thing."

"Yes, and she scampered off without even a good-bye, so sudden. What happened?"

"Apparently she choked on a chicken bone," explained Nelson.

"I recall we had chicken for dinner last evening, but I did not sleep well so I am not sure of anything today. I will ring if I need you, Nelson."

"Of course, Madame, and do try and get some rest. Perhaps you would like a drive around the lake to relax a bit later in the afternoon."

"If so, I will ring. Thank you Nelson, you are always on top of things."

"Yes, Madame, I try to please." He strolled across the gardens to his apartment above the garage as if he suddenly had control of the entire world. He had put a dog in the ground, unearthed a scandal of finance, and felt on top of things!

Chapter Nine

Alfred boarded the 7:02 a.m. train to London. He had not slept a wink all night and Margaret decided that he should have a chat with Tony about their business transactions. He called Tony and they arranged to meet at his club. Alfred wanted Margaret to go with him but she refused.

Tony was relaxing with a lager and lime, reading a newspaper, when Alfred appeared. "What is on your mind old boy? I have a busy afternoon and can only spare a bit of time. All seems to be going smoothly and we are raking in the money and all the better for it," said Tony with a grin.

Alfred got right to the point, nervously. "A peculiar friendship has taken place. Apparently Louise and your two children shared a compartment with Alma and Eric on the way home from London after the birthday celebration at your new town home."

"I am following you, Alfred, but who the hell is Eric?"

"He is a nobody, but happens to be staying at Alma's home and has taken up with Louise."

"Oh for God's sake, stupidity reigns and Louise is the queen of stupidity." Tony gulped down his lager and lime and ordered another. He ordered nothing for Alfred.

"I do not really know a thing about this Eric except that he is from Atlanta," said Alfred.

"Well, what is all this to-do about anyway?"

"Alma is afraid that Louise and Eric will figure out that you are the Smythe and Alma and I are the Boeld of Smythe and Boeld, and Louise will know that we are partners in business," said Alfred.

"Perhaps this could happen, but what do they know that could be harmful to us?" asked Tony.

"Well, you have become quite wealthy recently and so have I and she may figure out that you are doing very well and she is working at the library with the two little girls and perhaps connect the dots that you have made a great deal of money in a very short time and she could want more money from you. Margaret thinks she might hire an attorney," said Alfred, wiping his brow with his handkerchief. "It was Margaret who made me call and come to see you." Alfred looked around the club, which exuded posh serenity, wishing he could be a member.

"I see what you are getting at. It is not a problem. I will send Louise some extra money each month and perhaps that will keep her content. All is going well with our plan and there is no reason to switch oars now, but get that oaf out of your sister's house and away from Louise," ordered Tony.

"Yes, I told Alma to give Eric his walking papers," replied Alfred.

"Very well then, let's get on with our lives!"

Alfred wiped his brow and shook Tony's extended hand.

Chapter Ten

The social season in Ambleside was in full swing and Alma's social life was based on attending just the proper luncheons and dinner parties. Alfred and Margaret were hardly ever invited to the parties, which concerned Alma, because that did not reflect well on her. Alma was the true star. She knew exactly how to handle everything, keeping the conversations on a light note while admiring the dresses. She always had a smile on her face and a wave to a friend on the other side of the room. Her beautiful blue eyes did not miss a trick.

Alma had not told Eric to leave the house. Eric was really no trouble, so meek and mild and most attentive to her. She actually thought he might be in love with her and that gave her great delight. She simply could not boot him out. While she was concerned about the financial situation becoming a scandal, she felt that having Eric staying in the house enabled her to keep an eye on him.

Alfred told Alma about his meeting with Tony and that Tony was going to pony up a bit more money for Louise each month and that should keep her quiet. So things were copacetic at the moment. Alma was somewhat relieved. She was at her best when she stayed in the present and did not worry much about what might happen.

Alma wasted no time in telling Margaret that it was her duty to entertain and that a small dinner party would be proper. Margaret was not enthusiastic but knew she must obey Alma.

Alfred and Margaret's party went smoothly, most fortunately. The guests mingled on the back terrace. "Margaret my dear, this is such a lovely evening and your garden is in full bloom. However the crows have certainly made themselves at home with all their droppings," said Alma in disgust.

"I must thank you for sending Nelson and Eric over to make things look better. You do recall that Gerry, my dear gardener, passed away in April and I have not replaced him," said Margaret.

"It was my pleasure. By the by, ask Freddie to take pot shots at the crows. He loves to do that. It reminds him of the war," said Alma with a boisterous laugh. "I like the crows, Alma. They are very bright and interesting." Alma turned away and went to chat with Maggie Campbell. Maggie wintered in Spain and was more interesting than her boring sister-in-law.

As the party ended, Nelson was promptly there to drive Alma home. "Nelson, whatever possessed you to take Eric over to putter around in Freddie's garden?"

"Well, Madame, Eric has become most interested in gardening and since the festivities were to be there this evening, it seemed like a nice thing to do."

"Hmm, I see," said Alma, who was wondering if she was losing touch and things were going on behind her back. "Nelson, please do keep close to home except for your morning trips to the market, as I never know when I may need you to drive."

"Of course, Madame." The remainder of the drive was in silence.

The phone rang in the morning. Bertha answered and came to awaken Eric as the call was for him. Eric was already dressed and ready to go to town with Nelson, and so he picked up the phone in the hall telephone closet. "Yes, good morning to you too and I am on my way into town and will meet you at the fountain shortly."

Louise was on her morning tea break from the library and met Eric at the fountain with the most beautiful smile Eric had ever seen. "Well, what are you so pleased about, Louise?"

"I cannot believe it, but my check from Tony is triple the usual amount and was sent express. He included a note saying that he did not think the girls were dressed properly for the birthday celebration and that I should buy them each new party dresses and new jumpers and perhaps they needed new trainers for the school year. The check he sent could buy us all new wardrobes and then some. I know he has a new job and has left the bank, but I never thought he would become so successful so quickly, though he is very smart. He was first in his class at Oxford and received a special ribbon around his neck at graduation. He also suggested that I have the bricks mended in the back garden, as the girls could trip and fall as they run around so much, and that I should not allow any friends to come over until the bricks are repaired."

"Oh, how very nice for you my dear, you work hard and deserve the best. I am happy for you."

While strolling they came upon a refreshments cart. Louise ordered a triple chocolate cone. Eric was content with plain vanilla – "no sprinkles, please." Louise smiled to herself. Afterward, Louise went back to work at the library. Eric had made plans to meet Nelson at the open market, so he started on his way. Nelson was waiting for him with the produce for luncheon and dinner. Eric sat in back as Nelson directed him to do. He felt uncomfortable in the back seat with Nelson driving, but Nelson always insisted that he was to ride in the back of the large black car. It was larger than any Eric had ridden in before, especially in the back. "What kind of car is this?" Eric ventured. "A Bentley, 1970," Nelson responded proudly. Eric had never heard of a Bentley. He didn't know what to say. "And how was your visit with Louise?" asked Nelson.

"Very pleasant and Louise had good news," said Eric.

"Oh really, and did she tell you what it was?"

"Yes, she did, and I am so happy for her," exclaimed Eric.

"Well, how good is this news, old boy?" asked Nelson.

"Very good. She received a very large check from her ex-husband Tony to buy the girls more clothes and to have the bricks fixed in the back of her house."

Nelson drove on with a big smile, quite enjoying this new intrigue. "It is a lovely day, eh Eric?"

"Oh yes, very nice," said Eric.

Chapter Eleven

Nelson went up to his apartment, fixed himself a cup of tea and sat in his chair by the window looking out over the gardens. He was rather content with his job, but had thought so many times how nice it would be if he didn't have to "Yes, Madame" all the time. He felt that he was worthy of more. Or was he? He knew that he was gay and had been all his life. No one else knew; it was his secret. But, he thought to himself, the world is changing and being gay is a bit more acceptable and so many brilliant and charming men are gay and have wonderful lives. Why can't I be one of them? All I need is to acquire some money so that I can set up my own housekeeping and live as I like and not pretend to be someone else in this uniform day after day, year after year.

He thought how lovely it would be to have his own flat in London and live as he chose. He felt confident that the time was now! He had overheard the conversation between Madame and Mr. Alfred and so was privy to the fact that there was some kind of fraudulent money scheme going on between Mr. Alfred, Madame, and Mr. Tony. AH HA, he thought, if I can find out where Mr. Tony has his office I will confront him with my inside information and blackmail him. Oh my, he thought, am I really up to all this? As he thought about it, he gazed out his window and saw Eric strolling up the driveway with a basket of fruit. Nelson chased down the stairs and stopped Eric before he reached the front door.

"Good afternoon, Eric, and where have you been?"

"Oh hello, Nelson. Louise invited me for tea after she left the library and I met her two lovely daughters again. You may recall that Louise and the girls were on the train with us when I first came to England."

"Eric, why don't you invite Louise to have an early tea with us at The Village Tea Room tomorrow," suggested Nelson.

"Well, that might be possible, as tomorrow Louise only works in the afternoon and her girls are at sailing camp all day. Yes, that would be pleasant. You make me feel welcome, Nelson. Thank you." Eric went on into the kitchen to deposit the fruit. "See you tomorrow morning," said Nelson with great satisfaction.

Eric put down a bowl of milk for little Lucy. Bessie and Bertha were very fond of the new house cat and took good care of her for Eric, who had rescued her, half starved, from the bushes.

Eric and Louise arrived at The Village Tea Room just as Nelson was parking the car. They made small talk until Nelson said, "Louise, Eric tells me that you are planning to tidy up the bricks in your back garden. Do you have a reputable person to do the work?"

"Actually I do not. Do you know of someone who might not charge too much and does good work?" asked Louise.

"Well," Nelson said with a smile, "I happen to be a very good bricklayer and a decent handyman and would be happy to do it for you for very little as I enjoy taking off the grey gloves and getting my hands into the earth when I have time off."

"Oh, how super. And when could you start?"

"Well, I must come over and establish what must be done, get the materials and then I can start the work," said Nelson.

"Oh jolly good, I will be at the library this afternoon and the girls at sailing camp, but you can go over anytime as the back gate is always open and the kitchen door does not latch properly. Perhaps you could take a look at that also. Since Tony left I haven't been in the mood to do much fixing," Louise said with tears in her eyes.

"Most understandable, Miss Louise," said Nelson. They all had a second cup of tea, finished off the remaining biscuits, and went their separate ways.

Nelson delivered Alma to her afternoon garden party hosted by a couple from Paris who were renting a lovely home on the lake and seemed to know everyone. Madame did not speak kindly of them after their first party in early June; she thought they were a bit overbearing and lacking in interesting conversation. When Alma had asked if they had enjoyed the Paris opera season, they said they had been on a cruise most of the winter and heard only "Rigoletto" and a poor production of "Aida" and were giving up their tickets for the coming season and thinking of renting a house in Arizona for the winter. They had not been in America for two years and were eager to see their son, who had married a girl from Arizona.

Alma told Nelson that she would stay only one hour. Nelson drove over to Louise's house and spotted some mail on the hall table. It confirmed the last name was Smythe. He saw an envelope with Mr. Tony's office address.

Nelson returned to collect Alma and helped her into the back seat. There was a brief silence while Nelson was trying to figure out his thoughts. "Madame, may I assume that you do not have luncheon plans tomorrow as you have not mentioned any to me?"

"And Nelson, why would you ask?"

"I was hoping we could have luncheon together tomorrow."

"Nelson, this sounds like a very improper invitation. What may I ask, prompts this honor after all these years?"

"It is a personal matter, Madame," said Nelson.

"It never occurred to me that you had personal matters, but of course you must. How interesting. I should be delighted to hear about them. I do hope they are spicy as I love intrigue, though it has slapped me down a few times, but I always manage to come back and have such a glorious life and you are like part of the family, Nelson, so please join me for luncheon on the terrace tomorrow. By the by, you need not wear your uniform since it is so warm. I usually had my luncheon, when I am at home, with dear little Sophie on the chair next to me. I do miss her, but one cannot dwell on past mishaps. Be a dear and tell cook that there will be two of us for tomorrow's luncheon."

Nelson was seated comfortably on the terrace when Alma arrived wearing one of her free-flowing dresses. Nelson at first thought that it was a nightgown. "Oh, there you are. Now come to the table and we will have a nice luncheon. Is this the first time we have lunched together?" asked Alma.

"Yes, Madame."

"Oh, I do wish we had done this sooner. It is so important to communicate. My sister in law, Margaret, has no skills and is truly a total bore. By the way, Nelson, I have always wanted to ask you why so many call you Pinky?" Alma asked with a bit of a giggle.

"Well, Madame, it was actually your brother, Mr. Alfred, who started it. One day he was admiring my driving suit and liked the maroon color, which you picked out, and he said, 'We shall christen you Pinky of Boeld Manor.' He thought it was a great joke, very pleased with himself, and we both laughed. The name stuck to me like sticking plaster."

"Oh for heaven's sake," sighed Alma. "Freddie has always been a bit of a buffoon. Just call him Mr. Freddie and see what happens." Finding herself enjoying the time with Nelson, she asked Bertha to bring out a nice bottle of summer wine. Bertha served it and Alma turned from the view of the water and looked at Nelson with her piercing blue eyes. "Are you in love with me, Pinky? And if you are, do not worry about it. Many men have been in love with me, but I choose to live by myself."

"Of course, Madame, that suits you so well."

Alma turned her head abruptly and said, "And how would you, of all people, know that?"

"I don't really know, Madame, how I know. I just know that I have enjoyed living alone." Nelson stood up and asked to be excused and thanked Alma for the delicious luncheon, even though he had only a few little bites. Alma sat and stared at the lovely lake, had a few sips of the wine, thought about her past and knew she was always going to be alone.

Back in his apartment, Nelson looked at his maroon uniform hanging on the closet door and decided to stay in his casual clothes, as Madame would not need him until she wished to go to Mr. Alfred's supper party. He looked at himself very carefully and saw much to admire. He stood at different angles, looking into the mirror. He did this often, smiling and posing a bit for himself. He was pleased with what he saw. But this time he stopped, stood still, and wondered if the mirror would be his only friend.

Chapter Twelve

Alma wore aqua blue for Alfred and Margaret's supper party and, as usual, looked charming. Nelson waited outside Alfred's home along with the other drivers. They smoked cigarettes and made small talk to pass the time until the party was over. This evening ended quite differently than others. After midnight, Alfred came stumbling down the stairs from the front terrace, without his dress jacket or tie and with his shirt hanging outside his dress trousers. He was calling for Pinky and bumping into all the cars. Nelson located him and pulled him into the back seat of their car. Alfred said he wanted to be with his friend from London and have a drink. He told Nelson that he would be the next president of the bank. Nelson sat quietly and hoped Alma would come quickly and take charge.

Alma finally appeared and told Nelson to put the lap robe over Alfred's head until all the cars had left the party. Nelson did as he was told and Alfred seemed to be passive, just drooping into a lump; only a few groans could be heard. Alma left briefly and returned and told Nelson to get Alfred out of the car and back into the house.

Alma, entirely in charge, ordered all the outside lamps turned off and all the doors locked and all the windows closed. Margaret appeared and fell into Alma's arms with tears of desperation. "Margaret, get a grip on yourself and be of some help. Your husband is completely out of control and you should call the ambulance and put him in hospital until we see fit to release him."

"Why does he need to go to hospital, Alma?"

"Oh, just do as I say."

Tony appeared and came up to Alma asking if there was something he could do to be of help. Tony was the only guest left; Alfred had invited him to spend the night and enjoy a Sunday in the Lake District, as it would give him a chance to see his two girls. Tony had been pleased to attend the party and make small talk with some of the clients who had invested quite heavily in the partnership. He made a wonderful impression on them with his humor and good looks. Alfred did not want Tony to be the star and was feeling left out. He drank too much brandy and started to tell everyone that he was the boss and Tony worked for him. Tony tried to salvage the situation but Alfred only made things worse and openly accused Tony of stealing money and declared he had tried to make things right, but Tony was a very bad boy. Most of the guests thought it was a joke of some sort until Stephen Lorde came forward and announced that he was a prime investor with Tony and wished an immediate accounting. He asked to have his car brought to the front and departed without another word.

The party was over. Tony punched Alfred while in the kitchen in hope of shutting him up. Alfred emerged from the kitchen with blood dripping from his jaw after throwing his glass of brandy at Tony and calling him a crook. Alma, at this point, quickly ushered the guests into the smaller parlor, started playing the piano and shortly suggested that all go home. It was then that Alfred managed to get himself out the front door, stumbling down the outside stairs and Pinky came to his rescue.

They decided not to call an ambulance, but to put Alfred to bed in his own home. He had passed out and Alma decided that it was a family matter and to be kept that way.

The next morning was lovely and warm with a clear blue sky. Alma and Nelson arrived at Alfred and Margaret's house at 7 o'clock and found not a creature stirring. "Nelson, please park the car and find a way into this house."

"Yes, Madame, I will try."

The door was unlocked so Alma and Nelson entered. "What a dreadful mess. It looks like a murder scene and no one is stirring. I will go upstairs and see what is going on," announced Alma. As Alma climbed she came eye to eye with Tony. "Well, at least one mouse is stirring. Nelson, please let us get some coffee and I must sit down," said Alma.

Nelson brewed coffee in the kitchen, which was also a mess, and found a tray and proper napkins and brought the tray out to the small terrace. "Nelson, you might as well join us as this is a most difficult situation and perhaps you can brief us as to what happened outside last evening."

"Thank you, Madame, I will join you but I am not sure that I can put any light on the happenings."

"Just start at the beginning and work it like a puzzle. I am very good at puzzles. Do you like puzzles, Mr. Tony Smythe?"

"No, I do not, Mrs. Boeld, I am strictly a factual and straight-on kind of guy."

"Well then, Nelson, how did Alfred get so bloodied up?"

Tony interrupted. "Mrs. Boeld, there is no need to beat around the bush. It is obvious that your brother Alfred became totally unhinged last evening and has put us all in a very embarrassing position. It is not a puzzle, Madame."

Alma uncrossed her legs, crossed them again and turned the other way so her back was to Tony. She needed time to think.

"Well, perhaps we should all have a little meeting together, since you are still here, Tony, if I may call you Tony?"

"You have already addressed me as Tony several times, Mrs. Boeld."

"Is your coffee still warm? If not, I am sure that Nelson can manage to brew us both some hot. I think that cold coffee is simply a disgrace and most irresponsible. Tea always works so well for me," said Alma as she slumped deeper into her comfortable wicker chair. Nelson went into the kitchen to brew hot coffee and tea. Alma leaned back in Tony's direction, turned her head and stared at him with her piercing blue eyes. "Tony, you simply have to get us all out of this mess that my stupid brother, Freddie, has put us into. What are we to do?"

"Mrs. Boeld, I have been pondering this very predicament most of the night and early morning and I believe I can settle this entire situation without a lot of fanfare and without the ruination of your family name."

"How can you do this?"

"Well, I can fix the books, and if an accounting takes place, it will all appear in order." Tony stood up, looking Alma straight on, and said, "but your brother, a prime investor and unfortunately a horse's ass, will take the brunt of the situation. You, Mrs. Boeld, will also take a great loss. Steve Lorde, whom I have known for years, has asked for an accounting of his money and if we nip this in the bud and I am able to put affairs in order, he and the others will come out all right. However, you must realize that Alfred will be left with practically nothing when the other investors receive their disbursements. I will stay on as chairman of the board and manager of the firm. I have invested the monies extremely carefully. You and your jackass brother are no longer partners or investors. I want nothing to do with either of you. That is what I will do, Mrs. Boeld, and there is no more conversation to be had about it. Case closed. I will go back to London on the next coach and commence putting things in order. I would advise you to tell Alfred to keep his mouth closed if he wants to avoid an investigation and hence a jail sentence for himself."

"Oh, good God, Tony, if I may call you Tony, you are a brilliant crook. I do not know what to say, and I am not often at a loss of words, but I simply do not know what to say. Would you like my driver to take you back to your flat in London, as the express train runs so infrequently?"

"Mrs. Boeld, that would be most helpful, as I can work in the car and will have this all cleared up by tomorrow morning. Do not discuss this with anyone and just keep Alfred under wraps!"

Nelson had the car ready. He helped Tony with his small overnight bag into the back seat. Nelson started up the car and they were off to London. Nelson realized that the car was very low on petrol and suggested they stop at the first station. Tony agreed and offered to pay for the petrol.

Alma started slowly up the stairs and saw Alfred trying to find the banister. "Freddie, stop, you are about to fall. Stop!" screamed Alma.

"Alma, are you still here? What is going on?" asked Alfred as he caught himself on the banister and landed with his feet on the top step and his head down the stairs. Alfred righted himself and said, "The whole place is upside down. I am quite an acrobat, aren't I Alma?"

"You are a damn fool," she responded. Alfred began to whistle and wave his arms about. Alma said to herself that it would be a blessing if he just toppled down the stairs and broke his neck.

Chapter Thirteen

Eric continued to enjoy his stay in Alma's home. He was becoming fond of everyone and felt relaxed and welcome. He liked walking into town, meeting Louise during her breaks from the library, and wiring off the daily local weather predictions to *The Altoona Daily News*. He was quite proficient with the wire machine now. His knowledge of the predictable weather patterns in Altoona was sufficient for the forecasts. "Cloudy with a chance of rain" seemed to be the norm.

On Sunday morning Eric was feeling particularly relaxed after tea with Bessie and Bertha. Nelson had driven Alma somewhere quite early. Little Lucy was in the kitchen and snuggled in an old blanket Bessie had found in a closet. She embroidered a large L on it. Eric had become very fond of little Lucy and wondered if he could take her to America, but Bessie persuaded him that she would be better off in Ambleside.

Eric decided to bicycle to Louise's house, as it was a lovely crisp morning. When he arrived at her house, her car was in the driveway. He knocked on her door. Millicent and Suzanne answered the door together and both burst into tears. "Where is your Mum?" asked Eric. "She is sick and cannot get out of her bed. We thought you were Daddy. He was supposed to come for a visit today but he never called."

A Fine How Do You Do

They both hugged Eric and cried some more. "Have you had your breakfast, girls?" "No and Mum is sick," cried Suzanne. "Well, let's see what I can do to cheer you all up." Eric called for Louise. Louise recognized Eric's voice and said that she would be downstairs in a minute.

Eric and the two girls sat close to each other on the couch. Louise came down in a bathrobe and sat on the floor by the fireplace with her head facing the hearth. "Louise, what is the matter?" asked Eric. Louise did not answer or move her head. The girls moved to the floor and cuddled up next to their Mum. All three began crying at the same time.

Millicent suddenly burst out, saying "Daddy never called to make plans for today. I think he might be dead and I must write an obituary for him. An obituary is for dead people who never come to visit anymore and it goes in the newspaper and then everyone knows that they are dead. I write obituaries for people who are not dead yet too," said Millicent.

"Dear girls, that is not the case, perhaps your Daddy had some business and is too busy to call you," said Eric. "Let's try and call him, where does he live now?"

"In London," they said together.

"Do you know his telephone number?"

"Yes, but there has been no answer."

"Well let's try again and see what happens." Eric dialed the telephone and let it ring several times but there was no answer. "We will keep trying to call and in the meantime, how about some cereal?"

The drive to London went swiftly and Nelson kept his eye on the road, though he could not help but notice how busy Tony was in the back seat, and Nelson enjoyed watching him in the rear view mirror. His facial expressions did not change as he was writing notes throughout the entire drive. When they arrived at

Tony's townhouse in London, Tony invited Nelson to come in. As they entered the telephone was ringing.

"Hello, Daddy, I thought you were dead and I have already written your obituary. Do you know what an obituary is?"

"Yes, Millicent, I do, but you are talking to me so you know that I am alive and not dead and I love you and Suzanne very much and will see you very soon, but I must go to Zurich tomorrow and will bring you both nice presents."

"Daddy, why are you going to an icky-zoo?"

"Not an icky zoo, dear one, to Zurich in Switzerland. Now go and comfort your Mum and all will be fine. I am sorry to be in such a rush and miss our visit together." Tony hung up the phone and threw his head back against the leather chair. "Nelson, my new friend, I presume that you do not have a family, am I correct?"

"No, Mr. Tony, no family at all, just me, myself and I."

"Well," said Tony with a wink and a smile. "We must get to know this threesome a bit better. How about a lager and lime?"

Chapter Fourteen

"Madame Boeld, Tony here." Alma was completely dismayed by everything that had happened and did not know what to say to anyone. She almost put down the telephone before replying, "Yes, this is Alma Boeld. What in the world am I to do now that you have ruined my brother, ruined me and my entire life and where is my car and my driver?"

"Mrs. Boeld, please try and listen for a moment and I will explain how I am going to get this mess all together. You must keep calm and get your brother to stay at home and do not talk to anyone. Is this understood?"

"Yes, Tony, I hear you and will listen. I have no choice."

"Thank you for your confidence. I am flying to Zurich today and will be gone for at least two days to straighten out this mess that your brother has created and I will be in touch with you when I return to London. I will have some papers for you and your brother to sign. Nelson will take me to the airport and will bring your car back after he drops me off," announced Tony.

"My oh my! You have taken my car, my driver and all my money! Who do you think you are?" screamed Alma into the phone.

"I am all you have, Madame Boeld, so grin and bear it. I am not interested in your complaints."

Nelson drove Tony to the airport and was pleased that Tony sat beside him in the front. They smiled at each other and made plans to meet again after Tony returned from Zurich. Nelson drove back to Ambleside and enjoyed every minute of the drive reminiscing about their most unexpected evening together.

Alma was on the terrace slumped in a chair when Nelson returned and found her. "Well, Pinky, what is going on? I had to call Elizabeth to come fetch me and bring me home as Freddie was a mess and Margaret had locked herself in the bedroom and would not answer."

"I have no idea what is going on, Madame. I only do as I am told and concentrate on driving safely. When will you be wanting the car next, Madame? I need to wash it up a bit."

"Forget about any washing. We must go to Alfred's right now and make sure that he is being put in hospital where he cannot do any more damage," said Alma, pushing herself out of the chair. "I dare say that you do not admire my coiffure today," she said as she puffed up the cushion.

"No, Madame, I mean you look a bit tired today, Madame." Alma climbed into the car and began to cry. She was sobbing so badly that she began to choke and started to scream and call for help. Nelson stopped the car and went into the back seat. Alma clung to Nelson and would not let go. "Madame, what shall I do?"

Alma did not answer right away but took a few deep breaths. "Get the car going, straighten your tie and forge ahead. Where is your cap?"

"I left it in London, Madame," said Nelson as he returned to the driver's seat. He could hear Alma muttering "A fine how do you do."

Alfred was sitting alone on a back garden bench and could barely get to his feet upon the arrival of his sister. "Alfred, sit down and stay on that bench until I tell you to get up. Now listen to me

Freddie. You are in big trouble after that performance you put on. You must see no one and do not answer the phone. Stay in this house and wait for me to tell you when to breathe next. Is that understood, you idiot?" Alma's blue eyes stared right into Alfred.

"But why are you so annoyed with me, Alma dear, was it not a lovely party?"

"No, it was a disaster and he robbed us of all our money. Freddie, you are the dunce of all time. Please go up to bed. You need to rest and sleep."

Chapter Fifteen

Tuesday morning was bleak; the forecast was cloudy with a chance of rain. Eric stayed in his bed and was aware of some goings-on, but chose to stay in his room and not get involved. He suddenly felt lonely and missed Martha. He never meant to leave Martha, as he loved and cared for her, but this venture had been so much more than he ever could have imagined. It was taking on a life of its own and Eric was grasping it and hanging on for all he could. Every day was a holiday for him and he still felt that he was on that merry-go-round. He had picked up some Wordsworth books from the library and was enjoying them, though he really did not understand all the strange words, but he liked the way they flowed along like a melody. He decided to ride the bike over to Louise's house and see if all had settled down. He was worried about Louise and her girls.

"Hello, Louise, are you here?" he asked as he knocked on the door. Suzanne came to the door and Millicent was in the kitchen trying to make some soup for her mother. Eric came in and quickly removed the pot of soup from boiling over. Millicent had gone for the bowls and not noticed how rapidly the soup was boiling.

Eric wondered why they were all home on a weekday. Louise emerged from her room and came to Eric with open arms. "I am a mess and so is my life and everything is a lie."

"Oh, my dear, what do you mean?" asked Eric.

"I mean that Tony is a fraud and all this money he is making is not honest money," explained Louise through her tears.

"How do you know this?"

"Because, I know Tony. I lived with him for 13 years and he never has been honest and is always looking for a way to cheat people and he looked down on everyone we met unless they had a lot of money. I sensed the minute that he sent that big check to me that he was up to something and then he did not come to see the girls and then he phoned that he is going to Zurich. I am not as stupid as he thinks I am. I know that he is up to no good. I took the check to the bank early this morning and they would not cash it and said that the account was closed. I left straight-away as I did not want to embarrass myself. I came home and went back to bed. Millicent is now saying that she will write my obituary and put it in the paper unless I get up and smile. Suzanne says nothing and just goes out to the garden and swings on the swing, back and forth. It makes me dizzy to watch her."

"Oh, my dear Louise, I do think that you have hit on something, as you are a wise lady," Eric responded. "I would suggest that you keep all your suspicions to yourself and see how this all plays out. I listened to lots of mystery and murder stories on the radio before I came here, and the best thing to do is to keep your mouth shut."

Louise looked at him strangely. "Mum, the soup is ready and I need help getting it poured into the bowls," said Millicent. Eric hugged Louise and said, "I didn't mean to scare you. I will help you serve the soup and, well, with other things." Louise smiled and then burst into tears. Then they all sat at the table and held hands before trying the soup. Millicent wondered if she would have to write any more obituaries.

Eric bicycled back to Alma's house and went into the kitchen to see if Lucy had come down for her milk. Bertha and Bessie were sitting at the large and sturdy kitchen table and Bertha had little Lucy on her lap. Eric joined them. "You look a bit out of sorts, Eric dear," said Bessie. Eric put on a smile and said, "I think little Lucy is happy here, but I wonder where little Lucy came from. She has probably been more places than we have." All three giggled. Lucy jumped under the kitchen table and rubbed up against everyone's legs. They heard the front door slam and Alma's voice screeching "Is anyone here?"

"Yes, Madame," said Bessie as she darted out to the front door. "Oh Bessie dear, you both are such a comfort to me. You are the only people I know who are trustworthy and worthy of my time at all," said Alma, hugging Bessie. "Let's make some tea and sit around the kitchen table. I haven't sat around the table in so long and it would comfort me."

"Yes, Madame, of course. I have just baked some biscuits and we will sit around the table with Bertha and Eric and have a jolly time with Lucy."

"Lucy who?"

"The little cat that Eric found and brought home."

"I am unable to have a jolly time," complained Alma, "but I will try my best. Our life is in shambles, but do not worry, you will not lose your jobs and you will stay on with me as you always have, through thick and thin," she said in a cracked voice.

"Yes, Madame, where else would we go, this is our home, isn't it?"

"Of course it is, and always will be." Alma spotted little Lucy under the kitchen table and insisted that Lucy have Sophie's old bed and that it be put back in her bedroom. She would have Nelson drive her to the pet shop in town and they would buy Lucy a proper collar and little bows for her and cushions to be placed throughout the house. She would have a proper bath before moving up to Alma's bedroom. Alma insisted that Lucy not be let

A Fine How Do You Do

outside. Nelson was summoned and off went Alma with Lucy in a covered wicker basket to town. Bessie, Bertha and Eric stared at each other and all covered their faces.

The telephone rang while Alma was in town. Margaret was phoning for Alma. Margaret told Bessie that as soon as Alma came back from town she must come right over to their home as Alfred had taken ill and seemed to be unconscious and unable to speak. Bessie told Bertha and Eric about the call and they poured another cup of tea and just sat there looking at each other. "I do wish that little Lucy was here," said Bertha. They all nodded their heads, and took a sip of tea and a nice warm biscuit.

Margaret had the sense to call Dr. Mellini, the very prominent doctor who summered in Ambleside. His main practice was in Rome. Dr. Mellini came to the house and was examining Alfred when Alma arrived and exclaimed, "Is he alive, Margaret?" Margaret said that she did not know anything and that the doctor had closed the door to their bedroom and had not come out.

"Oh, for the sake of God, Margaret, open the door, go in and find out what is going on. What is the matter with you?" asked Alma as she pushed Margaret out of the way, opened the door and went over to the bed.

Dr. Mellini was talking to Alfred. Alfred was to hold up two fingers if he wanted to say yes, and only one finger if he wanted to say no. "Are you able to hear me, Mr. Boeld?" Two fingers went up. "Are you in pain?" One finger. "Very well, I have called the ambulance and you will go to hospital for some tests, is that satisfactory with you, Mr. Boeld?" Two fingers went up. Alma smiled, as she was delighted that Alfred would be in hospital and would not be around while this financial mess was being cleared up and so would not be part of any further trouble.

"A very wise decision, Dr. Mellini," said Alma and instructed Margaret to pack up the essentials for Alfred. "Thank you, Dr.

Mellini. We do apologize for bothering you and do so appreciate your prompt attention to my brother. I hope we did not interrupt you from some social occasion," said Alma.

"Oh, no, Madame Boeld. We live a very quiet life and do not go to many social occasions. My wife is so pleased that we are included in some, however," said the doctor. Alma responded, "You and your wife are most charming and I will make it a point to entertain you both as soon as Freddie is back on his feet."

Chapter Sixteen

On Wednesday the weather had cleared and Eric rode the bicycle to the library to wire the week's weather to the Altoona paper. His mind wandered as he pedaled along the narrow path. He wondered how Martha was getting along, but put the thought out of his head almost immediately. All was going so well and he did not want to confront his mind right now. For years he never really had to confront his mind with anything at all as Martha took over everything and he just went to the office at *The Altoona Daily News* and wrote the weather predictions. He had the same grilled cheese sandwich for lunch every day at the luncheonette. He could count on either chicken or pork chops for his supper with Martha.

Arriving at the library, he parked the bicycle, greeted the receptionist with a tip of his tweed cap and asked if Miss Louise was here. The receptionist explained that Louise had been called to the girls' school as apparently Millicent had written all over the blackboards "God is dead, save the Queen." Eric wired off his weather reports and bicycled back to Alma's house. When he arrived, Lucy meowed and greeted him. Eric took her up to his room and decided to just sit there with Lucy and wait to see what was going to happen.

Eric heard the car come into the garage and saw that Nelson was back. He wondered where Nelson had been. He decided to knock on Nelson's door, but Nelson did not answer. Eric took little Lucy into the kitchen. Bessie asked, "Well, Mr. Eric, how be you on this fine day?" "Oh very well, thank you." Lucy jumped right up on the table. "Oh, our little baby is back!" exclaimed Bessie. Lucy's pink bow around her neck was in total shambles.

Eric took the opportunity to call Louise's home on the kitchen phone. Louise answered and began to laugh hysterically. Louise explained to Eric that Millicent had been sent to the headmistress' office and Louise was full of laughter at all the commotion and attention Millicent had created. She was not concerned and took delight in detailing Millicent's escapade, and invited Eric to join them for a late afternoon tea. Eric pedaled over to Louise's house, not knowing what to expect.

The phone rang just as Louise was serving the tea. It was Tony, but Eric could not hear the conversation. When Louise hung up she was smiling. She reported that Tony had returned from Zurich and arranged to be in Ambleside this weekend to see the girls. He wanted them to come into London but both girls had birthday parties to attend in Ambleside.

"Oh, for the sake of heaven, Margaret, I cannot hear a thing you are saying and you do not know what you are talking about!" shouted Alma. Margaret stopped talking and brought Alfred to the phone to speak with Alma. Alfred had been sent home from the hospital since all his vitals were in order and he was continually shouting for Margaret and trying to get out of bed. He seemed in control of himself at home, but totally confused about what had happened. "What happened to Tony? I wanted him to stay for the weekend," asked Alfred.

"Freddie, we cannot discuss it now. You need to rest. All I can say is that you are getting off easy as he has saved us all from an investigation and we could all be sitting in jail," said Alma.

"But where is all my money, Alma?"

"GONE, Freddie, GONE. And you are the cause of the whole fiasco."

"Who, me?"

"Yes, Freddie dear, you are. It will be quite rough on all of us and we will discuss it later. I am going to call Tony and set up a meeting with us all and he can explain himself. In the meantime, please get some rest and call no one. This is strictly a family matter. Do you understand that, Freddie, and for the sake of God do not let Margaret leave the house."

Alma was annoyed that Tony was not answering his phone. Finally she reached him and told him what was on her mind and would he please come to her home and discuss the situation. She told him that Alfred had been hospitalized and this was all due to the ruination of their lives. Tony agreed to meet with them in Ambleside on Saturday only because the plan was most convenient for him, enabling the visit with his daughters. Tony suggested to Alma that Nelson come into London on Friday evening and bring him to Ambleside on Saturday for their meeting. Alma reluctantly agreed to that, and to put Tony up for the weekend. Tony knew that Alma was well aware that she was in no position to call the shots. Tony knew his game plan, and the Boeld family would be indebted to him for a very long time.

"Oh hello, Elizabeth, my dear, so nice to hear your voice and what can I do for you on this beautiful day, my dear?"

"Oh, not really a thing at all, Alma dear. I wondered if you were going to the Westcotts' garden party next week and if I could borrow your lovely French blue shawl and then go along with you to the party?"

"I will be wearing that particular shawl. However, I will be delighted to have Nelson collect you and then we will go to the

Patty Dickson

party together. We can discuss our social life later, Elizabeth," said Alma quite abruptly.

"Is something wrong, Alma? You sound flustered."

"Yes, that is exactly what I am. Flustered is a fine word. It has an interesting ring to it. Take care of yourself, Elizabeth." Alma hung up the phone, went to her closet and picked out a hat matching the shawl she was not lending to Elizabeth for the Westcotts' garden party.

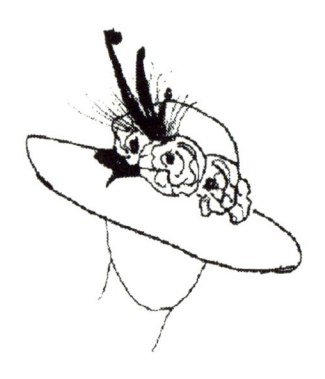

Chapter Seventeen

Nelson drove to Tony's town home just as Tony was arriving. They hugged and remarked how timely things had worked out for them. Once again, Nelson admired how beautifully appointed Tony's place was, with comfortable lounges, antique tables and a very private back garden. "Let's open a bottle of wine and sit in the garden," suggested Tony. "That would be just what the doctor ordered after the drive into London," responded Nelson.

Nelson had been pondering the financial fiasco and decided, after a substantial sip of wine, that he must confess to Tony that he had overheard about it in a most clandestine manner. He told Tony he had actually considered blackmailing him in order to get a payoff, escape his chauffeuring existence and live comfortably as a gay man. He told Tony the entire story.

Tony leaned back in his garden chair and almost tipped over with laughter! "Well, dear boy, I assume you now realize that your idea was most elementary! Oh my, how the plot thickens, my dear Nelson! So we would have met one way or the other. However, your little plan would not have worked and here we are, by hook or by crook!" They smiled and raised their wine glasses to each other. Tony asked Nelson about his life. Nelson told him that it had been most uneventful and unsatisfying but he had endured it all these years, as he had no escape. Tony confessed that he also had suspected he was gay for many years. He tried to live as a straight man with a wife and two children, but the marriage had not worked out. He felt somewhat guilty that he had brought unhappiness to his wife and two daughters. In the beginning he felt that he would do better as a banker and financial investor if he appeared to be a straight man. He admitted to Nelson that he had experienced some very interesting encounters with men since his divorce from Louise.

Nelson and Tony went out for a late dinner, walked around Belgravia and enjoyed a pleasant evening together. Nelson brewed the tea the next morning and Tony poached the eggs. "Are you going to wear that pink uniform in the car today?" asked Tony.

"Yes, Mr. Tony, I am. This is who I am today," said Nelson with a sly smile.

"Well, that will have to change."

"I presume there will be a lot of changes after your meeting with the Boeld family this afternoon," said Nelson as he poured the tea.

"Yes, you can bet on me," said Tony with a nod and a big grin.

"Good afternoon, Mr. Tony Smythe. Please come in and make yourself comfortable in the front parlor. Tea will be served as soon as Alfred and Margaret arrive."

"Thank you, Mrs. Boeld," said Tony. He sat in the straight chair in front of the desk by the window, removed papers from his briefcase, got up to take off his jacket and suddenly noticed a small cat under the desk.

"Well, hello, little kitty, and what can I do for you?"

"Oh, so sorry, that is only the kitchen cat and she does not belong in here at all," said Alma. Bessie arrived with the tea tray and Alma ordered her to remove Lucy to the kitchen. Alfred came in without knocking, followed by Margaret. She was holding a handkerchief to her nose.

"Do you have a cold, Margaret dear?" asked Alma.

"Perhaps."

"Go sit in that comfortable chair by the window. The last thing I need is a cold," said Alma. Margaret sat in a straight chair, the only chair by the window. She was too nervous to close the open window.

With everyone seated, Alma declared: "We all know Mr. Smythe and I think it would be a good idea if we allowed Mr. Smythe to try and explain all the matters concerning our former business with him."

Tony stood up, presenting himself with astonishing flair and charm. Alma could only throw darts at him with her piercing blue eyes, hoping he would land on his bottom.

"Thank you, Madame Boeld. It is with great regret that we must have this meeting. As you know, the privacy of our business was destroyed by actions of Mr. Alfred Boeld, which led to the necessity to end our business partnership. I went to Zurich and met with several investors and paid them all off and also paid off the investors from France and the USA. Most of the investors are old schoolmates from Oxford and I personally cannot afford to lose them. I will continue my financial investing but our business together is finished. It was necessary to pay off other investors according to the current rate before we were investigated. Mr. Stephen Lorde from London is a very proper gentleman and has been a loyal investor of mine. As you will recall, last week at the party he heard all of Mr. Alfred Boeld's accusations towards me and would have prompted an investigation immediately had I not gone to Zurich on the spot. I arranged the books so as to avoid an investigation that would have ruined us all and most likely would have meant you, Mr. Alfred Boeld, would be having bread and tea as your main diet in jail."

Tony began to wander around the room as he continued talking. "You all have received letters from my office stating that our business and financial relationship is legally terminated. You will sign them and return them to my office by mail and there will be no further dealings. By the way, Mr. Alfred Boeld, if you are thinking of a lawsuit against me, put it right out of your head, as you are the named president of the firm as you originally requested. It is very clear from the letters sent to you, Mr. Boeld, that you have no holdings and your account is completely wiped out. Madame Boeld is in the same position and I can only wish you the best and assume you have other holdings to fall back upon," said Tony as he sat down at the desk.

"So, my business with the Boeld family is over. I thank you, Madame Boeld, for your hospitality and will say 'good day' to you all. I will not impose upon you for dinner but do thank you for the opportunity to spend the night. I will leave in the early morning to visit my family."

Tony gathered up his papers, put on his jacket and left the house. Alma, Alfred and Margaret sat upright in their chairs not knowing what to say.

"Margaret, why are you sitting in front of the window if you have a cold? Have you no sense at all?" asked Alma as she looked out the window to see Nelson opening the front door of her car for Tony to enter. "Freddie, do something. Nelson is taking the car and Tony is in the front seat. Freddie, do something!"

Alfred raced out the door but the car was already down the driveway. He returned laughing, and said, "Alma, I bet you don't know what those Americans say when something happens like this, do you?"

"No, Freddie, I do not," admitted Alma.

"They say, I think we got screwed." He laughed again.

"Freddie, that is less than amusing. Take Margaret home and put her to bed before she spreads her cold all over the house."

Alfred was disappointed that his American jest was not well received by Alma. He gathered up Margaret and went on his way. Alma went into the kitchen and found Bessie on her hands and knees washing the floor. Little Lucy was sipping a bowl of milk and scurried under the table when Alma came in.

"Oh, Bessie my dear, I know not what will become of us all!" said Alma as she collapsed in a chair and began to weep.

Bessie came out from under the table. "Begging your pardon, Madame, where did you say you were going?"

"Oh nothing, Bessie dear, just bring me some soup. I think I will take a warm bath."

"That is a fine idea," said Bessie as she went down on her hands and knees, continuing to scrub the floor.

"I will be upstairs. Please bring a fresh bowl of milk for Lucy. She should be in my bed where it is cozy and safe."

Nelson drove Tony to Louise's house on Sunday to collect the girls and take them to the park. Eric and Louise were seated at the kitchen table pondering a jigsaw puzzle when they arrived. The girls heard a car drive up and scurried to the window. "It is a fancy one, Mum, who could it be?" Tony stepped out of the car and Nelson followed. Millicent ran to the door and opened it. "Daddy, Daddy, you have come home! Oh, I just knew that you would come someday. Now, Suzanne and I can stop crying at night. We have a promise to each other that we both will cry every night until you come home, but now you are here."

Louise sat very still at the table and Eric did not move either. "May I come in with my friend, Nelson?" asked Tony.

"Yes, come in Daddy," said Millicent. "We are doing a puzzle and we are not very good at it. You don't like puzzles do you, Daddy?"

Suzanne asked, "Did you bring any presents, Daddy?"

"No, not this time. Now, tell us all about the birthday parties," said Tony. Louise and Eric had not moved and just stared down at the puzzle. Eric finally got up and said, "Well hello, Pinky, how nice to see you. What a surprise!"

"Hello Mr. Eric, a pleasure to see you too."

"Well, we all seem to know each other and that is just dandy," said Tony.

"Why did you call that man Pinky, Uncle Eric?" asked Suzanne.

Nelson interrupted and said, "It is a little joke because my pants and jacket are maroon, which is a dark pink." Nelson, for the first time, was ashamed of his attire.

"Oh, very funny," said Millicent, "sort of like a clown."

"No, Millicent," said Tony. "Nelson wears a uniform because he has an important job driving Mrs. Boeld to various places, and all respectable chauffeurs wear uniforms. My uniform is a grey suit and Nelson wears a maroon suit for his work."

"Oh, I see," said Millicent. "Just like Suzanne and I wear our blue skirts to school. Mum does not have a uniform."

Louise took a deep breath and finally spoke. "Hello, Tony, please sit down and join us for supper if you wish. Eric and I have been preparing a stew and it is almost ready. Eric and I met at the library. He is a famous weatherman and wires weather conditions around the world to newspapers."

"How do you do, Mr. Eric," said Tony extending his hand for a shake. "Daddy, let's all have stew now, like a big family," suggested Millicent, twirling her spoon in the air.

Suzanne and Louise pulled up enough chairs for everyone and they all sat around the small table. Before they started to eat, Millicent suggested that everyone hold hands while she said the grace. "Thank you God, for this stew and that Daddy is here and now I won't have to write any more obituaries. Amen."

Tony cautioned, "Millicent, you must stop writing obituaries. There are many other interesting subjects to write about."

"I used to write about people who didn't really die, but just went away, so it is all right now. Let's eat and we can tell you about the birthday parties. You start Suzanne, because I need to be the last one as my stories are always more interesting and we must save the best for the last," said Millicent, picking up her spoon and looking at her mother for approval.

"Millicent, that is very rude and unkind to your sister. Now you go first and Suzanne will go last," said Louise. Nelson decided he would never wear his uniform again and that Millicent could write an obituary for his uniform. However, he would tell her that news at a more appropriate time.

Chapter Eighteen

Alma chose to wear a black silk suit topped off by a bright red feathered hat for Margaret's burial service. It was not an easy task for her to remain upright while trying to keep Alfred from falling down. He kept trying to steady himself by hanging on to the red feathers of her hat. There were only a few close friends at the graveside service and the minister was an old friend of the family. Alfred finally settled himself on the ground at Alma's feet, clutching her ankle. Alma straightened her hat, saying a silent prayer of thanks to God for coming to the aid of the family in such a welcome way.

Pneumonia had set in very rapidly and Margaret had died in her sleep eight days ago. Margaret's personal possessions and all her money went to Alfred; she had no heirs. Margaret's father had been a very successful textile merchant owning a small factory in Ireland. Mr. Browne, the attorney, discovered that the father had set up a trust fund for Margaret years ago, but no one knew about it until Margaret's death. Perhaps Margaret herself was unaware, as no withdrawals were ever reported. The trust had increased in value and Alfred was a wealthy gentleman today. Alma was taking good care of Alfred and had requested that Mr. Browne come to dinner next week and write a will for Alfred.

"Good evening, Mr. Browne, and thank you for taking time to join our family at this very sad time," said Alma. She decided to have the dinner at home as it would be more comfortable for everyone. It was certainly more comfortable than Mr. Browne's office, which Alma had scouted out and was a mere hole in the wall.

"Thank you for the dinner invitation," said Mr. Browne, who was dressed entirely in brown. Noticing that, Alma could hardly keep a straight face as she met him at the door and ushered him into the drawing room. After all were seated he declared: "I realize this is a very sad time for all of you, but it is most important that a will be created to protect your family. I am aware that this was not the case for Margaret. However all went, as should be, to the surviving spouse, Mr. Alfred Boeld. Now, it is secure that Mr. Alfred inherits the estate of his wife, Margaret MacCaley Boeld. The other assets were disclosed to you in the letter from the Trust Department at The Bank of Scotland regarding Mr. MacCaley's estate. As you know, this is a rather large trust fund and, with permission from Mr. Alfred Boeld, I think it proper that we ask for an accounting from all years back. This accounting may take some time, but it is most essential to do this background report. We wish to make sure that it was handled in an honest and forthright fashion. Do you all agree?"

Alma and Alfred nodded in approval. Alfred leaned toward Alma and said too loudly in her ear, "I do not care for Mr. Browne's brown suit and shoes. Margaret never liked brown." Alma gave Alfred a glance that he immediately recognized was an order to stand up. She led the way to the dining room.

"I hope you enjoy fresh trout with a caviar sauce. It is one of my favorites and I personally taught dear Margaret how to serve it for her very first dinner party," said Alma, patting her eyes with a lace hankie. "This dinner is in memory of my beloved sister-in-law whom we all shall miss so very deeply," she said most convincingly. "Freddie, please find the appropriate white wine and bring it to the table. Bessie will pour, as you have been so unstable on your feet that I dare not trust you with expensive wines! Oh, Freddie dear, it was only a little joke. Do cheer up!"

"Yes, Alma dear, I will do my best to do whatever you think is proper. It seems to be raining and I hope all the lovely flowers are not falling apart on my Margaret's grave. I want to drive over right now and make sure that she is warm enough and the flowers are alive. She was never warm enough and that is why she caught that pneumonia," said Alfred with tears running down his face.

"Of course, Freddie, I understand and why don't we all go over after we finish the trout course?"

"May I take your arm all the time we are there, as it will be very lonely for me?"

"Of course, Freddie, I am always here to support you and keep you afloat," said Alma, who did not like deaths of any sort as she had seen too many of them during the war. However, she was determined to believe that Margaret's passing was a particularly good omen for the Boeld family.

Mr. Browne had drawn up wills for both Alma and Alfred according to Alma's suggestions prior to the dinner meeting. The wills were signed at the dining table as Alfred had chosen to drink his dinner and not even touch the lovely trout with caviar sauce. The wills stated very clearly that all of Alma's possessions and money would be left to Alfred and all of Alfred's earthly possessions to Alma. Margaret's inheritance from her father would be put into a joint account from which Alma and Alfred could draw upon at any time. Mr. Browne agreed that Alfred was not a responsible person and Alma was very pleased with this arrangement, which she had carefully manipulated. Alma and Alfred both signed the legal agreements.

A Fine How Do You Do

Alfred wanted to go to the gravesite to visit Margaret, but Alma said it was too damp and that Margaret was sleeping comfortably and the morning would be a better time for a visit. Alfred asked Mr. Browne to take him to Margaret's grave and said he would allow Mr. Browne to sit down near her. He told Mr. Browne that his suit matched the dirt on Margaret's grave. Alma suggested that Alfred retire for the evening if he continued to act like a lunatic. Alfred nodded, rose and meandered around bumping into furniture; boo-hoos could be heard from all over the house. Finally, Alfred fell into a guest room bed and was out for the evening.

Alma and Mr. Browne discussed the situation by the fire in the front parlor and Mr. Browne agreed that Alfred should sell his house and move into Alma's lovely home and give Alma the proceeds of the house sale and she would promise to care for him throughout his lifetime. He would draw up the papers and be back tomorrow for all signatures. Mr. Browne suggested that the money Alfred received from Margaret's father be converted into bonds. A document would be drawn up by Mr. Browne tomorrow to guarantee this arrangement. Alma was most confident that she could arrange for Alfred to sign anything she suggested, as Alfred needed a steady and caring crutch and she was that.

Bertha came to the door and gave Mr. Browne his walking stick, cap and some wrapped-up trout from dinner. Bertha also gave Mr. Browne a flirty smile and curtsy while presenting him with an unopened bottle of wine. Mr. Browne bowed to Bertha as she winked at him. Bertha lifted her skirt and turned away quickly. Mr. Browne departed with a smile on his face. He was full of glee at finally managing to have some business and could charge a somewhat handsome fee and perhaps be back in the social scene once again.

Three summers ago, Mr. Browne had consumed a great amount of brandy, misbehaved and dropped his trousers at one of Alma's supper parties. He had been flirting most ostentatiously with Bertha all evening. Since that episode he had not received an invitation to any social occasion. His phone rarely rang and his good clothes were being munched away by moths. He knew he was now being manipulated by the infamous Madame Boeld, but Alma promised that she would arrange for him to be invited around again. He and Alma had an unwritten pact and both would gain from it.

Alma kept to herself more than usual, as she was quite worn out from all the recent happenings. So many images were going through her head she was quite dizzy from it all – losing all her money, Margaret dying from pneumonia, discovering the mysterious trust fund. Suddenly she was wealthy once again. It was an emotional merry-go-round. Dealing with the most commonplace Mr. Browne was a tremendous bore, but it would pay off for Alma. Now Alfred would be moving into her house. She climbed into her warm bed and pondered if she should simply stay in bed tomorrow or perhaps order a new hat.

Chapter Nineteen

Eric picked up some groceries, met Louise at the library at the end of her work time and walked home with her. He had been working on the broken bricks on her back terrace that Nelson had abandoned and was able to piece many together and make the terrace somewhat level. They had tea together and Eric departed before the girls arrived home.

He was most concerned about the loss of money for Alma and Alfred and disturbed that Tony had been involved. Margaret's untimely death due to pneumonia was upsetting him as well. He wondered if he should leave Alma's home and decided to ask her if she wanted him to depart. When he met with Alma a bit later she told him that it was quite convenient for him to stay on for a while, as the finances would be worked out shortly and she hoped he could help around the garden and to please stay out of her way until she was feeling more like herself.

Eric crept upstairs and went into his bedroom. Alma gazed out the window and discovered that the sun was shining brightly and the sky was clear blue. She felt a bit better but decided to rest for the afternoon and order a new hat tomorrow. Her customary milliner was in London, but this young girl with her own shop in town was very obliging. She took her shoes off, plumped up her pillows and enjoyed the breeze and sunshine coming into her bedroom as she rested comfortably. She decided that a snappy beige straw hat with a perky garden green bow and large pastel flower would now be appropriate, as Margaret was buried and the mourning period was almost over.

Eric felt a bit lonesome in his bedroom and decided to return to Louise's and continue the work on the terrace. Being outside in the sunshine would cheer him up. He was on his hands and knees placing bricks around when he heard, "Hello, Mum, we are home but Suzanne fell down and has a bloody knee. She is sitting by the tree crying."

"Millicent, how could you leave your little sister by the tree?" asked Louise as she ran out to Suzanne.

"Hi Uncle Eric," said Millicent. "I want you to tell me more about that old lady who died. Did you know her and did she have snow white hair and wear wire glasses and carry a beautiful cane?" Eric had to gather his thoughts. "She was called Margaret and I first met her at my birthday party. She was married to Mr. Alfred Boeld, who is Alma's, I mean, Mrs. Boeld's brother," explained Eric.

"What did she look like when she was dead?"

"Oh Millicent, of course I did not see her when she was dead."

"Well, how do we know that she really died?"

"There was a service at her graveside and all the family was there," said Eric as he pieced more bricks together.

"I will write an obituary about it," said Millicent as she picked up her schoolbooks, went back into the house and up to her bedroom. Louise came in with Suzanne, who was recovering from her fall. "Where is Millicent?" asked Louise. "She is writing another obituary," said Eric with a smile of amusement.

Chapter Twenty

Nelson was sitting in his apartment recalling all that had happened. Never had his life been as complicated, with so much emotion involved. He sat and looked out the window and tears came to his eyes. He did not know how to handle his emotions. He had always dressed in his uniform and it dictated his behavior. He suddenly felt he had become a real person and was in a state of shock. He was very fond of Tony and Tony seemed very fond of him. Bertha appeared at Nelson's door and told him that Mr. Smythe was on the kitchen phone. Nelson raced down the stairs and to the kitchen.

"Pinky, how are you dear boy?" asked Tony. "Oh, just fine and you, dear boy?" Both laughed. "So how is everything going at the Boeld Estate and how is the Witch of Ambleside?"

"All is a bit of a shamble and Madame has been out of sorts, but other than that, all is fine. Mr. Alfred is selling his property and I heard Madame talking on the telephone to a designer about fixing a suite upstairs for Mr. Alfred to occupy."

"Oh, very clever of her to keep him under her nose and control. Wonder who will be the next body in the morgue."

"Oh, please do not say that, Tony, I have had more than I can handle for a while."

"I have some business partners I must meet so I must buzz off now," said Tony, hanging up the phone.

Nelson sat down with Bessie and Bertha and was offered a cup of tea, which he accepted. He drank the tea but did not start a conversation. The three sat together as they had for many years. "We are sort of a family, aren't we, Pinky?" said Bessie. "Yes, we are," said Nelson. Bertha looked at Bessie and both shook their heads.

Alma spotted Alfred in the driveway from her bedroom window and could tell from the way he was stumbling around that something was wrong. Alma made a beeline for the kitchen just as Alfred stumbled in and fell into the nearest chair. "Now Freddie, just sit back and take some breaths. You must have some breakfast even if it is late afternoon and we should be having tea, but you are all off schedule. Now, eat your eggs and toast."

"No," said Alfred. "I do not like to be bossed around. Margaret would not approve of you bossing me around. Margaret never bossed me around. She was my best friend and now she has gone, all due to a bad cold. I do not understand what happened. I will have more hot tea and then I want to go home. Give me the keys to my car so I can go and have a visit with my Margaret. I have missed her."

"Freddie, you have not been yourself, but of course you must visit Margaret and do you want me to take your arm so you will be steady on your feet?"

"No, I want to go alone. Where is my jacket?"

"Freddie, your jacket is in the closet and Nelson will drive us to the cemetery."

Nelson drove and Alfred saw the fresh dirt and knew that was where they buried Margaret. He went over to the grave and fell upon it and cried like a baby. "Margaret, speak to me and tell me what to do. I am lost." Alfred began to take off his clothes and dig in the dirt. Nelson and Alma had to drag him away and get him in the car. They brought him back to the house. Nelson helped him bathe, get into his dressing gown and told him to go to bed.

Alma was called to the telephone to find that Tony was calling. "Madame Boeld, good afternoon, Tony Smythe here."

"Well, Mr. Smythe, I had hoped never to hear from you again. What in the world do you want?"

"Madame Boeld, a client of mine is most interested in purchasing the home of Mr. Alfred Boeld."

"Oh really, Mr. Smythe, then you must contact our estate agent. I do not wish to deal with you directly and it is not proper that I do."

"Very well, Madame Boeld, I will do just that, but thought I would give you the advantage of a private deal and save you the commission."

"Mr. Smythe, a private deal with you is a deal with the devil and I have had enough of you," said Alma and hung up the phone. She smiled to herself. She had upstaged Tony Smythe. Alma immediately called the estate agent and told her to raise the price on Alfred's property.

Chapter Twenty-One

Alfred awoke in the morning to find that his hands were a bit dirty and thought perhaps he had neglected to bathe before retiring. His nightshirt however was clean and still pressed. It bothered him to be so confused. He rang for Bertha.

"Bertha, why are my hands and my knees so dirty?"

"Well, Mr. Alfred, you are having troubling times but all will be all right. Freshen up and come down for breakfast. Madame sent Pinky over to your house to pick up some clothes and I will bring them right up to you now that you are awake and chipper. Would you like some soft-boiled eggs this morning, Mr. Alfred?"

"Yes, Bertha, that sounds very nice. But does everyone just eat eggs here?" Alfred did not feel chipper and remained quite confused.

"Well, good morning to you, dear Freddie. You look rested and back to sorts. Very good, as I have some interesting news for you," said Alma, who had barged into Alfred's room without knocking. "Why are my hands and knees so dirty this morning, Alma?"

"Well, my dear brother, you decided to scramble around in the cemetery yesterday and we brought you home, as you were very upset and not yourself at all, but that is over and today is another day," said Alma reassuringly. "Now, for the good news. The estate agent just called and a lovely couple from Paris wish to see your house and will most likely purchase it and would like all the furniture and will be offering a very handsome price."

"But where will I go, Alma? Oh … may I live with you, since my Margaret has gone away?"

"Of course you may, Freddie dear, and we will work all that out. The estate agent is on her way over to your house right now, as they are very anxious to take it over while the social season is still high. They have friends from Paris who summer here. You know how the French love to summer here and thank God they all stick together and we do not have to be troubled by them. Monsieur Grobet is in finance and Madame Grobet is an artist. They have a flat in London and a lovely apartment in Paris overlooking the Champs de Mars. What could be better? Freddie, we have luck on our side today, don't we?"

"Ah, rather, I guess we do, if you say so."

"Yes, Freddie, I know luck when I see it and today you are a very lucky gentleman."

"I don't want the eggs and I want to see that cute cat again that came up to my bed and snuggled with me," said Alfred.

Eric had been awake for some time and overheard the conversation about the potential sale of Alfred's house and that Alfred would be moving in. He never had to make choices, as Martha always took care of him and they never changed their life. Everything just went along as usual in Altoona. However, now that he had ventured out, he realized that he had to make some decisions for himself but he did not want to. He would be helping in the garden and perhaps that would be enough to let him stay on for a bit more time.

He went downstairs and into the kitchen, as he did not want to interfere with the family matters in the dining room. Bertha and Bessie were busy washing the dishes and did not turn to welcome

Eric immediately. Eric saw Lucy drinking her milk from a bowl on the floor near the back door. "Hello, dear Lucy, so glad to see you."

Bertha and Bessie turned around and welcomed Eric to the kitchen table and sat down with their tea and gave coffee to Eric, who ventured, "I guess that you both know that Alfred will be moving in soon."

"Yes, we do," said Bertha, "and thank the good Lord for it, as Bessie and I were worried about what might happen to us."

"Well, I was wondering if I should move on too."

Their eyes all met and Bertha said, "Mr. Eric, we all agree that we have become a sort of family, haven't we?"

"Well, you could say that, but I do have a real family in Altoona. I haven't talked about them, have I?"

"No, you haven't, but Bessie and I were wondering where you came from. I mean to say that we are awfully glad you are here, but we thought you might be a gypsy. You know there really are gypsies all over the place."

"Well, I am not a gypsy, I am a weatherman," said Eric.

"Do you have gypsies in Altoona?"

"No, not in Altoona. I do not know what goes on outside of Altoona and that is why I came here, to see what was happening in England. I had heard about England but I had never been out of Altoona," said Eric.

"We have never been anywhere either, but that is the way it is and we are content," said Bessie as they all raised their cups together.

"Well, this is a happy scene you three, what is going on?" asked Alma as she entered the kitchen.

"Oh, nothing much, Madame, we are just having a little sit-down."

"Eric, dear chap, you had offered to help with the gardening, did you not?"

A Fine How Do You Do

"Oh yes, and I would be happy to do anything you wish."

"Very good, and so convenient of you to be available. I saw Nelson washing the car. Please go and ask him to gather up some gardening tools and take you over to Mr. Alfred's house to spruce up all the shrubs and turn over the soil in the garden. Snip off all the dead flower heads so it looks alive and presentable. Bertha and Bessie, you two must go also and clear out all of the closets and bring Mr. Alfred's clothes back here. As for Madame Margaret's belongings, just discard her clothes but pack up all her jewelry and personal pictures and bring them back to the house. Make sure you bring all of Mr. Alfred's toilet articles. Have Nelson help you put the silver chest and silver coffee set and tray in the car. We can clear out other things tomorrow. That is all for now, so scurry off," ordered Alma before walking out to the dining room. She was delighted with the way everything was turning out. She sighed and straightened her back and smiled at herself in the dining room mirror. "You are a survivor and I love you!" she said to her image. She wandered out to the back terrace and collapsed in a chair. She saw the car leave the driveway with Eric, Bessie and Bertha all inside and knew it was a most fortunate day. She had no time to deal with a new hat today.

Bessie and Bertha returned from Alfred's house and were scrubbing the floor when Alfred came in with his dishes. "Mr. Alfred, you need not bother with that. We will do it," said Bessie.

"I always do the dishes, that is my job and I empty the wastebaskets when Margaret tells me," said Alfred with pride. Bessie and Bertha looked at each other and giggled. "That is most helpful, Mr. Alfred, and thank you."

"Oh, there is my kitty cat!" exclaimed Alfred. Lucy came running over to him and they sat in a kitchen chair together as Alfred fed her little scraps of bacon from his plate.

"Did you know my Margaret?" asked Alfred.

"Yes Mr. Alfred, we did, and we are sorry to learn of her passing,"

"Thank you and I am so sorry if I have caused any trouble here, I will be better soon."

"Of course you will be, Mr. Alfred, and we are happy you have decided to move in with us all."

"Oh, I am not moving in, I am just staying here until my Margaret comes back."

Lucy looked up at Alfred for more scraps but there were none, so she jumped down and scampered off. Alfred excused himself and saluted both Bessie and Bertha and went out to the terrace to join Alma.

"Well, Freddie dear, pull up a chair and let's enjoy the lovely sun and warmth. Are you feeling better now?"

"No, not really. I am waiting to go home."

"Freddie dear, this is your home now. Sit down and be quiet and enjoy the sunshine. I will bring you the newspaper so you can catch up on the happenings. I think we should plan a small dinner party for our friends. Who would you like to invite?"

"I like Elizabeth. We all need a good laugh, don't we? Perhaps those people from Paris who want to buy my house, if they have good manners and won't step on Lucy," said Alfred.

"Freddie dear, the sun is so good for you and you are full of good ideas. I shall plan the party when we are assured that the Grobets are buying your house," said Alma.

"Yes, that sounds just fine, Alma dear. I shall fetch my proper clothes."

"That is all taken care of and you will be dressed perfectly."

"May I sit next to you at dinner and on my other side put Elizabeth with the long hair. That will be very funny."

"Yes, that will work very well and everyone will be amused and have a grand evening." Oh my, Alma thought to herself, this is going to be a trying time, but I will weather the storm. She would find a free evening, call Dr. Mellini and invite him to the supper party, as he is a charming fellow and will prescribe some soothing medicine for Freddie.

The phone rang and it was the estate agent, Miss Carrolle, calling from Alfred's home. "Madame Boeld?"

"Yes, this is Alma Boeld."

"Madame, I have some very good news for you and your brother. The Grobets wish to purchase the house and take occupancy as soon as possible. They will be paying full price and would like all the furniture in the home except for the family objects that you have designated as not included. I have spoken with their financial agent, Mr. Tony Smythe, and a check can be drawn from their account as soon as all the papers are signed and in good order. I will be meeting with Mr. Smythe and Mme. and Monsieur Grobet in London tomorrow. I would like to bring over the contract papers for Mr. Alfred Boeld to sign within the hour so I am able to have everything in order for the meeting in London tomorrow."

"Absolutely not. This is too much of a rush and my brother is grieving the loss of his beloved wife and I naturally want Barrister Browne to examine the papers and witness all transactions. Alfred will give Barrister Browne power of attorney and we shall not be meeting with Mr. Tony Smythe. I will call Barrister Browne and he will be in touch with you. Thank you so very much, Miss Carrolle. You have been most efficient and my brother and I appreciate your kindness in respecting our privacy at this time. Barrister Browne will be in touch with you very shortly," explained Alma, hanging up.

She took a deep breath, picked up the phone and dialed Mr. Browne.

"Good afternoon, Mr. Browne speaking."

"Mr. Browne, this is Alma Boeld and most suddenly we have a full price offer on Alfred's residence and the papers need to be signed tomorrow in London at Tony Smythe's office. Will you be available to handle this affair and spare my dear brother from all this? It all has happened so very suddenly and Freddie is still very distraught but anxious to sell and will give you power of attorney. Is it possible for you to come over to my home, as Alfred has moved here, and he will sign the proper papers so that you may handle the sale for him. We do not wish to deal personally with Mr. Tony Smythe," said Alma.

"Well, ah ... I surmise this fortunate offer will relieve some of your financial troubles. I advise accepting the deal if I approve the contract. I can come over within the hour and draw up a power of attorney for me to handle this sale if Alfred agrees to the procedure."

"Very well, I shall alert Freddie and we will be ready to receive you within the hour."

Alma took her time going back to her brother on the terrace. She must put her thoughts in order and present this news in a most positive way. "Freddie, dear, I was thinking that we should go to that wonderful place that makes the most beautiful headstones and purchase a particularly lovely one for dear Margaret's grave site. We can put all the lovely flowers around and the stone will be carved beautifully and read 'Beloved wife of Alfred Boeld.'"

"Oh yes, Alma, when can we do this?"

"Tomorrow," assured Alma."

"Oh, my dear sister, you always think of everything and this is a perfect idea," exclaimed Alfred.

"Thank you, Freddie. Barrister Browne is on his way over to our home and we must sign some papers so you can sell your home to the Grobets and then tomorrow, first thing, we will go together and order the gravestone and it will be engraved with your name and Margaret's and will be the most handsome ornament in the cemetery and you can go there anytime you like, dressed in your best attire, and take lovely flowers to Margaret as often as you like."

"Oh, Alma dear, you always know what is best and this is the best idea you have ever had in your whole life. How will we pay for all this?"

"Very easily. Mr. Browne will arrange the sale of your house and then you will be able to afford the stone and more flowers."

"Oh, very good thinking, Alma, why didn't I think of that?"

"Freddie, the idea really came from you and you will plan it all when we go to the foundry where they engrave the stone just as you want it to be."

He stood and came over to Alma and gave her a big hug and told her that he loved her and please to never go away like Margaret did. Alma breathed a sigh of relief and promised him that she would always be his caretaker and that he need not worry about anything anymore. "That is me, worry free," said Alfred as he saluted Alma and suggested that they have a glass of Dubonnet. Alma called for Bertha to please bring three small glasses of Dubonnet and some cheese to the terrace.

The doorbell rang. Bertha balanced the tray with the Dubonnet and cheese and managed to open the door for Mr. Browne and his attaché case. Alma jumped up from her chair, welcomed Mr. Browne and suggested that they get right to business before having refreshments. Mr. Browne had drawn up all the necessary papers for the sale of Alfred's house and had given power of attorney to himself with Alfred's approval.

Chapter Twenty-Two

Alma was relaxing on her bed and decided to stay there and try to digest all that had happened in the last few days. Oh dear, she thought, things come in threes, and we have had two. The dreadful situation with the finances and then Margaret passing away. She relaxed a bit as she thought things looked clear and perhaps the triangle of situations would not apply. She had suffered through uglier scenes than these in the war. She threw the covers aside and went over to the window and looked out upon her lovely property. Soon the inheritance from Margaret would be in order and the money from the house sale would be deposited. Life would surely be more comfortable. She would do anything to maintain her wellbeing and place in society and would face the day with all the energy she could muster up. Yes, all will be fine if I can just keep my hands on the wheel. I am the Captain of this ship and always will be.

She heard a knock on the door and was startled from her thoughts. "Is that you Bertha?" "Yes, Madame, I have your toast and tea here." "Thank you Bertha dear, I wish to have a word with you." "Yes, Madame, I hope we have not done anything to disturb you." "Heavens no, Bertha. You and Bessie are part of the family and you have been most patient and diligent. I want you to know that my brother Alfred will be staying here indefinitely. Actually, he will be moving in permanently today," said Alma, avoiding eye contact with Bertha.

"Yes, Madame, we have brought all his personal belongings over here, as you asked, hung up all his jackets and trousers and will iron the shirts that we found rather poorly pressed in his closet," said Bertha most proudly.

"Yes, I imagine that is the case, as dear Margaret had no decent help and was not very mindful about caring for things. Did you notice how she let the sofa and the chairs just go to ruin in the front parlor?" asked Alma.

"No, Madame, I took no notice of that," said Bertha, though she had indeed noticed.

"She also neglected the garden and almost everything around the house. It is all over now and the house will be sold and Alfred will be amongst us here, so let us carry on and make the best of it all," said Alma with great satisfaction.

After finishing her toast and tea, Alma went downstairs and found her brother walking about. "Now, Alfred dear, you are looking properly spiffy this lovely morning."

"I do not like the word stone, can't we call it something else?" asked Alfred.

"It is a stone and will always be a stone but you will have anything your heart desires inscribed on the front of it and that is what makes is so very special, as it is your stone and no one will have a stone like it anywhere in the world and it will just be for you and Margaret as she is buried there."

"Yes, I know and can we go there now?" Alma nodded and said, "Bertha, please call Nelson and tell him that we will be ready in one half hour to go and see Mr. Evans about the stone for Mrs. Alfred Boeld's gravesite."

Nelson was promptly in front of the house dressed in his pressed uniform, having polished up the car. "Good morning, Mr.

Alfred and Madame," said Nelson as Alfred and Alma climbed into the back seat.

"Alma, that angel with the lovely wings reminds me of Margaret and I want that one," he said pointing to a very large angel as they drove into the cemetery. "Then you may have the angel, Freddie dear. Go and tell Mr. Evans what engraving you want and I will wait in the car." Alfred entered the office by himself.

"Oh Nelson, it seems like a day does not go by that we don't have some incident of sorts. I do hope that we will be back to normal very soon, but what is normal and who can define it?" asked Alma.

"Well, you have a very interesting point, Madame, and I have often wondered about that myself."

"Oh, you have, how interesting, Nelson, and what have you come up with?"

"Nothing yet, Madame."

"Well, work on that one, Nelson."

"Yes, Madame, I will try."

They sat in the car in silence waiting for Alfred. Nelson could see Alma in the rearview mirror, straightening her hat and pulling the veil down over her face.

Chapter Twenty-Three

Nelson stood in front of his mirror and began a conversation with his image. "Look old boy, you are not getting any younger and you have no life. Now take the leap and do something to give yourself a life and some enjoyment." But he was anxious about taking any steps to make it happen. He wanted most desperately to do it. Tony called and was planning to come from London on Saturday to see his girls and wanted to have dinner with Nelson after he delivered the girls back home. He would have to check with Madame to make sure that she did not need him to drive her somewhere on Saturday evening. Yes, he would bite the bullet and tell Madame that he needed Saturday night off and that was that. He would call Tony and tell him that he would be delighted to spend Saturday evening with him. He realized that he actually could do this. He went to the kitchen and dialed Tony's number. Tony answered immediately.

"Tony, Saturday evening is fine."

"Did you tell Madame Boeld that you will not be available for Saturday evening?"

"No, not yet, but I will right away." Nelson decided not to change back into his uniform and just stay in the gardening clothes. He and Eric had pruned some of the trees and weeded some of the flower beds. Nelson sat down at the kitchen table feeling very proud of himself. "Cheerio, ladies, and how are you?" he asked Bertha and Bessie.

"Well aren't we the cheery sort, you must want some tea and toasts."

"No thank you, not just now, but shortly I hope."

Nelson went into the dining room and Alma was standing over piles of silverware scattered all over the table. "Oh, hello, Nelson, I am sorting out all the combined silver, some just do not match well and others are tarnished. I doubt they will ever be of use. Margaret did not take care of things."

"I do not mean to interrupt you, Madame," said Nelson, "but I wish to ask, I mean inform you, that I will not be available for you on Saturday evening." Alma stood up. "My heavens, Nelson, you sound like you are on stage in a play. What is the matter with you?"

"Nothing at all. I have a social engagement for Saturday evening."

"Aha, a lady friend is on your dance card. How very nice and where did you meet her?"

"No, that is not it at all," said Nelson.

"Oh well, fortunately, I do not think that I will need you on Saturday evening."

"Thank you Madame, I appreciate it." Nelson backed out of the dining room, through the swinging door into the kitchen, falling into Bessie's lap.

"Welcome to my lap, Pinky dear, and what is this all about?"

"Oh, please excuse me, Bessie, I am a bit jittery," said Nelson.

"Well you are acting like a youngster on his first date," said Bertha as both women giggled. "Please do not say that," said Nelson. Bessie and Bertha had overheard the conversation in the dining room and so knew that something was going on, as Nelson had never asked for an evening out. "Well, Pinky, whatever you are doing, we hope it is pleasant," said Bessie.

A Fine How Do You Do

The doorbell rang and Bertha pushed Nelson out of the way. She opened the door to find a lady with a big briefcase and large darkened glasses. She wore a tilted beret with her blond hair curling around it.

"Good afternoon, and may I ask who is calling?"

"Yes, I am Miss Carrolle, the estate broker, and I would like to see Mrs. Boeld." Alma heard the voices at the door and came right out. "I was expecting you, Miss Carrolle. Please come right in and excuse my appearance, but I am busy sorting out the family silver," said Alma.

"I came to deliver the signed papers for the sale of Mr. Boeld's house. All is in order. The Grobets will take occupancy in six days. They so enjoy The Lake District and have a number of friends already summering here. Mr. Browne stated that six days was enough time for you to clear out personal belongings. Is Mr. Alfred Boeld here?" asked Miss Carrolle.

"Yes, he is and please make yourself comfortable in the parlor."

Alfred heard voices and was on his way downstairs. He spotted Miss Carrolle and her big sunglasses, very trim suit and snappy beret, and thought she was a famous actress. Miss Carrolle stood up and went over to him. "How do you do, Mr. Boeld, and congratulations on such a successful sale of your lovely home." Alfred was intrigued with Miss Carrolle. "Thank you and would you care for tea?" he asked, not letting go of her hand. She began to twitch and tried to loosen the grip but Alfred kept hanging on and then put his left hand over his right for a better grip.

Alma came to the rescue and asked Miss Carrolle to please sit down in a comfortable single chair. Alma pulled Alfred's shirt and pushed him onto the couch. Miss Carrolle sat upright, massaging her hand, before opening her briefcase. "Here are the papers, Mr. Boeld, for the sale of your house. They are all properly signed by the buyers. I must be going now."

Alfred paid no attention to the signed papers or any of the business conversation. He could not take his eyes off Miss Carrolle and followed her to the waiting cab. Alfred noticed her very slim legs as she stepped into the taxi. He waved good-bye and she waved back and smiled.

Alma, who had also come out, said with great satisfaction, "Freddie, you have a check here and you must deposit it tomorrow in the account that has been established for us." Freddie turned around and said, "Miss Carrolle is very pretty."

Chapter Twenty-Four

Eric and Louise were sitting in Louise's kitchen, having prepared a healthy vegetable soup and reminiscing about their long walk in Grizedale Forest and how enchanted they were with some of the sculptures along the way. "Louise, this is such a beautiful place to live and I like spending time with you. I want to thank you for letting me spend time with you." Eric realized that his statement was a bit awkward, but he meant what he said. He found himself thinking about Martha while walking and wished she could be here.

"I like spending time with you too, Eric." Louise had found herself thinking about Tony when the girls were little and they would go to Grizedale Forest and all bicycle around for the afternoon. The top on the pot began to jump around and Louise stood up. "It smells lovely and should be ready any minute so I will turn it down very low until the girls return."

Just at that moment they heard car doors slam and the girls came rushing in carrying packages. They heard the car depart quickly and Eric noticed the disappointment on Louise's face. Millicent came in first and let the door go slamming right into Suzanne's packages. Suzanne said nothing and picked up her presents and hugged Louise. Millicent said nothing and went straight to her room. Louise asked Suzanne how she spent the day and Suzanne replied "with my Daddy." A few minutes later Millicent appeared in a lovely green velveteen dress with a white lace collar and new Mary Jane shoes. "Remember when that dog in the coach train made a puddle and ruined Suzanne's shoes, well that dog ruined my shoes too, but now I have new ones and so does Suzanne and we both have new party dresses."

Millicent whirled around and landed in Eric's lap. "I remember that incident also, Millicent, and that is when I went to get a mop and fell and hurt my foot." Millicent stared at Eric and was deep in thought for a moment. "I did not know you hurt your foot. Is it all right now?"

"Yes, it is, and your mother and I had a lovely walk this afternoon and my foot does not hurt any more at all." Suzanne had fallen asleep on her mother's lap. Louise told Millicent to take off the lovely dress and save it for a special party. Suzanne woke up and went to sit in her usual place at the table. Louise served the soup and Millicent appeared in a pink tutu with a paper crown on her head. Louise remained quiet and did not comment on Millicent's outfit.

Tony combed his hair while driving to Alma's house and tried to brush the cookie crumbs off the front seat. Nelson had decided to wear the old tweed jacket that Alma gave him several years ago. He decided not to wear the tie. He looked at himself in the mirror and smiled. He thought he looked quite attractive and was excited about seeing Tony again. He saw Tony's car pull up by the garage and he went downstairs and looked around. All seemed quiet in the house so Nelson was comfortable walking out and getting into Tony's car.

"You act as if you are running away from school, Nelson. Calm down, we are just going on a dinner date and all is perfectly safe." Tony smiled at Nelson, leaned toward him and held his hand.

"Yes, you are right and I do not mean to be nervous. I was very relaxed when we were in London but now in Ambleside it is a bit different."

"Yes it is, but we won't be in Ambleside forever. We will talk about it over dinner."

"Where are we going for dinner, Tony?"

"Oh, just an old hangout of mine with very good food. It is a friendly pub and you will like it." They pulled up in front of The Cuckoo Brow Inn and parked. Tony took Nelson's arm and they entered the pub. The noise overwhelmed Nelson but Tony kept his hand and led him up to the bar, where a fellow turned around and said to Tony, "Alright, mate, how are you? And how are things in London town? You've been making yourself scarce."

"Hi Benny, and good to see you again," said Tony, patting Benny on the back. "Nelson, this is my old pal Benny." Nelson shook hands with Benny.

"Any friend of Tony's is okay with me," said Benny. Nelson smiled and sat on a stool and looked around. Tony and Benny slapped each other on the back several times. Benny said, "A new one now, is it?" Tony responded quietly, "Well it could be, mate, we'll see how it goes." "And how is your family?" asked Benny. "Oh, just fine, thanks." Nelson was fascinated with all the people having such a good time.

Tony ordered two lager and limes. Nelson downed the drink like water and Tony said "Watch it, old boy, these can creep up on you." Nelson was not paying attention and was fascinated with all the hustle-bustle and laughter and everyone slapping each other on the back. He slapped Tony on the back. "How about another one of these lager and limes, Tony?"

"Coming right up," said Tony. They each had another drink and then sat down for dinner in a private booth. "Well, what do you think, Nelson?"

"I think it is a wonderful place and I like it."

"And do you like being out and about and seeing how the other half live?"

"What do you mean, the other half?" asked Nelson.

"I mean regular people. Not like Madame Boeld and all her friends."

"Yes, it is very different. I am not used to this sort of fun. I spend so much time alone or just with Bessie and Bertha or with Madame and I don't know what else is happening. All of Madame's guests are very different from the people here," remarked Nelson, taking another swig.

Tony laughed and said, "I will show you around, my friend, and you will find a whole new world. Would you like that?" Nelson did not know what to say. He asked, "Do they have kidney pie here? I have not had a kidney pie in so long."

They both ordered kidney pie and Nelson enjoyed every bite. "Tony, this has been the best evening of my life."

"Oh, just you wait my friend, this is just a starter."

Tony drove Nelson back to the house. Nelson was relieved that all seemed quiet in the household. "Thank you, Tony, it was a very special night and when will I see you again?"

"The night is not over, if you will allow me to stay in your apartment. It is late for me to drive back to London."

Nelson felt frozen. He wanted to say how grand that would be but could not express himself at all. He just sat in the car and then began to cry.

"Let's get out of the car, Nelson, and go up to your apartment and talk."

"But, Tony, suppose Madame should see your car?"

"Do not worry yourself about Madame Boeld. She is no threat to me. You know very well how it all went and that she owes me big time," said Tony.

A Fine How Do You Do

Nelson smiled, opened the car door and said, "Welcome to my humble abode."

Tony left Nelson's apartment before dawn so as not to cause any suspicions with Madame, Bertha or Bessie. However, Bessie was up very early and noticed a strange car leaving the driveway. For whatever reason she did not mention it to Bertha. Nelson was cleaning up his apartment and heard little Lucy meowing at his door. He let her in and gave her a small saucer of milk. Lucy drank all the milk and then curled up on the unmade bed and fell asleep. While dressing himself, Nelson felt like doing the same thing.

He went out to make sure Madame's car was neat and tidy and had plenty of petrol to take Madame to church. Nelson reminisced about the evening and realized that he had some serious thinking to do. Tony had suggested they go off to Paris for a holiday. Tony said that Paris was practically void of Parisians in the summer and lots of the restaurants are not open and unfortunately it was crawling with tourists from all over the world but they would have a wonderful time and it would make Tony happy to introduce his favorite city to Nelson. Tony spoke of a charming little place they could stay on the Left Bank. Nelson was now determined to make something of his life and this was a wonderful start. He would muster up his courage and ask Madame for a week's vacation and she need not pay him for that week. He would suggest that Mr. Alfred do the driving while he was away since Mr. Alfred had already moved in and had little to do. Nelson told Tony that all Alfred did was open bottles of whiskey and sit in the garden and then throw the bottles in the trash bin by the garage so Madame would not know.

Yes, he would not waste time and would approach Madame this very morning after he collected her from church, as he wanted to speak with her when Alfred was not around. Alfred hardly ever left his bedroom before noon. Nelson looked out his doorway, which he had left open for little Lucy to come and go, and spotted Eric who was about to get on the bicycle.

"Good morning to you, Mr. Eric, and where are you off to?"

"Oh, good morning to you, Nelson. I am going to the fresh market and see what is left from yesterday before church starts and everything is picked over. You know, I do the shopping now, unless it is a party and then Madame and Bessie take over."

"Oh, I see, well there are a lot of changes around here," said Nelson.

"Oh yes, now that those Italian gardeners do not come anymore, I do the gardening also – with your help, which I appreciate very much. I have never done much work in the yard or gardens so I am most grateful for your advice and help, Nelson."

"Ah, pas de quoi," Nelson said and smiled, as he had just learned that French phrase from Tony.

"Huh?"

"Oh that is French for 'you are welcome'," said Nelson with a newly found assurance.

Putting down the bicycle, Eric decided to see what Bertha and Bessie were baking for breakfast. Nelson decided that it would be advantageous to approach Madame about his holiday while on the way to church instead of afterward, when she would be carrying on about all the hats and who was there and not there.

Chapter Twenty-Five

Louise was determined to sit down and quietly read the letter from Tony she received in the mail yesterday. She realized that she had upset the girls before and did not want to do that again. She opened the envelope and took a large sip of tea.

"Dear Louise, Your check is in the mail and my apologies for the mix-up last month. It was necessary for me to close out certain accounts and that is why your check was unable to be cashed. I hope in time that I will be able to increase your child support but at the present time it is not possible. The girls seem fine and as we always thought, Millicent is certainly her own imaginative and vibrant person while dear Suzanne is as sweet as ever. You are a very caring Mother and I will be in touch when next I am able to see the girls. Fondly, Tony." Louise folded up the letter and held it close to her. "Hmmm, well that is that," thought Louise, and tore up the letter.

Eric was working on Louise's brick terrace and Louise thought it was taking so long for him to repair it. "Is everything going along well with the terrace, Eric?"

"Oh yes, but I have to figure out the drainage and slope of things and how to place the bricks properly. I want it to be right for you."

"I am sure you will do a most proper job and it will be just fine and if you will excuse me, I am going to have a lie down with my book and I will see you next time you are able to come around and thank you."

Louise went upstairs and collapsed on her bed, pulled up the soft blanket and wondered what was in store for her and what kind of a life she would have after a failed marriage. Actually, it was not much of a marriage, as she never really understood what Tony was doing financially and he was always on the phone or not home at all. He had taken a flat in London because he said that he was working such late hours trying to provide for the family. Tony was basically a mystery to her. She turned on the telly and found herself absorbed in a program about ladies with more problems than she could ever imagine. She heard the girls come in from the Sunday sailing group and knew they needed baths and clean clothes. She went downstairs to greet them. "Hi girls, how was your day?"

"Oh, it was just beautiful, Mum. The lake was like a mirror and we sailed for a long time and I handled the rudder. It was so smooth that I barely needed to work at all! Suzanne was not in my group so I do not know what she did."

"So, Suzanne, how was your day?"

"It was just beautiful Mum, but I really want to stay home with you."

"Well, you both know that is not possible during the week as I have a job at the library but if you want to stay with me on Sundays, I would very much like that."

"But I could help you at the library during the week."

"No, dearest Suzanne, that is so thoughtful but not possible as the library hires only adults and you must go to school and be with the other children."

"But Mum, I want to be with you," said Suzanne, throwing herself onto Louise's lap. Millicent went over and hugged them both. Eric came in through the back doorway. "Oh, what a lovely scene, I wish I had a camera and a picture of you all like this." Millicent pulled Suzanne to her feet, saying "Suzanne, come upstairs with me. Mum brought me a book from the library about a pig and a spider and you would like it. I will read it to you." Suzanne went back to Louise and looked into her mother's eyes and said, "I do not like pigs and spiders." Louise smiled and told the girls to go upstairs and read the book. Millicent grabbed Suzanne's hand and pulled her upstairs. "What is this all about?" asked Eric. "It's a book about friendship and Suzanne will love it. She just doesn't know that yet," said Louise, wiping a tear from her eye while giving Eric a most friendly smile.

Chapter Twenty-Six

Nelson shined up the car once again, even though it did not need it. He drove up to the front door, stepped out and waited to open the car for Madame, who had not yet appeared. Nelson was concerned that she would be late for church. Then she emerged, exclaiming, "This blue feather for my hat is not the right match for my dress but we must get along or else all will wonder why I am not sitting in my usual pew."

"Good morning, Madame, and the feather is fetching and compliments your beautiful blue eyes."

"Nelson, you are always such a comfort."

"Thank you, Madame, and should we wait for Mr. Alfred?"

"Just get going please, Nelson."

"Yes, Madame of course." He realized this would not be a good time to bring up the possibility of a holiday for himself so he tried to be attentive to Madame. "Is Mr. Alfred feeling well?"

"Who knows what goes through Freddie's head and how he is. No wonder poor Margaret died of exhaustion."

"I thought she died of pneumonia, Madame."

"Just let me off here, I see Elizabeth and I will walk up with her."

"Very well, Madame, and I will be here to take you home after the service." Alma pounced out of the car and waved toward Elizabeth and they walked up and into the church together.

Elizabeth looked around with a wide smile to see how many people noticed that Alma had invited her to sit in her pew.

Nelson was parked when the service was over. Alma signaled him to wait while she greeted friends and spoke of her grief about losing her dear sister-in-law. Alma signaled Nelson to pull up and they would go to the cemetery and take the altar flowers to Margaret's grave, with some of the congregation following, as the minister had suggested. Nelson loaded the flowers into the car.

Alma could not remember which way to tell Nelson to turn once inside the gates of the cemetery, as she had not been there since the burial. Nelson recalled the path and assured Alma that he knew the spot. A very large stone angel with her wings outspread suddenly appeared before them and Nelson stopped the car.

"Why are we stopping here, Nelson?"

"This is the grave of your brother's wife, Madame."

"Oh, dear Lord, save us all, this cannot be true, are you sure this is the spot?"

"Yes, Madame, and I suggest you get out of the car, lead the congregation around the site and just pray with your head down while the flowers are being distributed. Come directly back to the car, as you need not chat with anyone due to your grief."

"Oh dear God, Nelson, why was I not informed that this monstrosity was being erected?"

"Would it be that Mr. Alfred took it upon himself to arrange things?"

"Yes, that is it. Freddie has lost his mind with grief and somehow the angel of the Lord appeared before him and created this dreadful embarrassment. He never would have done this in his right mind. Is there a brolly in the car, Nelson?"

"Yes, Madame there is always a brolly in the car in case of rain or a hot sun."

"Well, for God's sake please fetch it immediately."

"Yes, Madame, right away."

"Run Nelson, before the rest arrive." Nelson brought the umbrella around and Alma immediately took his arm, opened the umbrella and whispered in his ear, "You are not to leave my side." "Yes, Madame," answered Nelson with great satisfaction that he was being most helpful and appreciated.

When they arrived home Alma found her brother on the back terrace with little Lucy licking scraps from his plate. "Isn't she just the very cutest little kitty you have ever encountered, Alma?"

"Yes, Freddie she is quite adorable but you are not." Alfred recognized that voice tone and it always meant that he was in trouble. Even though he was only 18 months younger than Alma, he was never in control. It was always Alma who made decisions for him and bailed him out of trouble in school and almost always did his homework, while he bounced a ball outside to see if he could bounce it more times than the day before. The Boeld family was very prominent in Oberammergau and Alma liked the attention of the Bavarian people and her social position there, so she covered up for her brother. As time went on, he never asked what Alma did during the war and showed no emotions about it.

Alma interrupted Alfred's meditation: "Freddie, look at me and tell me why you ordered that enormous angel for Margaret's tomb?"

"Oh, did you see her and doesn't she look just like Margaret?"

"Yes, Freddie, she is just like Margaret, but do tell me how much it cost."

"They called our bank to make sure I could pay for it before they erected it and I guess the bank said it was proper, so there she is!" Little Lucy jumped into Alfred's lap and began licking her paws. "Alma, are Bertha and Bessie sisters?"

"No, they are cousins, their mothers were sisters."

"Oh, how very nice and now they are part of our family aren't they?"

"Yes, they have become part of the family, why do you ask?"

"Because they like me," said Alfred with a slight smile. Alma left him on the terrace, looked up Dr. Mellini's telephone number and dialed it. "Doctor, so sorry to disturb you on a Sunday, but I am very concerned about the condition of my brother, Alfred, whom you know."

"Yes, I remember him well. What seems to be the matter?"

"I think he might have had a stroke or something that has altered his mind, as he has become so childlike."

After a few seconds, Dr. Mellini said, "Madame Boeld, you should seek another opinion, but the fact remains that the situation with your brother will not change no matter how many tests are performed. The best thing to do, in my opinion, is to keep his brain active with puzzles or whatever appeals to him, and give him meaningful tasks. The death of his wife is certainly a factor in all this and it all may pass if he finds new interests. The grieving process is very different for everyone and this may be what is going on, so I would suggest that you give him time to grieve and see how his health may improve."

"My, Dr. Mellini, that is a lot of wisdom very quickly spoken and it does make some sense. Would you consider coming over at your convenience and having a conversation with Freddie?"

"Yes, I will do that if you wish. As you know we only summer here and are planning to return to home soon, so would this coming week be convenient for you? In fact, perhaps tomorrow? Would it be convenient if I arrive approximately 2 p.m.?"

"Yes, and I do so appreciate it, so we will see you tomorrow."

"Yes, Mrs. Boeld, and tell your brother that it is a friendly visit."

"Yes, I understand."

Alma returned to the terrace and found that Bessie had brought the tea and small cakes out. "Isn't Bessie like family, Alma?" "Yes, Freddie, she certainly is." "I am so glad you like Margaret's angel." "Yes, Freddie, Margaret's angel is lovely." "So will you let me stay here, because I am real family, aren't I?" "Yes, Freddie, darling, you are my brother."

Alfred smiled and dipped his little cake into his tea. He dropped a bit of cake onto the terrace and Lucy came scampering over to it. "Isn't little Lucy just the cutest little kitty you have ever encountered and just like family?" "Oh my yes, Freddie, she most certainly is."

Chapter Twenty-Seven

Alma called the bank. The check had cleared from the sale of Alfred's house and was deposited just as she had ordered, in a new joint checking account for herself and her brother.

Dr. Mellini came to the house and Bessie served tea on the terrace. Alfred kept reminding them that 2 p.m. was entirely too early for afternoon tea. Dr. Mellini apologized for coming at this hour, but it was the only time he had free because he and his wife were preparing to return to Rome.

"Why do you live in Rome?" asked Alfred.

"Because that is my home and I practice there."

"Well, sport, what do you practice, cricket?"

"No, Mr. Boeld, I do not attempt cricket, I am a doctor."

"But then what is it that you must practice?"

"I am a practicing doctor, Mr. Boeld."

"I used to practice bouncing the ball all the days of my life and I am very good at it."

"Well, that is a great accomplishment. Do you have a ball now?" asked the doctor.

"Alma, do I have a ball now?"

"No, Freddie, not right now, but we will get a new one tomorrow."

"Mr. Boeld, it was so nice to have this short visit with you both but I must be running along now," said Dr. Mellini. Alma walked him to the front door and they nodded to each other. Dr. Mellini said, as he went out, "A new one would please him." Alma went back to the terrace and sat to finish her tea. She looked over at Alfred and thought to herself this was not fair. Why did she always have to be the one to pick up the pieces and keep things in order? Alma finished her tea and went upstairs.

Nelson was in his apartment. He had tried several times to call Tony from the kitchen to explain why he was unable to approach Madame. He had seen Dr. Mellini leave the house so knew something was amiss. He decided to see Bessie and Bertha. When he arrived in the kitchen Alfred was making a ham sandwich. "Bessie and Bertha are not here, so I do not know what is for dinner. Do you know if there is a party and I need my dinner jacket?"

"I do not think so, Mr. Alfred. Madame would have mentioned it to me."

"Well, Pinky, I would like very much to practice my ball playing but I do not have a ball." Alfred looked at Nelson and waited for a reply.

"You would like a football, would you now? Very good, we will go into town and get you a football."

"Pinky, you are such a good chap, I like you a lot."

Even with the sale of Alfred's house, Alma was still quite concerned about her long-term finances. She decided to call Mr. Browne and ask him to contact the bank and have as much money as possible moved to her personal account. She would explain to Mr. Browne that Freddie was not competent to handle financial matters and all he wanted was a new ball and she was at her wits' end with trying to keep him from getting into all kinds of trouble.

She knew she could manipulate the barrister. She took off her shoes, opened all the windows and called Mr. Browne.

Nelson and Alfred returned with a new football. "Pinky, we were lucky that the little store on the corner was open." "Yes, Mr. Alfred, that little store caters to the visitors here in Ambleside and they seem to always be open." Alfred took his ball upstairs to show Alma. "How nice to have a ball now, Freddie. You must get some exercise too, so go outside and enjoy the nice air." Alfred went out and began to bounce his ball and was having a grand time.

"For the sake of God, Freddie, do you have to bounce that ball right under my open window? Go around to the garages and bounce it there." Alfred picked up his ball without a word and bounced the ball over to the garages.

Nelson had returned to his apartment and he could hear the ball bouncing. "Mr. Alfred, would you mind bouncing down by the third garage?" Alfred picked up his ball and took it over to the kitchen wall instead. Nelson went to the kitchen to try to reach Tony by phone once again. The phone rang and Tony answered. "Sorry, Tony, Alfred seems to be going through his second childhood and is bouncing his new ball against the kitchen wall and I cannot hear you very well, so please speak up."

"Well, he is not your worry. Have you informed Madame that you are taking a week's vacation?"

"I was going to do it this morning but it has been an upside-down sort of day."

"Well, get to it, old boy, as I have to arrange my business schedule as I will have some meetings in Paris when we go."

"Yes, Tony, I will."

"By the by, is Eric still going over to the house?"

"Yes, he is and I believe he is repairing the back terrace."

"Fine and well. Cheers! Call me when you have arranged things with Madame and keep in mind that Madame is in great debt to me and is not apt to complicate matters. I feel sure you will be able to take a week off." Tony rang off abruptly. Nelson was learning that Tony wanted things all in order very quickly and did not put up with any dilly-dallying.

Nelson was upset and confused. For years he had yearned for something different and all these changes in his life had come so suddenly. He simply was not prepared to be in control of it. Life was a lot simpler with just Madame to deal with, though she could be difficult and demanding. He noticed that it was now tea time and thought perhaps Madame would be on the back terrace and he could join her.

"Madame, I hope I am not disturbing you," said Nelson, quietly approaching Alma. "Oh, it's just you, Nelson." "Yes, Madame, just me." "Pull up a chair and Bessie will be here with tea in a few minutes. What is on your mind? You know, Nelson, now that I think about it, you are the only stable person in this house." "Thank you, Madame, and—" Alma motioned Nelson to stop, turned her back to him and began to weep.

"Madame, what can I do for you?"

"Nothing, thank you, Nelson, I just have so much to figure out."

"Madame, I was going to say the same thing to you, as I am in a total quandary about how my life will go on."

"What in the world are your troubles, Nelson?"

"Well, I have never asked for a vacation but I would like to go on vacation to Paris."

"Nelson my dear fellow, no one in their right mind goes to Paris in the summer. Why do you think they are all coming here?"

He paused, then plunged ahead. "I want to be honest with you, Madame, so I will tell you that Tony Smythe has invited me to go with him to Paris."

"Tony Smythe has done what?"

"He has invited me to go to Paris with him."

"Why in God's name would he do that?"

"We have become very good friends."

"Oh for the sake of God, now I have two total idiots on my hands. Next thing I will hear is that Bessie and Bertha are having babies. Please, Nelson do not confuse my life at this time and no, you may not leave for a week, as I do not know how Freddie is going to behave and very likely will need the car. But, for God's sake, what is going on with you and Mr. Tony Smythe?"

"I will tell Tony that I am unable to join him. I am sorry to have bothered you Madame."

"Pas de quoi, my dear boy. Do sit down and we will talk sensibly."

"I would prefer to chat with you another time, Madame."

"Things as usual, then," stated Alma. "Yes, Madame," said Nelson, wondering how he would tell Tony that Madame ran his life completely.

Chapter Twenty-Eight

"Hi, Mom, how's it going today?" asked Gail. "Oh, same as usual. Nothing changes in Altoona except your father is still away. However, I'm fine and there are four of us who go to Bingo at the Fire House on Wednesday evenings and then on Tuesday evenings we all go to Mary's house and watch the TV and have supper. We like the quiz games and we do pretty well! George called from the newspaper and said that they think Dad is in England, somewhere near London, and did I want to hire someone to track him down. George has been sending me Dad's paycheck payable to me, and says that his weekly weather predictions are all so correct. I guess he sends them in from somewhere. George is just going to let it all go on like this until a year is up and then he will have to assume he is not alive and I don't know what will happen but they will probably chase him down, wouldn't you think? Anyway, Gail, I do not think any further than a day and then I am not putting pressure on myself. How is dear little Norma?" asked Martha.

"She lost two molars at once and was so happy when the tooth fairy came and left some change. Mom, Norman and I want to help you out if you are getting strapped for money."

"No, dear, as I said, George is sending me paychecks and I do go in there every other day and clean the offices. And I have the job at the library. I just take it a day at a time."

"Would you like us to come to Altoona for your birthday?" asked Gail.

"Yes, that would be fun," said Martha.

"Okay, Mom, we love you and think about you every day." They each hung up. Martha was proud of herself and had managed to keep her spirits up and stay busy. She missed Eric very much but had reconciled herself that if he loved her, he would come home. She was amazed that he could be taking care of himself, wherever he was, as he was so dependent on her for almost everything. But how long could she wait? Maybe forever, as she did not have any other choice. After seven years, he would probably be declared dead anyway and that would be that. He either would come home or he wouldn't. Stormie her cat never complained and slept in the bed with Martha every night. Sometimes they listened to Uncle Bernie on her new radio but mostly they just cuddled together.

Alma was somewhat relaxed as the week went on. The bank sent her a notice that money had been transferred from the joint account to her private one. The only other money withdrawn from the joint account was a personal check from Alfred for Margaret's gravestone. The inheritance from Margaret's father was set up in a separate joint account with a restriction that Alma must approve any withdrawals Alfred might wish to make.

Alfred was content with his new football and managed to find his old stamp collection among the things moved over from his former house. He kept bringing the well-worn albums to Alma and showing her the most colorful stamps. Alma had no interest in the stamps but was happy that Alfred had found them and that they occupied his time.

Alma had not heard from Nelson again about the suggested trip to Paris with Tony Smythe and she prayed that she would never hear his name again.

Eric seemed very busy with the gardening around the property and was no trouble at all. He bicycled to do the market shopping each day and always consulted with her about what vegetables and fruits she wished for the day. She was pleased to have him staying on but thought it a bit odd that he never spoke of his family.

The telephone rang and Alma was delighted to hear from Elizabeth. "We have not chatted all week, dear Elizabeth, how are you?" "Very well, thank you and I hope things are going well for you, Alma dear." "Oh, yes, things are quieting down and Alfred seems happy here," said Alma. "Speaking of Alfred, perhaps you can advise me about the invitation from the Grobets for their housewarming affair. I cannot figure out if it is for dinner or just a garden party, can you?"

Alma had not been through the mail in several days and so now was scrambling through it while holding Elizabeth on the phone. There was no invitation from the Grobets. "Elizabeth, I received the invitation but did not read it carefully as it arrived when things were a bit busy here, and I was surprised that they moved in so quickly and were already giving a party," said Alma, hiding her fury, but presuming the invitation would arrive shortly. Certainly she and Alfred would be included.

"Well, they seem like most considerate people, as my invitation indicated that Mr. Tony Smythe will be fetching me and then kindly delivering me back home, isn't that considerate?"

"Elizabeth, did you say Mr. Tony Smythe?"

"Why yes, Alma, you remember the gentleman who told the Grobets about Alfred's house?"

Alma sat down on the straight chair as she though she might faint.

"Alma, are you there?"

"I will call you back later, Elizabeth."

Alma sat and pondered the scenario. Tony Smythe was like a spider weaving a web and Alma was caught in it. Had she met her crafty match? Alma was set on figuring out this puzzle. Aha, she thought, this is about Nelson. Or could it be something about the financial fiasco? No, she thought, it is about Nelson and the trip to Paris. Little wonder that Nelson has been so aloof this week. Yes, that is what it is and she would take care of it immediately. She could not afford to have Mr. Tony Smythe holding anything over her head. She called for Bessie and asked her to please go to Nelson's apartment and ask him to come to the house immediately, which he did.

"Nelson, we need to have a little chat. I have been under a lot of strain recently and I do believe that I was a bit hasty discouraging you from going to Paris. Paris is really lovely anytime of the year and it would be a wonderful vacation for you. You have been most loyal and have not requested any time off all the years you have been with me, so please make your plans and we will work out the car arrangement. Alfred seems more content now and perhaps he can do the driving for the week you will be away."

"Thank you, Madame and I very much appreciate your change of heart," said Nelson, turning away without further conversation.

"Oh, Nelson, I will need you to take me to the party at Alfred's former house. A French family by the name of Grobet purchased it and have moved in already."

"So I understand, Madame."

"How did you know that, Nelson?"

"Tony told me about it, Madame."

"Oh, I see. Well that Mr. Smythe certainly does get around, doesn't he?"

"It is my understanding that Tony introduced Mr. and Mrs. Grobet to the broker who sold the house to them," said Nelson.

"Ah yes, perhaps that could be, I do not recall all the transactions as it was a difficult time for Alfred and me in many ways."

"Yes, Madame, I recall that it was and you have weathered the storm very well and look as handsome as ever."

"Thank you, Nelson. You flatter me and I appreciate that at my stage in life." Alma was convinced Tony had constructed this whole scenario to force her into granting the time to Nelson so they could go prancing off to Paris together. She took the bait, as she had little choice. Tony had the upper hand and she would be his puppet if she wanted to save her reputation and pride. She acknowledged to herself that Tony had shielded them from a financial fiasco and this is the price she must pay.

Nelson wasted no time in calling Tony. Tony replied, "I figured you would be calling anytime now with good news. Shall we proceed with our Paris plans?"

"Yes, how did you know?"

"It was in the cards, old boy. Let's just say it was meant to be. By the by, I will be coming to Ambleside for the party the Grobets are giving next weekend."

"Yes, Madame just mentioned the party, and I will be driving Madame and perhaps Miss Elizabeth as we often do?"

"No, I will escort Elizabeth to the party."

"Oh, I see. You set this all up?"

"Yes, my boy. Tony here is a clever fellow," replied Tony, laughing.

"I should say so." Nelson felt both elated and confused. They said goodbye and hung up. Tony called Madame Grobet and advised her to invite the Boelds.

Nelson heard little Lucy meowing at his door. He opened the door and she ran right in and over to the fridge. Nelson poured her a small bowl of cream and she lapped it up and sprang onto his bed and made herself right at home.

A Fine How Do You Do

Alma called her millinery shop in London and made an appointment for next Saturday in order to have several hats created for the coming Fall season. Her appointment was at 4 o'clock and tea would be served to her while she viewed the possible styles and materials. She would bring samples of her fall suits being made so as the hats would match. She asked Bessie to fetch Nelson. "Nelson, dear boy, Alfred and I will not be attending the party at the Grobets' home. I will be going into London on Saturday for my usual Fall hat fittings, so will of course wish you to drive. We will be quite late arriving home. I assume you are free to do so?"

"Yes, Madame, of course. By the by, I met the Grobets' driver in our driveway and he handed this envelope to me and asked that you receive it straight-away." Alma took the envelope and tore it in half immediately.

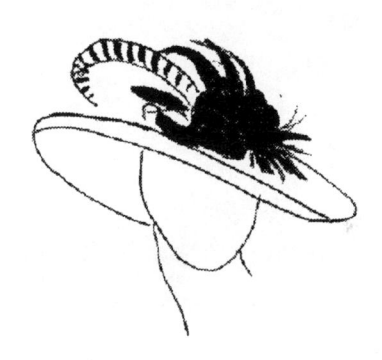

Chapter Twenty-Nine

Alfred was on the back terrace snappily dressed in some of his better attire and looking quite content. "Well, good morning Freddie dear, how are you and have you had your breakfast?"

"I am waiting for a phone call," said Alfred.

"Oh really, from whom?"

"The Humane Society."

"Whatever for, Freddie?"

"It's about Angel."

"And who is Angel?"

"Angel will be my new friend."

"What in God's name are you talking about, Freddie?"

"I wasn't going to tell you and just let it be a wonderful surprise."

"Freddie, surprises are not good for me, now tell me what you are up to."

"Well, I was reading the daily paper and the Humane Society has a beautiful dog named Angel and I am going to adopt her," he said proudly.

"Oh my dear God, I may never get out of bed again," said Alma.

"Oh, Alma dear, I never told anyone, but I always called my Margaret Angel. She would give me such a lovely smile and I loved her and miss her so much."

A Fine How Do You Do

"Freddie dear, stop upsetting yourself over a silly dog. What shall I tell Bessie to bring you for breakfast, soft-boiled eggs?"

"No, I won't eat any more eggs until the Humane Society calls me back and then I am going to go and pick up Angel and bring her home."

"Well, you are not going to put any stray dog in my car, so just forget about all this nonsense."

"I will take my old car. I have not been driving it since I moved in, but Nelson started it up and it is just fine."

"What sort of dog is this Angel?"

"She is a cairn terrier and someone dropped her off at the shelter," said Alfred.

"Oh, Freddie dear, how can we cope with a dog when we can barely manage our own lives? Now be sensible Freddie. Are you listening to me?"

"No, not really Alma, as I need to listen for the phone to ring." The phone rang and Alfred jumped up to answer. "Hello, Alfred Boeld here and who are you?"

"Mr. Boeld, this is Miss Caldwell from the Humane Society. I apologize for keeping you waiting, but, as you must understand, we need to do a background check on all prospects wishing to adopt one of our dogs or cats."

"Oh, yes, of course," agreed Alfred.

"Well, Mr. Boeld, we find that you have moved from a former address and are now living with your sister, Madame Alma Boeld, is this correct?"

"Yes, that is correct and Bertha and Bessie live here too."

"Are Bessie and Bertha cats or dogs?"

Alfred burst into laughter and turned to Alma and said, "They think that Bessie and Bertha are dogs and cats."

"Oh, Freddie, just hand me the phone…. Hello, this is Madame Alma Boeld and Alfred Boeld is my brother who has just recently moved into my home as his wife passed away and we have sold his former home. Bessie and Bertha are servants and have lived here all their lives."

"Well, Madame Boeld, are there other animals in the home?"

"No, just a stray cat who comes and goes as she pleases."

"I see, and who would feed the dog?"

"Anyone who is in the kitchen at the time, I suppose."

"Madame, we must make sure that the dog will have a good schedule of exercise and regular feeding times."

"Oh, for the sake of God, of course the dog will be taken care of properly," said Alma with great dignity.

"Mrs. Boeld, these are matters that we must cover as I am sure you must understand that we need to know that our animals are going to good homes."

"Miss Coldy—"

"My name is Caldwell."

"Whatever it is, you can be assured that the dog will be well cared for in my home. Mr. Boeld will be over immediately to adopt the dog from your shelter and we need not chat any more about it." Alma hung up and told Alfred to get his car and she would go with him to the shelter. Alfred said he wished to collect Angel by himself. Alma sat in a garden chair and hoped the remainder of the morning would be without startling news or disturbances. "Bessie, is breakfast on the way?"

Eric overheard the conversation as he was in the kitchen with Bessie and Bertha having coffee and waiting for the biscuits to bake. They were all so interested in the news about a new dog that the biscuits burned. Eric volunteered to eat them anyway.

Nelson appeared and joined in the conversation. All agreed that a dog was just what Mr. Alfred needed as he had been so morose since he lost Madame Margaret and a dog would cheer him up.

"Well, I have some news also," said Nelson.

"Really now, Pinky, what excitement could be entering your life?"

"I am taking some time off and going on holiday to Paris."

"To Paris?" they all said at once.

"Yes, to Paris," said Nelson with a big grin, "and very soon."

"Now wipe that smug look off your face and tell us about it, Pinky," said Bessie with a big smile.

"Well, you will find out sooner or later I guess. Mr. Tony Smythe invited me on the trip."

Eric, Bessie and Bertha all looked up in a startle. Bessie voiced their confusion: "You mean, the Mr. Tony Smythe that caused all the financial trouble? You know, dear Pinky, that we hear almost all that goes on here as the kitchen door is never closed and Madame hates Mr. Tony Smythe."

"Well, so be it, that is my plan. I have never had a holiday and I am very excited about the trip," said Nelson with glee.

"Of course you are and we wish you all the best and hope you both come home safe and sound."

"Thank you and I will see you all later," said Nelson.

"Oh, Pinky, do come back soon, as you will want to meet the new dog. By the by, if you are driving you might pick up some dog food and perhaps a nice bone as a welcome present for Angel."

"A very nice thought, Bessie, I certainly will do that."

"Oh and perhaps if the little store on the corner is open, do pick up a fluffy bed for the dog and a fancy collar and leash. Madame has a charge there." Nelson tipped his cap and went on his way. He decided to stay in his driving uniform as they would recognize him at the store and he would be able to charge all the items to Madame without trouble. It disturbed him that no one seemed to recognize him out of uniform and were so very attentive when he was in uniform. "Well, all this will be in the past very soon," he thought to himself and walked with a bit more of a prance.

Nelson arrived home with the goods for Angel and found everyone in the kitchen. Alma was petting Angel and giving her scraps. Alfred had poured himself a brandy and suggested a toast. "And here is to Angel. Cheers to my new friend and addition to our family. I love Angel already and I know that my Margaret loves her too. I will take her to Margaret's grave tomorrow and she can see the angel I had installed on top of the grave. It is a beautiful angel and looks just like my Margaret, doesn't she Alma?"

"Oh yes, Freddie, it is quite an angel." Alma turned to Bessie and rolled her eyes and Bessie winked back.

"So now we are all family, aren't we, Alma?"

"Yes, Freddie, we are all family."

Chapter Thirty

Millicent and Suzanne were planning what to wear when their father came to pick them up on Saturday. He had promised to take them on the boat trip around the lake. "Do you think he will really come this time, Millicent?" asked Suzanne.

"Of course he will come, don't be a worry wart. Mum says she has heard he is coming out for a party later, so he will come and get us for the boat ride around lunchtime. He will leave London very early in the morning. Mum also said that Uncle Eric told her that Daddy was taking a trip to Paris with Madame Boeld's driver."

"Why would he do that? He knows how to drive himself!"

"I have not figured that out yet," Millicent acknowledged. "Now, I think that we should wear our matching outfits that Mum just bought for us, so in case you wander off people will know we are sisters and that you belong with me."

"I won't wander off, but I like that outfit. It has a sailor collar."

Millicent rolled her eyes and said, "That is why I chose it for us."

"Are we going to Paris when Daddy goes?" Suzanne asked.

"No, but I have heard so much about Madame Boeld from Uncle Eric, I want to meet her. We have only met her driver with Daddy once and I don't remember his name."

"I remember his name, Millicent. It is Nelson."

"You are right, now I remember too."

"Oh, here comes Mum. I will put the tea on." They sat at the kitchen table and looked over the books that Louise had brought home for them.

"Mum, why is Daddy going to Paris with Madame Boeld's driver when he knows how to drive himself?"

"I have no idea, dear, and let's not dwell on it. I suppose you could ask your father when you see him on Saturday."

"We're going to wear the outfits with the sailor's collar because we are going on the boat ride," said Millicent and Suzanne at the same time.

"A very good choice," said Louise.

"Mum, can we read some of the books you brought home?" asked Suzanne.

"Yes, certainly," replied Louise. "I will be upstairs, but have a good time. I will be in my room if you need me and be sure and turn the kettle off."

"Oh, Mum, I almost forgot to mention that Uncle Eric brought us some beets for supper," said Millicent, leaving the kitchen while balancing one of the library books on her head.

"Elizabeth, dear, I am so sorry not to have called you back earlier," Alma said.

"Are you well, Alma? I have been so worried as you hung up the phone so abruptly the other day."

"All is fine, Elizabeth, and we have been busy as bees as Freddie has adopted a lovely cairn terrier named Angel from the Humane Society and frankly she has taken over the household."

"Oh, for heaven's sake, Alma dear, all you need is another mouth to feed over there."

"Well, Angel is here and seems to be settled in and Freddie is beginning to come around and is making more sense of himself since Angel arrived," said Alma.

"Splendid. Oh I must tell you about the party at the Grobets. It is a garden party and apparently relatives of the Italian gardeners have done a remarkable job with the gardens. I am sure that you and Alfred will be anxious to see what they have done to the house," said Elizabeth.

"We have decided not to attend. I have no interest in seeing the house nor the gardens and Freddie is certainly not up to revisiting his past life with Margaret, as he seems to be doing well and I do not want him to go into a depression or whatever might happen. Freddie is so unpredictable," said Alma.

"Yes, of course, I do understand."

"My dear, let us chat again tomorrow. I wish to make sure that Queenie has everything she needs," said Alma.

"Who is Queenie, Alma dear?"

"The new dog, of course."

"Well then, who is Angel?"

"Oh, call her what you like," Alma said and hung up the phone.

Nelson decided to stay in his apartment because he did not know how to handle any more questions that Bessie, Bertha or Eric might have for him about the Paris trip. He certainly did not wish any more conversations about it with Madame. He decided to call Tony and ask his advice. "Tony, Nelson here."

"Yes, nice surprise, what's up dear boy?"

"Well, I am not sure how to handle our trip to Paris with everyone here."

"So you've been talking with the help in the kitchen?"

"Yes, as well as Eric and of course Madame."

"What's said is said and you need not go on about it. Tell them you will bring back perfume for the ladies and silk ascots for Eric and Alfred."

"And we have a new dog. Actually, it is Mr. Alfred who has a new dog. Everyone has fallen in love with her and Mr. Alfred is so pleased and seems to be much better. She is a cairn terrier and her name is Angel."

"Well, here's to Angel and her new home and we will bring the chien a French bone." Tony laughed, but Nelson did not. "I am leaving London at the break of dawn and will stop in at your apartment on Saturday late morning as we must get you a passport. I am taking the girls on the lake boat ride and then I will go to the garden party at the Grobets."

"Madame has decided not to attend the party and I am to drive her into London on Saturday for some hat fittings in the afternoon," said Nelson.

"Not a surprise, my dear Nelson."

"Why do you say that?"

"You will learn, my dear Nelson, that Tony Smythe is always a step ahead of the crowd. So it seems that I will be going one way on Saturday and you the opposite so we will not meet. I must ring off now as I have deals to put together before we leave for Paris. Go to your postal office there in Ambleside and get the proper forms to apply for your passport." Tony hung up.

Nelson went down to the kitchen to have a cup of tea with Bessie and Bertha and perhaps little Lucy and Angel. The kitchen was Nelson's retreat and the only place he truly felt comfortable.

Chapter Thirty-One

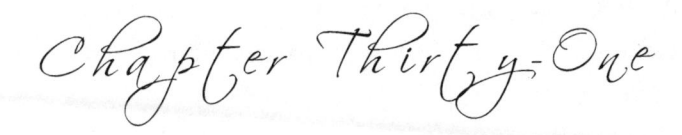

"Good afternoon, Millicent, and thank you for being so punctual for our meeting," said Mistress Bloom.

"I am never tardy," said Millicent, looking straight at her.

"Well, a lot of the girls are tardy for this very important meeting before school resumes next month. Are you looking forward to the new school year?"

"Yes I am, Mistress Bloom, and I have read all the required books for the summer reading."

"Very good, Millicent, and how was your summer holiday?"

"It was not really a holiday as we didn't go anywhere."

"Tell me what you did that was of interest to you."

"Well, I wrote in my diary a lot and my sister and I went to sailing camp and we learned how to sail."

"How very nice. And did you go on family outings together?"

"No."

"Why not?"

"Because we do not have a Daddy anymore," said Millicent, looking out the window.

"Oh, that must be a great sadness for you."

"It is a sadness for Mum and Suzanne."

"And for you?"

"I wrote an obituary for him."

"Oh, he passed away?"

"No, we see him in London and when he comes here," Millicent said, looking directly at Mistress Bloom.

"Well, let's talk about what particularly interests you about coming back to school."

"I can't think of anything in particular right now, Mistress Bloom, but do you like Winnie the Pooh?"

"Oh yes, I certainly do."

"How old were you when you were one?" asked Millicent.

Mistress Bloom smiled and said, "I had just begun."

"How old were you when you were two?"

"Almost new. And my dear Millicent, how old were you when you were three?"

"Almost me," replied Millicent, and rushed over and gave Mistress Bloom a hug and burst into tears.

"Millicent, you are a very clever and bright girl and I hope we will become good friends as the year goes on."

"We are friends already and I will write about you in my diary."

"Millicent, I want you to know that you can call on me anytime you wish to do so."

Millicent looked around Mistress Bloom's office. "Mistress Bloom, may we have our next conversation out in the garden? I can see from this window a very large tree with lots of beautiful leaves and when the breeze blows I can see the leaves dancing and I would rather have a visit there than in this dreary office of yours."

"That is a wonderful thought, Millicent, and perhaps we can have tea and little sandwiches too, would you like that?"

"Yes, but I do not like cucumbers."

Chapter Thirty-Two

"Oh, the sun is glorious out here, Alma, isn't it?" Elizabeth exclaimed. "Yes, I guess as much and you describe it all so well. I want to thank you for coming over, as I have no driver now that Tony and Nelson have gone prancing off to Paris. What do you make of all that to-do, Elizabeth?"

"My dear, I think that we should not think about it at all and hope that they enjoy their little holiday together."

"Elizabeth, you know very well that there is something going on with Nelson and that dreadful Tony, do you not?"

"No, Alma, I know nothing, but must admit that it has me puzzled. Let's just enjoy this nice breeze and I will tell you about the garden party at the Grobets."

"Oh, you mean Alfred and Margaret's former home?" asked Alma with a sarcastic tone.

"Yes, dear, but try and move on and accept that it belongs to the Grobets now and frankly Alfred was damn lucky to get out of there and find a good buyer and move in with you. Everyone at the party felt great relief for you that it all worked out so well."

"Elizabeth, I have never heard you say 'damn' before!"

"Well, it will not be the last time. I feel it gives me freedom and it helps me release my feelings."

"Elizabeth, are you seeing a psychiatrist? This all sounds so unlike you," said Alma.

"Is Tony a psychiatrist?" asked Elizabeth.

"Elizabeth, he is a cheat and a thief, and pay no attention to his ways."

"Well, Tony and I sat on the couch together at the party and he put his arm around me and told me that I was beautiful and I needed to get out of my shell. He also said that he was off to Paris with Nelson," said Elizabeth with great glee.

"For the sake of heaven, Elizabeth, get your wits about you and realize that Tony is a conniving social climber among other rotten traits."

"I know that you are always correct, Alma, and I always take your advice, but I must confess that he gave me the tingles," said Elizabeth, putting her hankie to her nose.

"He gave you what?"

"You know that tingling feeling when someone compliments you?"

"Elizabeth, this is an absurd conversation. Drink your tea," Alma said, shaking her head.

Eric went into the kitchen and found Bessie and Bertha polishing the brass and silver. "Madame has so much silver now with Mr. Alfred's coffee sets and table silver, it takes forever to keep it all polished."

"I stopped in at Louise's and the girls were there alone as it was too windy today for them to go to sailing class."

"Yes, Eric, and what is the matter? I can tell that something is bothering you," said Bessie.

"Well, Millicent, you know, the older one, is very clever and says all sorts of things, and she asked me if she could come over here and meet Madame."

"Why would she want to do that?"

"She seems determined to find out why her Daddy is in Paris and took Nelson with him to drive when her Daddy knows how to drive very well. She cannot figure it out and she is determined to get some answers. I told her that I had no idea why and she gave me a dirty look and told me that I would make a very poor spy," explained Eric.

"She sounds like a little pistol," said Bertha.

"Well, she really wants me to bring her over here to meet Madame and ask her why."

"Lordy me, Eric, I would like to be a fly on the wall for that get-together," said Bertha.

"Actually, Millicent remembers meeting her on the coach from London as we all shared the coach when I first arrived but they never spoke and Millicent remembers what Madame wore and that she had little Sophie with her and that Sophie piddled on the floor of the coach and ruined her party shoes and that Madame had a hat with a big feather in it and also that she had a bottle of Dubonnet."

"My, that little one would make a very good spy!" The two women laughed and looked at Eric. "So what are you going to do?"

"I guess that I will ask Madame if it is all right to bring her over and perhaps we could all have tea together." They heard the car doors slam as Alma and Alfred came in with some canned soups and a leg of lamb. "This should do us for a couple of days and then you can make up some lamb stew," said Alma. "You three look like you have seen a ghost, what is the matter with you all?"

"Nothing at all, Madame, I guess that rubbing all this silver is tiring for us."

"Well, when you have finished, why not wrap up some of the larger pieces and put them away, no need for them to stay out and tarnish so quickly."

"Yes, Madame, an excellent idea," said Bessie.

"I will help you put the larger pieces in the closet," said Eric.

"Very well then," said Alma, and started out.

"Madame, may I have a word with you if it is convenient?"

"Why of course, Eric, but you know you are welcome here for a bit more time so do not feel you must leave just because we have had some turmoil going on and anyway, you are such a help with the gardening and shopping and never cause any trouble and we all are so fond of you."

"Thank you, Madame, that is very kind of you but that was not what I wanted to ask you."

"Well, out with it then, we cannot stand here all day."

"Do you think that we could sit on the terrace, as it would be more comfortable to explain it all there."

"I see no reason why not," said Alma, with a bit of mystery in her voice. "It is lovely out here in the late summer, my favorite time of the year, except all the parties die down and we don't have much to gossip about anymore," she said with a laugh.

"Do you recall the mother and the two little girls on the coach when we first met each other?" asked Eric.

"Yes, I do, but they did not say much except it was from the elder girl that I learned you had a birthday. I also know that their mother, Louise, is Tony's ex-wife and that she works at the library and that you visit her from time to time and are fixing up her back terrace as Tony is not supporting her properly. Their father is a dreadful rascal and I do hope that the little girls are doing all right."

"The girls are doing fine. Suzanne, the youngest, has taken the divorce much harder than her sister Millicent, who is a very independent girl and most imaginative. She is very inquisitive also," said Eric. "Well, Millicent remembers you from the train and asked me if she could pay you a visit."

"Really, how interesting, it might be entertaining, so let's have them all for tea some afternoon."

"Oh, I think that Millicent would rather come alone," said Eric.

"Why not have her come around tomorrow at four? I should like to see what this little girl has up her sleeve."

"I believe that would work out with their schedule as they go to sailing camp in the mornings and Louise could drop her off here around four o'clock."

"Very well, then, I shall have Bertha make up some cucumber sandwiches and we will have a little tea party. Perhaps Lucy and Angel will join us also."

Eric rode the bike to Louise's house, finding everyone gardening together. "Suzanne, the biggest plants go in the back and the little ones in front," Millicent told her. "I don't care where the big ones go, I want all the yellow ones here and then the purple ones there." Then the girls saw him. "Oh hello Uncle Eric," they said in unison.

"I have an invitation to present to Suzanne. Suzanne, would you like to go to the traveling circus tomorrow? It is only in town for two days and we could go tomorrow."

"Oh, yes, Uncle Eric, I would love that. We can see all the animals do tricks and see the clowns and maybe there will be a big fat lady too!" She ran over to Eric and threw her arms around his neck. She could see Millicent still on the ground planting flowers and she stuck her tongue out at her. Millicent laughed and said, "You are a silly girl, Suzanne."

"Now, for you, Millicent," said Eric, "you have an invitation to tea at Madame Boeld's tomorrow."

"Oh my, how interesting this will be. I thank you so much. It will be a very important meeting and I must take notes so that I will remember everything about it. Are you going to be there too, Uncle Eric?"

"No, Suzanne and I will be at the circus."

"Mum, I will pack a case with my party shoes and my party dress and a ribbon for my hair and when you pick me up at sailing class I can change my clothes in the car and you can drop me at Madame Boeld's house for tea. And then I will call you to come and get me as I know for a fact that Mrs. Boeld does not have her driver this week."

Suzanne stared at her mother but her mother and Eric both turned away.

Chapter Thirty-Three

Tony rented a bright blue two-door Ford convertible after their plane landed in Paris in late morning. Nelson was fascinated with everything, as he had never been out of England and had only imagined what Paris might be like. "Tony, this is more beautiful than I ever imagined, but isn't the traffic simply awful?"

"Yes, and all the roundabouts can drive one bonkers. But do remember that you are used to the quiet of dear Ambleside, so this must seem like quite a madhouse to you," said Tony as he honked the horn at an elderly woman with her dog on a leash trying to cross the street. She shook her walking stick at Tony and continued crossing, causing Tony to slam on the brakes. Nelson put his hands over his eyes and said, "Everyone is driving on the wrong side of the road!" Tony laughed and said "that is what the French say when they come to England."

Since they had departed London on an early morning flight they had the entire afternoon to sightsee around the city. "Oh, here is my favorite café and what good luck as that car is just pulling out." Tony pulled into the parking space with one turn of the wheel. Nelson had slumped down in his seat.

After lunch they drove around the Eiffel Tower and then to the Louvre where they parked the car and spent the rest of the afternoon. They ended their first day in Paris at the Moulin Rouge. At the small hotel on the left bank that Tony had stayed in many times, they received a very warm welcome. They had a small room with a little balcony overlooking the street and Nelson was fascinated with all the couples walking arm in arm, laughing and sometimes stumbling right into the street.

Tony had a meeting with some clients the next morning and had instructed Nelson to do a bit of shopping. He bought picture books for the girls and a little bottle of perfume for Louise. He bought some lovely sachets for Madame Boeld and at the last minute he decided to buy Bertha and Bessie some sachets also.

He was fascinated with the Marais district and stopped for a coffee at Les Chimères. He thought he could be quite happy just sitting there for many an hour. On his way back to meet Tony at the hotel, he passed a little shop with French berets and bought himself a navy blue one. The young shopkeeper spoke a little English and helped him with the money. Tony had given him directions and the address of the hotel, so Nelson had no trouble walking back. He put on the beret and felt very independent and comfortable and nodded to people as he passed by. The young lady at the hotel desk admired his beret and came over to him and placed the beret at an angle, saying "Now, Monsieur, you look as a true Frenchman!" She kissed him on both cheeks. Nelson did not know how to react, so he just bowed and said "Merci."

Tony returned. After an onion soup lunch, he suggested that since it was such a lovely afternoon they take a ride on a Bateau Mouche and view Paris from the river. Tony had made reservations for dinner at the restaurant atop the Eiffel Tower.

The next morning they started out for Normandy in Tony's rented car. The little hotel had packed a lunch for them and Tony had bought a bottle of table wine.

"Oh Tony, I wish this trip would never end. I have never been so happy and felt so free," said Nelson, placing his hand on Tony's knee as he was driving. Tony smiled and said, "My dear boy, this is just the beginning."

Chapter Thirty-Four

"Oh Mum, I forgot to put my slip in the bag," said Millicent. "It will be fine, just keep on your undershirt and pull the dress on now, as we are almost there," Louise responded. "It isn't proper and I want my slip," pleaded Millicent. "We will turn around and go back for the slip," said Louise. Millicent was glad to go home as she could also wash her face and hands and put on a little cologne that her father gave her for Valentine's Day. She also picked up a box of candy that Eric had brought over for Louise. Now she was ready to go. "Thanks, Mum, it is fine now."

When they arrived at last at the Boeld home, Louise told her daughter, "I hope you have a nice time and call me when you want me to come and fetch you. Do remember your manners and do not hold the tea cup with both hands."

Millicent blew her Mum a kiss and went briskly up to the front door. She saw the very large doorbell and pushed it.

"Good afternoon, you must be Miss Millicent."

"And are you Bessie or Bertha?"

"I am Bessie and Madame Boeld is waiting for you on the terrace. We have tea and some lovely cucumber sandwiches made especially for you."

Millicent stopped immediately and leaned up to Bessie's ear. "I do not like cucumber sandwiches but I brought a box of candy just in case you had the cucumber sandwiches."

"Do not worry and say nothing to Madame. I will warm up some biscuits with jam and clotted cream, how would that be?"

"Oh, very yummy, and so much better than those cucumbers. Oh, you have a dog, what is his name?"

"She is a girl and her name is Angel. Now, come along to the terrace where Madame is waiting for you."

"It is nice of you to come to tea with me, Millicent, and please sit down," said Alma.

"This is a beautiful house. I have never been in such a beautiful house before and you are quite beautiful too, Madame Boeld. I thought you would have a hat on with feathers," said Millicent as she twirled around.

"We only wear fancy hats at a fancy tea party and this is not a fancy tea party. Just two new friends together. One friend is very young and very pretty and the other is very old and not so pretty anymore."

"Oh, yes, Madame Boeld you are still very pretty and I remember you from the train and you had a beautiful hat with a big feather."

"Yes, I remember you also and my dog piddled on your shoes."

"It doesn't matter because my Daddy bought me new party shoes. Where is that doggie from the train? I saw a different one in the hallway."

"Well, little Sophie ate a chicken bone and died but now we have Angel and she is a lovely dog and will not piddle on your new party shoes." Millicent immediately pulled her feet up under her on the chair. "Now, tell me all about yourself and why you wanted to meet me again."

"I wanted to meet you again for many reasons," Millicent said. "I think that you must be a very interesting person and I was fascinated with you on the train, but you never spoke to me. I understand that Eric lives here now and Eric comes to visit us very often so you see we have things in common. Do you remember my Mum?"

"Yes, I do."

"But you never spoke to any of us, only Eric."

"We will make up for that slight oversight now and have a lovely conversation all about you and your sister and your Mum." Bertha came in with the tea and biscuits with clotted cream and strawberry preserve. "Oh, you must be Bertha, I am Millicent Smythe and so glad to meet you. Mr. Eric has told me all about you and Bessie and how much he likes you both. I have met Nelson only once when my Daddy came over to our house. Do a lot of people live here?"

"Alfred, my brother, lives here too, Millicent. His wife just died and he sold his house and moved in with me."

"What was her name?"

"Her name was Margaret."

"When did she die and was there an obituary in the newspaper?"

"Yes, there was one but very short."

"Well, I write obituaries and I could write one about her but I would need to know more about her."

"Why in the world do you write about dead people, Millicent?" asked Alma.

"Well, they aren't always dead, sometimes just people who are not really dead but have just disappeared."

"Oh, I see, a very interesting hobby is it?" asked Alma.

"I wrote an obituary about my Daddy and he is not really dead. You must know lots of dead people, Mrs. Boeld," said Millicent.

"And is that why you wanted to come over for tea with me, to talk about dead people?" asked Alma with a big laugh.

"No, not really, but this is fun and I love the clotted cream. I have never had clotted cream."

"Let's talk about something pleasant now," Alma suggested.

"Have you ever been to Paris, Madame Boeld?"

"Yes, many times, and if you and I become good friends I might take you to Paris someday."

"You would take me to Paris?"

"Well, we will see how things go."

"Oh, Mrs. Boeld, I would carry the bags and help you go across the street and be a wonderful helper."

"Yes, I believe you would be."

"Oh, thank you Madame Boeld, I knew you were a wonderful person the minute I saw you. And when we go to Paris we can wear fancy hats with feathers."

"Yes, and we can go to the Opera and museums and you will learn a lot about life outside of Ambleside and London. Do you visit your Daddy often in London?"

"Sometimes, but he is in Paris now with your driver, Nelson, did you know that?"

"Yes, I do know that, and you have been wanting to ask me about that all afternoon, haven't you, my dear?"

"Why did Daddy take your driver when he knows how to drive?"

"Well, I think that they are good friends and just went on holiday together."

"But he could have taken Suzanne and me," Millicent said, looking away.

"You will have many trips and I am sure that you enjoyed sailing camp didn't you?"

"Yes, but I miss him and we hardly ever see him and it would have been fun."

"Would you like to come back for tea again and we can get to know each other better?" asked Alma.

"Yes, I would like that. I have no grandmothers. They both died and that is when I started to write obituaries. You seem like you would be a snappy good grandmother. Maybe Bessie could be Suzanne's grandmother."

"Well, you must bring Suzanne next time. Now it is getting dark and you should call your Mum to fetch you. Go in the kitchen and Bessie will hand you the phone."

Alfred came down the stairs with Angel. "And who are you, little girl?" he inquired. "I am Millicent and I am Madame Boeld's new granddaughter and we are going to Paris together."

Millicent spotted her mother in the driveway and ran out to the car. Suzanne was in the back seat. Louise asked Millicent if she had a pleasant visit with Alma. Millicent replied with one simple sentence: "She is my new grandmother and she is going to take me to Paris!" After a slight silence, Millicent asked her mother if she had ever been to Paris. Louise answered that she had not, but that she certainly would go one fine day. Suzanne asked if she could go too. Millicent asked Suzanne if she enjoyed the traveling circus. "Yes," said Suzanne, "and I liked the pony ride best. And I brought you these two balloons. What do you have for me?" Millicent thought for a moment and said, "Bessie wrapped up some delicious cucumber sandwiches for you."

Chapter Thirty-Five

Alma was at her desk sorting out the mail when the phone rang. "Yes, this is Mrs. Boeld and who is calling?"

"Mrs. Boeld, this is Dr. Franklin from the American Hospital in St. Cloud in Paris and I understand that a Mr. Nelson Davies is employed by you in Ambleside, England, is this correct?"

"Yes, for well over ten years now, what has happened?"

"There was an automobile accident involving Mr. Davies and a Mr. Anthony Smythe. Both were brought here by ambulance. Mr. Smythe's rental car was in the accident. There is no answer at his London address. Does he have family in Ambleside?"

"Yes, he does. His ex-wife and two children."

"Do you have a telephone or an address for them?"

"No, not offhand, I will have to get it for you. How are the two gentlemen?"

"Mr. Davies, who was in the passenger seat, is unconscious but with no apparent serious injuries. He has some open wounds on his face and legs and they have been treated. Mr. Smythe was driving and, according to the police report, made a left turn into the oncoming traffic and three automobiles were involved in the crash. He is unconscious and has some very serious wounds on his face and we are not yet sure about the condition of his legs, as they were trapped in the wreckage of the car and they had to wait for the hospital emergency to come with proper equipment to release him from the wreckage. He is now in hospital but the condition of his legs has not yet been established."

"Oh, how dreadful, but I am not sure that you should call Mrs. Smythe just yet. It might be best if a good friend broke the news to her so as not to upset the children too terribly much. Her very good friend happens to be staying at my house and if you think it appropriate, I will contact him and he can go over to her home and break this terrible news to her." Dr. Franklin hung up before Alma could say anything else.

"Bessie, Bertha, come here immediately please."

They both came running and found Alma shaking in her desk chair and her head down on the desk. "What has happened, Madame?" they asked in unison.

"Oh my, this is a disaster and we must handle it all very carefully. You both must help me with this as it is just terrible." Alma told them what had happened and both burst into tears.

"Is Eric around?"

"Yes, Madame, he is out in the garden doing some work."

"Well, go get him and tell him to come in."

Eric came into the library and found Alma in tears. "What has happened?"

"Oh, Eric, I do not think I am up to all this."

"What do you mean Alma?" He hardly ever called her by her first name but it just came out.

"Oh, Eric, I am ever so thankful that you are here, as a dreadful accident has happened to Nelson and Tony. They are both in hospital in St. Cloud, which is just outside of Paris."

"What happened, Alma? Please try and settle down so I know what has happened."

Alma told Eric the particulars and that Dr. Franklin thought it best that he tell Louise. Alma held her head down with her handkerchief over her face but peeked out at Eric to see his response. Eric did not respond. He never had to handle anything such as this. Martha always took care of everything and he just did his weather report at the office and then they had supper, watched the television and listened to "Uncle Bernie" on the radio and went off to bed. Eric thought about it all and realized that Louise was very much like him and was never really in charge of things. He liked Louise and wanted to protect her from this horrible news. He thought about it for several minutes until Alma declared, "Eric, did you hear me?"

"Yes Alma, I did, and I am trying to think what to do."

"Well just tell her about the accident and that Dr. Franklin is in charge and he will let us know what is going on."

The phone rang and Alma answered it. "Oh, Louise dear, Eric is right here." Louise told Eric that Dr. Franklin had found her telephone number and had called her about Tony and that he was in a terrible accident and that they had taken X-rays of his legs and both legs were broken in several places and that he was not responding well and could not move or feel anything in his legs or feet.

Eric asked her if the girls knew and she said she had not told them. She said she was going to bed now and the girls could fend for themselves and she had made them some soup and muffins and that they were watching the television. Eric said that the girls needed to know and that Louise must comfort them. Louise said she was distraught and needed to go to bed. Eric said that he would come over in the morning and take the girls to camp and she should call the library and tell them that she was ill and could not come in. She said that she had already called and said that she was ill and told Eric not to bother her when he picked up the girls. Louise hung up and Eric was at a loss.

Alma, who had sat through the conversation, told Eric that he had handled it all very well and there was really nothing more to be done today, so they should both have a lie-down and relax and would he please join her and Alfred for dinner at six. Eric said he would join them for dinner and now he wanted to go back to his gardening.

Alfred came downstairs for dinner with Angel at his heels. He found that no one was about and went into the kitchen to feed Angel. He noticed that the dining room table was set for three and wondered who the guest might be. Bertha and Bessie were sitting very quietly at the kitchen table with a cup of cold tea in front of them and not chatting at all.

"Well, this is a dismal scene. What is the matter with you two spinsters anyway?"

"Alfred, this is no time for smart remarks, sit down and we will tell you."

"I want to feed Angel, and here comes little Lucy too." Neither Bessie nor Bertha moved a muscle. Alfred began to whistle. "Alfred, if you are going to whistle, at least do a tune."

"Very well, anything to make the spinsters happy." He began to whistle "God Save the Queen" and put some scraps from the fridge in Lucy's bowl and leftover lamb in Angel's bowl. "Now, should I sit down with you or leave?"

"It is up to you, Mr. Alfred, do as you like."

"Well then, I will sit down and just stare at your beautiful faces until you tell me your secret."

"It is not a secret, it is bad news. Mr. Tony and our dear Nelson have been in a terrible accident in Paris."

"Why are they in Paris?"

"They went on holiday together."

"Well, they didn't invite me and I haven't been to Paris in years. What did you say about an accident? They were both in a bad car accident in Paris?"

"Yes, Mr. Alfred." He began to whistle again and left the kitchen.

Alma came downstairs and looked very glamorous in a long black dress with a red shawl.

"Alma, did you know that Tony and Nelson went off to Paris and had an accident?"

"Yes, Freddie, I know all about it."

"Well, I don't. Why didn't someone tell me they were going to Paris?"

"Freddie, the point is that they have had a terrible automobile accident and are in hospital." Alma stared at Alfred with her eyes wide open and eyebrows raised.

"In Paris?"

"Yes, Freddie, now shut up. I am exhausted and am going to pour myself a glass of Dubonnet."

"Who is coming to dinner, Elizabeth?"

"No, I invited Eric to join us."

"Why don't I ever know what is going on?" asked Alfred.

Eric came down the stairs and Angel and little Lucy came running out of the kitchen together. "They seem to be friends," said Eric.

"Yes," said Alfred. "Except no one ever tells me anything and I should know what is going on. Even those two in the kitchen won't talk to me."

"Freddie, go make yourself a cocktail and sit down," Alma declared.

Eric sat down and smiled at Alfred. "I suppose you know more than I do, Eric, do you? And did they invite you to go to Paris?"

"No, Alfred, they went on holiday by themselves."

Bertha announced that dinner was ready. The three sat in silence and ate. "Oh, my favorite dessert, apple pie, did you make this Bessie?" asked Alfred. "Yes, for us all," said Bessie. "Thank you, Bessie," said Alma, "you always know what to do. Mix the sour with the sweet don't we?"

"We try, Madame."

Eric remained quiet and ate very little.

Chapter Thirty-Six

Eric pedaled to Louise's home the next morning. Louise was still in her bed. "Come on girls, it is a lovely day and the lake should be just fine for your sailing class."

"We are coming, Uncle Eric, and could you get the sandwiches I made for our lunch out of the fridge please?" asked Millicent. Eric found only two sandwiches, wrapped in newspaper. "Suzanne, your shirt is on backwards, turn it around," said Millicent. "I like it this way," said Suzanne. Millicent glared at Suzanne and Suzanne pulled her arms out and fixed her shirt. She ran to Eric and took his hand.

Eric suggested, "Now, ask your Mum to come down and we will all go together." Having heard the commotion, Louise struggled down the stairs. "Just get in the car and I will take you to camp," mumbled Louise.

"But, Mum, why are you going to drive in your pink nightgown?"

"I want to drive in my pink nightgown and maybe even in my blue one too."

"Mum, does that mean that you have lost all your proper clothes?"

"No, it means that I may have lost my proper mind. Go get in the car." Both girls climbed in, and they left. Eric decided to wait at the house for Louise to return. He went out to the back terrace and decided to put more bricks in place. He thought the terrace looked rather nice and was proud of the job he had done and thought that some more flowers around the borders might cheer up the whole scene. Louise returned and seemed in better spirits and came out to the back terrace in her pink nightgown.

"Louise, please go and put on some decent clothes."

"I am not indecent, just uncomfortable," responded Louise.

"I will now leave. Call me at Alma's later if you need me."

"Thank you, Eric."

Eric whistled as he pedaled his way back to Alma's. His mind began to wander and he wondered how everything would turn out and what would become of everyone as no one seemed secure and he was worried. He had always been secure and had never had to worry about anything except getting the weather report into the *Altoona Daily News* on time. Martha took care of everything. He began to think about Martha and wondered how she was making out. His thoughts went back to Louise and the girls. Martha was always all right and they very rarely had any troubles.

Eric spent the next two days working around the gardens and generally cleaning up Alma's property, which was in a bit of a shambles. Alfred was in the habit of leaving the newspapers on the terrace and they eventually blew all over the place. Eric would gather them up and tell Alfred that he really should take them back inside to discard. Alfred looked at Eric and told him not to boss him around. Alfred reminded Eric that he was family and Eric was not. While Eric was working he heard the phone ring and Alma answer but could not make out the conversation. Alma appeared on the terrace and summoned Eric to come in.

"Eric, that was Nelson. He has been released from hospital as his injuries were superficial and he is mending nicely." Alfred then appeared and wanted to know what was going on. "No one ever tells me anything," complained Alfred. "Freddie, please be considerate and stop acting like a baby boy." Alma explained that Nelson was returning to England on Sunday and perhaps Alfred could pick him up at the station. Alfred said that he could do that and then he would be the first to hear all the news. Alma rolled her eyes and gave Eric a humorous smirk. "Ha, ha," said Alfred. "I shall dress in my dinner clothes and then he can call me Blacky." "Alfred," said Alma with a sigh, "You are a complete ninny and you will do no such thing." Eric laughed to himself.

The next morning at breakfast, Alma declared: "Freddie dear, thank you for all the driving you have handled while Nelson was on holiday. Now that the end of summer is closing in on us, of course the social scene will end except for all the regulars like Elizabeth and the Millers and now the Johansons, who seem to have settled in nicely. Actually they are young, interesting and most polite and seem to enjoy us. Anyway, we always carry on, don't we, Freddie?"

"What did you say, Alma dear, do you need to go and have some dress fittings?"

"No, Freddie, I do not and never mind anyway."

Eric waved to both as he went out the door and onto the bicycle. He found going to the market was great fun and he met many nice people there. It was a social occasion. He, Bertha and Bessie were becoming such good friends and had such comfortable times together in the kitchen with little Lucy and Angel. When he was in Altoona, Eric did not particularly care for tea but now he enjoyed it, finding it settling.

Eric arrived at Louise's house with some fruit and tarts. All were dressed and had the picnic basket ready for the boat ride on the lake. The girls were finished with sailing camp and had not yet started school. "So off we go for a lovely day on the lake. Hurry up, Suzanne," said Louise. "Suzanne is such a slowpoke, I do wish she were more like Millicent and could fend for herself better. Ever since Tony had the accident I have lost patience with everyone. I even get annoyed with people at the library and in the market."

"Louise dear, you are under a lot of stress and have a lot to deal with right now."

"Eric, how come you are always so relaxed and nothing ever seems to bother you?"

"Well, I guess I never have to deal with stress so I guess I am just that way." They looked at each other and smiled.

"Eric, you have been so good to us all and I never say thank you, but I mean thank you."

"It is okay, Louise."

Millicent came over to the car with the picnic basket. "Where is Suzanne?" asked Louise. "She wants to stay home and wait for Daddy to call," said Millicent.

"Oh my, she must not remember the conversation last evening at supper, when I told you girls that Tony's legs are paralyzed and he cannot do things for himself."

"Suzanne knows that, but she does not understand why he cannot use a telephone," said Millicent.

"Eric, perhaps you can convince her to hurry along and we will discuss this all later, as we do not want to miss the boat," suggested Louise. Eric went inside and came out with Suzanne's hand in his. "I want my hankie," said Suzanne. "Here, Suz, use mine," said Millicent.

Chapter Thirty-Seven

"Oh, hello, dear Elizabeth, so nice to hear your voice today, and how are you?"

"I am fine and have had the fire going in the hearth today as it is getting so cool. The summer seems to be closing in and the cooler weather approaching. I presume that you are not too sorry to learn of Mr. Tony Smythe's unfortunate accident. You never liked him, did you?"

"Oh, Elizabeth, please do not think that way at all. He was a bother, but only for a short time. Yes, it is a shame about the accident and of course Nelson was hurt also but will be released from hospital and back on Sunday."

"What do you think happened to them?" asked Elizabeth.

"I do not know but it was a bad accident and Tony was driving a rental car and crashed it up. He is a very irresponsible person as we all know and it is just a shame that Nelson got himself involved with him. It has caused such an inconvenience."

"Alma, would you and Alfred like to come for supper on Saturday? I have no help now so we will be on our own and I will make my lovely cheese soufflé for us. Would six o'clock be convenient?"

"Why how very thoughtful of you, dear Elizabeth, that sounds like a most relaxing evening and it will give Bessie and Bertha a little break, but please do not refill dear Freddie's wine glass too often."

"We all understand, Alma dear."

The phone rang as soon as Alma set it down. "Hello, Mrs. Boeld, this is Millicent, do you remember me?"

"Yes, dear child, you are the extraordinary girl who writes obituaries," said Alma.

"I do lots of things besides writing obituaries and you told me that we could go to Paris and I would love to go to Paris. Did you really mean it that you would take me to Paris?"

"My dear Millicent, I understand that your father has been in a very bad accident in Paris and I am so very sorry to hear that news." Millicent burst into tears and hung up and went to her bedroom and cried into her pillow. Suzanne heard Millicent crying and brought her a hankie and snuggled next to her. Millicent knew right away that she should not have been so rude as to hang up, so she got up and went to dial the phone once again.

"Hello, is this Madame Boeld?"

"Yes, Millicent dear. We must have been disconnected and I am so sorry that my phone was not working properly."

"Oh, Madame Boeld, it was not your telephone that was out of order, it is me who is out of order. Could I come for tea one afternoon soon?"

"Yes, of course, would tomorrow be too soon for you?"

"Oh, Madame Boeld, tomorrow would be just perfect. Should I bring some cookies?"

"Thank you for offering, but Bessie and Bertha bake all the time and I feel sure that they will come up with something to please us, so please come around four thirty. Will your Mum be able to bring you?"

"I have a new bicycle and I know the way now as I ride by all the time hoping that you will be in the gardens but you never are there."

"I will see you tomorrow, my dear child, at four thirty and we shall have a grand tea together." Alma put the phone down quietly, and went to her favorite chair on the back terrace, put her head back, looked up to the clouds and smiled.

Millicent was excited about her visit with Alma. She had been practicing her curtsy and wondered what to wear. She decided on her new party shoes and her white and green striped pinafore. She rode her bike over to Alma's and rang the doorbell. Bertha answered the door and told Millicent how nice it was to see her again. Millicent made a very deep curtsy for Bertha. "My, what a lovely young lady you are, Miss Millicent."

"Thank you, Bertha, and you are a lovely lady too." Bertha smiled and announced Millicent's arrival to Alma. Millicent went right up to Alma, who was seated, and made the deepest curtsy she could. Millicent's face almost ended up in Alma's lap and they both giggled.

"Well, good afternoon, Millicent, and please come and sit next to me, right here."

"Thank you Madame Boeld."

"Millicent dear, I am so very sorry about your father's accident." Millicent began to cry and buried her head in Alma's lap. She kept crying and Alma began to rub her back and Millicent put her arms around Alma's neck. They hugged each other and

Millicent looked up and said, "Madame Boeld, will you be my new friend?"

"Yes, dear, I already am your new friend and you are my new friend."

They sat up and Millicent smiled. "I love your house and all the beautiful things you own. That silk fan over there is beautiful with all the blues and greens in it, where did you get it?"

"I bought it in Paris many years ago, long before you were born."

"I sometimes wish I had never been born," announced Millicent.

"Oh, Millicent, you must never say or think that. Life is a long journey and yours has just begun and things will change and you will change and grow and you will have a wonderful life. I know how upset you are now, but things will be all right," Alma said with a smile, "even though this is a difficult time for you and your Mum and sister."

"Yes, it is and I am the strongest of them all, you know, and I am only twelve. Do you remember that we met when we were coming home from my birthday party with Daddy in London and we all met on the train?"

"Of course I do and Eric was on the train also."

"So, we really are friends already," said Millicent.

"Yes, we are," said Alma with a smile.

Millicent spotted an old picture of a little boy in a silver frame on the table. "I did not know you had a little boy. What is his name?" asked Millicent.

"His name was William and he was my younger brother," said Alma with tears in her eyes.

"I think he died didn't he?" asked Millicent.

"Yes, he died in the war fighting for a cause he hated," said Alma.

Millicent wanted to know if they wrote obituaries way back then, but sensed that this was not the time to continue the conversation.

Alfred came down the stairs and said, "Alma dear, aren't we going to have dinner at Elizabeth's soon?"

"I would like you to meet a friend of mine, Millicent Smythe." Alfred stopped in his tracks and said, "Did you say, Smythe?"

"Yes, Tony Smythe's elder daughter, Millicent."

Alfred looked at Alma with total amazement. "What is she doing in our house?" he bellowed, pointing his finger at the girl.

"We are new friends, Freddie."

"Well, I do not need any new friends especially with the surname of Smythe. I am going out to bounce my ball. When did you say Pinky was returning?"

"He asked if you would pick him up at the train station on Sunday which is tomorrow."

"Oh, very good, I know the days of the week, Alma. Maybe things will get back to normal when he returns." Millicent went over to Alfred and put out her hand out to shake his and he turned away and said, "I am going to take Angel out now." For the first time in her life Millicent was at a loss for words.

Chapter Thirty-Eight

"Alma, I still do not know why you had that child of Tony Smythe's over for tea," said Alfred.

"Freddie, she is a lovely girl and is in great pain about her father's accident and needs comforting."

"But why did she come to you?"

"I do not really know but in a way we are kindred spirits I think."

"What does that mean, Alma?"

"Watch the road, Freddie, you are swerving all over the place. Just pay attention to your driving." All had gone well at Elizabeth's little party. "You were most polite and enjoyable this evening, Freddie."

"I'm going to marry Elizabeth."

"Then I suppose I will be a bridesmaid. But for now, keep your eye on the road. You must pick up Nelson tomorrow so drive carefully now," ordered Alma.

"Does she need money, Alma?"

"No, nothing like that at all. Concentrate on your driving so we do not end up in a heap too, one bad accident is enough. Freddie, look out! That auto is stopped right in front of us. Put on your brakes, Freddie!"

Alma and Alfred got out of the car to see what had happened. They went up to the window and looked in to find that a boy had fallen asleep and was crouched down in the driver's seat. "Well, thank God there is nothing serious and we will call the village police as soon as we arrive home."

Late Sunday afternoon, Alfred returned from the station with Nelson and joined Alma on the back terrace. Nelson went up to his apartment without conversation except a thank-you to Alfred and a promise that he would wash the car and get petrol later. He did also ask Alfred to let Madame know that he was back and did she need him to drive tomorrow. "Well, Freddie, how did he look and did he seem upset?" asked Alma. "I don't know," said Alfred, waving his arms about in frustration.

Nelson threw himself on his bed and cried very quietly. He knew that his life had changed forever and he could not abandon Tony. His fingers were grasping the spread and he buried his head in the pillow and fell asleep. When he awoke it was dark and he was hungry. He went into the house kitchen and Bessie and Bertha were both asleep with their arms resting on the table. Awoken by his entrance, they jumped up and went to hug Nelson. "Welcome home, Pinky! We were waiting for you and have made some lamb stew for you and have kept it warm for hours."

"It is wonderful to see you two and I am hungry and thank you for waiting up for me as I fell asleep."

"Do you want to talk about it all or just relax now?" asked Bessie.

"I think that I will enjoy your company, eat the stew and then tomorrow we can talk. Is everything all right here and where are little Lucy and Angel?"

"Angel is with Mr. Alfred and little Lucy has not come home yet. She must be chasing some mice."

"It's comforting to be home and I need some sleep so I will eat the stew, say thank you and good night." He gobbled up the stew and then he went around the table and placed a kiss on each one. Bessie and Bertha told Nelson that they missed him and prayed for him. Nelson blew another kiss to each as he went back to his apartment. Little Lucy was now at his door with a mouse.

Eric stayed for supper at Louise's. Afterward, since it was dark, Louise put the bicycle in the car and drove Eric back to Alma's. Eric observed, "Nelson must be back. His light is on."

"What does this mean, Eric?"

"Simply, it means that Nelson is back and we will have to wait until tomorrow to see what news there is."

"The doctor has not called me in two days so I have no idea how Tony is doing."

"I know, Louise, and it is upsetting, but drive back home and I will be in touch with you tomorrow." Eric took the bicycle out of the car. Louise drove very carefully back to her house. Millicent was up and sitting in the kitchen.

"Why are you down here, Millicent?"

"I just wanted to make sure that you came home."

"Of course I came home and I will always come home to you and Suzanne," said Louise as she kissed Millicent on top of her head.

"You will never have a car accident will you Mum?"

"Hopefully not, my darling, and don't you worry your pretty little head about it."

"I want us all to be safe and to have everything be all right. Madame Boeld said that life is a journey and changes all the time and everything will be all right. Is that true, Mum?" asked Millicent.

"Yes it is and Madame Boeld is a wise woman. Now, let's go up to bed and say prayers together." They both put on their warm nighties as the nights were getting cooler. "Mum, I don't want to say prayers tonight." "Why not?" asked Louise. "I don't know why, I just don't."

Everyone in Alma's house was awakened by thunder and lightning and the sound of heavy rain. Angel found refuge under Alfred's bed and little Lucy curled up tight by the open hearth in the kitchen. It was two o'clock in the morning and everyone wandered about in their nightclothes. Bessie and Bertha made tea and heated up some biscuits. Everyone huddled around the kitchen table.

"I wish I had a picture of us all, it looks like an air raid," said Alfred. Alma glanced at him and said, "Nothing like an air raid, Freddie, just a storm." Nelson sat quietly in a straight chair away from the table.

"Pinky, are you warm enough over there?"

"Yes, thank you, Mr. Alfred, I am."

Suddenly all the lights flickered but did not go off. Then came a very loud crack of thunder and Bessie and Bertha hugged each other. Alfred moved very close to Alma. "Well, we are all safe and sound and we can go back to bed soon," said Alma. "Bertha, please find all the extra blankets you can and distribute them around. I am fine and do not need more blankets. Thank goodness we still have the electric, so at least we can see where we are going."

"Where are we going Alma?" asked Alfred. "Back to bed Freddie. That is the warmest and safest place to be," said Alma. Nelson said, "I shall make a dash for it back to my room."

The next morning was clear and the sun was shining. "Well, at least no damage done except the garden is a shamble, but we are all in one piece," said Alma.

"I like to be at the kitchen table," said Alfred. "I feel safe here."

"You are safe here, Mr. Alfred," said Bertha. Alma declared, "Now, we will all have a hearty breakfast and get on with the day."

"Oh, I like it when we are all huddled together and I hope we have another storm very soon," said Alfred. Crows were squawking outside and upsetting Lucy and Angel. "Freddie, go up and dress, and see if you can help in the garden to clean up the mess."

"Alma, you are so clever, you made a rhyme and do not even know it."

"Freddie, you are so full of nonsense," said Alma as she went up the stairs.

Chapter Thirty-Nine

"Hello Tony, I can hear you quite well. We had quite a storm last night but everyone is all right this morning and how is everything going along at the hospital?"

"Well, other than fifteen nude Parisian dancing girls up and down the corridors, all is quite normal."

"Tony, you sound good! That is the first little joke you have made since the accident," remarked Nelson.

"Well, what else can I do? Legs do not work, so best to keep the brain dancing. Nelson, is Eric around?"

"I do believe he is here."

"Would you please give him a message for me?" asked Tony. "I have been doing some thinking, that is, between dancing with all the girls here, and I think that Eric should deliver the news to Louise and the girls that I plan to be back in London soon but will be in hospital for a while and everything will be fine. When I am back in London you could drive the girls to hospital and we will have a little tea party. I will send you some money to buy gifts for them. I do not want to upset them and want them to be assured that I will be fine very soon."

"I understand and think that is a good plan. No need for the girls to be too upset and good to give them a positive forecast."

"Yes, exactly, and Louise is very sensitive and cries at the drop of a hat, so we must keep the news upbeat," said Tony.

"When will you be back in London?" asked Nelson.

"I do not know but I think I will be transferred there very soon. I need you to be with me," said Tony.

"I want to be there for you and I am going to work it all out. I must."

"I know you will work it out, and remember that money is not a problem, so quit the job with the Madame if you need to."

"Yes, Tony. I will contact Eric. By the by, any new reports from the doctor?"

"Well, actually yes and not too positive. My left leg may get the feeling back but they fear that my right leg is totally paralyzed and I may never have the use of it again. However, they can do great things and a young woman came to my room with a very positive attitude and good bedside manner to cheer me up. I would like to hire her for my business as I do believe she could sell ice to an Eskimo!"

"Oh, Tony, you are so brave and I just know that everything will be all right."

"Not everything, Nelson dear, but maybe good enough to keep life going."

"Tony, you know I will always be at your side."

"I don't want you only at my side, dear boy."

"Oh, Tony, get some rest and we will chat after I get in touch with Eric." Both laughed before hanging up.

Nelson immediately burst into tears. He thought he must be strong and positive and take on responsibility. He had always taken orders and this was all so new to him. Nelson went over to the kitchen and found Bessie washing the supper dishes and Alfred drying them. "Well, hello Bessie and Alfred," said Nelson. "I am glad we are all together."

"We are getting married," said Alfred with a big laugh. "Only jesting, but I love Bessie and Bertha. They are my best friends."

"That is very nice, Alfred. Have either of you seen Eric?"

"He is in his room. I heard the bath running. Why do you want to see him?" asked Alfred. Nelson did not answer. "Nelson, why do you want to see Eric?"

"Mr. Alfred, it is about Tony," explained Nelson.

"No one ever tells me anything and I do not like secrets and I want to know about that Tony Smythe. I hope he never walks again," said Alfred.

"Mr. Alfred, please leave the kitchen," said Bessie.

"I am going to tell Alma on you. You have to be nice to me and you should know that Tony Smythe is a bad boy," said Alfred as he kicked the door.

"Mr. Alfred, I suggest that you stop right now and go find something else to do," said Nelson.

"I do not want something else to do and this is my house, not yours. You and Eric think you own the place and it is my house and Alma's house and she makes all the rules and you don't," screamed Alfred.

"Mr. Alfred, get a hold on yourself and quiet down. We all know that you are the boss and we respect you, so just quiet down and act like a boss," said Nelson as he went out the door.

"Thank you. Now everybody go away. Bessie and I have important things to do," said Alfred. Bessie threw down the kitchen towel and gave Alfred a very nasty look and went up the back stairs. Alfred was alone in the kitchen. Not even little Lucy or Angel came to comfort him. The house was dark and quiet. Nelson left a note on Eric's bedroom door asking him to knock on his apartment door in the morning.

As dawn was breaking, Nelson went to the house and heard Eric speaking with Alfred, who was in the dining room pouring some brandy.

"Good morning, Eric, may I speak with you for a few minutes in my apartment?"

"Of course," said Eric, and they walked out. Alfred, being alone, started to cry and called for Alma. Alma came downstairs and said, "What in the world is the fuss about down here?"

"They are mean to me and will not tell me what is going on and I am the boss here and they are not telling me what is wrong with Tony Smythe."

"Freddie, you simply must learn to be kind and to be a gentleman. You act like a child so much of the time."

"Margaret told me that I was her baby and I told her that she was my angel."

"Freddie, are you drinking brandy for breakfast?" Alfred said nothing and went upstairs and closed his door without a word. Alma threw back her head and wondered what else today would bring. She thought she might invite the precocious Millicent for luncheon tomorrow. She dialed and Louise answered the phone. "Oh, how very thoughtful of you to call, Madame Boeld, do you have any news about Tony?"

"No, dear, I do not, but I was wondering if you and the girls would like to come for luncheon here tomorrow. I know it is short notice and we will have a simple lunch together."

"Thank you so much for thinking of us but I have a job at the library and the girls must go to the school to get their books for this year."

"Well, perhaps another time," said Alma.

"Thank you, Madame Boeld, I hope so."

Eric and Nelson were seated in Nelson's apartment. "This is a very comfortable apartment. How long have you been here, Nelson?" asked Eric.

"Going on about twelve years now," said Nelson. "I want to speak with you about Tony Smythe, Eric. You have heard about his accident haven't you?"

"Yes, of course, and we are all so very sorry about it all," said Eric.

"Tony thinks it best for you to inform Louise of his condition in person instead of over the telephone from Tony at the Paris hospital." Eric pondered this request and was not entirely comfortable with it.

"May I ask you how Tony is and how bad is the news?"

"He is in good spirits and feels that he will make good progress and will be back in London very soon."

"Is that the message he wants me to give to Louise? If so and that is all, I will convey that to Louise. They are all pretty upset over the accident and Louise mentioned that she had not heard from the doctor in two days. How bad is it, Nelson?"

"I do not really know."

"I understand. It is a tragedy and I will do all I can to help the family."

"How very kind of you, Eric," said Nelson. Nelson and Eric shook hands and Eric went out the door and walked around the grounds. He heard a meow and little Lucy came scampering over to him. Eric bent over, picked up little Lucy and took her to his room.

The phone rang in the house and Alma picked up. "Oh hello, Elizabeth, how kind of you to call. By any chance, do you feel like a little adventure?"

"Oh, I'm fine, I do just feel a bit lonely and tired from time to time and there are no invitations in the mail."

"Well, we know the season is almost over and we have to find things to occupy us for the winter months. I do wish I had the funds to go on an ocean voyage, wouldn't that be nice?" suggested Alma.

"Yes, it would Alma, but where would we go?"

"I would go almost anywhere without Freddie. He is so very tiresome and childlike. I do not know how Margaret coped with him."

"Oh, as you may well know, I do not have the money for long travel and do not really know if I could manage a trip. My hip is very painful and the doctor said that I should see an orthopedic surgeon about it."

"Very well, let's not talk about that. It was just a pipe dream anyway," said Alma. "Elizabeth, would you like to come to lunch here on the day after tomorrow?"

"Oh, yes, that would be fine. Alfred is always so flattering to me and at our age that is very nice."

"Yes, Elizabeth, Freddie is very fond of you." Alma rang off and smiled to herself. She realized that she still could control some situations and that Elizabeth would be a grand babysitter for Freddie.

The weather was warm enough to have luncheon on the terrace and Elizabeth arrived wearing a very short skirt and a flowing blouse. "My, Elizabeth dear, you look so young and charming. Where did you purchase that lovely costume?"

"I did not purchase it, I remodeled it," she said with a big laugh.

"You are most clever. I hope you like Bessie's vegetable soup. She made it fresh this morning from vegetables that Eric picked up. You know that he goes each morning and picks up all the nicest and freshest things. He is really a wonder and I do hope he stays on, as he is no trouble and so very pleasant and has been a tremendous comfort to Louise and the girls since Tony's accident."

Alfred appeared on the terrace in a velvet dressing gown. "How nice of you to come, Elizabeth, and I am delighted to see you. I miss my Margaret very much but would you marry me?"

Alma and Elizabeth looked eye to eye and did not know what to say. Elizabeth managed, "Freddie, you are very charming but I cannot marry at my age. I like living alone and do enjoy company and visiting my friends."

"Well, I want to marry you," said Alfred who would not sit down and just stood there with his hands in the pockets of his fancy robe. Bessie had overheard the conversation and came to the rescue, pulling out a chair for Alfred.

"Oh, thank you, Bessie, what do you have for us?"

"Some fresh vegetable soup, Mr. Alfred." She returned to the kitchen.

"Oh, yes, very nice." Alfred sat down and winked at Elizabeth. "Do you know how to wink, Elizabeth? I taught Margaret how to wink and we winked at each other all the time."

"Bessie, is the bread ready?" Alma called out.

"Yes Madame, perhaps you would ask Mr. Alfred to come and fetch it."

"Alfred, do give Bessie a hand and fetch the bread."

"I will do anything for Bessie and Bertha. I want to marry them too." Alfred went into the kitchen.

"Alma, Alfred seems a bit disoriented today. Why is he in that dressing gown at this hour?" Alma sat and said nothing at first, as all of a sudden her mind was going back in years. "Elizabeth dear, please excuse me but my mind is clearing a bit and I do believe that I was told that when Freddie was released from the prison camp and then left the hospital in care of me the report said that he had some brain damage but could manage and therefore did not need any more medical care. I, myself, had only been released from the prison a few days before I went to fetch Freddie and we were so happy to reunite that we just went on with things and tried to pull our lives together. We sold our family home in Oberammergau and bought this house. We had just settled in when Margaret came for a summer and stayed at the Inn. They met and married all in one month. Margaret had a bit of money and they purchased their house and all seemed to go well until Margaret died."

"Oh, poor dear Alfred, that is such a tragic story."

"No, it is not, Elizabeth. Life is like that. You are just lucky that your life has been so simple and protected."

"We were in the mountains in Villars, Switzerland, during the war," said Elizabeth, "and my brother and I learned how to ski."

"How very nice for you."

"Yes, it was most pleasant," said Elizabeth, gazing off onto the garden below the terrace. "You were lucky that the recent storm did not absolutely ruin your garden, Alma."

"Yes, thank goodness for small favors." Then Elizabeth and Alma screeched as they heard two gunshots. "Elizabeth, get down on the floor behind that chair!" Elizabeth, shaking all over, did as she was told. Bessie and Bertha came running out to the terrace with their aprons over their heads. Alma was standing behind a wooden pillar and began calling for Alfred. There was no answer. Finally, Alfred appeared with two dead crows.

"Where is the gun, Freddie?" asked Alma.

"I put it back in my auto. I always keep it in my auto, Alma," said Alfred calmly while his dressing gown absorbed the crows' blood. Bessie and Bertha walked slowly over to Alfred and Bessie began blotting his legs with her apron. Bertha took the crows and threw them over the railing as far as she could. As she turned back she screamed at the sight of Elizabeth huddled into the size of a pillow behind the chair shaking like a leaf. Nelson had heard the shots and run to the house, bursting in the front door and meeting face to face with Eric.

"Eric, we will take Mr. Alfred upstairs, put him in a tub, and you stay with him, and do not let him leave his room. I will look for the gun." It took both Eric and Nelson to maneuver Alfred upstairs and into the tub. Alma met Nelson coming down the stairs. "Nelson, get the gun out of Freddie's auto and hide it in your apartment. We will deal with it tomorrow."

"Yes, of course, Madame."

Patty Dickson

Bessie and Bertha were mopping the hallway when Elizabeth appeared in total disarray from her hideout. "Alma, do let's have some tea. It would hit the spot right about now."

"Yes, of course, Elizabeth dear, but please do not mention spots. Just look at the carpet!" said Alma, throwing her arms high in the air while collapsing into a chair. Alma put her hands upon her head and decided that tomorrow would be a perfect day to purchase a new hat after she and Nelson had disposed of the gun.

Chapter Forty

In the night, clutching his pillow, Eric started to scream for Martha. He awoke and caught himself before he screamed loudly and found that he was in a sweat and his pajamas were wet and he felt rather faint. He turned on the light and looked at the clock. It was two-thirty in the morning. He was wide awake and wanted to escape somewhere. He was not comfortable. He did not know what tomorrow, or actually today, would bring and he was afraid. He stepped out of bed and poured a glass of water, wiped his brow and changed his pajamas. He wanted to be with Martha and in his own bed in Altoona where he felt safe. He had been most comfortable here but all of a sudden he felt lost and confused.

His mind caught up with him and he recalled that he had called Louise and asked her to have a picnic lunch with him down by the lake during her lunch break. They decided to meet at the boat landing at noon. He needed to formulate how he would tell Louise about Tony's condition. He was most annoyed that he had agreed to do this for Tony and disliked him greatly for being such a coward. However, he had agreed and must go forward for the sake of the girls and Louise. Martha would know how to handle this situation. He missed Martha and began to feel guilty about his disappearance. This was supposed to be just an escape for a short while and a fancy to discover other places. He had never even considered getting involved in anyone's problems or family. It was just a little getaway from Altoona, not from Martha. He loved Martha and missed her and his daughter, Gail, and his granddaughter, Norma. He had missed Norma's birthday. He was surrounded by guilt. He climbed back into bed and just stared at the ceiling until he drifted off to sleep again.

He awoke when he heard Nelson starting the car. He got up, dressed himself and took the bike into the village and purchased some vegetables as well as items for the picnic. As usual, all went onto Madame's account and Eric felt he must reimburse Madame for the picnic items. He biked back to the house and dropped off the produce with Bessie. They wished each other a good day. Bessie looked at Eric and asked if he felt ill. Eric replied that he did, but would be all right and not to worry.

Louise was waiting for Eric by the landing and had already spread out the blanket for their picnic. Louise had brought some Swiss chocolates for a treat. "You picked a great day for a picnic, Eric. The sun is lovely and there is no wind."

"Yes, a lovely day, Louise. How are the girls?"

"Oh, pretty well, I guess. Millicent is back to writing her obituaries and has written about ten for Tony. Her latest one was that he was a clown in a circus and the circus was having a special memorial service for him."

"What does she do with all these after she writes them?"

"She tears them up into the tiniest pieces and flushes them down the toilet. I told her that she might clog up the drains and she said that God would not let that happen."

"Well, let's hope that God is listening and takes care of it all," said Eric.

"Suzanne is very quiet and sticks to me. She sulks and then holds my hand and tells me that she loves me."

"Oh, Louise, this is a very difficult time and my heart goes out to you, my dear girl."

They sat quietly and Eric opened the wrappings and sorted out the picnic. "It looks just lovely, Eric. It must be a special occasion as these sandwiches are that very pricy liver pâté and such lovely sweets also. Did you hit the lottery?"

"No, I did not hit the lottery and there is no special occasion. However, Nelson asked me to talk with you."

"Why would Nelson want you to talk with me?"

"He thought it would be a good idea if I could explain to you in person about Tony's condition from the accident. Tony asked Nelson to ask me to do so. It may sound a bit complicated but that is how it is. Tony did not want to do it over the long-distance telephone. Nelson says he is in good spirits but the medical report is not very good. His legs are the problem. His left leg will recover feeling but his right leg may remain paralyzed. That is really all they can tell right now. He will be in the Paris hospital for a while and then to a hospital in London. When Tony thinks it appropriate, Nelson will bring the girls in to see him in London. He is in good spirits, Louise, and the money will continue. He is hopeful that you will not be too upset and to know that all will be all right," Eric said and took a deep breath.

"Is that all he said?" asked Louise.

"Yes, basically, that was what he wanted you to know."

"What does all this mean, Eric?"

"I cannot answer that, dear Louise. I think you must go on and keep your spirits up for the girls and keep a positive attitude."

"Oh Eric, life has just turned upside down since Tony left. I could not imagine all this would happen to us. What did I do to deserve all this?"

"You did nothing, it just happened. Perhaps the girls could make get-well cards and Nelson will mail them to him at the hospital. Nelson will be the one who knows what is going on."

"Oh really, what exactly is Nelson to Tony?" asked Louise.

"Let's put it this way, they are more than just friends," said Eric as he rearranged the picnic case.

"I think I know what you mean," said Louise. Eric looked into Louise's eyes and said, "I truly do not know."

"What am I going to tell the girls?"

"Nothing, he is their father and he loves them. Nothing has changed there."

"Does everyone know Tony is queer?" asked Louise with her hands over her face.

"Louise, I just do not know and please do not dwell on this subject. You have the girls to bring up and you must be strong and just concentrate on them and your wellbeing."

"Oh Eric, I hope you will be my friend forever." Louise looked at Eric and he looked away. "Eric, what is the matter? You will be my friend forever won't you?"

"Of course, you and I will be friends forever, but I am going to have to go home soon."

"Oh, please do not ruin the picnic. We haven't even had the sweets yet."

"Yes, let's have the sweets."

They each picked a sweet and looked toward the lake and the reflections of the mountains on the water. "Isn't it funny how everything is upside down in reflections?" Eric smiled and offered another sweet to Louise. Louise took his other hand and put it to her mouth and kissed it.

"You are a very sweet man."

"And you are a very sweet girl."

They packed up the picnic basket and Louise walked back toward the library. Eric rode the bicycle to the library and sent off the weather reports for the coming week. Louise came into the library and went over to Eric. "It was a wonderful picnic, Eric. I will be fine and thank you for being my friend." She took his hand and squeezed it.

Chapter Forty-One

Louise sat the girls down in the kitchen the next day and told them about Tony's legs. "Will he walk again?" asked Suzanne. "I do not care if he walks again ever or never or at all or anyhow or anywhere," said Millicent.

Louise and Suzanne stared at her. "So, what is the matter with you two?" asked Millicent.

"That is wicked of you to say," scolded Louise.

"So what?" said Millicent. "Okay, I will send him some cards and weave him a basket. I know how to weave. They taught us to weave on days we could not sail."

"That would be nice, dear," said Louise.

"I do not know how to weave but I know how to draw. I can make pictures and we can mail them to the hospital. How will you get a basket to the hospital, Millicent?" asked Suzanne.

"I don't know. Mum, how can we get a basket to the hospital?"

"Well, I think it will work out very nicely. We can put everything you make in the basket and Nelson will take it to the hospital when your Daddy comes back to London."

"Mum, can you take us to get paper and pens and the straw so I can start the basket tomorrow?"

"Yes, we will drive to that specialty store where they have all the art supplies." Millicent stuck her tongue out at Suzanne and went outside with her jumping rope. Suzanne and Louise folded the laundry. "You are a good little helper, Suzanne." She replied, "Yes, I know I am and Millicent is not a good little helper, is she Mum?" Louise said, "Not as good as you are."

The phone rang and Suzanne answered. "Hello, I am Suzanne, who is calling please?"

"Good afternoon, Suzanne, is your sister Millicent at home?"

"No, she is skipping rope outside."

"Would it be possible for you to summon her to the telephone?"

"Are you her new teacher from school?"

"No, I am Madame Alma Boeld"

"Oh, I know who you are. You are the fancy lady with the beautiful house and Millicent went to tea with you."

"Yes, your sister came to tea and I hope that you will come to tea."

"When can I come to tea?"

"Well, how would Thursday be for you both to come and have tea with me?"

"I will have to ask my Mum. We have to get some things to make for my Daddy who is in the hospital in Paris and he can't walk."

"Would you ask your Mum to call me back please, Suzanne? And please ask your dear Mum if she is able to join us for tea also."

"I will and goodbye."

"Who was that on the phone, Suzanne?"

"It was Madame Boeld and she wants us all to come for tea on Thursday."

"How very nice, does she wish me to call her?"

"Yes, can we go?"

"Yes, we can."

Millicent came in with her jumping rope and threw herself on the sofa. "I am exhausted and do not wish to be bothered. I am going to my room."

"Do you want to go to tea at Madame Boeld's?" asked Suzanne.

"What did you say?"

"I said we can go to tea at fancy Madame Boeld's."

"What are you talking about?"

Louise came in and explained the conversation to Millicent. "Why did she call you, Suzanne? You don't even know her. I am her friend."

"Suzanne answered the phone, you were outside," said Louise. "I will call Madame Boeld and tell her that we all would be delighted to have tea with her on Thursday. Now, go upstairs and pick out the dress you will wear and make sure that your party shoes are clean and that you both have starched slips to wear under your dresses. Oh, and also pick out ribbons for your hair and I will iron them."

"Good afternoon, Madame Boeld," said Louise. "I understand that you called and so kindly asked us for tea on Thursday."

"Yes, I did and I do hope you will be able to come."

"We would be delighted to join you for tea."

"Very well. I will expect you at four o'clock on Thursday," said Alma and abruptly hung up.

"Bessie, are you there?"

"'No, Madame, this is Bertha."

"Bertha, we are having seven for tea on Thursday. Please make some sugar cookies and a lovely chocolate torte and use all the best china teacups and the small linen tea napkins. Perhaps the larger tea napkins would be more suitable."

Alma thought that Elizabeth would add to the group nicely and called her. "Elizabeth, will you come for tea on Thursday at four?"

"Why, yes I can. What is the occasion?"

"Nothing really, just Louise, the two girls, Alfred, Eric, you and me," explained Alma.

"Do you mean Tony's ex-wife and those girls?"

"Yes, of course. They are a lovely family and I think that we should spend more time with young people."

Nelson, Eric and Alfred were all helping on the grounds to remove debris from the storm. "We can all join together for the good cause," said Eric. "Yes, it is only proper that we all pitch in," said Nelson. "Well, I am tired now of all this raking and picking up and I was the first one out here so I am going in now," said Alfred.

Nelson suggested, "Oh, on your way, Mr. Alfred, would you be kind enough to take the wheelbarrow full of brush and dump it in the pile next to the garage?"

"I am not going that way," said Alfred as he walked off.

Alfred went into the kitchen and found Bessie and Bertha scrambling around polishing silver and preparing for the tea party. "Who is coming for tea?" asked Alfred. "Your sister has invited Miss Louise and her two daughters and Miss Elizabeth, and you, Eric and the Madame make seven for tea, so we are bustling around as you can see."

"Oh, that will be nice, as I wish to marry Elizabeth."

On Thursday at precisely four o' clock in the afternoon the doorbell rang and Alma answered the door. "How lovely to see you. I am pleased that you are so prompt."

Millicent pushed her mother aside and curtsied in front of Alma. "Madame Boeld, I would like you to meet my lovely mother, Louise Smythe, and my little baby sister, Suzanne."

Alma was most amused at Millicent and rather admired her impertinence. "How nice of you to come. Suzanne, will you take my hand and we will all go onto the terrace, as it has cleared up so nicely from the storm," said Alma. Suzanne did not know what to say and clutched her mother's hand.

"Come along dear Suzanne and I will show you the lovely nest that the little robins have made during the summer and was fortunately not demolished with the wind and the storm."

"Oh, I love birds, where is the nest?" she asked and rushed over to Alma. The doorbell rang and they all turned around to find Elizabeth at the open doorway. "Hello, hello, Elizabeth here!" she exclaimed, entering by herself. Alfred was coming down the stairway dressed in his yachting jacket and white trousers. He wore a navy blue captain's cap.

"Good afternoon everyone. I am Alfred and I live here. Alma is my sister. I welcome you to our home and please introduce yourselves to me."

"I am Millicent and I am the older sister of Suzanne and my mother is the beautiful lady in the blue frock. We all met on the coach train from London last spring and Madame Boeld's dog wet the floor and ruined my party shoes. But we have all had more troubles since then and we cry a lot. What do you do, Mr. Alfred?"

Alfred stood in silence.

"Oh, hello, dear Elizabeth," Alma said, restoring order. "So very nice of you to come to tea. Do you know the Smythe family, Elizabeth?"

"I do not remember their names," said Elizabeth.

"Oh, do come right in and we will go onto the terrace and get to know each other," Alma said, as she was quite looking forward to this gathering as things had been a bit tiresome lately and she was most interested to see how Millicent would handle herself and if she really wanted to invest time with her.

"Do sit down as we are most fortunate to have help with the cleaning up of the storm mess and we can enjoy the clearing weather." Louise sat on a double couch and Suzanne sat next to her. Alfred took a chair next to Elizabeth and Millicent waited to see where Alma would sit. Alma chose a chair and Millicent kept standing. "Do sit down, my dear Millicent. Bring up that straw chair and sit by me." Millicent carried the chair to next to Alma and was most interested in its straw.

A Fine How Do You Do

Millicent declared, "I know how to weave straw and I have made baskets but not any chair seats. I am going to make my Daddy a straw basket and we are going to collect cards from all over town to send to him in hospital. He was in an accident and his legs are all broken and he may never walk again." Suzanne burst into tears and buried her head in Louise's lap.

"We all hope that he will walk again dear, and we will pray for his recovery," said Alma. "Now do come over here, dear Suzanne, and I will show you the bird nest."

"I think that personal cards in my basket would be better than prayers," said Millicent.

While lifting Suzanne's head from her lap, Louise said, "Madame Boeld, it was so kind of you to invite us and we all are naturally so concerned about Tony's situation, but we intend to go on with our lives and hope that he recovers and will be able to be with the girls once again for visits."

"I would like to do all I can to help you during this uncomfortable time," Alma said as she went over to Suzanne and took her hand. "Now I will show you the bird nest, but we must sneak up quietly. It's right above your head, in the beams." Suzanne tiptoed along Alma's side.

Bertha arrived with the teacart and Bessie carried the chocolate torte and the sugar cookies. "Oh my," said Suzanne, "I have never seen such beautiful pastries." Bessie passed the cookies and Suzanne took three and tried to pick up a fourth and dropped all of them on the floor. Millicent ran over to Suzanne and helped her pick them all up.

"She was just trying to get some for me too and dropped them by mistake," said Millicent, looking at Alma. Alma looked at them both and said, "I have dropped many a cookie in my life. It is perfectly all right and the little baby birds will welcome the crumbs."

"Mr. Alfred are you a business man?" asked Millicent.

Alfred did not answer right away but looked down and swept the crumbs off his shoe. "Yes, I mind my own business," said Alfred.

"Do you know my Daddy? He is a business man in London and all over the world," bragged Millicent.

"Yes, I know of him but I did not know that he had such a fine family until I met you today." Alma smiled with great pride that Alfred had handled himself so well. Then she realized Eric was not present. "Where is Eric? Bessie, will you please see if you can find Eric?" Bessie said she would search the house.

Elizabeth asked the girls when they started school. Suzanne said, "In two or three weeks I think and I will be glad to get back to school."

"And how about you, Millicent?" asked Elizabeth.

"I do not care about school but I go anyway. I like to write stories and obituaries and would like to travel around the world."

"I feel sure that you will be able to do anything you want to do, Millicent," said Elizabeth.

"And what about me?" asked Suzanne.

"And you also will be a very happy person," said Elizabeth. "Perhaps you girls would like to come to my home for tea next week."

"I would like to come to your house for tea and I won't drop the cookies on the floor," said Suzanne.

"Perhaps you could come after school, Suzanne, and we could bake the cookies together."

Suzanne smiled and ran over to Elizabeth and threw her arms around her neck.

"Oh that would be such fun, just you and me?"

"If that is what you would like, then that is what it will be. Just the two of us baking cookies."

Alma smiled and knew that she had, once again, created an agreeable party.

"It was very nice to see you, Miss Millicent and Miss Suzanne, and I always like to see Elizabeth, but I have things to do and Angel needs me," announced Alfred. He walked over to Elizabeth and gave her a wink and kiss on the cheek. Elizabeth giggled a bit, while calling Alfred a flirt.

"It has been a lovely afternoon and we so enjoyed the tea and being with you, Madame Boeld," said Louise.

"Must you all run so soon, but I suppose that you must, since it is getting a bit dark and cooler."

Bessie returned and reported that she had found Eric fast asleep in his bed. "Poor dear," Alma said. "He tries to be so helpful."

Elizabeth went over to Suzanne and whispered in her ear, "Do you like surprises?"

"No not really. All my surprises are bad, like in Goldilocks."

"Well, we will have nice surprises for you when you come to tea and we bake cookies together."

"Oh, that would be so special," exclaimed Suzanne. Elizabeth leaned down and gave Suzanne her hands, pulled her up and gave her a hug.

Millicent went over to Alma, curtsied and said, "What a delightful time, thank you so very much and I hope to see you again very soon, Madame Boeld. May I come for a visit on my bicycle?"

"Millicent, do not be so forward. You must never arrive at anyone's home uninvited," said Louise with a look that Millicent knew so well. "Come girls, we must be off."

Alma smiled and gave them a wave as they walked toward the front door. Millicent turned her head back toward Alma and blew her a kiss. Alma blew a kiss in return.

Alma sat down again and began to hum an old song she suddenly remembered from Bavaria that her mother sang to her so many years ago. She remembered the words in German and began to sing aloud and dance around holding her skirt in her hand. Bertha and Bessie came out to the terrace to pick up the tea things. "Oh come and dance with me, you two old friends." Bertha and Bessie looked at each other and joined Alma, and the three of them danced and sang.

Alma finally sat down after many swirls and said, "My oh my, what fun that is. We must dance and sing more often."

"Yes, Madame, it is inspiring and good for our souls having the young around," said Bertha. Alma looked at the two of them and said, "It certainly is and we will do it more often now."

"We love to see you enjoying yourself, Madame, just like the old days." Alma smiled and said, "Just like the old days." Bertha and Bessie took the trays away. Thoughts of the old days went through her head. Some of the old days were wonderful to recall and others too frightening.

Chapter Forty-Two

"Good to hear your voice, Tony, and how are you doing today?" asked Nelson.

"I am glad to be back on British soil. However, my feet have not touched the ground. Too much time for me to be alone and thoughts blowing in and out of my mind have taken a bit of a toll on me. Fortunately, I have been able to still do business and make some money and things look quite proper there. I am considering putting the townhouse on the market. If I ever get out of here the stairs will be too much and I would be better off in a nice flat. I am talking to agents," announced Tony.

"I was wondering about that and it seems like a good idea," said Nelson. Tony interrupted: "I would like to see you but do not bring the girls, I do not want them to see me like this."

"I wasn't planning to bring the girls. I saw Eric and he said that the girls have made some cards for you in a straw basket made by Millicent. I will bring them in when I come. Madame had the girls and Louise for tea last week."

"And what was that all about?" asked Tony.

"I really couldn't say," said Nelson.

"Madame Boeld always has something going in her screwy head. How dare she fool around with my family when I cannot even confront her," said Tony angrily.

"I think that it was quite a pleasant little tea party and they all enjoyed themselves."

"Was Eric there too?"

"No, no, Tony, Eric did not go but he sees Louise and the girls from time to time and he told me about it."

"Oh, what the hell. When are you planning to come?" asked Tony.

"I will come on Thursday, in the afternoon, as I know you have all that therapy in the morning. I can do some errands for you, check on the townhouse and spend the night there and go back on Friday."

"Actually, that is a good plan, as I will ask the agent to meet with you on Friday morning at the townhouse and she can take a look around and give me a price to sell."

"Right. That will work," agreed Nelson.

"Hey, maybe she could line up a few flats for lease to show you that are suitable for invalids and cripples. I will ring her up and set up something."

"Very well, Tony. What would you like me to bring when I come?"

"What a loaded question that is, my friend. How about one new leg and a bottle of wine?"

"No problem, let's talk tomorrow, and keep your spirits up."

"I surely will. Way up," Tony said with a sarcastic laugh.

Nelson went to the house kitchen as he always did when he didn't know what else to do. "Well, good afternoon Pinky, what are you up to?" asked Bertha. "Not much. Madame does not need me on Thursday and Friday so I will drive into London and visit with Tony."

"Oh, Pinky, we will make some special little cakes and tarts for you to take in for Mr. Tony," Bessie said. "What a grand idea," said Nelson. They all turned around when they heard a

A Fine How Do You Do

whistle blowing. Alfred appeared with a whistle in his mouth and continued blowing it. "Mr. Alfred, what are you doing with that whistle?" shouted Bertha. "I am blowing it, you simpleton."

"Now, Mr. Alfred, please do not address any of us that way."

"Well, then don't ask me funny questions."

"How about a nice cup of tea, Mr. Alfred?" asked Nelson.

"How many cups of tea and biscuits do you have each day, Pinky?" asked Alfred.

"Why do you ask, Mr. Alfred?"

"Because I am paying for them," said Alfred with his nose in the air.

"I see. Well, why don't you just write out a bill for 30 cups of tea and 60 biscuits a month and Madame can deduct it from my salary," said Nelson.

Alfred looked at Bessie and Bertha, who had turned away and were giggling. Nelson held his ground and just stared at Alfred.

"Have any of you seen my pet Angel?" asked Alfred.

"Yes, she is over there in her little basket by the cupboard," said Bertha.

"Oh," said Alfred and he left the kitchen. They could hear Alfred blowing his whistle outside. Angel perked up her ears and started to scratch the door. Bertha let Angel out and the dog ran to Alfred and jumped into his arms.

Eric rode the bicycle to the fresh market and then to the library to wire the weather report to the Altoona newspaper. Louise did not appear so Eric rode back to Alma's house. Alfred was in a pair of shorts squirting the hose all around the gardens and at Angel, who seemed to enjoy the game.

"That looks like lots of fun, Alfred."

"Oh yes, it is fun and Angel loves to play Squirt."

Eric went upstairs and noticed that Alma was not in her room and the door was wide open. Eric thought that something was peculiar in that Louise had not appeared at the library and now Alma was nowhere to be seen. Eric decided that he was probably overreacting and all was in order, so he went into his room and started to look over his clothes. He took out his gold watch and cufflinks, buffed them up a little and wondered why he had not worn them recently. He decided to put them on as they would certainly catch Alfred's eye. His shirt did not have the proper cuffs for the gold links but the gold watch looked very handsome on his wrist. He went downstairs to see Bertha and Bessie. They were busy making up a basket for Nelson to take into London for Tony.

"Bertha, have you seen Madame this morning?"

"Oh yes, she decided to go to the hairdresser, so Nelson has taken her and Alfred will pick her up."

"I do wish I could be helpful with the driving but I do not have an international driver's license."

"Mr. Eric, you are always very helpful and Bertha and I were just chatting and hoping that you will not be leaving for a while as you are always so sensible and seem to add a calmness to the house when things get a bit snappy."

"Oh, thank you both and I do enjoy it here, but I must be thinking about returning to Altoona and my Martha."

"Mr. Eric, this is the very first time you have mentioned Martha. Do tell us about Martha."

"Martha is my wife and I love her very much and I miss her." Eric looked down at his watch and Bertha noticed the watch for the first time.

"Is that a new timepiece, Mr. Eric?"

"No, it belonged to my father and I have gold cufflinks also. I just felt like putting on the watch this morning."

"It is a lovely watch," said Bertha.

"Thank you, Bertha. I feel like time is running away," said Eric. As he helped load up the basket of goodies for Tony, he turned and said, "I'm going out to the front garden and look for Mr. Alfred."

A moment later Alfred came into the kitchen dripping wet with Angel behind him. "Bertha, please give Angel a bath. She was playing Squirt and then she rolled in the garden dirt," said Alfred. "Hah! I've made a poem!"

Bertha and Bessie looked at each other. Angel shivered on the kitchen floor.

"Never mind, ladies, you are busy packing the basket so I will rinse off Angel," said Alfred, pouting. Eric heard this as he returned to the kitchen. He took off his gold watch, put the leash onto Angel, picked up a towel and pulled her outside to hose her down. Then he brought her inside with the towel wrapped around her. Bessie finished packing up the basket for Tony. Alfred went outside.

"My, your hair looks just lovely and it is a bit shorter, isn't it, Madame?" asked Bertha as Alma came in through the kitchen doorway.

"Yes, we thought it might take some years off me and I would look a bit more casual."

"It is most becoming, isn't it, Bessie?" She agreed. "My yes, you look lovely."

"And what happened to Angel?" asked Alma.

"Mr. Alfred was playing with her outside and she needed a bit of a scrub, so she is drying off."

"So that is what he was doing. He was to collect me up at the hairdresser but Nelson came instead and I did not know why." She went upstairs.

Nelson came into the kitchen. Bertha asked about his day. "I went to fetch Madame as I saw that Alfred was in his shorts and sopping wet and then over to Louise's to get the things the girls made for Tony. Madame and Louise had a brief conversation and then we dropped Louise at the library as she was running a bit late. I will take that basket for Tony as soon as you have it ready."

Bessie was cleaning the floor where Alfred and Angel had dripped all over. "My, things seem to happen all at the same time," said Bertha as she sat down with her feet stretched out in front of her. "I will go out and do some gardening and then go to the back garden and trim some of those bushes that were smashed in the storm," Bertha said. "There is much to be done now since Madame let the gardeners go. Mr. Alfred really must find something to do with himself, he is such a nuisance and does not help out at all."

"I heard that, Bertha, and it was very naughty of you to say and I am going to tell Alma on you. I never liked any of you anyway," said Alfred, who had slipped back into the kitchen. No one said a word. Alfred saw that Angel was dry and went over to her, took her leash off, kicked her, leaned down, picked her up and began to cry. Angel licked Alfred and snuggled close to him.

Chapter Forty-Three

"You are so tardy, what happened?" complained Tony. Nelson told him about the traffic and that he had so much to do before he could get away and how Alfred is such a nuisance.

Tony laughed. "More than a nuisance, a total nitwit. I hate to admit it, but taking his money was child's play and he truly never knew what was going on with that financial scheme. Fortunately, I shoveled us all out of that mess with only a scratch, but Alfred took the brunt of the loss. Did you know that after Margaret died they discovered that her father had left her a bundle?"

"No, really?"

"Yes, really, but your Madame managed to get control of it and that is why she keeps Alfred under wraps, so to speak. Madame Boeld is a very interesting person and I sense that things were not always pleasant for her. I know nothing of her past but would bet it is rather raunchy."

"Well, perhaps we will know one day," said Nelson. "Now, I have some thoughtful gifts for you. See this basket?"

"Yes, it is a very handsome basket," sighed Tony.

"Millicent made the basket all by herself and stayed up half the night to finish it so that I could bring it to you today."

"Millicent has been weaving? For God's sake, has she gone mental? People in mental homes weave."

"Tony, she learned to weave when the weather was not good for sailing this summer."

"Oh, that makes sense, how dear of her! She is a pistol, isn't she?"

"Yes, she and Suzanne are very different," said Nelson.

"Millicent has always been more like me and Suzanne, a simple but pleasant child, very like her mother."

"Here are some pastries from Bertha and Bessie."

"How nice this all is, but we must get on with some business," said Tony. "Actually it is getting quite late, so you must whip over to my townhouse and let her in."

"And who is her?"

"Oh, sorry, Miss Judith from the realty firm. She has been through the house and we have agreed on a price. Show her through and she will figure out what furniture to include in the sale. Now, here is the good news. There is a simple flat, four bedrooms, that she thinks might suit us," said Tony.

"For both of us?" asked Nelson.

"Yes, is that a problem, you want more bedrooms?"

"No, I just had not thought about moving."

"Well, think quickly, because that is the plan."

"But we never talked about me moving in with you."

"No, we didn't, and we never discussed cracking up the car and we never discussed losing my leg either."

"You have not lost your leg."

"Well, it is still attached but good as lost. You will move in with me, won't you, Pinky?"

"Not if you call me Pinky."

"Great, then it is settled. I will never call you Pinky again and you will move in with me."

"Tony, you are a beast and always will be, and yes I will always take care of you."

Tony reached out and touched Nelson's cheek, smiled and said, "How did you become so lucky? Hey, let's get two cats. We will call one Limpy and the other Pinky."

Nelson put his new French beret on at the proper angle and opened the door. "Hey, Pinky, the French couple might want to buy you, too." Nelson smiled and was on his way.

Nelson returned from his real estate venture and was most excited as he entered the hospital. He awakened Tony from a nap and spread out all the papers on the bedside table. "I have great news. Your townhouse is almost a done deal, as Miss Judith had her clients with her from Paris and they will buy it as soon as possible. The flat in Belgravia is lovely and is on two floors and has an elevator. Can you imagine an elevator in a private house?"

"Nelson, what about the furniture? I am so helpless."

"The Paris couple will buy whatever does not fit in the new flat. You are making money on the deal as the new flat is much less than what the townhouse will fetch. Miss Judith will be over here tomorrow morning for you to sign all these papers. So you best be awake and look them all over carefully," explained Nelson.

"I knew it would all work out, now all we have to do is get the cats," said Tony as they hugged each other.

"So Pinky will be your cat and Limpy will be my cat," said Nelson.

"No, they will both be ours. Everything is going to be ours from now on," said Tony.

"Let's open up the goodies in the basket. I bought a bottle of wine and two plastic glasses," said Nelson. They uncorked the bottle, poured the wine and toasted each other.

"They give me so many meds that I will probably pass out from this first sip."

Nelson began to unpack the basket. "Here are some lovely pictures made by Suzanne, and look at the delicious biscuits from the two B's."

"The two B's, who be them?" asked Tony jokingly.

"Them be Bessie and Bertha."

"Well, three cheers to the two B's and all the rest of the cheers belong to us."

"Oh for heaven's sake, there is a gold watch in the basket, how very strange," said Nelson.

"A gold watch? Who would pack a gold watch for me?" asked Tony. Nelson turned the watch over and saw initials. "It belongs to someone, but I cannot make out these initials," said Nelson. "Well," said Tony, "now we have a new house and a mystery gold watch. Not a bad day after all, eh Pinky?"

"You promised not to call me Pinky, you cripple."

"All right, all right, it is a deal, no Pinky, no cripple. So, not a bad day, eh mate?"

"A great day, mate," said Nelson as they clicked the plastic glasses.

"Don't shatter the crystal, mate. Now, I want you to take back some presents for my girls. Tomorrow I will ring up that store, Children's Closet. That pretty lady, Sylvia, owns it and she will pick out some nice things. You know where it is?"

"Yes, right around the corner, and they always have such pretty window displays."

"Oh, look at these cards that little Suzanne made! My oh my, each card has a picture of a little girl with tears running down her face. Now here is a card from Millicent that says 'Please Get Well Soon so we can go skating. You can use this little basket for mail. It will be perfect for collecting all the mail won't it? Love, Millicent, your lovely growing up girl.'" Tears came to Tony's eyes. "How will I ever make all this up to them?"

"Don't worry about that now, Tony. It will all work out."

"Oh here is an envelope from Louise. Pictures of the girls this summer. I will have them put in a frame."

"Well, I guess I should be heading off to your flat. I am rather tired with all this excitement," said Nelson.

"I will call you in the morning and you can be here when I sign all the papers."

Nelson went down the hall and took a sharp breath as he entered the lift. Thoughts scampered through his head. He could hardly keep up with them. He felt better when he left the hospital and could draw a big breath. He drove carefully back to Tony's townhouse. He began to think about the gold watch; perhaps it might be Eric's. But how did it get in the basket and why? He would call the house and surely the mystery would be solved.

Nelson dialed. "Madame, Nelson here, how are you?"

"Very well, thank you, and yourself?"

"All is coming along with Tony and sorry to disturb you so late, but I am calling about a gold watch we found in the basket I brought in to Tony that Bertha and Bessie packed up with some biscuits."

"Oh, for the sake of heaven, it belongs to Eric. He has been frantic about losing it," exclaimed Alma. "So you have it with you in London, Nelson?"

"Yes, Madame, I do have it and I will bring it back to Eric tomorrow when I return."

"Just a moment, Nelson, I am a bit confused. How did it end up in London?"

"I cannot explain how it came to be in the basket, but the important thing is that it is safe and I will bring it back tomorrow," said Nelson.

"Hmmm, a most unusual happening. Alfred has notified the police and reported it as a robbery."

"Well then, Alfred should notify the police that it has been found and all stop worrying and know that it is safe and it will be back in Eric's possession tomorrow."

"I will speak to Alfred right now and tell him to notify the police that it has been found," said Alma.

"Thank you, Madame and good evening to you all."

Nelson rang off. Alma called upstairs, "Freddie come down here."

He appeared at the top of the stairs. "What is it Alma, have more valuables vanished?"

"No, Freddie, the watch has been found and all is fine, so I will call the police and tell them that the watch has been found and tell Eric also."

"Oh, pooh, I like excitement and am sorry it has been found."

"You can go to bed now, Freddie, and read that mystery story from the library I checked out for you."

"Yes, Alma, but will you come and say prayers with me?"

"Oh for the sake of heaven, go to bed and pray for yourself."

"I will pray for you too, Alma, and also that Angel comes back."

"What do you mean, has Angel run off?"

"Maybe and maybe not."

"Freddie, you must stop playing these silly games with me, as I never know when to believe you."

"It is true that I do not know where Angel is."

"Well, put on your jacket and take her leash and see if you can find her."

"Yes, Madame, Sister Alma, Queen of Ambleside, I will go on a hunt."

Alma sat on a chair in the front hall, put her head on her arms and wondered if it was worth the money from Margaret's father to put up with Freddie. Dear Freddie, she thought. It is not his fault as he was so badly injured in the war and his brain has not been proper since. It is my duty to take care of Freddie, she convinced herself for the umpteenth time.

Eric heard the commotion, came out into the hall and went downstairs to find Alma slumped in the chair.

"Eric, is that you, why so it is. Nelson found your watch in the basket that Bessie packed up for Nelson to take to Tony."

"I had wondered if that had happened. There was so much going on in there. Oh what good news. So Nelson called you? I assume he will bring it back tomorrow. How very nice of him. He must have realized how worried I was about it."

"Yes, he will bring it home tomorrow. By the by, have you seen Angel?"

"No I have not. Isn't she with Mr. Alfred?"

"No, Alfred is out looking for her."

"Perhaps she came to the kitchen door and is in the kitchen with Bessie and Bertha."

"Oh Eric, that is probably what has happened. I do not know why I didn't think of that. Alfred seems to always have some problem going on and I am too tired and old to be mothering him."

Eric went into the kitchen and found Angel curled up under the kitchen table. He returned to the hall to tell Alma.

"Eric, it is such a wonder that we met and that you are here, isn't it?" said Alma.

"Yes, it is, and you have been most kind and hospitable to me. And thank you for the good news about my watch." Eric went into his room and gave a large sigh of relief. He knew that the watch would be his ticket back to Martha.

Alma remained slumped in the front hall chair next to the telephone with her shoes off and relaxing for a moment when the phone rang. "Yes, this is Alma Boeld and to whom am I speaking at this hour?"

"Alma, my dear Alma, this is your old friend, Bernard from Oberammergau."

"Oh, dear heavens you are alive after all these years? Thank the Lord you are alive. I have prayed for you for years. Oh, Bernie, you are really alive. I cannot believe it. Where are you?"

"I am in London. I am working in a hospital and I happened to be taking care of a Mr. Tony Smythe and we began talking and when he heard I was from Oberammergau, he mentioned your name and I almost collapsed. He gave me your phone number." "Bernie dear, oh my, we will arrange a visit for you here in Ambleside as soon as possible!"

"I have not taken any time off in six years so I hope they will excuse me for a few days. May I stay with you?"

"Of course! Freddie and I will be so happy to see you and we will rejoice in the fact that you are alive."

"Oh, Freddie made it through the war, did he?" asked Bernie.

"Yes, he did and is living with me, as his wife died. Oh enough now, we will catch up when you arrive here. I can hardly think at the moment. Call me tomorrow and we will sort out the details."

Alma sat back in the chair and began to cry and pray. Dear Lord, thank you for watching over us and sending dear old Bernie to me. She decided to make plans immediately for a festive reunion.

Bernie called Alma the next day and they made plans for him to come for a visit the following weekend.

Chapter Forty-Four

"What a lovely dinner and what a gay old time we are having," said Alma. "All my favorite people are here ... you, Freddie dear, our new and beloved friend, Eric, and Nelson my trusty driver and our beloved Bertha and Bessie and my old sweetheart from school, our dear Bernie. Bernie, I had given you up for dead when I never had responses to my letters."

"Oh, Alma, all the pensiones were taken over by the Nazis. I joined the resistance and was captured and held until the war ended. Your brother William was in the same camp as I, but I heard he had pneumonia and died. Were you in the resistance, Alma?" asked Bernie.

"In a way, but I was arrested and in prison with prostitutes and dirty people until the war ended."

"Why did they arrest you, Alma?"

"I was branded a spy and never had a trial but just put in a horrible cell with nine other women. It was a miracle that I survived the filth and diseases around. Many of the girls died without any medical care at all."

Nelson said, "I have never heard any first-hand stories about the war and I am at a loss to know what to say, except that I thank the Lord you all survived."

"I heard about the war back in Altoona," said Eric.

"I was in the war," said Alfred proudly. "And I was a prisoner and had to wear a very itchy uniform and all they did was ask me questions all the time. I got sick and a nice man took me with him and he had a gun and we slept in the forest for a long time and then some other men came with guns and put us in a truck and I don't remember anything else until Alma came to get me in the hospital. I was just a lad and really too young to be a soldier, wasn't I, Alma?"

"You were a fine soldier and I am proud of you," said Alma, saluting Alfred.

"I just want to find Angel now. Do you think that they came and took her to the forest?"

Alma rolled her eyes and Bernie nodded at her. "Let's go look for Angel," said Bernie.

"Oh yes, we need to be together in case they come after us with those long guns," said Freddie.

"No one is coming after you, Freddie. The war is over and the world is at peace and you should be at peace too."

"I will be fine when we find Angel."

"Right, get your coat and her leash and we will take some torches and go look for her once again."

Nelson excused himself and went up to his apartment. Bernie took a torch and went out into the darkness while Alfred was getting his coat, and he saw Angel by the light from the kitchen door. He went over and put the leash on her just as Alfred came out.

"Alfred, is this your Angel? The dog appears just fine and has come home to you."

"Oh, how wonderful!" said Alfred as he began to whistle and run to take the leash from Bernie. He burst in through the kitchen door and said "BOO" to Bertha and Bessie.

"Good lord, dear boy, do not startle us that way."

"I found Angel and all is okay and the world is at peace, so we never have to go to war again, so there!" exclaimed Alfred.

Bessie and Bertha looked at each other and smiled. "Yes, Mr. Alfred, all is well with the world and don't you worry about things like that."

Alfred had found his bouncing ball and he whistled as he took Angel up to his bedroom. "Angel," said Alfred, "if you wander off anymore, I shall punish you." Angel looked up at Alfred, who said, smiling, "just jesting you silly little doggy girl." Alfred took her into the bedroom and they curled up on the bed together. "I wonder what Margaret is doing tonight, Angel?" Angel snuggled close. "Good night, Margaret, I miss you." He put his bouncing ball on the floor next to the bed. He began to whistle a marching song and then began to cry.

Alma had come up to check on him, heard him crying and came into his room. "Freddie, you are okay, now stop crying and be a big boy." Alma went over to the bed and gave him a kiss and a hug.

"I love you Alma and so does Margaret. Angel loves you too, so don't go into the forest or they will shoot you. They shot Ralph and I was all alone."

She pulled a blanket partway over him and returned to the parlor, where she and Bernie sat for a few moments just looking at each other.

"It has been a long time, Alma, and the world has changed and so have we."

"Yes, Bernie it has, and I cannot believe that we actually are sitting here together in Ambleside."

"Let's have a brandy to cheer each other and to celebrate our surprise reunion." Just at that moment, Bessie appeared and asked, "Would you like some brandy served, Madame?" Alma and Bernie laughed and then said in unison "Bring on the brandy, Bessie!"

Alma and Bernie reminisced about their youth in Bavaria. Their skiing days, participating in the Passion Play in Oberammergau, and then parting ways when Bernie went off to university. A silence came over them as neither wished to bring up the war years.

"A bit more brandy, Alma dear?"

"Yes, Bernie just a drop, and let's turn on the Victrola and dance."

A Strauss waltz was on the record player and they began to dance right through the doorway onto the terrace and whirled around until they both became dizzy.

"My, Alma, you have not missed a beat and I have not waltzed in ages."

"It is just grand and let's not stop. I will put the needle back on the beginning of the record."

They danced around and did not seem to tire at all. They were startled when Bessie appeared and asked if they would care for coffee. They said no thank you and just kept on dancing.

Alfred appeared downstairs some time later as he kept hearing the scratching of the needle on the end of the record. "Alma, what are you and Bernie doing on the lounge chair?" There was no answer from either of them. "Alma, answer me, it is the middle of the night and the needle keeps scratching the old record and it woke me up. Alma, Alma, please wake up!"

Bernie awoke. "Alfred, we were dancing and just stopped for a bit of a rest."

"My watch says four-thirty in the morning and what is the matter with my sister?"

"Your sister is just fine and dandy and so am I, so go back to bed."

"You always bossed me around when we were growing up in Oberammergau and I did not like you then and I still do not like you," complained Alfred.

"Alfred, we are all good old friends who all love and care for each other, so just go back to bed."

Alma suddenly awoke and said, "My, what time is it?" She looked around and spotted the empty brandy glasses and heard the scratching of the needle on the record. "Freddie, do be a dear and tend to that Victrola."

Alfred did as he was told and went back to his room. Alma and Bernie had a good laugh and smoked a cigarette, blowing smoke at each other and laughing some more.

"Bernie, you take the blue room upstairs and we will meet for breakfast. What is the hour?"

"It is four o'clock."

"Heavens, way past tea time!" exclaimed Alma. They both laughed and stumbled up the stairs and blew a kiss to each other as they entered their separate bedrooms.

Chapter Forty-Five

Bessie and Bertha prepared a lovely breakfast, but Eric and Alfred were the only ones at the table. "Well, we have eggs and biscuits for all, so have a nice breakfast," Bessie declared. Just at that moment Alma appeared in a royal blue dressing gown, and Bernie handsomely dressed in a country tweed jacket with an open shirt and smart trousers.

"Good morning to you all," said Alma and Bernie in unison. Everyone smiled at one another and gobbled up the eggs and biscuits.

"What a gay old time we had last evening. Now what is on the docket for today?" asked Alma. Eric broke the silence and said "I am joining Louise and the girls at the art exhibit in the square at noon. You probably know most of the artists, Alma."

"Yes, I most likely do. Let's all go together, as I would like to see Millicent and little Suzanne and their dear mother again."

She asked Bessie to call for Nelson, and Alma asked him to join them. "Thank you, but no. I must do some private work in my apartment, but will be pleased to drive you into town and fetch you."

"Yes, that would be fine, Nelson. Let's all meet in the front hall in one hour. That should give us time to pull ourselves together." Alma called for Bessie and Bertha. "Ladies, would you care to join us at the art exhibit in the town square?" Bessie and Bertha looked at each other and nodded. "Yes, Madame, that would be a lovely treat for us." "Well then," Alma said, "we are all set. The sky looks a bit grey, so bring a wrap and perhaps a brolly. Come along, Bernie dear," said Alma, taking his hand.

Eric spotted Louise and the two girls at the art exhibit and went over to them. Millicent was staring at a very contemporary watercolor and turned around when she heard Eric's voice. "This painting looks like three clowns turning somersaults and the plaque says it is called 'Dancing Angels.' What does that mean?" asked Millicent as she looked at Louise and Eric.

"I do not know," replied Louise.

"Well, someone here must know what it means," said Millicent as she spotted Alma and scampered off.

"Well, fancy meeting you here, Madame Boeld. I want you to look at a painting over there as I do not understand the title of it."

They walked over and studied the watercolor. "I would call it 'The Midnight Waltz'," said Alma with a twinkle in her eye. Eric said that he liked it but did not know what to call it. Louise said that it looked like a very happy painting but she could not think of a title. Suzanne said it was all mixed up with colors.

"Well, this is a most interesting painting," Alma said. "I will put on my glasses and see if I can read the artist's name. Ah. His name is Alfred Boeld." Alma took Eric's arm as she felt faint and then burst into tears. "Oh, for the sake of God, how can this be that Alfred has been painting and none of us knew?"

"This is a lovely painting," said Bernie.

After a decent interval, Alma and her group returned home. "Freddie, are you here?"

"No," replied Alfred from upstairs.

"Oh, Freddie dear, we have just been to the art show and we saw your painting and we all think it is just too grand for words. Please come down and tell us all about your painting."

"I cannot do that. My paintings all belong to Margaret and she tells me what to do."

"Freddie, we saw your watercolor of the dancing angels at the show. Why didn't you tell us that your wonderful painting would be on display?"

"Because Margaret told me you would steal it, just like you did the money that her father left her. Where is that money anyway, Alma?" asked Alfred as he came downstairs.

"Oh, Freddie, you know very well the money is safe. No one even knew about it until after Margaret died and you should not worry about it at all," said Alma with great confidence. "We should have a chat when you are up to it, Freddie dear."

"Margaret tells me what to do, not you," said Alfred as he picked up Angel and went back up the stairs. "Where is that Bernard fellow? He cannot be trusted," shouted Alfred from upstairs.

"Bernie is a true gentleman and he is right here. I would trust him with my life. Now stop this behavior, Freddie," shouted Alma as she headed for the Dubonnet in the dining room. She poured herself a small amount and downed it in one swallow. She wondered why her feet were swollen, and then remembered dancing the night away with Bernie.

Chapter Forty-Six

Alma thought it was a particularly lovely Sunday morning in Ambleside, with a clear blue sky and only a few crows flitting about. The house was very quiet and Alfred's bedroom door was closed. She collected yesterday's unread mail and the phone rang as she was passing by the telephone table.

"Oh good morning to you, Elizabeth, and I am well, thank you. How are you and how do you expect to spend this lovely day?"

"Alma, I thought you knew that Alfred asked me to join him on a boat trip on Lake Windermere today. I naturally thought you knew about it."

"How very thoughtful of Freddie. I have not seen him yet this morning. I assume he is still in his room. Do pop over and we will work it all out and have a lovely day," said Alma. "I have not been on the lake in quite a while and I do have such wonderful memories of my first love affair in the castle gardens after a lovely boat ride and a picnic luncheon with too much lovely wine!"

"I am not surprised at all, Alma. They are beautiful and most romantic gardens, though probably overgrown and fading by this time of summer. I will not leave the boat as my left ankle is not yet healed from my fall at the Wellingtons' garden party, but fortunately it does not bother me to drive the car. Alfred asked me to come over to your house about ten o'clock and it is that now," said Elizabeth hurriedly and hung up the phone.

Alma heard the doorbell and went to answer it but Bertha arrived first. Millicent was at the door with a beautiful basket of flowers. She was wearing a pale yellow cotton sundress, white sandals and a very colorful straw hat with real flowers. "A very good morning to you, Miss Bertha; I have come to call on Madame Boeld."

Alma overheard the conversation and came to the front hall. "I hope I have not come too early, Madame Boeld, but I wish to have a conference with you," announced Millicent.

"A conference, my dear, what sort of conference?"

"Should I take off my hat?" asked Millicent.

Alma shrugged and said, "It is a charming hat, my dear, do as you like."

"My school starts very soon and I am quite bored with all the subjects and I really want to study how to be just like you," said Millicent as she presented Alma with the basket of flowers.

"What a charming basket and lovely flowers," exclaimed Alma.

"I made the basket for my Daddy but decided to give it to you and I made him another one," announced Millicent with pride.

"How very interesting," said Alma. "What is prompting all this, Millicent dear?"

Millicent looked at her feet for a moment, pushed back the hair that was falling in her face, and said, "I have decided to leave home as my Mother is dreary and my little sister, Suzanne, is even drearier. I want to be just like you and I think that if I could move in with you and watch all you do, I could be a beautiful lady when I grow up," explained Millicent with tears running down her face.

"Millicent, come in, wipe away the tears and let's sit down and talk this over," said Alma, completely taken aback. Alma led her to chairs on the terrace. "Well, my dear Millicent, this is a fine how do you do, and how do you plan to carry this all off?"

"I will pack up my clothes and move in here and work in the kitchen with Bertha and Bessie and carry your breakfast tray to you and then go to the library and see my Mum and read books there and then come back here for tea with you and listen to you and all your friends and learn to be a proper lady. I plan to go to London very often and visit my Daddy and help him learn how to walk again and I will go to all the museums and libraries in London and help Daddy in his new flat and then come back and see my Mum and Suzanne for tea or supper and then come here. I will also chat with Uncle Eric and learn all about the United States. I will help Mr. Alfred to be a happier person and teach him how to weave baskets if he will teach me how to play croquet."

"My, oh my, dear child, you most certainly have planned a very busy schedule and put yourself in a fine how do you do, haven't you?"

Millicent smiled, rose from her chair and curtsied for Alma, saying "I do not really know what a fine how do you do is, but whatever it is I will do it."

Alma could think of nothing to say at the moment except "Yes, a most interesting how do you do, my dear child." Her head full of thoughts, Alma got up and went inside. Millicent followed.

The doorbell rang and Bertha opened the door to Elizabeth, who was carrying a large picnic basket. "Good day, Miss Elizabeth, please come in, and may I take the basket from you?"

"No, no. It is a picnic for Mr. Alfred and me on the Lake Windermere boat ride."

Millicent said, "Let's all go on the boat ride together and have a lovely day and I am sure that the gardens will still be most beautiful, Miss Elizabeth."

Nelson drove them to the lakeside, with Millicent and Eric following on bicycles. When they arrived at the landing, Alma gave Millicent the money for their tickets and she ran ahead to get outside seats in the stern of the boat. Millicent thought it would be less windy in the stern.

"You were very smart to get these good seats in the stern, Millicent dear," said Alma.

Nelson made sure that all would find room on the boat. They all waved as he drove away.

"This is such a treat for me, Alma dear, and a perfect way to spend a Sunday afternoon," said Bernie.

Bertha and Bessie went inside the cabin to organize the picnic. Alfred had brought his trumpet and began blowing it on the deck. The captain came over to him and said he must stop, as musical instruments were not allowed on the craft. Alma apologized to the captain.

Eric took a seat as far from the edge of the craft as he could find and did not want anyone to know that he never learned to swim. "Such a gentleman you are, dear Eric, to leave the best seats for us," remarked Elizabeth. Alma looked at Eric's pale face and smiled, as she knew why Eric took the safest seat. Millicent sat next to the railing. Alma took off her hat and gave it to Eric, who amused all by putting it on his head.

"Oh, what a grand day this is going to be, isn't it, Madame Boeld? Is this a fine how do you do sort of day?" asked Millicent.

"Today is just a perfect day," answered Alma, breathing in the clear cool air.

Millicent looked puzzled but threw her arms around Alma's neck, saying, "I am quite grown up for a twelve-year-old, you know." She sat down and smoothed her dress down over her knees as her mother had taught her to do. She smiled at Alma and said, "I would like to call you Madame Almama. May I call you Madame Almama?"

"I have been called many names in my long life so I suppose another silly name would not bother me," said Alma with a smile.

Bessie and Bertha brought out an arrangement of sandwiches. "I am not hungry," said Eric, who had turned very pale.

"Eric, the boat is not even moving yet, what is bothering you?" asked Elizabeth.

"Uncle Eric can't swim. Mum told me that."

"Now that would be a fine how do you do should you fall overboard," laughed Alma.

Eric turned a pale shade of green and said he had to leave the boat and would go to the library to do some work.

"Eric is a sissy," sang Millicent. Eric turned around, smiled at Millicent and sat down in the boat again.

The boat started up and Millicent went over and took Eric's hand. The wind was cool and the water very calm. Bernie leaned back and gazed at Alma with a smile as the wind ruffled her hair, wondering what kind of life they would have had without the war.

Elizabeth was busy cutting up the sandwiches in little even pieces. Alma rested her head on the back of the seat, thinking that the day had certainly turned very fine. As Captain John was starting up the boat, a group of noisy crows swooped down over the stern. "I should have brought my gun," Alfred declared. Elizabeth tried to shoo the crows away with a tea towel but they managed to snatch most of the sandwich pieces. Everyone was in such a good mood that they started laughing, all except Elizabeth, who kept waving the tea towel at them.

Chapter Forty-Seven

"For God's sake, Pinky, how could you have fucked this up so badly?"

"Tony, I confirmed everything with the movers yesterday and they said they would be here at 2:30 this afternoon and if you call me Pinky one more time you can spend the rest of your life on this sidewalk, sitting in this wheelchair until some bum comes by and robs you blind."

"I agree, Pinky, that I have entirely too much cash on me, but just call them and see where the hell they are. The very presentable people of Belgravia are not used to unshaven invalids hanging out in wheelchairs on their sacred sidewalks," said Tony.

"Oh, here comes the truck now, Tony. I cannot wait for you to see the new flat and I have made floor plans for the furniture. The Paris couple have bought everything that I did not think you needed in the new flat."

"Did you say needed, Pinky?"

"Well, three bicycles and should I go on?"

"You are most correct, my life will be very different. Do you know a cheap dope peddler in the neighborhood yet?" asked Tony with a raucous laugh.

"I am still searching that one out," Nelson answered sarcastically.

"This whole scenario is a pain in the ass. I hope to hell that I do not see anyone I know on their way home."

"Not to worry, Tony, they will not recognize you with the blanket wrapped around you and your feet hanging out."

"I could be starting a new trend for the West End, you know," Tony said.

"A very good afternoon to you, sir," said a casually dressed young man walking by with his very small hairless dog.

"And a good one to you also," said Tony.

The truck stopped and three burly men jumped out and began taking out Tony's belongings.

"Tony, I am going to take you upstairs in the lift and you can supervise and check off items as they bring them in and I will stay out here with the van."

"Sounds like a good plan to get me off the street. By the by, Pinky, your slip is showing," said Tony, followed by his famous raunchy laugh. Nelson ignored the remark.

When the movers departed, Nelson observed, "All the furniture is in place and it all looks very elegant. However, I think that the dining room table should go the other way around."

"Why not," said Tony. "We go the other way."

"And that blue chair should be moved so that the wheelchair can be close to the balcony with this great view."

"You know, dear fellow, your life was not entirely wasted before you met me as you have a fine eye for decorating. I like the way all is fitting in and I really do think this is all just perfect."

Tony pushed himself all around without much trouble and gave thumbs up to the arrangement of furniture. "You have made this room for the girls so very pretty. They will love it. I presume this room off the kitchen is for Claudia. Where is she anyway? I thought she would be here already and brew up some tea for us."

"She has just quit one job and is packing up her things to bring here and move in. She will be here shortly and I must scurry back to Ambleside," announced Nelson.

"And leave me with the young thing?" said Tony with wink.

"Yes, you are on your own now, dear boy," said Nelson.

"Hey, back up please, what did you say?"

"I said that you are on your own with Claudia's help. Madame is planning another party this weekend and her old friend Bernie is arriving again," said Nelson.

"Yes, I know all about your Madame's Mr. Bernard," said Tony. "He hands out pills and water at the hospital. He is a decent fellow," said Tony with another wink.

Chapter Forty-Eight

"My dear Millicent, you have been here each morning and for afternoon tea every day for over a week and we have talked a great deal about your young life and all the sadness you are now experiencing. I am grateful to say that my childhood in Bavaria was simply lovely and I was a free and happy child. However, as life goes on, things change and you must learn to adjust and to handle certain circumstances that seem very unhappy at the time. You cannot escape by running to another place and hoping things will be better. You are twelve years old and need your mother and sister and also your father, so you have two very welcoming homes as is! You will find that what seem like huge problems today will be worked out with your family and your family needs you. It is a wonderful thing to be needed and you must 'step up to the plate,' as the Americans say. Does this all make any sense to you, my dear child?"

"Yes," said Millicent. "It means that I cannot come and live with you."

"That is correct. But it does not mean that I do not care for you. The proper way of life for you is with your dear Mum and sister and to be with them until you are of age to go to university," explained Alma.

Millicent sat in the chair and crossed her legs back and forth several times. Alma began to cross her legs several times also. They began to giggle and crossed their legs as fast as they could to keep up with each other. Alma dropped her shoe and the game was over.

"May I still call you Almama?" asked Millicent.

"I see no reason why not, as silly as it is," said Alma.

"It is not silly to me," said Millicent. She leaned down and put the shoe back on Alma's foot.

"Now, as you have helped me with my slipper, you will help your Mum with all her shoes and troubles and comfort your dear sister and help your Daddy with his shoes that hopefully will take him walking again."

"I think I can do it, if you will be my Almama."

"Now, get on your bicycle and go on home for your lunch and give your Mum and sister a big hug."

"I want to stop at the lake first and feed the ducklings," said Millicent as she slowly headed for the door. As she opened it she came face to face with Nelson. "Hello, Nelson, I have not seen you for a long time and have not heard from my Daddy. How is my Daddy?"

"He moved into his new flat and has a nice bedroom for you and Suzanne when you visit."

"Will you take me to London to see him?"

"Of course I will," said Nelson, excusing himself and announcing to Alma that her hairdressing appointment was 10 minutes ago and the engine was running. "Thank you, Nelson," said Alma, looking at him as he held the door open. As she stepped into the car her shoe fell off. "Oh for the sake of heaven, this is the second time this morning that my shoe has left my foot." "So sorry, Madame," said Nelson with a smile.

Nelson waited in the car during the hair-styling and took a snooze. He had not been sleeping well recently. He was awakened by Madame knocking at the window. "Nelson, let us go to that little shoe store on the main street. Do you have enough shoes, Pinky?"

"Yes, Madame, thank you."

"Well, in my mind, no one ever has enough shoes. Occasions occur that one does not expect and one must have the proper shoes. You park the car and come with me and we will both have new shoes."

"Yes, Madame, that will be fine."

Nelson could not carry all the packages after the shopping, so Alma held two bags as well. "We certainly made their day worthwhile, did we not?"

"Yes, Madame, it appears you are most satisfied with your purchases."

"I am not the only one to be satisfied, as we have two pair of patent leather party shoes for the girls, a lovely afternoon flat softy shoe for their mother and new leather ones for Freddie and what else do we have, Pinky?"

"We have two pair of sturdy slippers for Bessie and Bertha and you so kindly encouraged me to accept the yachting shoes."

"Why did you pick the yachting shoes, Pinky?"

"Because you suggested that I might need them someday and that I should always be prepared."

"Ah yes, and that is why I bought the silver evening slippers. Now, Pinky dear, are you planning a new life?"

"I do not know yet, Madame."

"How is your friend Mr. Tony Smythe?" asked Alma.

"He is coming along very well, thank you. He is out of hospital and in a very nice flat."

"I shall need you this weekend as Mr. Bernard is arriving by coach from London on Friday and will be here for the dance party at the Yacht Club on Saturday evening. Miss Elizabeth will be having a luncheon on Sunday and Mr. Alfred and I will host a simple Sunday supper party. You may take Mr. Bernard back to London on Monday morning and please have the car back by Tuesday for luncheon."

"Yes, of course, Madame, and I do appreciate your kindness." Alma smiled to herself and felt rather satisfied with the day so far.

Nelson went up to his apartment and called Tony. "Tony, I was with Madame today and I will ask Louise if the girls could come into London on Monday and back on Tuesday."

"It would be swell to see them but what about my leg? They will be sure to notice," said Tony, looking down at his useless leg.

Millicent found that Louise had come home for lunch and so they chatted. "Do you get bored with your job, Mum?"

"No, I do not, and you know that I have always loved to read and books are my friends. Some old friends and some new ones, so no, I am not bored."

"Well, do you hope that Daddy will come home?"

"I have accepted the fact that he will not be coming home here as he has a new home of his own in London," said Louise, turning her head away from Millicent.

"Well, then, Mum, what is bothering you and why are you always so dreary?"

"So you think that I am dreary, do you, young lady?"

"Yes, and so is Suzanne."

Louise smiled and said, "Millicent, you are a wonderful girl and so is Suzanne, but you have different personalities and you will gain from being with each other and learning to respect each other."

"Oh, I do not want to hear anymore about what I should do," said Millicent and she went outside. She climbed onto her bike but did not know where to go. Her morning visit with Alma had been disappointing and her mother was as tiresome as ever. She thought that the only thing left for her to do would be to join a circus and learn to ride the elephants and train the tigers. She decided to call her father and ask him how to join a circus. She came back in the house and asked Louise if she had Daddy's new phone number.

"Yes, I do, as he called and told me that Nelson would be taking you both to visit him in his new flat on Monday and bring you back home on Tuesday."

"Why didn't you tell me this news before?"

"You did not give me a chance to tell you, as you were too busy about yourself."

"You hate me, don't you, Mum?"

"No, my darling, you are just growing up a bit early for your age and hard to follow sometimes," said Louise.

"Now I do not have the new clothes that Nelson brought back from Daddy," announced Millicent, looking out the window.

"Why not, where are they? What did you do with them?"

"I cut them into pieces and threw them into the trash."

"That was very stupid of you. You will have to figure out what to tell him when Suzanne arrives in her lovely new clothes and you will wear whatever you want."

Millicent thought for only a minute until she came up with an idea. She would go back to Alma's on her bike and ask Alma for a fancy hat to borrow. "Now Millicent," said Louise, "before you entertain any other wild ideas, please clean up the table and kitchen while I return to work."

As soon as she could, Millicent darted out of the house onto her bicycle and over to Alma's. She sang a little song as she pedaled and thought that this had turned into a nice adventure. Upon arriving she found Eric and Nelson in the garage. Nelson was polishing up the Bentley and Eric was on his bicycle with a bunch of carrots and some radishes. They seemed to be having a serious conversation.

"Hello, Uncle Eric and Nelson, is Madame Boeld at home?"

"Yes, Millicent, she has just returned from her hair-dressing appointment."

Millicent smiled and gave each a very deep curtsy. "Almama, are you home?" she yelled as she barged into the front hall.

Bessie came running out and said, "Miss Millicent, you must not be bursting in like that. It is not polite. You must be announced."

"I am so sorry," she said and fell into Bessie's apron and began to cry. "And what is all this about, Miss Millicent? Why are you crying like a baby?" asked Alma as she came in from the garden. "Bessie, take these flowers and I will see what is bothering this little blossom. Come here my dear and tell me what has happened." Alma walked briskly over to Millicent and pulled her head upright and said, "What on earth are you up to?"

"I need to borrow one of your hats like you had on in the train when we first met."

"Just be quick and tell me what you are up to now, you silly child."

"I cannot tell you quickly, could we sit down?"

"Meet me on the terrace. I have something for you. And then we must talk quickly, as I have many things to do," said Alma, who waved Millicent toward the terrace, found the right shopping bag, and went out and joined her.

Millicent declared, "I want to borrow the blue hat you wore on the train."

"Have you been invited to a costume party, dear one?"

"Yes, that is it and I need a fancy hat."

"Well, if you have been invited to a fancy party you need more than a hat. Will you wear these?" and from the bag she took out Millicent's new shoes.

"Oh, Almama! Are those for me? New party shoes?"

"Yes they are, and I also have new shoes for your sister and your mother."

Millicent leaped up and clutched her prize, but then her expression changed. "I will have the best hat and shoes," she said, "but I have outgrown all my clothes and so I will look very strange."

"No, you can go as a gypsy. As you said it is just a costume party. Now, I will fetch the hat and some costume jewelry, and you will need to run along as I am preparing for a party weekend."

Before leaving, Millicent put on the costume jewelry so she would not lose it, placed the blue hat firmly on her head, and fitted the bag with the shoes into her bicycle basket. Then the little gypsy carefully rode home.

Louise had left Tony's phone number on the little telephone table and Millicent dialed him in London. Tony picked up after only one ring.

"Daddy, it is me, Millicent. How are you?"

"Just fine and dandy and I will be seeing you on Monday."

"Daddy, can I bring all my stuff to your new flat?"

"Why would you do that, my little plum?"

"Because I will take care of you and I need my stuff with me."

"You only need a few things for staying the night."

"I am coming to live with you."

"Who told you that one?"

"I just want to."

"Hell no, little plum. You stay with Mum and Suzanne. That is where you belong."

Millicent wanted to ask him about the circus but he hung up too quickly.

Alma was having her afternoon tea and heard the front door open. "Who might that be?"

"It is me, Eric."

"Well, how very timely, do come out and have a cup of tea."

"I will and thank you."

"I have not seen you in a while, Eric dear, what in the world have you been doing besides supplying us with delicious fruits and vegetables each day?" Eric removed his cap and then put it back on. "Please relax. You can leave your cap on or off, whatever suits you."

"I seem to be very comfortable in my cap. It was the first thing I purchased upon arriving in the airport."

"Yes, I notice that you wear it almost all the time. It is most amusing that we are chatting about caps, as I just loaned Millicent a very large and busy hat for her to wear to a costume party."

"Louise did not mention anything to me about a costume party. The girls are going into London to see their father and Louise was most upset that Millicent has lost the new clothes her father sent her. Nelson is driving them in on Monday with your friend Mr. Bernard and then will bring them back home on Tuesday."

Alma sat still for a moment and then began to laugh. "Well, I must be aging. I used to be able to see through everyone, but this Millicent is a devious little creature."

Chapter Forty-Nine

Alfred was in bed with a summer cold and most unhappy that no one was responding to the ringing of his bedside bell. "Well, Angel, I will gather up your leash and we will go for a walk. I am most bored with this bedroom and no one is paying any attention to my bell." Alfred put on his cap and the leash on Angel and then decided to take his car into town as he did not feel like getting dressed for a walk.

His car spit and snarled a bit but Alfred pushed it into gear and they roared out of the drive. He had put the top down, as Angel loved the wind in her face. Alfred decided to drive over to Elizabeth's house.

"Alfred, what in the world are you up to? I can see from here that you have pajamas and no robe on. Is Alma in trouble?" asked Elizabeth.

"Yes, Alma is in trouble."

"What sort of trouble, Alfred dear, please speak up."

"She is always in trouble and she took all my money and I have no home and no one answers the bell."

"Oh, Alfred, do not carry on like this. You are fine and you should go home and have some hot tea and a nice warm bath." Angel jumped out of the car and ran to the front lawn and did her business. "Alfred, please come and take care of your dog."

Patty Dickson

Alfred started up the car, turned abruptly and motored rapidly down the drive. Angel ran up to the porch and turned on her belly and waited for Elizabeth to open the door.

"Do come in and have some nice chicken salad, Angel dear." Angel wagged her tail and followed Elizabeth into the kitchen. Elizabeth put some of the chicken salad on a plate and filled a bowl with water. "Well, this is a fine how do you do," said Elizabeth. Angel perked up her ears and jumped directly into the lap of Elizabeth.

Nelson heard the ring of his new telephone, which Tony had given him. He knew it was Tony, as he had no other friends who would be calling him. "Everything is going so well, Nelson, and we certainly made the proper move. I have met the two gentlemen who lease the flat above me and they are charming fellows. Both named John, isn't that amusing? Jack the elder is owner of a lovely antique shop down the street and Johnnie is working at BBC and travels from time to time. They always stop in to see if I need anything. Claudia is efficient but not amusing. Anyway, I have a bright idea of what to do with the girls when you bring them on Monday. I was unpacking some of my books and old papers and came across the memorabilia from my days at Oxford. I would love to take the girls to Oxford for the day and we can pack a picnic. Do you think you can leave Ambleside very early so as to get here for this outing? It would be great to take them atop the Church of St. Mary for the wonderful view and then of course to my Trinity College and to The Prince of Wales for a pint and some fish and chips for an early supper. I have never taken them to Oxford and I think that it would be a grand day. Of course, I will fill the tank for your Madame Boeld and we can hope for a clear day."

"Yes, Tony, that sounds just grand and I will tell Louise that the girls do not need any fancy clothes."

"They have not as yet witnessed my new vehicle of travel and they will be a bit put off by it, so an outing is in order. So, very good, Pinky my pal, and I look forward to seeing you all on Monday," said Tony, hanging up the phone.

So now it is Pinky my pal, thought Nelson.

Chapter Fifty

"Freddie, you must stop this ridiculous behavior and take on your role of a gentleman if you wish to stay in my house."

"I do not wish to stay in your house, I wish to stay in my house," said Alfred.

"Freddie, gather your wits about you. You forced Elizabeth to take care of your dog and you have been acting most troublesome for the last few days. What is the matter with you?"

"Alma, you have been bossing me around since we lived in Bavaria and I am tired of it."

"You must forget all this nonsense and prepare for the weekend. Bernie is coming for all the festivities and is looking forward to seeing you. The parties are all arranged and, as an extra man, you may escort Elizabeth to the dance at the Yacht Club, so be certain your attire is ready."

"Oh, this will be fun. I only wish Margaret could be here to enjoy the dancing but I will be most polite to Elizabeth," said Alfred. "Margaret never could master the dance steps. She was always off balance and kept stepping on her skirts as she never bothered to have the proper shoes or the skirts were just too long," said Alfred with a smile.

"Run along and take care of Angel," said Alma, pointing her finger at Alfred. He stalked out, waving his arms in the air.

A Fine How Do You Do

The telephone rang. Alma answered. "Madame Boeld speaking."

"Madame Boeld, my name is Miss Stern, at your bank in London. Your brother telephoned me earlier today and he wants to withdraw all the money in your joint account, but does not have your approval in writing to do so. I am speaking of the account that was acquired from Margaret Boeld, the late wife of Alfred."

"I am well aware of the account and of course I have not given approval to such a withdrawal. As a matter of fact I did not even know he had been in touch with you," said Alma.

"Madame, I apologize for suggesting such, but your brother seems a bit unstable."

"Yes, he is a huge responsibility to me and needs constant supervision. He is totally irresponsible and I have to care for him twenty-four hours a day. He has moved into my home as you probably know and as a matter of fact, I should like to discuss this situation with you and Barrister Browne, as I will be needing more funds to properly care for my dear brother. You have no idea how I worry what he is up to all the time. What is your name by the way?"

"I am Dorothy Stern. And I will tell your brother that the money is not available."

"Of course you must do that immediately, and it saddens me so greatly that it all has come to this. I may have to hire a companion to tend to him. And please be certain to notify me if my brother ever makes such a request again."

After they rang off, Alma thought to herself that Freddie always finds a way to scramble matters just when they are finally falling so nicely into place. But perhaps not this time. Alma was most adept at rearrangements.

Eric spotted Nelson in the driveway and gave him a whistle. He had almost forgotten how to whistle. They met in front of the first garage as Nelson had started to polish up the Bentley. "Nelson, please tell me what I should do."

"What is the situation, Eric?"

"Madame is insisting that I go to the Yacht Club dance as she says I would be an attractive extra man. What does an extra man mean?"

"It means that you will be available to dance with the ladies."

"I am not a good dancer and have danced with no one but my Martha."

"Oh, get a grip and just dress properly and talk about the weather. Nothing like new experiences, eh Mr. Eric," said Nelson with a smile as he kept polishing the car. Nelson was delighted not to be included in the festivities and satisfied listening to all the gossip. He would need to rest up for his trip on Monday. "That sure is a handsome car," Eric said.

The sound of a bouncing ball caught the attention of both Nelson and Eric. "I wonder how Mr. Alfred is feeling, as he bounces his ball when he has worries, which is most of the time," said Nelson.

"I like it here and I have no worries, but I only feel comfortable with Louise," said Eric.

"And I am most comfortable by myself," said Nelson.

"We are like a big family here but we really do not know each other at all. I will be going now as I must get to the library before it closes," said Eric.

"What is it that keeps you so busy at the library, Mr. Eric?"

"I write the weather reports," said Eric abruptly. It occurred to Nelson that he and Eric had something in common. They both had secret lives.

Chapter Fifty-One

On Monday morning Louise was up very early and breathing a sigh of relief that she would not have to explain the loss of Millicent's new clothes to Tony. She had packed up two small suitcases and also some pictures of the girls taken at sailing camp. She pondered about enclosing a note and decided not to do so.

She heard Eric's bicycle arrive. He entered without knocking. "Louise, Nelson will be here soon to pick up the girls," said Eric. "Yes, they are all dressed and ready to go. They have already been to the fresh market to buy some fruit for their father," said Louise. "Well, here they are!"

"Hi Mum, we are back and the money you gave us was just enough to buy Daddy a freshly baked peach pie and I told the girl to put it in a special box as we were going to see the Queen and I think she believed me," said Millicent."

"Do we look pretty even though we have on our sailing clothes?" asked Suzanne.

"Yes, dear girls, you are both just darling and beautiful but do remember my saying 'Pretty is as pretty does.'"

"We will remember, Mum." Both girls came over and gave Louise and Eric hugs. Nelson pulled the car into the drive and the girls popped into the back seat. Mr. Bernard was in the front. Once off, he slept most of the way to London. There was very little traffic and Nelson delivered Mr. Bernard to his flat, and soon parked the car near Tony's flat.

Tony was just outside the front entrance and Suzanne spotted him first. "He is in a wheelchair, Millie," she said.

"Hi Daddy, we are so glad to be here," said Millicent and both girls ran over to him and gave him big hugs. Millicent stopped to watch the well-dressed men and women walking by.

"I love you both and am so very happy to see my two best gals and my, how grown up you both look."

"I had my hair cut in layers just for my visit with you," said Suzanne.

"Now, tell me Suzanne, is that like a chocolate layered cake or what?" asked Tony.

"It is just cut in layers," said Suzanne.

"I am going to let my hair grow down to the floor," said Millicent.

"Well, whatever do you think I should do about my hair?" asked Tony.

Suzanne and Millicent said in unison, "But Daddy, you have no hair."

"Ah yes, you are both observant and honest. They had to shave my head but my hair will grow back soon. Now, you both come into the elevator with me and Suzanne, you may have the first turn to steer my new bicycle."

"Daddy, this is a push chair not a bike," said Suzanne.

"Oh, for heaven's sake, how could the shop make such a stupid mistake?" said Tony with a laugh.

"Daddy, we are not stupid and we know that your leg does not work yet and this is a push chair," said Suzanne. "We will take turns pushing you all around," added Millicent.

"Oh you girls are a pretty pair and I love you both. I would gamble that no one in the whole world has two such beautiful pushers."

Once at the floor, the girls ran into the new flat, leaving Tony in the foyer. "Oh, Daddy, the beds are like cushions and the spreads are just glorious," exclaimed Millicent. "Oh so glorious," said Suzanne as she began to cry. "Just stop that, you baby," said Millicent.

Monday was a particularly clear day and fine weather for the drive to Oxford. "Oh, Daddy, this Oxford is a beautiful place. It does not look like a school at all," exclaimed Millicent.

"It looks like an old city," said Suzanne.

Nelson parked and they all took turns pushing Tony about. "Did you really go to university here, Daddy?" asked Millicent. "Yes, I did and they were the best years of my life," answered Tony.

"Daddy, I am taking a vow right this very second that I will come here and become a great lady writer," said Millicent.

"And I will come here too and be with Millicent," said Suzanne. Tony looked over at Millicent and she just rolled her eyes.

Tony knew for certain then and there that Millicent took after him and dear Suzanne had her mother's sensitivity, lack of drive and dependence. He would have to think about all this. He realized that he never had time for family, what with his wheeling and dealing and great desire to make money. He decided he needed to supervise the girls. He knew that Louise was a dear girl but he never loved her and never would have married her, had she not been so needy and loving and kind to him. He felt too guilty to leave her then, especially after he had forced her to make love to him in the back of his old car. It was not a good marriage and it was not her fault. Yes, he had a mission and he would follow through and be a good father to his girls.

The sun was going down and everyone was worn out from all the sightseeing around Oxford. They settled into a booth at The Prince of Wales Pub. "Daddy, I have never been in a pub before. I like it and all these people seem to know each other. It is like a big party but why is it so dark?" asked Millicent.

"Well, that is the way pubs are. Now, I will order fish and chips and a lager and lime for Nelson and myself, as he will be along shortly."

"I have to go to the loo," said Suzanne. "Come along with me Suz, we will go together," said Millicent, taking Suzanne's hand. "When can we go home, Millicent?" asked Suzanne. "Hurry up and don't let Daddy hear you say that. The loo is right here and wait for me."

When they returned, Tony said, "Oh, how pretty my favorite girls are and so grown up now. I am so happy that you are here and we will have lots of weekends together after your school starts. We will chat on the phone every evening and I can help you with your homework and you can tell me all about school and what you are doing."

Millicent responded, "I have all these postals you just bought me about Oxford and I want to make a scrapbook of all our visits together and I will write under each picture."

Nelson entered the pub and spotted Tony and the girls immediately and sat down with them. "Do not forget to get the film developed, Nelson," said Millicent. "I will have the pictures developed in Ambleside, so you can pick the best ones and we will give the others to your Daddy," said Nelson with a laugh.

"I know what that means," said Suzanne. "I always get the hand-me-downs. But this time I have the pretty dresses and Millicent does not because she cut up all the dresses you sent her and threw them in the trash," said Suzanne, looking right into her father's eyes.

A Fine How Do You Do

"Is that true, Millicent?" asked Tony.

"Yes, it is, and I am ashamed of myself. I was just in a bad mood and lost my senses."

"Well," said Tony. "That certainly was a stupid thing to do, but let's forget it and enjoy the fish and chips."

After their supper, Tony declared, "Home again, home again, dear little ones." At the flat, Nelson arranged the wheelchair near the front door of the car and Millicent and Suzanne each took an arm and settled Tony in the chair. "Now, we get to ride in the lift again," said Suzanne.

"It was a perfect day in Oxford, wasn't it Daddy?" exclaimed Millicent. Suzanne jumped onto Tony's lap and hugged him. "Yes, it was and now you both go and shower and jump straight into bed."

"We have never used a shower. I want to go into it with Millicent," said Suzanne. Tony stared at Millicent with a questioning expression. "I am the big sister," said Millicent as she took Suzanne's hand.

Chapter Fifty-Two

Nelson returned to Ambleside on Tuesday, dropped the girls off with Louise, and then went to see Bertha and Bessie. They were still cleaning up from the party weekend.

"You are home, Pinky, and how was merry old London?"

"All went very well, thank you Bessie, and how are you two after the weekend here?" Bessie and Bertha looked at each other and said in unison "We are old and tired!"

"Do tell me all about the festivities," said Nelson. They wiped their hands on their aprons, poured three cups of tea and sat down at the table. "Poor Mr. Bernard could hardly keep up with all the parties and we had to wash his shirts along with Mr. Alfred's and iron them all each day and he never had breakfast. He slept very late and appeared for luncheon and then had a lie-down 'til tea time and then another rest 'til the evening. He is a very handsome gentleman and always smells of expensive shave lotions and polishes his own shoes," said Bessie.

"But he combs his hair way over as he is balding and he looks funny," added Bertha.

"He slept on the drive back to London. And how was Mr. Alfred?" asked Nelson.

They both giggled and Bertha said, "He wore the starched white dress shirt with a red striped bow tie and his white dress jacket and black pants all day and night and told everyone that he was the master of the house and the only person allowed to drive. He told everyone that Alma had a driver but she preferred him to drive the cars and that the driver was useless. He dressed Angel in a pink frilly skirt and a pink bow stuck in her hair."

"And how about Madame?"

"Oh, Madame was so charming and wore a beautiful blue evening dress to match her eyes and many couples came back here after the party at the Yacht Club and we had to scurry and get back in our clothes and serve little crepes and brandy. Madame danced with all the men on the terrace til after midnight and kept pinching Mr. Bernard's cheeks when he looked like he might be falling asleep on the lounge. Mr. Alfred kept playing records on the Victrola and carrying Angel around on his shoulder as he was dancing with Miss Elizabeth."

"And how about Mr. Eric?"

Bertha and Bessie looked at each other and Bessie said, "Well, we don't think he was very comfortable in the evening outfit that Madame rented for him and he kept pulling at his pants and trying to straighten his bow tie. I had to tie it for him in the kitchen before the party and he told me he wished that his wife, Martha, was here."

"And what of the supper party hosted by Mr. Alfred last evening?" inquired Nelson.

"Oh, that was a bit of a nuisance, as we had prepared a lovely duck dish with wild rice and all the trimmings and Madame cancelled it at the last minute as she neglected to remember that there was a special twilight concert at the Anglican Church and everyone seemed to want to go to it and then would be too tired for another party."

"How did Mr. Alfred take to the cancellation of his party?"

"He told us that he never had planned a party and that Madame was all mixed up and Margaret would not have wanted him to have a party and that he wasn't going to the church either. So we had supper with Mr. Alfred in the kitchen and he wanted to scramble the eggs, so we let him, and he drank a bottle of open Champagne left from the night before and danced all around the house with Angel," said Bertha. "Fortunately, we helped him upstairs before Madame and Mr. Bernard came home from the concert."

"Where is Madame now?" asked Nelson.

"I brought up her tray earlier and she has not come downstairs," said Bessie.

"Do you think I might have a biscuit and another tea?" asked Nelson. "And then I will go and clean up the car."

"Pinky, dear friend, we will all have a bit of that fine duck we cooked up, so sit down," said Bertha.

"Bessie, Bertha, where are you lazy girls?" Alma said loudly as she walked toward the kitchen carrying her breakfast tray. She pushed open the kitchen door with her shoulder. Bertha was just putting the plate of duck on the table. "Is that the second duck we planned to have for Alfred's little supper party on Sunday?"

"Yes, Madame, it is and a tasty one it is too," said Bertha.

"Well, what are we waiting for, Christmas?" Alma asked.

"Certainly not, Madame," said Bessie. Nelson pulled up a chair for Madame. Alma nodded without looking at Nelson. The kitchen door opened and Alfred appeared with Angel in his arms.

"Is that another duckling?" asked Alfred.

"It happens to be just that, Alfred," said Alma.

"Well, why are we not sitting at the dining table and dining like normal people?"

"Yes, of course, we must dine like normal people," said Alma with a caustic look at Alfred. They carried their plates to the dining room.

"Is this breakfast or luncheon, Alma?" asked Alfred.

"It is whatever suits you, dear Freddie."

"I hear that the Americans call this brunch," said Nelson.

"Well then, brunch it will be. What a silly word but the duck will not know the difference," said Alma. Everyone smiled at the little joke. Alma rose and then returned from the kitchen with a bottle of red wine and five wine glasses. "Would you please do the honors, Pinky, and uncork this thing?"

"Thank you, Madame, I will be happy to do so," said Nelson. "I wanted to do it," said Alfred and grabbed the bottle from Nelson. "Please do so then, Mr. Alfred," said Nelson, handing Alfred the bottle. "No, I have changed my mind, it is your job." "Thank you, Mr. Alfred," said Nelson as he uncorked the bottle and poured a bit in Alma's glass for her to taste.

"Yes, a perfect compliment for the duck."

Nelson filled everyone's wine glass. "Cheers to all and here's to brunch," toasted Nelson and sat down. Bessie and Bertha raised their glasses together and smiled at Nelson.

"A very amusing name, brunch, so very American. They bunch old words and letters all together and somehow make new words that are not in any proper dictionary. So now we have brunch. Most amusing," said Alma, slightly slurring her words. After that declaration she ate her brunch quietly and quickly excused herself.

Chapter Fifty-Three

Eric spent Monday and Tuesday delighted that the festive weekend had come to an end and he hoped that he never again had to wear a tuxedo outfit. Wednesday brought a lovely cool morning and he inhaled the fresh air. Eric felt a bit homesick on Wednesdays because that was the day he and Martha always went into town and played bingo at the firehouse. He took the bicycle to pick up the vegetables and fruit for the household and then on to the library to wire the weather report to *The Altoona Daily News*. Louise was already at her desk. Louise saw Eric enter and beckoned him to come over. Eric waved back and she met him halfway and suggested that they step outside.

"Eric, when I came in this morning, this wire was on my desk. I could not help but read it as I had no idea who it was for." She handed the wire to Eric and he read it several times and then sat down and put his hands to his head. Louise excused herself and went back to her desk.

Eric left the library, went down to the lakeside and sat on a bench. He read the wire several more times. The wire was from George, his boss at the newspaper. It read: "Eric, this is the wire number you have been using for the weather reports so I hope you receive this without any trouble. Your reports have been right on target for each and every day, so I have just let things go along and have been sending your paycheck to Martha. Otherwise I have had no recent contact with her. However, Eric, I must know if you plan to return home soon as this arrangement cannot continue indefinitely. I feel sure you understand the situation. Please contact me personally and explain. Our contact will be held confidential. Sincerely, George."

Eric was actually surprised that this message had not come sooner. He admired George for being so kind and knew that he must give George an answer quickly.

Eric went to the wire machine and wired the weather reports to George and said that a personal letter to him would follow. This would give him time to think it all out. Eric could see Louise looking at him and he went over to her desk. "Thank you, Louise. Would you like to join me for a picnic lunch by the lake?"

"Yes, Eric, that will be fine, as the girls are going on a picnic with their sailing group and will not be home until late afternoon. I'll meet you at noon."

Eric bicycled back to the house and went into the kitchen with the fruit and vegetables. "Mr. Eric, you look like a ghost has hit you," exclaimed Bertha. "It has," said Eric. "Bertha, would it be too much to ask you to pack a small picnic for me and a friend?"

"And would that friend be Miss Louise from the library?"

Eric looked up and said, "Yes, it would."

"Sit down, Mr. Eric, and take a load off your feet."

"I cannot sit down right now. I must go upstairs and get my wits about me." Eric left the kitchen. Bertha and Bessie looked at each other and began to giggle. "My oh my, Bessie dear, we are busier patting all their backs than cooking for them."

"I bargain he has heard from his wife," said Bessie. "Well then, he may be leaving soon. Such a nice chap and no bother," said Bertha. "Let's pack him up the remainder of the duck with some bread and add that bit of wine from the carafe for his picnic," said Bessie.

Alfred barged into the kitchen and pointed at Bessie. "I am taking inventory of everything in my house. So count up all the table linens and all the silver pieces. I want it all reported on paper to me by five o'clock this evening."

"Mr. Alfred, we take our orders from Madame."

Alfred stuck out his tongue and put his forefinger to the side of his nose and said, "Well, then I will do it myself," darting out of the kitchen.

"I think he is losing his senses," said Bessie.

"This household is a fine how do you do," said Bertha.

"But it is the only household we have," said Bessie. They smiled at each other and gathered together a picnic for Eric. They added some cookies and fruit along with the duck and bread and covered it all in a wicker basket with a stripped cotton towel. They placed two fresh pink posies from the garden on the top.

"Let's have a cup of tea," said Bertha. There was no answer from Bessie. Bertha turned around and found that Bessie had collapsed on the floor. "Oh dear God in heaven, Bessie, wake up." Bertha raced into the dining room and screamed for Eric. Eric came running. Bessie was breathing but not responding to Eric. Eric told Bertha to call the police and the ambulance. They put cold compresses on her forehead. Alfred came running in and started to cry. "Oh, shut your mouth you fool," said Bertha. The kettle was boiling over and howling like a wolf. "Turn it off, Alfred," said Eric. Alfred did as he was told and sat in a chair and cried. "I love Bessie, what is the matter with her. Is it all my fault?" Alfred said, quivering.

The police and ambulance arrived at the same time. Bessie was still unconscious and they immediately put her in the ambulance. As the ambulance started up, Nelson arrived home with Madame, who had purchased a snappy new black felt wide-brimmed hat with a green ribbon around it for the Fall season.

"What in the world is going on? Alfred must be sick," said Alma, racing to the ambulance. She looked in and saw it was Bessie. Alma directed Nelson to follow the ambulance. Nelson saw that Bertha was frantic with concern. "Madame, should we take Bertha with us?" "Yes, of course."

The police entered the house as the ambulance pulled out toward the hospital. Eric and Alfred were standing by the door.

"And who might you two be?" asked the policeman.

"I am Alfred Boeld and this is my friend and butler, Mr. Eric. I am master of the house."

"Can you tell us what exactly happened?" the policeman asked.

"Neither of us were present when it all happened, but apparently Bessie, the cook, collapsed on the floor," said Eric.

"We have two cooks and I am the master of the house," said Alfred.

"Yes, officer, there are two cooks here and they are very close cousins. Bessie went off in the ambulance and Bertha went with Madame and Nelson, the chauffer," said Eric.

"I can hear an American accent. Where do you live in the States and why are you here?" asked one of the policemen. "I am a friend of the family and just visiting but plan to return home very soon."

"Oh, I see. May I please see your passport, sir?"

"Yes, of course. I will go upstairs and get it."

"You can always spot an American. They 'get' things, not 'fetch' things," said Alfred. "I am master of the house, but Eric is a fine fellow even if he talks funny."

Eric returned with his passport. A policeman looked it over and said, "Have a nice trip back to the States, sir." Both policemen tipped their hats and departed. Eric picked up the picnic basket and went off on the bike to meet Louise.

Alma and Bertha went directly to the emergency room. The doctor asked if there was a member of the family present. "Yes, that would be me, Bertha."

"Madame, I admire your hat but I must ask you to wait outside," said the doctor.

Alma gave the medical man one of her famous looks of disgust. "We will be in touch very soon. I must return to my obligations at home at once. But do you, by chance, know Dr. Mellini?" Alma asked the doctor.

"Yes, of course, everyone here knows Dr. Mellini."

"Very well then," Alma said. She spotted Nelson in the lot with the car still running. Nelson stepped out of the car and said, as she drew close, "Madame, if you do not mind, I would like to disconnect the dangling tag from your hat."

"Oh, for the sake of heaven, that new shopkeeper is not well trained at all. I must speak to Mistress Rogers about her."

Bertha was at Bessie's bedside weeping. "Miss Bertha, please go into the hall for just a minute. My nurse is coming in and we are going to check Miss Bessie's vitals," said the doctor.

"Her vitals, what are vitals? I do not think we brought any vitals."

"You just step out, dear lady. Vitals are pulse, heartbeat and things of that nature."

"Oh, I see," said Bertha as she stepped into the hall. Bertha noticed there was a chapel down the hall and went into it. It was a lovely small chapel with very colorful windows. She prayed to God to please save Bessie and to please give her strength. She sat there for quite a while and was almost asleep when she heard a voice. "Miss Bertha?"

"Oh, my dear sir, I know you are a friend of Madame Boeld's."

"She called me and asked me to come to the hospital to examine Miss Bessie."

"So kind of you to come and how is my dear Bessie?"

"She will be fine in a few hours. Her blood pressure was much too low and we are giving her drips and medication to bring it back up to normal."

"She is not going to die?"

"No, my dear lady, she will be around for a long time, but we will prescribe some medicine for her. Do you know if she takes any medication at this time?"

"Oh, no sir, we are Irish you know and never need any medications."

"Well, my dear lady, she needs medication now, and I will write a prescription and I suggest that you make sure she takes it," said Dr. Mellini. He smiled at Bertha and came over and put his arms around her. She burst into tears and said, "May the Lord bless you, doctor."

"And may the Lord bless you and Miss Bessie also. Now I must leave, as when Madame Boeld called we were just leaving for London and then on to Paris."

"Of course, doctor. We mean to be no trouble." Dr. Mellini hugged Bertha and gave her a kiss on her cheek.

"Now I know the Lord heard me and my Bessie will be alright," Bertha said to herself as she went to her cousin's bedside and rested her head on her bosom and was prepared to stay the night with her.

Eric and Louise had a very short picnic and Eric talked only about dear Bessie. He rode the bicycle back to the house and went upstairs to examine his gold cufflinks and gold watch. He heard the car drive in and came down to the kitchen. Alfred heard the car and also came down. Nelson went into the kitchen while Alma was still admiring her new hat in the mirror. They all sat down at the kitchen table with their heads bent down.

"Well, this is a fine how do you do," said Alma. "Dear Bessie in hospital with Bertha at her side and the rest of us waiting around to see who will put the kettle on for tea."

Alfred looked at Alma and said, "it is not proper to wear a hat like that in the kitchen, Alma."

"Well, what sort of hat would you prefer I wear? Do you have a dunce cap for me?"

"I am sorry, dear Alma. I hurt your feelings, didn't I?"

"Freddie dear, just sit down and wait for your tea and be most grateful that our dear Bessie is going to be well very soon."

Chapter Fifty-Four

Eric rode the bicycle to the postbox and posted his letter to George. He knew that the letter was vague but he needed more time to figure out his plans. He promised George that he would be in touch as soon as he figured things out and appreciated how generous he had been. Eric missed Martha and their daughter and her husband and the chubby little granddaughter. He knew in his heart that it was time to return to them. He decided to sell his gold watch and cufflinks and had them in his pocket. He had purchased only a one-way ticket in the States. He wanted to give everyone some presents before he departed and of course buy some things for Martha. If he brought her some nice presents she might not be too angry with him.

He had often biked by the Thrift Shop on the corner and decided to stop in. His eyes immediately landed on a lovely set of four china teacups and saucers. They were very fragile and he wondered if they would pack properly. He knew Martha would love them. A lady came over to help him. "Are you visiting here, sir?"

"Yes, I am staying with Madame Boeld."

"Oh my, we all know Madame Boeld, and as a matter of fact her driver brought in a large box of lovely things she wished to sell just a while back."

"I have a gold watch and some gold cufflinks to sell," said Eric.

"We do not take gold items, but there is a pawn shop around the corner."

"Oh, thank you. I will go there and return later." Eric decided that he would go first to the Travel Bureau right next door and see about tickets. He went outside but stood still, feeling paralyzed.

He decided to see if Louise was free for lunch and perhaps she could help him make some sense of all this. He biked over to the library and spoke with Louise. She smiled at Eric and put her hand in his and said, "You are a dear chap but a most confusing fellow. Come to the house around noon."

As Eric was parking the bike back at Alma's, he saw Nelson drive in with Bertha, Bessie and Alma. He ran over to the door and opened it before Nelson left the driver's seat. "Bessie dear, how do you feel?"

"It was just a little spell and I am fit as a fiddle and sorry to have caused such a fuss."

Alma said, "It was not a fuss, Bessie, and you must take your medicine. Now, go upstairs and rest until we fix a bit of lunch. Bertha and I will fix something, won't we dear?" asked Alma.

"Oh, yes, Madame. I will gather up the vegetables and fruit that Eric brought."

"I did not bring them today. I am so sorry."

"What is the matter with you, dear lad?" asked Bertha.

"Nothing really, I will get them now," said Eric.

"Nelson, please drive Mr. Eric to the fresh market and do see if they have any soups today. Now I must sit down. This is all too much for an old damsel."

Nelson and Eric drove off to the fresh market. "And what happened today that you neglected to pick up the fresh foods?" asked Nelson. "I am just a bit distracted and confused today," replied Eric. They picked up the fresh vegetables, some fruit and several containers of homemade beef soup.

Alma was on the telephone when Nelson brought in the fresh goods. "Miss Olga, did you say? Olga, of course, you are Bernie's dear sister, are you not, and what did you say happened?"

There was a dead silence and Alma burst into tears. "When did this happen?"

Alma fell to the floor in a pool of tears. Nelson raced over and picked up the phone.

"Hello, hello, this is Madame's driver and Madame has just fainted. Please give me your number quickly and I will call you back." Nelson wrote the number down, hung up the phone and yelled "Bertha, come quickly!" She did, and he said, "No sense in calling Dr. Mellini, he has gone to Paris. Place this compress on her forehead and I will give her sniffs of the salts," said Nelson.

Alma regained consciousness quite quickly. "Where am I and what are you two doing lurking over me like hungry turkeys?" she asked.

"Madame, you fainted while you were on the phone."

Alma tried to get up and Nelson suggested that she stay put for a few more minutes. Bertha gathered up some lounge pillows and put them under her feet and head. "I have Miss Olga's telephone number and we will call her back when you feel ready."

"I am ready and we must phone Olga. I think she said that dear Bernie passed away during the night."

Nelson dialed the number and Olga answered. Alma and Olga talked for a while. When Alma hung up, she crossed herself and burst into tears. "I loved Bernie. He was my first dancing partner in Bavaria when we were young." She wiped her eyes with a napkin Bertha brought to her. "And now he is my last dancing partner."

"Heavens to Betsy, Madame, you will be dancing again in no time."

"No, I will never dance again." No one said a word and Alma cried and cried some more.

"Now," said Alma after a few minutes, "we do not have all day and we have things to do. Bertha, where is my new black felt hat with the green ribbon?"

"Upstairs, Madame."

"Well, make sure it is brushed and have my black suit pressed and please find that green print Hermes scarf that I have had for years. But first let us all have a glass of sherry. What is that bouncing noise I hear from outside?" asked Alma.

"I believe that is Alfred with his ball," said Nelson.

"Well, Nelson, be a good chap and go out and bounce with him."

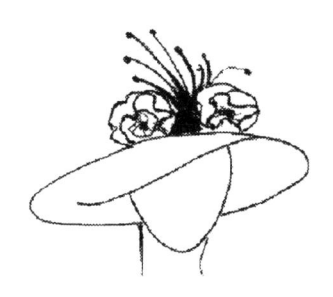

Chapter Fifty-Five

Louise was at home when Eric arrived on his bike. The girls greeted him, but remained entranced with pictures of the Queen on the telly. "Mum, take a look at the Queen and all the carriages and prancing horses. Can we go to the palace in London one day?" asked Suzanne.

"I would think that would be a nice thing to do with your Daddy," said Louise.

"Oh, yes, I will suggest it to Daddy for our next visit," said Millicent.

"Let's all go out on the back terrace. Eric has finished all the work and now the bricks are all even and we will not trip anymore," said Louise, taking Eric's arm.

Eric and the girls admired the terrace while Louise went upstairs to freshen up. When she came downstairs, Millicent and Suzanne were both in tears on Eric's lap. "Uncle Eric told us that he has to go back to America very soon," Millicent said, looking sadly at her mother.

"But he will give us presents before he goes," announced Suzanne.

"And we will give him presents too," added Louise. Eric turned to her and said, "Yes, unfortunately I must return to my home and my family. This has been a very long business trip and now I must make plans to leave."

Louise smiled sweetly and said, "Yes, it has been a long business trip and I hope it was worthwhile."

"Shall we have a party with presents and a cake?" asked Millicent.

"What about ice cream, we always have ice cream, don't we?" asked Suzanne.

"We will have all the trimmings," said Louise.

"It will have to be on a weekend as our school starts very soon. We go to Daddy's some weekends so let me get a calendar and I will write down a date," said Millicent.

"I do not know when I will be leaving, so we can set the date later," said Eric.

"I always know what I am doing, don't I Mum?" said Millicent.

"You are just a smarty pants," said Suzanne.

"Thank you, I like it that way," said Millicent.

"Well, I have the new dress from Daddy to wear for our party and you do not because you took scissors to it," said Suzanne.

"It will be a picnic party so it doesn't matter," said Millicent. Both girls looked at Louise.

"Now, how about a lovely salad and some honey buns for luncheon? You girls stay out here and Uncle Eric and I will put it all together."

Louise and Eric went into the kitchen and began preparing the lunch. "Oh dear, this is so awkward, I am sorry," said Eric.

"It is not awkward. We knew that you were only visiting and we became friends and hopefully always will be friends. It is not like a divorce for heaven's sake."

"I know, but I neglected to tell you that I never told Martha that I was leaving in the beginning."

"Now, that IS awkward, Mr. Eric," said Louise, pointing her finger at him.

"Do not scold me, please. I feel so embarrassed to even tell you this."

"Well then, the first thing you must do is to call Martha and tell her you are coming home."

"Suppose she is very angry and does not want me anymore?"

"Oh, Eric dear, what a fine how do you do you are creating. Now, just sit down and stop cutting up the tomatoes into such tiny pieces. There will be nothing left of them."

"I am so sorry, Louise."

"I am not the one to whom you must apologize."

"What shall I do, Louise?"

"Eric, you have been such a comfort to me these past two months and now the tables are turned, aren't they?"

"Well, yes, I guess you could say that. It is most unfair of me."

"As they say in the American movies, get a grip and get on with it," said Louise, looking straight into Eric's face. Eric started to laugh and hugged Louise. "You are an adorable lady, Louise, and I will miss you so much."

"What is taking so long with lunch, Mum?" asked Millicent as both girls burst into the kitchen. "We are solving the world's problems," said Louise.

The girls looked at each other and darted back to the terrace. "I sometimes do not understand grownups, do you, Millicent?" Millicent looked at Suzanne and shrugged.

After lunch, Eric rode back to Alma's and went up to his room. He sat on the bed and held his head in his hands. He decided to remove his suitcase from the closet and put it on the luggage rack by the window. He took off his jacket, hung it up and looked out the window. He stared out for quite a while and then decided to have a nap. He could not rest comfortably and went to get his gold watch and cufflinks out of his jacket pocket. He put them back in his suitcase and put the suitcase back in the closet. He went back to the window and stared out for a long while. He finally threw himself on his bed in tears and fell asleep.

He was disturbed by a knock on his door. He rose to open the door as Alfred burst in. "Eric, have you seen my Angel?"

"No, I have not. Is she hiding again?"

"I do not know where she is. Will you help me find her?"

"Well, Alfred, where should we start to look?"

"I do not know. I thought you would know."

Eric put on his shoes and jacket and he and Alfred went outside and looked all over the property. Angel was nowhere to be found. Alfred started to cry.

"Now, get a grip, Alfred. Why would Angel leave? She has a happy home here. Do not worry. She will come home." Eric took Alfred's arm and they walked toward the kitchen. "I bet she is in the kitchen with Bertha and Bessie. Have you looked there?"

"Yes, but no one is in the kitchen and Alma is in her bed asleep and no one is helping me," said Alfred.

"Why would Angel run away? She has everything she needs and wants right here. Do not worry, Alfred, we will find her."

"You are a swell pal, Eric, I like you better than Pinky."

"Alfred, everyone here is your friend and friends help each other."

"I already know that," said Alfred.

"Okay, now give Angel another call." Alfred called for Angel but she did not appear. Alfred had his dog whistle and blew it several times. Angel and two other dogs came scampering and jumped all over Alfred.

Eric was tired and wanted to go back to his room and lie down. "Now you have to figure out where these two strays belong," said Eric with something of a laugh.

"Alfred, is that you with your damn whistle again?" shouted Alma from her bedroom window.

"Maybe and maybe not," responded Alfred.

Eric excused himself and went back into the house through the kitchen door. Bertha and Bessie were there. "How about a nice cup of tea, Mr. Eric?"

"That sounds like just what the doctor ordered," said Eric.

"Oh, please do not mention anything having to do with doctors, please, Mr. Eric."

"Sorry, Bessie," said Eric as he sat down and stared out the window. Bertha brought the tea over. "Now, Mr. Eric, we do hope you are not feeling ill. We have had enough trouble for today."

"No. I am not sick, just sad."

"What is the trouble, Mr. Eric?"

"I will be going home very soon."

"Well, you have had a lovely holiday and I do suppose you must get back to your work."

"Yes, that is it," said Eric, picking up his teacup. "My, these are lovely teacups, aren't they? My Martha loves old teacups. I must try and get her a set to take home."

"Oh yes, everyone loves the English teacups. That would be a grand gift to take home. Where is it that you live, Mr. Eric?"

"In Altoona in the USA, rah, rah, rah!!!"

"Oh yes, Altoona," said Bertha and looked at Bessie. "Well, Mr. Eric, they will all welcome you home, I imagine. Perhaps even a gather at the pub for you?"

"Oh, no, nothing like that in Altoona. The best that can happen is that our minister will tell me that I have not fulfilled my pledge as promised."

"Oh, about the money, eh?" asked Bessie.

"Well, yes, sort of like that," said Eric.

Chapter Fifty-Six

Nelson had not slept well for three nights and was barely functioning when Madame called for him to drive her to and fro. He had not even stopped in to see Bertha and Bessie in the kitchen. He had neglected to shave for the last three mornings. He looked at himself in the mirror and decided that he would cultivate a new look for himself and perhaps a moustache would be a good start. He was certain that Madame did not need him this evening, as she had already retired and the house was dark. He decided to pay a visit to Tony's old pub. He hoped to meet a few of Tony's chums there. He liked them and hoped for a chance to bump into them again.

He drove to the pub and parked in the back so no one passing by would see Madame's distinctive automobile. He walked around to the front and went in.

"Well, Pinky, we wondered when you would return and join us for a pint."

"Thank you, chaps," said Nelson.

"And is this a new moustache or is the light bad in here, Pinky?"

"The moustache is new and I quite like it," said Nelson.

"Take a seat, lad, and tell us about our pal Tony."

Nelson ordered a lager and lime while twitching his new moustache. "Tony is doing well and has a new flat in London."

"That's old news, mate. What is he up to now?"

"He is getting along quite well despite the fact that he cannot walk," said Nelson.

The bartender leaned in. "We know all this from our pals in London but we would like him to pay up here. He owes since last April."

Nelson took a large slug of his lager and lime and said, "Here's to you, mates, and that is why I am here. Tell me what he owes and it is on the table for you." Fortunately, Nelson had cashed his paychecks from Madame and had the necessary money. Nelson paid up and they all lifted their mugs to him. The group suggested a toss of the dice and Nelson knew he had to leave. He had no idea about dice games and had just spent his entire pay.

He excused himself and drove back to his apartment. When he arrived all the lights were on in the main house. He parked and started upstairs to his apartment. Bessie came running out and called, "Pinky, come here, come right now." Nelson ran over to the kitchen. Madame was in her dressing gown.

"Nelson, you seem to be taking up wandering about at night with my car. I want it to stop or you may take the nearest door."

"So sorry, Madame, I thought the house had gone to sleep and I wanted to check out a bit of a rumble I have been hearing in the engine and thought this a quiet time and then we could schedule an appointment at the garage tomorrow to have them check it out."

"Well, enough of that tall tale, Nelson. Go up and help Mr. Alfred down the stairs. We must take him to hospital as he is suffering great pain in his side and it might be his appendix. Bessie called the doctor and he said to bring him in, so scurry and let us be on our way."

Nelson went upstairs with Bessie and Bertha. Eric appeared in the hall in his pajamas. "What is going on?" asked Eric.

"Eric, please, put on your clothes and help me get Mr. Alfred down the stairs. Bessie and Bertha, both of you go downstairs and be with Madame," ordered Nelson. They obeyed and found Madame in tears in the kitchen.

"I cannot go on like this. My dearest and oldest friend, Bernie, has left me forever and now all this turmoil. I will be the next in the basket," Alma announced as she rose from the chair.

"But now we will manage, so everyone hustle," ordered Alma. She went upstairs and put on her gardening pants and a bright blue cashmere jumper matching her eyes. She admired her image in the mirror and knew that she still had her good looks even though all around her seemed to be crumbling. "Bessie and Bertha, you dears, stay home and pray while brewing tea."

Nelson started the car and they went to hospital. Alma went in ahead as Eric and Nelson waited for a wheelchair for Alfred. Alma met the doctor and asked to see his credentials, as she did not know him.

"Madame, I am on duty in the emergency room this evening and have been here for twelve years and we are rather busy."

"Well, that will do for now. Please tend to my brother immediately." Alfred was admitted and examined. They decided to keep him overnight though the doctor did not think it was his appendix but more likely a bad case of indigestion. They looked in on Alfred and he seemed to be sleeping comfortably.

Nelson drove Alma and Eric back to the house. "Now, let us all have a glass of summer wine and sit on the terrace, as it is a lovely warm night and there will not be many of them left this season," said Alma, who was somewhat relieved to hear that Alfred would remain among the living. "Eric, please ask the B's to bring some cheese, jam and biscuits as supper was a while ago. How amusing that we have two boys and two girls in the house and then me, the old bat in a hat."

She looked into the distance at the evening sky. Her thoughts turned to Bernie and how she wished she could have attended his service. Her new hat would have been most suitable for the occasion. She wondered where they buried him. All was peaceful and no one spoke. The silence comforted them all as they sipped their wine and dabbled with the cheese and biscuits.

All of a sudden, Angel came scampering to the terrace door and whined to be let out of the house. Bessie opened the screen door and Angel darted out with Alma's new black hat in her mouth and the green ribbon trailing.

"Oh, for the sake of heaven, that canine is a menace. Get her in the house and do not let her out of the kitchen." Bertha ran out and grabbed Angel by the collar and put her in the kitchen. Alma picked up her hat. "A bit of stitching and a good press and the hat will be good as new," said Bessie. Alma said, "It IS new" and began to laugh. There was a pleasant silence again for a few minutes.

Eric excused himself and gave Alma a smile. Nelson had nodded off in the lounge chair. Bessie and Bertha were finishing off the wine, cheese and biscuits. "What a fine how do you do this evening turned out to be," said Alma. "Oh, begging your pardon, Madame, but we never had our supper so we are a bit hungry," said Bessie. Nelson awoke, stood up and said "I will check out the car rumble first thing in the morning." Alma gave him a wink, a nod and a slight gesture with her finger and said, "Good evening, Pinky." Nelson went quietly to his apartment.

Alma pushed herself up from the lounge chair. She stood very still, bowed her head, crossed herself, and looked up at the stars. As she entered the front hall the phone rang and it was Elizabeth.

"Alma, I have been ringing you for the last two hours. Did I miss a supper party this evening?"

"Oh, I am sure there was a lovely supper party somewhere, Elizabeth, but it was not here my dear."

Alma hung up, climbed the stairs to her bedroom and opened the window for some night air. The crows were conversing loudly around her window. Alma smiled as she climbed into bed, pulled the covers over her, said a quick prayer for Alfred and thought about waltzing with Bernie.

Chapter Fifty-Seven

Eric left the library after sending the Altoona weather report to George and brought the fresh vegetables back to the house. "There was very little fresh fruit, Bessie, so I did not get any." Eric had been in deep thought for days but had not discussed his return trip home with anyone except Louise. Louise had invited him for lunch again today. Eric accepted as he felt comfortable with Louise and he hoped she would guide him as to how to handle his departure.

When Eric arrived the girls were going through magazines and cutting out pictures of American movie stars. Louise had not arrived home as yet. "Uncle Eric, have you ever seen a real live movie star?" asked Millicent. "No," said Eric. "What is America like, Uncle Eric?" asked Millicent. "It is nice," said Eric. "Well, what is so nice about it and is it better than here?" she said. "Oh, no, no. Just different," said Eric. He decided he would not stay, as he had a terrific headache now. "Please tell your dear Mum that I am not feeling well and must go back to my room." Millicent said, "That is strange, Uncle Eric, you seemed fine when you came in."

Eric sat on his bicycle, waved goodbye, and started to ride back to Madame's. He passed the Travel Bureau and decided to go in. It was very crowded with tourists and he was told to come back later as they were about to close for lunch. He had placed his gold watch and cufflinks back in his jacket pocket, so when he spotted the pawn shop he parked his bike and entered. The gentleman was most courteous. "They are both made in America and very handsome, sir."

Eric nodded in agreement and said, "I would like to sell them. Can you tell me what they are worth in dollars?"

"Yes, I will appraise them and figure out a price for you. I cannot do it today, but if you return on Thursday, I should have a price for you. Would you like to leave them with me?" asked the gentleman.

Eric said he would do so, and asked for a receipt. Meanwhile, Millicent decided to bike over to Alma's as she wanted to know what was wrong with Eric.

Eric was bicycling when he spotted the Thrift Shop. He went in and was most disappointed to find that the teacups he had admired had been purchased. He did not see anything else that he thought Martha would like. He rode back to Alma's and noticed Millicent's bike by the kitchen door. Eric went into the kitchen and found Millicent sitting at the table with Bessie and Bertha. They were all looking at a paper map of the world and pointing out countries to each other.

"We found Ireland and now we have to unfold the map to find the United States," said Millicent. "There!"

Bessie declared, "It is so grand. I had no idea it was so big, did you, Bertha?"

Bertha was astonished and asked Eric where Altoona was located.

"Somewhere there in the middle of America. It is in the state of Pennsylvania and is not an important place," said Eric.

"If you come from there it must be wonderful," said Bertha.

"Millicent, what are you doing here and why are you not at home with your mother?" asked Eric.

"Mum came home and we swallowed down some soup and she took Suzanne for her physical exam for school. I was bored so I biked over here to see if you were feeling better."

"Mr. Eric, you look like you could use some nice hot tea," said Bertha.

"I will set it all up and serve the tea," exclaimed Millicent.

Eric sat down and began to pet Angel, who was tied up to a chair leg. Bessie put water on to boil, placed the silver tray on the table, polished it quickly, placed the lovely china teacups on the tray and cut up some lemons.

"This a real tea party and I want to be the hostess. My Mum taught me all about being a hostess and I know how to stick my little finger out while holding the cup perfectly still," Millicent declared. They all laughed and Eric stepped on Angel's tail by mistake. Eric took one of the biscuits from the tea platter and gave it to Angel. The front door slammed and they heard the voices of Alma and Nelson. "Anyone home?" asked Alma.

Millicent raced out into the hall and threw her arms around Alma. "Oh, Almama, I have missed you so much. We are just preparing tea for you and I am the hostess."

"My God, you almost knocked me down. What on earth are you doing here?"

"I came for a little visit. Aren't you happy to see me?"

"You are very tan and it is not good for your skin to get so tanned or you will end up like me with wrinkles and spots."

"I went sailing a lot this summer, but the classes have ended."

"Yes, I am happy to see you. Come and give me a hug."

Nelson brought in the packages of shirts and trousers that Alma purchased for Alfred and joined them at the tea table. Millicent acted as hostess and remembered to stick her little finger out when pouring the tea.

"Very nicely served, Millicent. However, you neglected the lemon," said Alma with a smile.

"Madame, how did you find Mr. Alfred this morning at hospital?" asked Eric.

"Nelson, you tell them as I don't remember the name of the disease," said Alma.

"Mr. Alfred has diverticulitis and is doing well. He will be coming home tomorrow and will be on a soft diet for a while and you all must remember not to give him any nuts."

"Oh, very well, we shall treat him like a baby," said Bessie.

"Yes, most appropriate," said Alma. "Eric dear, why such a sullen face?"

"Please forgive me, I am fine and very glad to hear that Alfred will be fine."

After a short silence Millicent said, "Almama, did you know that Uncle Eric has to go home to Altoona?"

"Oh yes, back to Altoona," said Alma. "Millicent, did you know that there was a famous battle there during their civil war?"

"No, Madame, that battle was in Atlanta," said Eric.

"It is too difficult to keep up with the Americans. They are always sticking their fingers in everyone else's pies."

"That is not fair, Madame. Are you forgetting the U.S. Army in World War II?" asked Eric.

"Heavens no, and that was a very rude remark of mine and I truly regret it. The U.S. troops were our savior and I was young." Alma paused and many thoughts went through her head. "I was involved for many years. I have nightmares about all those years. Our younger brother, William, lost his life. Alfred was with the resistance, captured and never has been himself since. I was in a prison for a long time for helping out the Allies. It was a terrible time. Let's not talk about it, especially in front of Millicent."

"Were you a spy, Almama?"

Startled, Alma looked at Millicent and said, "Yes. In a way I was a spy."

"I knew it," said Millicent. "My Daddy has books about that war and lots of spy stories. I want to be a spy too."

"Oh, for the sake of heaven, let's talk about parties or something else," said Alma.

"Would you please excuse me, Madame, as I have a very important errand to attend to before the stores close?" asked Eric. "Why, of course, Eric dear, scurry off and we will catch up later," said Alma, finishing her tea. Eric was upset over the war conversation and worried about his trip home, but realized that he could not part with the gold watch and cufflinks from his father. He arrived at the pawnshop just in time and rescued his belongings. He felt much relieved and enjoyed the bike trip and the cool air on his way back to Alma's.

"Let's have a party for Uncle Eric when he has to leave," said Millicent.

"That is a grand idea, is it not, Madame?" asked Bertha.

"Of course it is a grand idea," said Alma with tears in her eyes.

"I will wear my old clothes because it will be a picnic and Almama can wear the beautiful blue hat she wore in the coach car when we all met on the train."

"My oh my, we all met on the coach train. Just fancy that," said Alma.

"Yes, just fancy that," said Millicent and gave Alma a big hug.

Nelson thanked everyone for the tea party and went up to his apartment. He decided to call Tony and see how things were going, but Tony did not answer. Nelson relaxed on his bed and noticed the calendar on the opposite wall. He always crossed off each day but had not done so for three days. For some reason he noticed that today was his little sister's birthday, but Nelson was not sure where she was or how old she might be today. He had not seen Jennie since she went off to live with an artist at the age of fourteen. He now could recall the date of both his sisters' birthdays but it never occurred to him to try to contact them. He would have no idea how to contact them and he really did not want to. It was as if he had no family at all.

Nelson's father was a drinker and could not support the family. After Jennie left the house, his mother and baby sister Anna moved to Bath. Nelson stayed in the family home with his father. The rent was never paid and his father took off with a barmaid and Nelson was left on his own. The only thing Nelson knew how to do was drive a car.

He left home and took a job at a limousine service in London and enjoyed meeting the upper class and was fascinated by their conversations and lovely clothes. He was perfectly happy to wear the uniform and to have such a nice cap. He was able to rent a room and was content with his simple life and did not hear from any members of his family again. Arthur, the owner of the limo service, took a liking to Nelson and they spent many evenings together.

Arthur sent Nelson to pick up Madame Boeld at the train station one afternoon and drive her to her home in Ambleside. Nelson met Madame at the train and commented on her lovely tweed suit and beige hat. Alma thought Nelson was a most presentable fellow and offered him a job to move into the garage apartment and become her chauffer. When Nelson saw her lovely home he said he would be honored to become her private driver. She offered him a very slim salary, but Nelson liked the garage apartment and looked forward to being among some wealthy people. He never thought about his past or his family again and became the noble driver for the elegant Madame Boeld.

Nelson was startled at himself for reminiscing and decided to have a warm bath. As he stepped into the tub he thought about Arthur and how very nice he had been to him. Arthur had said he was sorry to lose Nelson as a driver but was happy that Nelson could start anew and wished him well.

After his bath he sat on the bed and dialed up Tony again. There was still no answer.

The next morning, Alma and Nelson set off to fetch Alfred home from hospital. Alma had instructed Nelson to find Angel, put her in the car and to stay in the car while she gathered up Alfred. Angel was delighted to go in the car and settled next to Alma.

"Nelson, where has this dog been? She smells simply dreadful and her hair is all tangled up. We cannot have her this way. I will go back in the house and call to see if that lovely beauty parlor for the dogs is open. What is the name of that dog parlor, Nelson?"

"It is called Pretty Pup, Madame." Alma went to call and Angel jumped into the front seat and nuzzled up to Nelson. Nelson put Angel on the floor and kept his foot on her leash until Madame returned. "Oh, so very lucky, they just had a cancellation and we will drop her off immediately and collect her on our way home with Freddie."

Alfred was waiting outside in a wheelchair and the nurse was lighting a cigarette for him. "What on earth are you doing with a cigarette, Freddie?"

"They had no cigars so Fanny brought me a cigarette and you are not allowed to smoke inside so here we are, aren't we, you cute little thing? I proposed to Fanny but she has a boyfriend already."

"Fanny, are you sure that it is time to release Mr. Boeld from hospital, is he well enough to come home?"

"Oh yes, Madame. He has been chasing up and down the halls peeping under sheets and causing a lot of disruption. He is certainly ready to go home, Madame. The doctor has signed his release papers and the instruction for his special diet is in his satchel."

Alfred took a puff of his cigarette and blew the smoke up in the air. "Onward we go!" said Alfred as he pushed the chair aside, took Alma's arm and climbed into the car with cigarette in hand.

"Put out that thing, it smells just awful. We are on our way to pick up your beloved Angel from the beauty parlor as she smelled simply dreadful. What a pair you two runts make," said Alma as she pulled out her handkerchief, which was drenched in Chanel cologne, and put it to her nose. Nelson smiled. He knew that he had made the right choice to come and live with Madame so many years ago.

Chapter Fifty-Eight

"Tony, so glad to catch you at home, I have called several times," said Nelson.

"I am getting about quite well now, thank you, and all is moving along in a spritely fashion. Claudia is not a bundle of joy and bosses me around but I am putting up with her, as she is useful. You must come into town and meet Flora. Guess where she is from?"

"A flower shop?" Nelson asked with a giggle.

"Ha ha, but wrong. Italy, of course. She is such a sweetheart and gives wonderful massages. I have taught her to play backgammon. I couldn't even get you to play backgammon with me, my dear Pinky."

"She sounds very nice. Where does she live and does she have a job?" asked Nelson.

"She has a flat in Bayswater near Paddington Station and gives massages in homes. I found her name in the telephone book and called her and it has all worked out very well."

"Oh, I see. Do the massages help you and the leg?"

"They surely do now, Pinky my pal. When are you coming in next? I want you to meet Jack and Johnnie who live upstairs and are most amusing. We can have a little supper party and Flora knows a bakery that makes fine kidney pies, so no trouble for you."

"Will Claudia and Flora be there also?" asked Nelson.

"Oh, yes, Flora is a delight and such a hooker, I mean looker."

"What about Claudia?"

"Pinky, my boy, you must learn the difference between them and us. Claudia is an ass wiper of sorts and not entirely proper, so when do you plan to come in?"

"I was talking to Louise and she was wondering when you wanted the girls to come in."

"Ah yes, I will call Louise and see if this weekend is okay. Are you free this weekend?"

"I will check with Madame and you check with Louise and see if this weekend is convenient."

Nelson hung up without another word, sat down on his bed and stared at his calendar. He particularly liked this calendar as it had beautiful pictures of places on the continent and he enjoyed imagining he was there. He noticed that he had again neglected to cross off the past few days. He had crossed off each day so regularly for many years and never before neglected to do so. He wondered why he had become so negligent now. He reached for his pen, went over to the calendar and crossed off the past days but not today. He picked up the phone and called Louise.

Millicent answered and recognized Nelson's voice. "Oh, hello, Nelson, how are you and when will you drive us to Daddy's again?"

"That is exactly why I am calling. Is your Mum at home?"

Nelson and Louise chatted a bit and Louise said that this weekend would be fine for the girls to go into London and that she and Eric would be taking a bike ride into town in a few minutes on this nice cool summer day. Nelson went down to the kitchen and had tea with Bessie and Bertha while waiting for Alma to come downstairs.

Alfred appeared dressed very handsomely in a tweed jacket and bowed to Bessie and Bertha. They stood up from the kitchen table and curtsied for Alfred, who clapped and said, "We are the top of society and we must live accordingly. I am feeling fit as a fiddle."

"But you must watch your diet as the doctor ordered," said Bertha.

"I will eat whatever you prepare and have the appropriate wine to go with it," said Alfred as he picked up Angel and plopped her on the kitchen table to show off her new hairdo and large pink bow.

"Mr. Alfred, you should get that dog off the table," said Bertha. Alma entered the kitchen in her dressing gown and swatted Angel off the table, giving Alfred a very stern look of disapproval. Alfred and Angel left the kitchen. "Madame, may I speak with you for a moment in private?" asked Nelson.

"I know what you wish to ask me but have you neglected to remember that I must go to church on Sunday morning very early as I am donating lovely flowers for the service in memory of Bernie. This is a very emotional time for me. Bernie was my dearest friend, Nelson, but I will allow it this once and from now on Mr. Tony Smythe must make his own arrangements to shuttle his girls around. You must be home to drive me to church and the car must be shining as I feel sure that everyone will be awaiting my arrival."

"I understand and thank you so much for your kindness," said Nelson.

Nelson called Tony and told him the plan. Tony was delighted that the girls would come in for the afternoon and rather relieved that they would not be spending the night. Tony did not mention any feelings about the fact that Nelson would be there only for the afternoon. Nelson was rather relieved and went up to his apartment and glanced at his calendar with a smile. He combed his hair, went back to the kitchen and helped Bessie peel the carrots for the beef stew.

Alma appeared in a lovely navy blue afternoon dress with a dark pink scarf and navy blue hat. "Nelson, I do not pay you to peel carrots, I pay you to wheel me around," she said with a slight giggle at her use of words.

"Yes, Madame, where would you like your wheels to carry you?"

"A sense of humor, how pleasant!" said Alma with a smile. "I would like to go into the village and pick out afternoon dresses for the girls to wear into London on Saturday." Bessie and Bertha stopped chopping and looked amazed at this remark.

"Oh, what a lovely idea, Madame, and with your smart taste the girls will look elegant."

"I also have some other shopping ideas but we will discuss all that in the car."

Alfred had been listening to the conversation from behind the screen in the dining room and now came in. "I have some shopping to do, Alma, and I wish to join you. I have decided to wear spats on my shoes from now on. They will go well with the outfits you bought for me."

"Oh, dear Lord, next you will be wearing an opera hat at tea time."

Alma and Alfred were ushered into the back seat by Nelson, who drove into the village and parked the car. "Now Alfred, you go along and buy whatever it is you want and Nelson and I will go shop for the girls and a few other items. Nelson, which direction is that little shop for children?"

"Right this way, Madame." They entered the shop and found Louise and Eric there.

"What a very pleasant surprise and for whom are we all shopping?"

"Oh, Madame, it is so very nice to see you and you have such lovely taste and Millicent admires everything about you and I am such a mouse." Louise burst into tears and sat down on a chair. Eric nodded at Nelson and Alma and he went to comfort Louise. Alma pushed in front of him and put her hands on Louise's shoulders. "Louise, my dear girl, get up and give this old lady a hug."

Louise got up and practically fell into Alma's arms. Alma felt her hands and they were freezing cold. Her face was pale and her body was limp. "My dear child, how long have you been so weak?" Alma asked Louise.

"I don't know, forever, I think."

"Nelson, get the car. We are taking Louise to hospital." Eric said that he wanted to go also and would hide their bikes behind the shop. They gathered up Louise and Alfred appeared. "What has happened?" asked Alfred.

Nelson brought the car around and they all piled in. Louise was crying in the back seat on Eric's lap. "Where are our bikes, Eric, I cannot lose my bike, as Tony will tell me how stupid I am. Millicent was carrying on so about not having proper clothes to wear to see her father and it upset me so that I almost collapsed."

"My dear, we are going to the hospital. You need a doctor," said Eric.

"I was in hospital until just yesterday and I feel fit as a fiddle now," said Alfred.

Louise picked up her head and looked at Alfred. "Who are you?" asked Louise and dropped her head again in Eric's lap.

"I am the master of the house and I know all about this hospital," bragged Alfred.

Nelson had called ahead and a stretcher and two aides were waiting for them. They took Louise away. Alfred wanted to go with her but Alma told him to get back into the car and be quiet. Alfred obeyed and went to the back seat and found Eric all slumped over and in tears. Alfred put his arms around Eric's shoulders and told Eric that he was a good chap and that everything would be fine. Eric looked up and said "Oh, it's you, Alfred."

Louise was admitted and put in the emergency room. Alma and Nelson went to the waiting room. "Nelson, take Eric and Freddie, get the bikes from behind the shop and go back to the house. Do not let Freddie out of the car until you get home. Then pick up the girls and tell them that their mother felt a bit faint and that I insisted she go to hospital and they are to come for supper and spend the night so to bring their toothbrushes," said Alma all in one breath.

"Yes, Madame, very good planning."

"Nelson, I had other plans in mind for today but one never can predict emergencies. Never mind, we will go for the fitting of your new blue uniform tomorrow. I am weary of this maroon one. It is quite dated. I decided that a snappy plaid cap would be so fitting for the Fall weather. Do you agree?"

"Yes, Madame, an excellent choice."

"After you deliver everyone at home, come back for me and I will be right here by the door. I have no doubt that they will keep Louise overnight. This hospital is becoming a second home for us," said Alma with a big laugh.

Nelson followed the orders. Suzanne was in tears on the floor and Millicent was on the phone with her father. Millicent told her father to hang on. She ran to the door and threw her arms around Nelson's neck. "Where is Mum?" she asked. "She has been gone so long."

"She is resting. She felt weak, so we took her to hospital, as she is just a bit over-tired from working. Now listen, girls, you are to get your nighties and your toothbrushes and I will take you to Madame Alma's to spend the night," said Nelson.

"Oh, how perfectly glorious, we can spend the night with Almama," said Millicent. "I want to go to hospital and sleep with Mum," said Suzanne. Millicent remembered that her father was still on the phone. "Daddy, I have to ring off now, as Mum is in hospital and we have to go to Almama's."

"Millicent, what in hell are you talking about?" The phone went dead. Tony hung up and dialed Nelson but there was no answer. He sat in his chair for a moment and then yelled "Hey, Babe, got a beer for the cripple?" Flora came in with a beer and jumped onto Tony's lap. "Thank God you are a bit of a thing or you would be wounding me," said Tony. The phone rang again and Tony picked up. "Why did you hang up, Millicent?"

"Tony, Nelson here. Do not worry as all is in control. Louise was a bit weak and we took her to hospital. I really have no information, but you can call the hospital. I am taking the girls to Madame's for the night."

"Oh, for God's sake, that woman will take over my family and I am so damn helpless," said Tony, holding back his tears.

Millicent and Suzanne packed their little bags and ran to the car. "When can we see Mum?" asked Suzanne. "Oh, perhaps tomorrow," said Nelson. Suzanne began to cry and asked Millicent if she was going to write an obituary about Mum. "No, Mum will be fine," said Millicent.

Everyone was sitting in the library when they arrived at Alma's, and a fire was burning in the fireplace. Millicent rushed over to Alma and threw her arms around her neck. Suzanne ran to Nelson and began to cry. "What a fine how do you do," said Alma as she stood up and put on a waltz record. Alfred jumped up to dance with Alma. Millicent danced by herself and Eric picked up Suzanne and twirled her around in circles. "I am getting dizzy," said Suzanne as she began to cry again.

Bessie came in with a large tray of greens and meat stew. Bertha carried a tray with the plates and silverware. They put the trays down and began to dance with each other. Nelson came in with a tray of glasses and a carafe of brandy. Millicent ran over and grabbed Nelson and began to waltz with him. The telephone rang and Alfred answered. "Yes, just a moment, Alma for you."

Alma answered and kept shaking her head. Everyone waited for the news. She finally hung up and said, "Louise is feeling better already. They found her to be quite anemic and she is having blood transfusions of vitamins. Her color has already improved but they want to keep her overnight and if all goes well we can collect her tomorrow and she should be fit as a fiddle.

"They made me fit as a fiddle," said Alfred, jumping up and down.

"Is anyone hungry?" asked Bertha.

All enjoyed the drinks and dinner and then kept on dancing. Millicent and Suzanne decided to sleep in the same bed together and fell asleep with their arms around each other. Eric went to his room and sighed with relief that Louise was in good care. Alfred took Angel up to bed with him. Alma was sorry that Louise became ill and felt quite guilty that she enjoyed the evening so very much. She fell asleep with visions of them all dancing around together, just like a family. Nelson went up to his apartment and crossed off today on his calendar with a smile of content. Bessie and Bertha had a sip of brandy by the fire, turned out all the lights and retired to their beds.

"They called from the hospital and told me that she was admitted yesterday. Why the hell was I not notified at once, Pinky?" asked Tony.

"It all happened very quickly and Madame was in charge and did a great job and we are on our way to pick her up now, so I must be going."

"That Madame of yours will be the death of me. She is a wicked woman and caused more trouble for me and my business than her little pinky is worth!"

"Louise had nothing to do with any of that. They are waiting for me, so I must go."

Alma, Eric and the two girls were in the car when Nelson arrived. "So sorry to keep you waiting, but Mr. Smythe called and was concerned why he was not notified about the admission of Louise to hospital last evening."

"Daddy does not live here so what could he have done?" asked Millicent.

"Now girls, let's all be very quiet and when we pick up your dear Mum, do not ask any questions and just tell her that you love her."

"Well I want my Daddy to know," said Suzanne.

"You are so out of it, Suz. Daddy knows, so shut up!"

"Why are you always so mean to me, Millicent?"

"I am sorry, Suz. Everything will be fine."

Nelson arrived at the hospital and Louise was dressed and waiting out in front looking very well and happy. The girls jumped out of the car and ran to Louise, who threw her arms around both girls and hugged them.

"Now, we shall go straight to my house and have a lovely brunch, as the Americans call it."

"What is brunch?" asked Suzanne.

"It is a surprise," said Alma.

Louise cuddled up with the girls and gave Eric a very meek smile. Marching music was heard as they drove up the driveway to Alma's house. Nelson stopped at the garage instead of the front door and helped everyone out of the car. Alfred appeared in a Nazi uniform and told everyone to line up and he would send them to camp. Alma stepped forward and said, "Freddie, this is no time for your fun and games."

"I have a gun right here and you all must obey me. I am Master of this house," said Alfred.

"Freddie, the war is over and we are all fine. You are safe here and please, dear Freddie, put the gun down," pleaded Alma.

"I like guns," said Alfred.

Nelson stepped forward and said, "Mr. Alfred, may I offer you a cigar?"

Alfred smiled and said, "Yes, that would be grand. Churchill likes cigars and I like Winston Churchill."

"Well, then, we are friends and not Nazis, yes?" asked Nelson.

"Of course we are friends and the Nazis must be spanked," said Alfred.

"My sister and I want to be with our Mum and you are a mean man in that costume and you scare me," said Suzanne.

Millicent clapped her hands, went over to her sister and held her hand. "Yes, Mr. Alfred, we both think you are a silly man."

"Where is my cigar?" asked Alfred, putting the gun down as Nelson handed him a stick. "This is a fine cigar," said Alfred as he pulled Angel on the leash and went inside the house.

Chapter Fifty-Nine

Bertha and Bessie set a lovely table and joined Alma, Eric, Millicent, Suzanne, Louise and Nelson for brunch.

"Oh, this is a beautiful happening," exclaimed Millicent. "I have never seen such lovely china and these goblets are quite heavy to pick up with one hand and I have never had eggs on a bun with yellow sauce before."

"Who can guess why this is called brunch?" said Alma.

"I think I know," said Suzanne. "Because it is not breakfast and not even lunch so they call it BRUNCH?"

Everyone clapped and Suzanne stood up from the table and took a bow.

"Very clever, the Americans, however a bit rough around the edges, but most amusing people," said Alma.

"Thank you for that backhanded compliment," said Eric and laughed.

"Oh, dear Eric, you have become so much a part of the household that I forget you are from the U S of A, and it is Atlanta, yes?"

"No, Madame, I am from Altoona."

"I give up, I shall never get that straight. My apologies, dear Eric. It is so easy when we are all from Ambleside, no one becomes confused. Why don't you just stay on and then you will be from Ambleside also?"

Eric stood, lifted his glass of Champagne and said to all, "I feel like family and these have been the happiest days of my life but I am going back to Altoona very soon."

"Why isn't Mr. Alfred sitting in his chair here?" asked Suzanne.

"I can hear you and am hiding here behind the screen, ha ha! I am a secret agent and I will arrest you all if you do not behave."

"Freddie dear, please open that other bottle of Champagne, pour for everyone, including the girls, and then come and sit next to me," said Alma, putting her head in her hands.

Alfred had exchanged his uniform for a plaid dressing gown. "My, how handsome you look, Mr. Alfred. May I bring you some eggs?" asked Bessie. Alfred sat next to Alma and nodded to Bessie, and then asked, "Alma, why isn't Elizabeth here?"

"Just a simple gathering on the spur of the moment," said Alma.

Louise tapped her glass with her spoon and stood and looked at Eric. "I do not make toasts very often but Eric deserves a toast from my heart." Tears filled her eyes, but she smiled and said, "He has been a friend to us all and he is a lovely gentleman and we shall all miss him and hope he will return soon with his family for another visit. And thank you dear Eric for everything you have done for the girls and me."

Louise started to sit down and then stood up again. She looked at Alma and said, "Madame Boeld, I have never known anyone like you and probably never will again. You are the most special, beautiful and generous person alive, and...." Louise began to cry and sat down.

"Well, this is a fine how do you do with tears flowing along with the Champagne. Let us have more Champagne and no more tears," said Alma.

Eric stood and lifted his glass to Alma. "Madame, I do not know how to thank you for your hospitality and your friendship and...." Eric began to weep and sat down.

"My dear boy, you have not yet departed, so we shall not dwell anymore on that subject."

Millicent raised her hand and asked Alma if she could be excused from the table. Alma nodded. Millicent jumped up and put a waltz record on the Victrola. Everyone but Alma rose, held hands and danced around in circles. Alma stayed at the table and wished this moment would never end.

"Now, Bertha, we must get everything in order quickly," said Alma as she stepped onto the terrace later that afternoon. She rang the bell and Bessie came out to the terrace. "One never knows when another catastrophe might occur. One must always be prepared," said Alma.

Bertha smiled and said that she agreed and had learned during the war that one must always be prepared. Bessie and Bertha busied themselves sweeping and cleaning up the terrace. "Let's not talk about the war anymore," said Alma, and she went in and dialed Louise, and Millicent answered. "How is your dear Mum this afternoon."

"She is in the kitchen boiling the water for tea," replied Millicent. Alma said she would be there shortly with dresses for them to wear into London. "Oh, I love to shop, may I come along?" asked Millicent. "I already purchased the dresses earlier this afternoon and have other stops to make today," said Alma as she hung up.

"Well, good day Nelson. Are we prepared to continue our shopping spree?"

"Yes, Madam, whenever you are ready."

"Well, fetch the car and let us be on our way before Freddie decides to join us."

"Madam, Mr. Alfred is in the car dressed in his plaid pants and no shirt. He claims it is too warm for a shirt and was most annoyed with me to suggest he change." Alma put her shoulders back, marched over to the car and told Alfred to get out of the car and go put on some casual clothes and please to learn how to behave. Alfred went off into the kitchen.

"Now, I do not think you need a new uniform do you, Nelson?"

"Actually, I was looking forward to a new uniform, but whatever you say, Madame."

"I say that we go to that proper gentleman's store and purchase some grey trousers and a navy blue blazer and some proper casual shirts for you." Nelson turned around and looked at Alma, who said, "Yes, let us go forward and pick out some proper clothes for you and then deliver the dresses for the girls. My hat is ready, so we must fetch it also from the shop."

Nelson was elated that Madame had chosen the grey trousers, several shirts and a very handsome blue blazer. He had become so accustomed to his uniform that this new attire was a great shock to him and he seemed to become a new person when he put it on. He turned around several times in front of the mirror in his apartment and hardly recognized himself. He began to play games with himself, turning around abruptly to see if he was still there. Then he kept bowing to himself and removing his new cap, and finally threw it on the bed as he decided to show off his new outfit to Bertha and Bessie. He did, and enjoyed how Bertha and Bessie had many giggles calling him "Sir Nelson."

Early Saturday morning, Nelson awoke abruptly with a hot flash and noticed that his bed was soaking wet, as was his forehead. His nightmare was very clear now. He had joined the circus and was forced to wear a clown suit and large floppy shoes. His boss was the image of Tony who was an animal trainer and carried a fierce whip. In the dream they seemed not to know each other, though every time Nelson passed him he smiled and cracked the whip.

Nelson bathed with cool water, dressed properly and went to fetch the girls.

"Is everyone comfortable?" asked Nelson. "Yes, Millicent and I like the back seat best," said Suzanne. "Of course you do and keep your feet on the floor and not on the seats," said Nelson. As the drive continued the girls were very quiet and Nelson was suspicious. "What are you girls up to?" asked Nelson. "I am writing a poem," said Millicent. "The title is 'The Lost Bracelet' and it goes like this:

> *I could have lost it flying my kite*
> *Or perhaps I lost it on my bike*
> *I possibly lost it bouncing my ball*
> *Or maybe it's not lost at all."*

"That is very good, Miss Millicent. You may have a future as a poetess," exclaimed Nelson.

"What should I be when I grow up, Nelson?" asked Suzanne.

"I think you could be anything your little heart desired if you worked at it," said Nelson, looking in the rear view mirror at Suzanne.

Suzanne smiled and said, "Then I will be a movie star."

Chapter Sixty

Millicent and Suzanne raced into Tony's flat and saw their father in the wheelchair. "Can you get up, Daddy?" asked Suzanne. "Well now, Miss Suzanne, the answer is yes." Suzanne stared at Millicent and Millicent stared at Nelson.

"Well, this is a fine how do you do," said Nelson as he went over to Tony and helped him out of the chair and over to the couch, which was piled with pillows. "We need to summon Claudia as she knows just how to arrange the pillows," said Tony.

Claudia came into the room and went over to hug the girls. The girls then looked at Nelson. Claudia asked the girls if they would like some ice cream and they said, "No thank you" at the same time. "Actually, it is tea time, Daddy, and we brought some shortbread that Mum made. We will go to the kitchen and fix it up."

"Very good," said Tony. "And how goes it with you, dear Pinky?"

"Pinky is not well, but Nelson is chipper and glad to see you," said Nelson with a sneer.

"Oh, Jesus Christ, what can I do to fix all this?" asked Tony. "This is so awkward for the girls and I do not know how to handle it all," said Tony and burst into tears.

The girls and Claudia were in the kitchen preparing the tea and the radio was playing. "Tony, get a grip old chap, face the music, be honest with the girls and things will fall into place."

"So, now you have graduated from chauffeur to therapist, have you?" Nelson looked at Tony and saluted. Flora entered the room and began rubbing Tony's back.

"I like the new paintings and the flat looks very cheery and comfortable," remarked Nelson.

"It is working out very well. I like the chaps upstairs and also the ones downstairs. So life is full of fun. Claudia and Flora have worked out schedules so one of the darlings is always here to stroke my back and sing and dance."

There was an awkward silence, broken by the girls entering with the tea and shortbread. "You girls look taller and are becoming more beautiful all the time," said Tony. "And you are as handsome as ever, Daddy," said Millicent. "May I sit on your lap?" asked Suzanne. "Sure thing, why not, just jump right up." Suzanne went over, gave him a big kiss and said, "I was only kidding, Daddy."

Millicent said, "We went to sailing camp all summer and Mum is all better now and we start school very soon and Eric is going back to America and Almama and I are having a party for him and you can come to it if you like, Daddy." Millicent poured the tea and Suzanne passed the cups.

"And who is Almama, pray tell?" asked Tony. Nelson turned to look out the window to avoid Tony seeing his face as he was about to burst into laughter.

"Almama is Madame Boeld. She is my new best friend and we are going to Paris someday."

"For God's sake, when did this all come about?" Tony asked as he looked over to Nelson, who was still looking out the window.

"Let's open the presents your Daddy has for you both," said Claudia as she opened the closet door and brought out four beautifully wrapped boxes.

"Oh, how exquisite," exclaimed Millicent. The girls opened the boxes and jumped up and down when they saw the contents.

"I have always wanted a red pocketbook and now I have one with a lovely jumper to match," exclaimed Millicent. "And I have a royal blue jumper and a beret to match," said Suzanne, jumping up and down.

"Here are two more boxes for you," said Flora. The girls opened up the boxes and each had a matching large bow for their hair. "Oh, Daddy, I will be the smartest-dressed girl in my class with all my new red things. Red suits me so well," said Millicent. "I like royal blue best, but when are you coming home, Daddy?" asked Suzanne.

"Oh, be quiet, Suz, you know that Daddy does not live with us anymore. Mum told you that a hundred times."

"Millie is right, Suzanne, Daddy lives here now," Tony said looking out the window as he wiped his eyes.

"Don't call me Millie any more, Daddy, please."

They had a tea party and played cards together. Suzanne was very happy when she won three games of rummy in a row. Nelson looked at his watch and said, "We should be moving on, Tony." Tony asked to be moved to the window where he could see the girls leaving.

He burst into tears when he saw Nelson in the middle holding his girls' hands. The girls were carrying their presents, now in paper sacks, with their free hands. Millicent looked back and saw Tony looking out the window. She alerted Suzanne and they both blew him a kiss. Tony opened his window and the girls could hear him saying "I love you beautiful babies!" over and over again. "Let's hurry up, Nelson!" said Millicent. "Daddy still can't walk and he needs some new clothes as he looks very sloppy," said Suzanne. "Your Daddy always finds a way. He is very imaginative. So don't you fret over that, dear child," Nelson said and then smiled. "Yes, girls, your Daddy is most inventive."

Tony stayed by the window and watched the girls until they turned the corner. He recalled Millicent asking him, not too long ago, when she was in her writing-obituaries stage, if he knew any dead people who were not really dead. He thought it was clever at the time, but now it was not amusing at all. He turned from the window and called for Flora and Claudia. "Flora, please put all these wrappings in the trash and let's get our act together and hop over to Jerry's Pub and liven up the place. It is Saturday night and the place will be jumping."

Chapter Sixty-One

Eric and Louise were sitting on a bench outside the library. The birds were chattering around them as they each had some crackers with their paper cups of tea. "The days are getting shorter and a bit cooler, have you noticed?" asked Louise. "Yes I have, and the days are getting short for me, my dear Louise, as I must plan my trip back home."

Louise was quiet and in thought. It seemed to her that nothing lasts forever and she had better realize it. "Please tell me if Nelson said anything about the girls' day with Tony. Millicent acted very strangely when she came home and Suzanne just wanted to sit on my lap and suck her thumb. It seems that Suzanne has reverted back to her baby days and Millicent is growing up so very fast. When I was ready to serve supper, Millicent appeared in this hat belonging to Madame Boeld. She asked me to bring it to the library and give it to you to return to Madame Boeld. I wonder what went on at Tony's?"

"Well, I did have a chance to chat with Nelson and he said that Tony cannot walk alone and has two ladies working for him in his apartment who seem to care for him. He also said that Millicent asked Tony not to call her 'Millie' any more, as she is now twelve years old, and Suzanne asked when he was coming home. Nelson did not have much more to report," said Eric.

A Fine How Do You Do

Louise put on Alma's hat and started to dance around until the wind took the hat right off her head and sent it twirling toward the water. Louise began to laugh but Eric interrupted, saying "I am going into the library now and send off another wire to George at my newspaper advising him that I am making plans to return home and to please wire my month's salary to my bank account so that I may have some money for traveling. I will ask him to tell Martha that my vacation is over and that I will see her soon."

"Eric, are you not going to contact Martha yourself?"

Eric did not reply as he threw some more crackers out for the birds and headed toward the library. Louise watched the hat being blown up and about, and wished she was as carefree as the hat.

Alma was sitting alone on the back terrace thinking that life had always been quite unpredictable and hoping that it always would be, as then she need not worry and just take life as it comes along. The social season was on its last leg and she thought that the farewell party for Eric should be a rather informal affair, but not a picnic. She had never been one for picnics.

She rang for Bessie and Bertha, who appeared promptly in their starched uniforms. "My, you ladies do keep up the presence of a respectable house!" They both smiled and curtsied. "As you both know, Eric is departing for Atlanta to rejoin his wife very shortly and we will have a party here at our home. I know we had discussed a picnic sort of party but I think an informal affair at home is more my style. I want you both to be seated guests along with Nelson. It will be a family affair. We shall have Louise, Millicent, Suzanne, Eric, Bertha, Bessie, Nelson, Freddie, Elizabeth and moi. Ten works nicely, n'est pas?"

"Yes, Madame, it will be just lovely," said Bessie, "but may I remind you that Eric is returning to Altoona not Atlanta."

"Of course he is and such a shame that he must depart, as he is such a pleasant fellow."

Eric entered the house and saw Alma on the back terrace. "Good afternoon, Madame, and how is life treating you today?" asked Eric as he sat down opposite Alma and rocked back and forth in the rocker.

"Life is life and that is all I know about it today," said Alma.

"Am I interrupting your thoughts, Madame?" asked Eric.

"No not all, the air is cooler and the summer is about over. I do like the change of seasons, don't you Eric?"

"Yes, I do," said Eric.

They both sat quietly and respected each other's silence. Alma heard the clock strike in the hall and said, "Eric, are you deep in thought or have you fallen asleep?"

"Madame, I am just trying to adjust my mind to leaving here and going back home and it is a bit of a puzzle to me."

"Well, dear Eric, it has always been a puzzle to me how you ended up here."

Eric laughed and said, "I guess I was in the right place at the right time."

"No doubt, dear boy!"

The phone rang and Alma answered. Millicent was calling to thank Alma for loaning her the hat but she had not needed it and Eric would return it to her. Alma told Millicent about the party and that it would not be a picnic but a little supper party. Millicent asked if she might make the place cards for the table and Alma thought that was a grand idea and suggested that she allow Suzanne to help also.

As Alma hung up, Alfred appeared with Angel in his arms and told Alma that they were on their way to pay a visit to Elizabeth. He needed to put petrol in his car and asked Alma if she needed anything from town. Alma told Alfred about the party and asked him to personally invite Elizabeth. "Oh, by the by, dear Freddie, would you stop in that nice gentlemen's store and see if they have a pair of knickers for Eric? Check also if they have the proper stockings and shirt. I want them for Eric as a going-home gift."

"They do not wear knickers in America, Alma," said Alfred.

"That is exactly why I want to give them to him," said Alma.

"I will buy him a picture book all about the Lake District to take home to show his friends and I will paint him a small picture also," said Alfred with enthusiasm.

"What a grand idea, Freddie!"

Alfred pulled Angel along on her leash and together they drove off. Alma went to the kitchen, where Bertha and Bessie were working, and asked them to please sit down. "Now, ladies, what do you suggest we serve for the party?"

"We have been discussing it and thought you might like to have a roast of beef with our special Yorkshire pudding, a mixed garden salad for starters and our delicious white fruit cake for dessert soaked in brandy."

"I could not have suggested anything better and it will be a lovely party for Eric." Alma smiled and blew each a kiss.

Chapter Sixty-Two

Alma hardly slept and awoke in the morning quite troubled. She was accustomed to sleepless nights and usually napped in the afternoon to catch up and very often realized that something was on her mind and she must try to identify it.

She went downstairs but, instead of ringing for Bertha or Bessie, went to the kitchen to make some tea. She sat at the kitchen table and looked out the window. Her mind was a blank until she began to recall the plans for Eric's going-home party. The plans were good and ten seemed a perfect number for the table seating. "Oh, my heavens, I know what it is," she said aloud, and then, rising, raised her voice. "Bertha, Bessie, are you awake?"

A moment passed and both appeared in their nightclothes. "Are you ill, Madame?"

"No, I am not ill but I am not imaginative and far reaching in my plans from time to time."

Bertha and Bessie looked at one another. "Is there perhaps something you wish to change about the menu for the party, Madame?"

"No, the menu is fine." Alma fetched her tea, sat down and asked Bertha and Bessie to sit with her. "Have you ever heard Eric speak of his wife?"

"Yes, we have. Her name is Martha and he seems most devoted to her. However, we have never figured out why she did not come with him and there never has been any post for Eric."

"Oui, tres etrange, and I have noticed that Eric is most confused about returning home. Actually, not only that, but how and why he arrived here in the first place is still a mystery. I am going to find out about his wife and his address in Atlanta and invite his wife here for a visit before he departs."

"Madame, he lives in Altoona, Pennsylvania, not Atlanta."

"Well, Louise will know and I will call her later and ask her if she thinks this is a good idea."

"Louise, dear, are you free for luncheon today?" asked Alma.

"Well, yes I am, if you do not mind having lunch at my home with the girls, as they are not back to school as yet."

"Nonsense, I shall have Bessie pack a picnic for us all, so bring the girls here and we will walk down to the lakeside."

"Is there anything the matter, Madame Boeld?" asked Louise.

"No, not at all," responded Alma.

"Well, Madame Boeld, I must apologize to you, as I lost the hat that Millie borrowed and asked me to return to you. I am very sorry and of course will try to replace it. It blew off my head while I was at the lakeside with Eric."

"Oh, that is grand and I hope it is floating around and finds a charming new head to land on. What a lucky hat to be so free! I think you did it a wonderful favor and it will have a much better life than being stuck in my closet," said Alma with a deep laugh.

Alma, Louise and the girls all sat comfortably on the picnic blanket enjoying the watercress sandwiches. Millicent was relieved that they were not cucumber. The sun was bright and the lake was sparkling. "Oh, I do wish we could go sailing, it is perfect day," said Millicent. "Next year, I will take more sailing lessons and then maybe Daddy will buy us a sailboat and we can all sail around the lake and discover things," said Suzanne. "That sounds just grand and I hope I am still spry enough to go with you," said Alma. "Oh, Alamama, you will always be spry as long as you wear your lovely hats," said Millicent. "So it is all about hats, is it young lady?" asked Alma with a laugh. "I want to be older and you want to be younger, so it must be all about hats," said Suzanne. "Well, if you say so Suzanne," said Alma. "Now, you girls run down to the lake and see if you can catch some frogs."

The girls ran off holding hands. "Louise, dear, I have a box for you and then an idea about Eric and his departure. May I discuss it with you?" asked Alma.

"Yes, please do, Madame Boeld. I did not sleep a wink last night as I know that Eric is most confused about going back home and I am so very fond of him and it upsets me to see him so befuddled," said Louise, looking at Alma with woeful eyes.

"I did not sleep well either, so we must chat about this situation," said Alma with tears in her eyes. "Now, my dear Louise, in this box is a captured hat that will be all yours and you may send it flying, keep it or let it go free."

Louise opened the box and pulled out the most beautiful hat she had ever seen. It was fine straw with brown and yellow ribbons. Louise immediately put it on and blew a kiss to Alma.

"It is perfect for you, my dear. Now we must talk business." Alma told Louise about her idea of inviting Eric's wife for a visit and to the party. Louise thought it was a grand idea and hoped that it would all work out. Louise told Alma about *The Altoona Daily News* and that Eric wired the weather reports regularly to a man named George and that George had wired Eric last week that it was time for him to come back to work. Alma said that she knew nothing about a wire machine but she would place a trans-Atlantic telephone call to *The Altoona Daily News* and speak to this George and find out how to reach Martha and ask her to come and visit.

Louise stood up and went over to Alma and gave her a hug and told her she was a brilliant lady and that she adored her, as do her girls. Alma stood up with a helping hand from Louise, straightened her straw hat with the striped ribbons and summoned the girls. "By the by, Louise, what is Eric's surname?"

"He is Eric Sanders and his wife's name is Martha Sanders."

"Thank you so much, Mr. George, and I hope I have not bothered you," said Alma quite loudly into the phone.

"Not at all, Mrs. Boeld, and I think your plans are very generous and most timely. In fact, I will speak with Martha, tell her about the surprise and make the airline reservations myself for Martha to depart two weeks from today. Am I correct that the airplane ticket should be from here to London and the coach ticket to Oxenholme, where I presume you will meet her train? I will also purchase two tickets back home," said George.

"Yes, that is all excellent," said Alma. "I will have my banker send the necessary amount to your account."

"Now, Mrs. Boeld, is this all to be a surprise for Eric?"

"Yes, hopefully, but if not, it will work out very well either way," said Alma with a feeling of great satisfaction. She poured herself a small glass of brandy, deciding to call Martha later, as now she was ready for a rest.

Very late that night, just before going to bed, Alma – taking note of the time difference – placed the call to Martha at the number George had supplied. The phone rang several times and a sleepy and surprised voice picked up. "May I please speak with Madame Martha Sanders?"

"Yes, I am Martha, has something happened to my husband? Is he alright?" Alma could hear crying and tried to calm her.

"No my dear, Eric is fine," said Alma. "He has been visiting in my home in Ambleside, England, for the past two months or so and is perfectly well. My name is Madame Alma Boeld and my brother Alfred and I live here."

There was a silence, and then Martha said, "I just now read my horoscope in our newspaper where my husband works and it said that I would receive good news today, so I hope you are the good news."

"Yes, Madame Sanders, I hope I am the good news."

"How did he get to your house?" asked Martha.

"I met him on the train and he had no place to stay so we invited him to stay with us," explained Alma.

"When will he be returning to me?"

"That is exactly what I wish to discuss with you," said Alma, but Martha angrily interrupted, saying, "I have no money for his trip and am in such shock over this whole adventure. He has taken off and left me in the lurch for months without a peep. I do not know what to say, Madame, what did you say your name is?"

"My name is Alma, and do you have any sherry or brandy in your closet?"

"Yes, I do and I am going for it right now."

"I am so delighted that you have a sense of humor, Madame Sanders," said Alma with a giggle.

"No, I do not feel any humor now. Why are you calling me?"

"Madame, I would like you to know that Eric speaks of you all the time and is devoted to you and wishes to return to his home with you," said Alma.

There was a silence. "When is he coming home?"

"Madame Sanders, would you consider coming to Ambleside and staying a few days here with us and then you and Eric go home together?"

"He isn't wounded is he?"

"No, no, nothing of the sort, my dear. We all thought that it might be a nice end for his vacation and a nice start for you both going home," said Alma.

There was a brief silence and then Martha said in tears, "This is all too good to be true, but how will I pay for it all?"

"I have spoken with your Mr. George at the newspaper and he is handling the whole trip, which we are funding, and you will leave shortly. He will call you with all the details. We are planning a lovely, very informal supper party for you both and it will be a surprise for Eric."

"Oh dear, Eric never has liked surprises. Once we gave him a surprise birthday party and he went upstairs in our house and locked himself in the bathroom," said Martha.

"Do not worry yourself and please know that we all are most fond of Eric and so very much looking forward to meeting you, dear Mrs. Sanders, and all will work out very well."

"Please call me Martha."

"And by all means call me Alma."

"The horoscope was right for once."

"My dear Martha, each day is a mystery and that is what keeps us going."

"You sound like a very nice and generous lady, Alma, and I thank you for this good news." Martha hung up and looked at herself in the mirror hanging over the hall table. She burst into laughter and tears at the same time.

She called her daughter. "Hello Gail, I am about to blow over," said Martha.

"What is the matter, Mom, are you okay?"

"I think I am or else I have had a fantastic dream and am in some sort of daze."

"Mom, just hold the phone for a minute." Norman was home and Gail wanted him to pick up the upstairs phone and listen. "Okay, Mom, what is this all about?"

"I just had a phone call from a lady in England and your Dad has been staying in her house all this time and she wants me to come to England and visit and have supper and then bring him home."

"Mom, this sounds crazy, who is this lady?"

"Her name is Alma," said Martha. "And George from the paper is handling all the arrangements for me to go."

"Mom, call George and get this all straightened out and call us back."

As soon as she knew he would be at the office in the morning, Martha called George and he explained everything to her and said he would arrange all the traveling plans for them both and not to worry about anything. Since George wanted Eric back to work as soon as possible, he suggested that she leave in two weeks, stay three days with Madame Boeld in Ambleside and then bring Eric home.

Martha was beside herself and could hardly believe what was happening. She looked in the mirror and thought she needed to get her hair curled and perhaps buy a new outfit for the trip. She totally forgot to call Gail back. She poured herself a cup of coffee and thought to herself that her waiting was finally over. The phone rang and Gail was calling. "Mom, Norman just spoke with George and all is on the level. I can't believe the whole story and you leave in two weeks. This is all so unbelievable and I am so happy for you, Mom."

"I will tell the library that I will be away for a few days and want to keep the job upon my return. One thing I have learned is that polishing brass, making pies and waiting for Eric to come home after work is not the way I wish to spend my days from now on."

Martha thought about the trip and that she must get a passport very quickly, and a new skirt and a nice dress for Eric's party. She put her head back on the chair and began to laugh until she could hardly breathe.

George called Martha once again and told her all about the flight. He said he had spoken with Madame Boeld again and she informed him that Martha need not take the train because her driver, Nelson, would meet her at the Heathrow airport outside London and take care of everything and drive her from the airport straight on to the house.

Alma was very pleased with her brilliant consideration of the situation, and that the outcome would be a joyous reunion party. Now she had no time to waste. She called Louise and asked to speak with Millicent.

"Hi Almama."

"Now, my dear Millicent, the table arrangements have changed for Eric's party as his wife Martha will be here so there will be eleven at the table instead of ten, which is quite an awkward number. However, it will be a joyous party and most interesting. You are making little place cards for each person, are you not?"

"Yes, I am," said Millicent, "and they will be lovely. Not too large but very colorful with little sketches on each one. Does Uncle Eric know that his wife is coming?"

"No, it will be a surprise party. I have spoken with Martha and she sounds most charming and overwhelmed about the whole trip."

"Oh, Almama, you always have the best ideas and I want to be just like you when I grow up."

"Well, my dear child, always be careful what you wish for."

Chapter Sixty-Three

"Good morning, Madame. Are you perhaps Mr. Eric's wife?" asked Nelson. "Yes, I am Martha Sanders," said Martha with a yawn. "How do you do, Lady Martha," said Nelson with a bow. "Let us pick up your cases and be on our way to Ambleside. Was your trip comfortable?"

"I have never been on an airplane and I was very uneasy. In fact, I have never been away from Altoona except to visit my daughter and her husband and little Norma. I brought pictures of little Norma."

"Well, Madame, it is simply grand that you came to visit and Eric will be overjoyed," said Nelson.

"Eric never gets overjoyed about anything," said Martha with another yawn. "But he better be glad to see me." They collected her luggage and started off to Ambleside. Martha slept. Just before they reached the house, Nelson stopped the car and woke her.

"Where am I?" asked Martha.

"Madame, we are at Madame Boeld's."

"Well, where is Eric?"

"Each morning Eric goes to market and picks out the fruits and vegetables for the day," explained Nelson. "And often he does other errands in town. He should be here shortly." Nelson was nervous about Eric's whereabouts and hoped he was not at the library.

"Well, I would like to meet Alma Boeld and then take a nap if I could."

As the car pulled around the drive, Alma appeared at the front door and stepped down to open the door for Martha. "Welcome to our home, I am Alma and so delighted that you have arrived safely. And you had no trouble meeting up with Nelson and his French beret."

"How do you do, Alma. I am sorry that I am so wiped out from the trip, but I must go to bed for a while if you don't mind," said Martha, who was feeling a bit faint.

"Not at all. Bessie will show you Eric's room and please make yourself comfortable."

Bessie appeared in her starched uniform and curtsied before Martha. Martha didn't know how to respond. They went upstairs and into Eric's room. Martha immediately threw herself upon the bed and clutched the pillow. She began to cry and held the pillow close to her. "Oh, Eric, I love you so much," said Martha, and before Bessie could remove her shoes, Martha was asleep.

Alma was at the bottom of the stairs and Bessie said with a giggle, "She is wiped out, what a peculiar saying."

"They are from America, my dear Bessie, and do not speak the King's English," said Alma, and she went to call Elizabeth. "Yes, it is true and Martha is upstairs resting and Eric has not returned from the market as yet," said Alma.

"I do not know how you manage to create all this and have a supper party too," said Elizabeth.

"I am a bit disturbed as it looks like rain and I do so wish to have cocktails on the terrace so Martha can enjoy our lovely gardens and countryside views."

"Alma, it will never rain on your parade, my dear," said Elizabeth as they hung up.

Eric arrived on the bicycle with all the fruits and vegetables and took them into the kitchen. "Ladies, why are you scurrying around so?" he asked. Bessie and Bertha did not answer. "Well, here are the vegetables and fruit you suggested to buy. Sorry I'm late," said Eric. "I will be off to the library to do my work."

"How long will you be gone?" asked Bertha.

"I will not be long, but I must speak with my office and arrange my trip home."

"You do know that Madame is having a small supper party this evening and you are expected," said Bertha.

"Oh yes, of course. Millicent planned the party and is doing all the place cards. She is such a clever girl and has changed so much since I have been here. See you gals later," said Eric, and rode off on the bicycle.

Bessie had arranged the curtains to darken the room but Martha was awakened in the afternoon by the door opening and hearing "Who are you in my bed?"

"It is me, Eric," said Martha as she jumped out of the bed and threw her arms around him.

Bertha and Bessie were very busy between setting the table and placing all the gifts that Alma had purchased for the guests and doing the preparations in the kitchen. Millicent and Suzanne arrived early. Millicent was wearing a lovely pale blue pinafore and went into the kitchen because she wanted to help Bessie and Bertha.

"I am anxious to see the place cards you made, Millicent dear," said Bertha.

"I have them here on the table. Some are very fragile and frilly. It took me all night to finish them and I never went to bed and it took me forever to get my hair in this fancy twist. I saw a picture of a girl in a magazine and I wanted my hair to look like hers."

"You look as pretty as a picture and your ribbons match your beautiful pinafore," said Bessie with a wink to Bertha. Suzanne asked what she could do to help and she received no response. She began to cry and left the kitchen. Bertha went after her and asked what the matter was. "No one ever asks me to do anything." "Well, I very much need your help with the silverware for the table," said Bertha. "Oh, Bertha, you are my new best friend and I will do anything you tell me to do," said Suzanne as she threw her arms around Bertha's waist.

Alma appeared in a lovely sapphire blue dress with matching shoes. Millicent went up to Alma and said, "We are both in blue and we did not even plan it." Alma smiled and said, "I am most anxious to see your place cards." Millicent placed the cards where Alma told her and Alma brought in the fresh flowers for the middle of the table. "Now, Millicent, you must take notice that the flowers must never be too tall. If they are too tall the guests cannot see each other across the table and no one can carry on a proper conversation."

Bessie and Bertha were a bit confused about what they should wear as they were guests but also cooks. Alma suggested that they wear their church dresses and then put on an apron for the cooking and take the apron off for the party.

Millicent greeted Eric and Martha as they came down the stairs. She curtsied and gave Martha a lovely bunch of flowers, saying, "I am so delighted to meet you, Madame Martha."

Suzanne rushed over to Martha, tripped on the rug and landed in Martha's arms. "Well, isn't this a fine how do you do," exclaimed Alma with a deep laugh as she came upon the scene. "I think we all know each other now, so do let's go onto the terrace so we can relax and enjoy the sunset." Martha was hanging onto Eric's arm and Eric leaned over to give her a kiss on the cheek.

"My, what a glorious home you have, Alma," said Martha. "No wonder Eric is so content here. This terrace is so beautiful and the sunset looks like it is just for us."

Elizabeth arrived just as Alfred came down the stairs and they went out to the terrace. Alma introduced everyone to each other and went over to Suzanne and asked her to come and sit on her lap. Suzanne was thrilled and threw her arms around Alma.

"Suzanne, what a lovely pinafore," said Alfred. "Everyone seems to be in baby blue except you and me, dear Suzanne. I much prefer navy and white and so do you, I see," said Alfred with a broad grin.

"This is an old one of my sister's and I wish it was pink," said Suzanne.

Bessie and Bertha came out with cheeses, biscuits and stuffed olives. They sported white starched aprons over their navy blue church dresses. "Now, we look like a handsome navy group," said Alfred as he began to sing verses from old British Navy songs.

"Were you a navy man, Alfred?" asked Martha.

"I do not think so. Was I a navy man, Alma?" Nelson appeared on the terrace before Alma could answer. "Oh, good evening dear Nelson," said Elizabeth. Nelson wore a navy blue jacket with white trousers.

"Well, it certainly seems that navy blue is the appropriate color for this evening," said Eric, who wore navy pants and a white jacket given to him by Alma.

"Now I am happy to be in navy blue," said Suzanne, and went over to sit on Eric's lap.

Louise arrived a bit late, as she had to close up the library that day. She wore a lovely white lace dress with feathered sleeves. "Doesn't Mum look just like a bride?" said Suzanne. Louise went over to Martha and leaned down to introduce herself and shake her hand.

"I am so very happy to meet you, Louise. You have two beautiful daughters and I am so enjoying them and everyone here," said Martha.

They all went in to supper and Millicent showed each one their place card.

"Nelson dear, please pour the summer wine for us all and I wish to make a toast to Eric and Martha," said Alma, holding back her tears. Alma asked Martha about Altoona and Martha asked Alma about England. Nelson chatted a little with Eric and the girls helped Bessie and Bertha with the plates. Eric finally stood up and thanked Alma for a lovely vacation and then kissed Martha on the cheek. Everyone else stood and raised their glasses to Martha and Eric. Alfred saluted Eric and they sat down.

After supper Alma led everyone back to the terrace. Bessie and Bertha were washing up the dishes after the party and finishing off the wine. They were doing a little jig together when Suzanne came in and asked if she could dance also. The three danced themselves onto the terrace where Alma and Martha were dancing to waltz records. Millicent was sitting on her mother's lap. "This is a special evening, is it not, Mama?" asked Millicent. "Yes, my darling, it is a very special evening for everyone but me." Millicent hugged her mother, put her head on her shoulder and picked up her skirt to wipe her mother's eyes.

"Come on, Mama; let's show off a bit and do a kick dance."

"What is a kick dance, Millie?"

"Hold my hand, Mum, and just do 1, 2, 3, kick your leg in the air."

Millicent and Louise began the kick dance and many joined in, kicking their legs in the air. Nelson had been very quiet all evening. He was deep in thought and had been drinking a lot of the summer wine. When the record stopped, Nelson stood up, raised his glass and said, "I would like to make a toast to my friend and employer, Madame Boeld."

Alma recognized immediately that he was stymied for words and said, "Nelson, I am the one who should be toasting you, my dear friend. Everyone loves and depends on Nelson!"

Alfred changed the record and came back with Angel in his arms. He had put *Der Rosenkavalier* on the Victrola and he began dancing with Angel. "Oh," exclaimed Alma, "Freddie and I always dance to this wonderful waltz, don't we, Freddie?"

"Yes Alma, always."

Eric stood up and reached toward his wife. "Martha, my dear, this will be our new dance together and we will always remember tonight as long as we live," he said, squeezing her hand.

"I want you both to stay here so we can always be a family like this," said Suzanne.

"You are most correct, my dear Suzanne, families are not always related to each other. Families may be created by caring friends all together," said Alma.

"Does that mean we all can be a family forever?" asked Suzanne.

"Yes, it does if you wish it to be," said Alma. Alfred was inviting everyone to go to the cemetery with him in the morning to see the beautiful angel on Margaret's grave.

Chapter Sixty-Four

Martha was overcome with the size of the angel on Margaret's grave. "Oh my, Alfred, you certainly must have idolized her and you must miss her so much."

"She talks to me all the time so it is like she is still here, but she really is in heaven," said Alfred as he placed the flowers from last evening's party table on her grave. Nelson said, "We must be moving on now as Eric and Martha have only a short time here. Millicent, Suzanne and I will take Martha shopping for presents for her family while Eric picks up the vegetables for the day."

"And after we go shopping we are all going on a boat ride around the lake and my Mum is packing a picnic for all of us!" exclaimed Millicent.

"Oh, how lovely," sighed Martha, who was holding Eric's hand.

"Well, you all look a bit done in what with all the day's goings on," said Bertha as everyone came in through the kitchen door. "Oh my, I have never had such a beautiful day in all my life," said Martha as she sat on a kitchen chair. "We shopped and bought lovely sweaters for our daughter and granddaughter and I picked out a warm woolen vest for me to wear when it gets cold in Altoona."

"I bought a key chain with a heart on it for Uncle Eric's keys," said Suzanne.

"And how was the boat ride?" asked Bessie.

"I have never seen such beautiful scenery and it was so quiet and like a beautiful dream and the picnic was perfect and dear Louise is so very charming," Martha said as she took Eric's hand.

"I have prepared some biscuits with jam and some tea for you all, so please go onto the terrace where Madame is waiting for you. Nelson told me that your tickets are all in order for the flight and you that you must be ready to leave by four o'clock in order to arrive at the airport on time," said Bertha.

"We have a late overnight flight back to the USA," said Eric with tears in his eyes.

"Uncle Eric, do not cry. I am always the crybaby," said Suzanne as she rushed into Eric's arms.

"Now, this is a fine how do you do, with Eric and Suzanne crying and Millicent blowing her nose and wiping her eyes and I have tears falling down my old wrinkled face," said Alma as she tried to pour the tea properly.

"Ah, it is tea time," said Alfred, appearing in his plaid pants with a striped shirt. "Freddie, go and make yourself look presentable. Either stripes or plaid, not both," said Alma with a wave to him. "I am presentable," said Alfred as he sat in the large wicker chair and put his bare feet up on the table.

"Please, you must excuse my brother. He was badly wounded in the war and sometimes does not behave properly," said Alma with a fierce glare at him.

"I am not wounded. I just like to do what I want and my sister is too bossy and Margaret says that I am handsome," said Alfred proudly.

"This is no time for antics, Freddie. Now put your feet down. Get up and I will serve the tea."

"I will pass the biscuits and Millie can help serve the tea," said Alfred.

"Please do not call me Millie, Mr. Alfred."

"Oh, you are all so proper and you think that I am a fool and I am not a fool. I like you all and Margaret loves me."

"Well, Alfred," said Martha, "I think you are a very nice gentleman and I am so happy to have met you, and I have enjoyed my visit so much with you and your dear sister and I want to thank you for allowing me to visit in your beautiful home. Oh, I saw by your pet dishes that you also have a cat. My, I mean our cat is called Stormie."

"Well, we hardly ever see little Lucy any more. Angel is the boss," said Alfred with pride.

Bertha appeared with the jam for the biscuits and Bessie brought out a small bottle of sherry. "Who would like a spot of sherry in their tea while we wish Mr. Eric and Madame Martha a safe trip back to Altoona?" asked Bessie.

"We all will have sherry and please join us, Bessie and Bertha, as you are part of this family," said Alma.

Millicent stood up, went over to Eric, gave him a big hug and kissed Martha on the cheek. Alma stood up and made a toast with her teacup, saying, "May you travel safely and return to our home next summer for another and longer visit."

Martha burst into tears and said, "Oh yes, we will and thank you."

Alfred appeared with a pile of presents and put them in front of Martha. Martha opened them to find a lovely picture book from the girls, a pair of knickers and matching socks and shirt for Eric, and lastly a beautiful painting of the view from the terrace at sunset. Alfred sat quietly and said nothing. "Freddie, you did it. It is lovely!" exclaimed Alma, clapping her hands. Everyone clapped and Martha began to cry. Alfred smiled and left the terrace. A few minutes later he could be heard bouncing his ball.

Nelson appeared and asked if their cases were ready to be put in the boot. Martha looked at Eric and said, "I must brush up on the English expressions before next summer."

"Yes, Nelson, we are ready to go home now," said Eric with a big smile and teardrops on his rosy cheeks.

Everyone waved until the car made the turn onto the road. "Now, let's all go back on the terrace and have a good cry and then a nice waltz all together," said Alma, using her tea napkin to wipe her eyes.

"Almama, may Suzanne and I have a spot of sherry in our teacups?"

"I see absolutely no reason why not," said Alma with a smile and tears on her cheeks.

"It has been a wonderful summer, hasn't it Almama?" said Millicent.

"But I wanted Uncle Eric to stay with us and I am sad to see him go away. My Daddy went away too," said Suzanne.

"I will not go away, Suzanne. You can always count on me to be around," said Alfred, who had returned to the terrace with Angel. "Let's all have more tea and put on the waltz records. Tomorrow we will all go for a picnic and a nice swim in the lake."

"For the sake of heaven, Freddie, Angel has devoured all the biscuits and there is jam and cream all over."

"Well, she should have some tea with sherry to wash it all down," said Alfred with a raucous laugh.

"Yes, she should and we all need more tea with sherry to wash our tears away, don't we Almama?" said Millicent.

Chapter Sixty-Five

Nelson delivered Martha and Eric to the airport and wished them a safe voyage home. Nelson decided to drive over to Tony's apartment and pay an unannounced visit. He did not know what he would find at this hour at night but he was anxious to know. Nelson parked and rang the buzzer. He put his beret at an angle, put both hands in his trouser pockets and managed to put on a wicked looking half-smile. He had been practicing this pose and was determined to keep it no matter what happened.

Claudia let him in and announced that Nelson was here. "Oh, Pinky has come up for air and decided to pay us a visit, has he?" asked Tony.

"Yes Tony, it is overdue, and I hope this is not an inconvenient time."

"Nothing is inconvenient for me, I am the miracle man," said Tony. They shared a hug as Tony lifted himself up a bit from the chair. Nelson resumed his posture and the half-grin. "Good God, Pinky, if I did not know it was you, I would swear Errol Flynn was here."

Nelson took a chair and asked where Tony would be most comfortable. "Are you kidding, old chap, comfortable is not in my vocabulary anymore," said Tony.

"I am sorry to hear that, Tony. I have been thinking of you and have called several times but there has been no answer."

"The damn phone is over there and I never make it in time. It needs a longer wire," said Tony.

Claudia and Flora came in from the kitchen and sat next to each other on the small couch, each with a pint of beer. "Hey, girls, how about a pint for me and Pinky?" Flora went into the kitchen and returned with a pint for Tony and one for Nelson.

"So tell me, Pinky, what goes on in the lake country?"

"Quite a bit, actually," said Nelson. He told Tony all about Eric and Martha and the supper party before they departed for the airport. Nelson told him about the girls and how well they were, but of course they missed their Daddy. Tony kept looking out the window and finally said, "I am a loser as a husband, as a friend and most of all as a daddy. I drink too much and forget to take the medicine and do not go to therapy and am pretty disgusted with myself. Claudia and Flora are my closest friends and we have a fine time together, don't we girls?" They nodded and slurped up more beer. "Neither of the broads can cook so we order take-away. I cannot remember the last proper dinner I had." Tony put his hands to his face, sighed, and asked Nelson how his life was going. Nelson said it was as usual.

All sat in silence for a few minutes and Flora turned on the telly. "Oh, this is such a cute program, Pinky, do you watch it? It is all about a bunch of sex-crazy girls and no guys." Flora and Claudia giggled as they snuggled up to each other.

"Tony, do you want your daughters to visit before they start school?" asked Nelson.

Tony looked at Flora and Claudia and then at Nelson. "Pinky, you are a very proper and caring fellow and I am so glad I know you. What do you think I should do?"

"I think you should do all you can to keep up with the girls. It is not about you all the time, Tony," said Nelson.

"When did all that change, dear chap? It is always about me. I am the money maker, I am the man of the family, I am a surviving cripple." Tony twisted in his chair and told Claudia to bring him another pint.

"Well, Tony, give it some thought and call Louise."

"Okay, I will be in touch. Thanks for stopping by."

While driving back to Ambleside, Nelson reviewed his life, and knew that, had his young life been different, he would not be Alma's driver. But he is Alma's driver and that is the way it will be. He was happy with his somewhat uncomplicated life and devoted to Madame. Bessie and Bertha were like family to him. And now he felt a certain responsibility for Millicent and Suzanne. He did not know how to be a father but he knew how to step in and care when needed. He arrived home and knew that it really was his home.

The next morning Nelson rode the bicycle into the village, enjoying the lovely morning air, and picked up all the vegetables for the day. Bertha would make a nice soup. Alma was on the terrace with her coffee and noticed the bicycle in the drive and was startled for a moment that it was Nelson, not Eric. Nelson took the produce into the kitchen for Bertha and Bessie to prepare and went to the terrace.

"Good day, Madame, and how are you feeling this morning?"

"It seems rather quiet without Eric, though he was never around much and certainly never in one's way. I guess I just miss him," said Alma and smiled at Nelson. "At least I can count on you, my dear Nelson, can I not?"

"You can most certainly depend on me, Madame."

"Well, anything new in the village?"

Nelson sat down, looked at Alma and smiled.

"Alright, my lad, out with it, what is on your mind?"

"I saw Louise and a young gentleman walking hand in hand toward the library."

"Oh really, what a scandal and totally overdue," said Alma with a big laugh. She leaned toward Nelson. "Who was he? Was he attractive and how old?"

"He had a mop of curly brown hair with a cap balancing on the top of the curls and he was carrying a paint easel."

"Oh, dear Lord, he sounds Irish. He must be a hungry artist of sorts," said Alma. "What news of Tony?"

There was an awkward silence. "Madame, I will always answer your questions when I can figure out a proper reply," said Nelson.

Alma smiled and nodded. "It will be reassuring when we hear from Eric and Martha."

Nelson gave Alma a reassuring nod and went to the village and purchased a box of Swiss chocolates. He went over to Louise's house. Louise threw her arms around Nelson and said, "I am so glad to see you. I feared I would never see you again after Eric left."

Millicent and Suzanne saw Nelson and came running to him. Nelson gave Louise the chocolates and the girls each took one. Suzanne liked the chocolate-covered cherries and Millicent liked the chewy caramel ones. Louise began to cry and threw her arms around Nelson again.

"Oh, stop this, Mum, you are fine and do not be a crybaby like Suzanne. I am tired of the two of you and if you do not stop all these boo-hoos I will run away."

Nelson suggested that they all sit together on the terrace. Millicent announced that she wished to ride her bike as it was too dreary on the terrace. Suzanne followed Millicent, leaving Louise and Nelson on the terrace. "My, Eric certainly did a grand job of fixing up and leveling the bricks here," said Nelson.

A Fine How Do You Do

"That can be a good metaphor, Nelson. We are now all like bricks and will not cry," said Louise as she pulled up her skirt to wipe her eyes.

"Louise, I only came over to see you because I care about you all," said Nelson.

"Oh, say, do you now, my dear Nelson," said Louise pointing her finger at him. "Do not think for one moment that I do not know what has been going on between you and Tony."

Nelson gave Louise a very stern look, stood up and said, "I hope you all have a very pleasant day." He tipped his cap and said, "I will let myself out." He could hear Louise sniffling and coughing as he departed.

Chapter Sixty-Six

Alfred came into the kitchen and joined Bessie for a cup of tea. "It is such a lovely morning, Alfred, why not take your Angel for a walk?" suggested Bessie. Alfred left the kitchen, put the leash on Angel and walked to the little park by the lake where they both sat down. The air was clear and the water shimmering in the sunshine. Alfred noticed a young couple holding hands and strolling toward him. He recognized Louise, waved and called her name. Louise waved and came over.

"Alfred, this is my friend Jimmy. He is from Dublin and he is an artist," said Louise quite calmly. Jimmy tipped his cap and Alfred began to giggle when he noticed all the red curls. He did not get up and pulled Angel closer to him.

"I am an artist too. Do you paint for food?" asked Alfred.

"I paint because I enjoy it and yes, if they sell, I buy what I need," replied Jimmy politely.

"I never need anything because Alma takes care of me and Angel," said Alfred with a big smile.

"Well, we must be on our way now," said Louise.

They walked along the lake and Jimmy stopped. "Here is a lovely spot for me to rest, smoke me pipe and ponder about the scenery," said Jimmy, giving Louise a little slap on the back.

"See you later," said Louise with a smile, and made her way to the library.

Alfred was practically galloping home with Angel at his heels. "Alma, Alma, where are you?"

"I am on the terrace with the morning post." Alfred went to the terrace pulling Angel on her leash.

"Why are you so out of breath and Angel all tangled up?" asked Alma.

"I saw Louise down by the lake with a Dublin lad who had a mop of red curls and is a painter and they were holding hands."

Alma sat in silence for a moment. "How very interesting," she said. "Bessie, Bertha, come here please." They appeared, drying their hands on their aprons. "How about a little tea party tomorrow? Apparently Louise has found herself a Dublin lad and I think we should meet him for the girls' sake as Alfred says they were holding hands down by the lake."

Bessie and Bertha began to giggle and looked at Alma, who was again looking at the morning post. "Yes, Madame, a little tea party. Would you like us to pop up some of our special popovers?"

"I will call Elizabeth and Louise and of course let's have the girls also. When you see Nelson, ask him to come also," said Alma with her head still in the post.

When Louise arrived home from the library the girls were going through fashion magazines. "Mum, we are all going to tea tomorrow at Almama's. She called and wants Jimmy to come too!"

"Oh, really, tomorrow is it?" Louise threw herself down in a chair and said, "Oh, how I wish Eric was still here."

Jimmy came through the door and noticed Louise in a heap in the chair. "What is up with your Mum, not feeling so swell?"

"She is fine and we are all going to Almama's tomorrow for tea," exclaimed Millicent.

"And who might Almama be?" asked Jimmy.

"Madame Boeld, who lives in the fancy house with Alfred," said Millicent.

Louise and Jimmy looked at each other and both began laughing. "This is a fine how do you do," said Louise between giggles.

"Mum, may we wear our sandals to tea?"

"You do not wish to wear party shoes?"

"Suz does but I am wearing sandals and, by the by, do you have a bra I may borrow?"

"Millie, what in the world has come over you? This is a tea party not a costume party."

The next afternoon, Suzanne saw a good chance to get the front seat in the car as she was ready to go and Millicent was fooling with her hair. Suzanne went down the stairs quietly and out to the front seat. Millicent came and sat in the back. "Almama always sits in the back seat and she looks at herself in the driver's glass. I can see myself in the glass now," bragged Millicent.

Louise came out and sat in the driver's seat. "Jimmy will be here any second now, so do not get restless. Millie, what happened to your lovely hair, did you chop it all off?"

"Heavens no, it is all done up with bows and twists," Millicent said, twisting the end pieces that were straggling.

"Oh, good, here is Jimmy," said Louise. Millicent was most pleased with herself as Jimmy would be sitting next to her. "Well, who do we have here, Miss Cover Girl?" asked Jimmy with a smile. "It is just me, Millicent." "Well, may I take the seat next to you or is it reserved?" asked Jimmy with a big smile.

"Everyone behave and we will be off to Madame Boeld's tea party. Girls, remember not to lick your fingers and take only one canapé at a time."

"Don't worry about me. I know to take me cap off in the house and behave like a proper gentleman," said Jimmy, tipping his cap.

Nelson was at the door to greet them and shook hands with Jimmy. Millicent raced past Nelson and went straight to the terrace where her Almama was sitting. She ran up and gave her a very deep curtsy. "All I can see of you is a mop of ribbons and bows, young lady."

Louise and Suzanne came in and Alma stood and welcomed them. "Madame Boeld, I would like you to meet my friend, Jimmy."

Jimmy put out his hand and Alma smiled as they shook hands. Alma said, "How do you do and welcome to my home. Please sit by me as I wish to be as close to that wonderful red hair as possible. So far we have a mop of ribbons and a crop of red hair. What will be next?" she asked with a laugh.

Alfred arrived dressed in green from head to toe. He was carrying Angel, who wore a large green ribbon around her neck.

"Well, this seems to be turning into a costume party," said Alma. Louise and Millicent looked at each other and Millicent stuck her tongue out at her mother ever so quickly that no one else noticed except Jimmy. Louise looked at Millicent with a stare that meant trouble. Millicent had seen that look many times.

Suzanne came in holding Nelson's hand. "Come over here, you pretty little princess," Alma said to Suzanne. Suzanne put on a big smile and ended up on Alma's lap. Suzanne stuck out her tongue at Millicent but Millicent was gazing at Jimmy.

Elizabeth arrived late as usual and both Nelson and Jimmy offered her their seat. "Elizabeth, take a seat on the chaise and rest your legs," said Alma. Jimmy introduced himself and admired her shawl. "Is it from Ireland?" Elizabeth nodded. "I thought as much," said Jimmy. Elizabeth asked Jimmy all about himself and Jimmy told her about his art studies in Dublin and that he was in Ambleside to do some painting before his classes commenced back home. He told her that he was staying at a public campsite by the lake and many poets and artists were there. He added that he came from a very artistic family and that his mother was an artist and his father a professor at the university. His sister was in London for the holiday and would be returning to Dublin soon also.

Bessie came in with the popovers and Bertha followed with a platter of cucumber rolls.

"I think I will be going into London next week, Jimmy, and would you like a ride to and fro to see your sister?" said Nelson.

Millicent spoke up quickly and asked her Mum if they would be going in also to see their Daddy.

"Yes, I believe so, I am waiting to hear from him to confirm." Nelson said that he had just spoken with Tony and "I should tell you all that he will be expecting you on Tuesday if Madame does not need the car." Alma immediately assured Nelson that she would depend on Alfred on Tuesday. The girls jumped up and down and Jimmy thought the plan was excellent. All the ribbons fell out of Millicent's hair as she was jumping up and down and Angel thought it a fun game to gather them up and chew on them.

As all were preparing to leave, Alma held Millicent's shoulder and asked her to wait. Alma told Louise that Nelson would drive Millicent home.

Millicent was in tears. She knew that Alma was annoyed with her and she tried to fix her hair so it was not such a mess. Alma returned to the terrace and found Millicent on the lounge in tears, her hair all snarled. She was using her skirt for a hankie and her underpants were showing.

"Sit up, young lady, and listen to your Almama."

Millicent sat up and put her hands in her lap, clutching her skirt. "We are going to have a little chat," said Alma, looking directly at Millicent. "Now go into the powder room and pull yourself together."

Millicent was barefoot and looked like a little orphan as she trotted off to the powder room. Tears came to Alma's eyes. Alma suddenly remembered that she had a very handsome leather journal she purchased in London years ago but never used. She knew now what it had been waiting for all these years. She went to her desk and rummaged through the drawers. She found it and clutched it to her bosom. She poured herself a glass of sherry and waited for Millicent.

Millicent appeared and Alma giggled. "You look like the cat who swallowed the canary," she said. Millicent stared at Alma, not really understanding what that meant or how to act.

"Come here, my dear child, and sit by me," Alma said, patting the couch cushion. Millicent sat down and stared at her feet.

"I do not like cucumbers but I do like to go barefoot. It makes me feel free," said Millicent, looking at the floor. "I know why you are upset with me, Almama, and I know I acted badly." She looked up at Alma and hugged her. "Do you still love me?" Millicent asked, with tears rolling down her cheeks.

"Well, my dear child, why don't you tell me why I am upset with you."

"Because I acted badly at the party?" asked Millicent.

"These questions are just the cover of your book. The story inside your book is what we must chat about," said Alma. Millicent looked troubled and confused.

They sat in silence. Alma sipped her sherry and picked up the journal and handed it to Millicent.

"There is no story in this book," said Millicent, flipping through it.

"It is waiting for you to fill the pages. It is a journal and it has been in my desk for many years just waiting for you to give it a home and write all your thoughts in it. It is like a diary," said Alma.

"I used to write obituaries, but I don't anymore," said Millicent, still flipping through the blank pages.

"You can write about your happy times and your troubled times and what you want for Christmas and how much you miss your Daddy and what makes you angry and about Jimmy and whatever else you want. A journal is like a friend who keeps all your secrets," said Alma, and put her arm around Millicent's shoulder.

Millicent smiled and hugged her new journal. "Almama, you are my best friend and my journal is my second best friend."

Nelson drove Millicent home and Louise was waiting for her in the kitchen. "I am sorry I caused trouble, Mum." Louise smiled as she came over and gave her a hug. Millicent gave her Mum a kiss and scampered upstairs with her journal clutched close to her. Nelson was still standing in the kitchen. Louise put her head in her hands. She decided to call Tony and tell him that the girls would be there on Tuesday. She dialed his number. "Is Tony there?"

"Just a sec. Tony, some babe on the wire for you," said Flora. Louise abruptly dropped the phone and hung up, put her head in her hands and ran over to Nelson in tears.

"Louise, if you wish, I will call Tony and confirm Tuesday, but I think it best if you try again," Nelson suggested.

"I think it best if Millie calls," Louise said. "Very well," Nelson said, tipping his cap.

The next morning, Millicent and Suzanne were out riding the new bikes Tony had ordered for them. "Hi, girls, some snappy new wheels have you now?" said Jimmy as he parked his bike.

"Yes, they are from our Daddy. He lives in London so you do not know him," said Suzanne.

"I talked to him this morning and we will all be going into London on Tuesday so maybe you will meet him. He is a cripple," said Millicent as she stepped up her speed. She made a figure-eight and ended up at Jimmy's feet.

"Wow, girl, you are a daredevil. You almost knocked me over," yelled Jimmy.

"But I didn't," said Millicent proudly as she pedaled down the road. Suzanne pedaled as fast as she could but could not catch up to Millicent.

"Yes, Pinky, Millie called and she sounds so grown-up. We will meet you at the aquarium in the London Zoo around three o'clock. It will be a long day for you and the girls all in one day. You will not be able to stay very long but it will be fine. Now, who is this fellow from Ireland who is coming along?"

"He is a friend of Louise's who is coming to meet his sister who is in London for the summer."

"Well, I suppose I will have to bring Flora and Claudia. I cannot get around without them. I will have to get them some appropriate clothes. Actually all their attire is zoo-appropriate," Tony said with a big laugh.

"It will be good to see you, Tony," said Nelson. "Right on, old chap, see you Tuesday."

Nelson sat quietly and reassured himself that Tony would no longer be a part of his life. He took the car and drove to the lake. The weather had turned cooler and the lake appeared darker.

Chapter Sixty-Seven

"Why didn't you tell me you were going to the zoo, Nelson?" asked Alfred. "I am just dropping off the girls to be with their father." "You mean Tony, don't you?" "Yes, Tony is their father," answered Nelson. "Well, I do not want to go and I hope that a lion attacks him and that they cannot save him," said Alfred, stamping his foot.

"Mr. Alfred, you do know that he is rather crippled now and his life has very much changed and he is no longer a financial threat to you or Madame," said Nelson sternly.

"I will go to the zoo another time," said Alfred, turning his back on Nelson.

Nelson went into the kitchen and found Bessie and Bertha having a cup of tea. "My timing is good, I see, may I join you lovelies?"

"Of course you may. We haven't had a tea time together recently and we have missed it, haven't we, Bessie?"

"Most certainly, we have. Sit yourself down and tell us what is new," said Bessie.

"I am taking the girls into London on Tuesday to see their father and I will go to the Tate for an hour while they are visiting. It will be a long day, as we are not staying over."

Bessie and Bertha looked at each other. Nelson smiled at them and they smiled back. "You have a good life here and Madame depends on us all," said Bertha.

"Yes, she does, and I am thankful for my job," said Nelson.

"Do you think you could gather the fresh produce every morning as Mr. Eric used to do?"

"Yes, surely. Of course I will do that."

"I think we all miss Mr. Eric more than we realized," said Bessie. "Do you think he will come for a visit next summer with his wife? I liked her very much."

"Yes, I do," said Nelson. "I feel quite sure they will return for a visit."

"It has been quite a summer with all the comings and goings," said Bertha.

Nelson nodded and went to wash the car for Tuesday's trip. He would simply wear proper afternoon clothes and his beret.

On Tuesday, Elizabeth collected Alma and Alfred and went, as they had planned, on the boat cruise around the lake. They loved this little excursion and were enchanted by all the scenery they knew so well. At one point Alfred began to jump up and down and called for Alma and Elizabeth to come to the railing. "Look, Alma, we can see the top of the angel on Margaret's grave. Oh, how wonderful this is," Alfred cried out and ran all around the boat telling the passengers about the angel and Margaret. Alma pulled her large straw hat down over her face, took Elizabeth's arm and went inside the cabin.

Nelson collected the girls and Jimmy and drove to the zoo in London. "Can my Daddy walk yet?" Suzanne asked Nelson.

"Suz, we all know he is a cripple, isn't he, Nelson?" asked Millicent.

"Why is he a cripple?" asked Jimmy.

Nelson cleared his throat and said, "Tony was in a bad car accident and most fortunately he survived the crash. His legs were severely damaged and he did not fully recover."

"You were with him, weren't you Nelson? Mum told me that you were with him," said Millicent.

"Yes, I was with him," said Nelson. There was silence in the car for several minutes.

"I am so looking forward to having you all meet my sister, Kathleen. She has brighter red hair than I do," Jimmy said with a laugh.

More silence followed. Millicent was very aware of the uncomfortable social atmosphere, but did not know what to do to fix it. She finally said, "When we meet, why don't we all make a circle and say our name and what we like to do. That is what we do in school," said Millicent.

"That is a grand idea. Do you all know that a circle means friendship?" asked Jimmy.

"Yes, of course we all know that," said Millicent. "And I cannot wait to meet Kathleen and see my Daddy."

"How will Daddy get in the circle?" asked Suzanne.

"We will all help each other, do not worry," said Nelson and sped up the car and took a deep breath. He could see Millicent staring at him in the rear-view mirror.

"I see Kathleen. She is talking to someone in a wheelchair and I'll bet that he is your Daddy!" said Jimmy.

"Oh, I see them too. Do let us out and you park the car, Nelson," said Millicent.

"Yes, Mistress Millicent, I will do so," answered Nelson with a grin. He could see that Millicent was learning a great deal from Madame. The girls ran up to their father and threw their arms around him and buried their faces in his lap. Tony's eyes were full of tears and he threw his arms around their necks. "Oh, my beautiful babies, I have missed you so much. Stand up and let me see you."

The girls stood up and Tony gasped. "I think of you both all the time," he said with tears in his eyes. "And you have gone and grown up on me."

Jimmy introduced himself to Tony and gave his sister, Kathleen, a big hug.

"Now we are going to make a big circle and all hold hands," Millicent said, "because we are all new friends."

"Here comes Nelson," said Tony. Nelson held hands and Tony said, "Now our circle is complete." Suzanne burst into tears and said, "No, my Mum is not here."

Tony did not want Claudia and Flora to stay, so Nelson dropped them off at Tony's home and drove on to the Tate. It was a cool day at the zoo and the animals were all in their outside areas. Jimmy found a good spot to sketch and Kathleen took lots of pictures of the animals and of the girls with their father.

Claudia and Flora appeared at the entrance of the zoo at five o'clock as Tony had requested. Tony explained to Millicent and Suzanne that his flat was being painted and cloths were piled and hanging everywhere but the next time it would be freshened and ready for them to spend the night again. Jimmy was pleased with his sketches and Kathleen said she had used two rolls of film. Suzanne had tripped over a silly rock in the path and was riding piggyback on Jimmy, much to Tony's chagrin. Jimmy put Suzanne down and treated everyone to scoops of ice. The girls watched Flora and Claudia push their Daddy in the chair down the street. Tony did not turn around.

When Nelson arrived with the car, Millicent jumped into the back seat and arranged herself so she could see herself clearly in the driver's mirror. Suzanne wanted to have the front seat next to Nelson. Jimmy had decided to stay in London with his sister and said he would phone if he planned to return to Ambleside. Nelson was rather annoyed that he did not get enough time at the Tate galleries.

Nelson was very quiet while driving the girls back from London but Suzanne spoke up. "Nelson, do you think our Daddy will come home soon?" Millicent could see that Nelson was looking in the car mirror and straight at her.

"Suz, you know that Mum said he would not be coming home and he has that pretty room for us in his new home, isn't that right, Nelson?"

"Yes, I do believe that is the arrangement," said Nelson with thoughts of his own disturbing boyhood.

Millicent could sense that this conversation was uncomfortable for all and she must come up with another subject. "Nelson, do you think that little Lucy will ever come home?"

"Well, that is an interesting question and I have asked myself that many times since she ran off. She often came home to my apartment after a night of hunting and brought me a mouse or two, but this time I have not seen her, though I thought I heard her several times and I went down my stairs very quietly, listened and stayed very still, but I never saw her."

"Oh, this is like a mystery story," said Suzanne, clapping her hands.

"I do hope I will not have to write an obituary for dear little Lucy," said Millicent. Suzanne began to cry and Millicent told her to "get a grip."

"So you are taking up American expressions, are you dear Millie?" Nelson asked. Millicent and Nelson laughed. Suzanne did not laugh, and asked, "But Nelson, do you think that little Lucy will come home?"

"Suzanne, I truly do not know, so from time to time we just have to wait and see and hope."

Louise was waiting up for the girls and asked Nelson if he cared to come in for a cup of tea. Nelson declined. The girls hugged their mother. "We missed you today, Mum. We made a circle and you were not there. A circle will never be complete without you," said Millicent, hugging Louise.

"Yes," said Suzanne. "It was a crooked circle."

"Tomorrow is a big day for you girls. You must go to school and gather up the new books that I bought for you. All the children will be there and they are having a picnic by the lake for all of you."

"Does this mean that the summer is over?" asked Suzanne.

"Yes, now back to work!" said Louise. The three of them made a little circle, hugged each other and went off to bed.

The next day, Millicent bicycled to Alma's after collecting her new books at school. "Almama, are you here?"

"Yes, out here on the terrace, just having a little catnap."

Millicent showed Alma her new books. "I never much fancied all my school books. My life taught me more than any school book," said Alma.

Alfred appeared with Angel in his arms.

"Is Angel sick?" asked Millicent.

"No, no. She just likes to be in my arms," said Alfred.

"I am so glad you have little Angel, Freddie. She reminds me of my little Sophie."

Millicent said, "Do you remember when little Sophie made the puddles on the coach train when we first met you, Almama, and our party shoes were all wet?"

"I most certainly do. That is when we met Eric on the train. My oh my, that seems just ages ago," said Alma.

"Why didn't you like your school books, Almama?"

"Well, it was a very difficult and upsetting time in Germany when I was young and the war was on."

"We do not speak of it at all, do we Alma?" Alfred said.

"No, we do not, Freddie."

"Do you think we could go back to Oberammergau someday and see our chalet and the pensione, Alma?" asked Alfred.

"Perhaps someday, Freddie," said Alma with a trembling voice. She rang for Bessie. "Tea time, Madame?" "Yes, and thank you Bessie," said Alma, her voice still unsteady. She wiped her eyes and said, "Now let us look at your books, Millicent."

"I was afraid you were going to call me Millie and I do not like to be called Millie."

"And I do not like to be called Freddie," said Alfred.

"For the sake of heaven, you have always been Freddie to me," said Alma with surprise.

"I am taking Angel to the cemetery to visit my Margaret," announced Alfred as he left abruptly. Alfred bumped into Nelson and knocked him down as he went out the door in such a rush. Nelson righted himself, brushed off his trousers and called out: "Madame, it is Nelson, may I come in with a surprise?"

"Of course. What is the surprise?" asked Alma as Nelson appeared on the terrace. "It is a letter in the post from Eric," said Nelson, still short of breath. Millicent jumped up and ran toward Nelson. "Is it for me?" asked Millicent.

"I would guess that it is for all of us," said Nelson, "but it is addressed to Madame."

"Oh, how lovely. Bessie, do go and fetch Bertha. I hope it is not bad news," said Alma as she opened the letter and began to read it to herself. She wanted to be sure it was good news before sharing it. Everyone sat quietly until Alma put the letter down.

"It is wonderful news. Both Eric and Martha are fine. Eric is happy to be back in Atlanta." Nelson interrupted gently with, "Altoona, Madame."

"Martha," Alma continued, "likes her job at the library. Eric says the weather is cool and they have a lovely early Fall season

A Fine How Do You Do

and the trees are turning all shades of red and brown. Their daughter, Gail, is having another baby in February and they will send pictures. He hopes we are all well and says to give his regards to everyone. He doesn't say anything about a visit to see us but I shall write him and invite them once again to visit next summer," exclaimed Alma.

"And Madame, do ask him to bring his daughter and her new baby too? Bertha and I love babies and we will take care of the wee one."

Alma sat with a large grin on her face and said, "Bertha, do I still have some of that lovely cashmere wool?"

"I was going through that bureau last month and I do think I saw some of it. It is a lovely baby blue," said Bertha.

"But suppose it is a girl?" asked Millicent.

"It will be a British blue blanket appropriate for any sort of baby," said Alma with a smile and a clap of her hands. "Now, let's all have a cup of tea."

"I do not want tea and I have to go home now," said Millicent as she picked up her books, ran out of the house and rode her bicycle home in tears. Everyone looked at Alma and did not say a word.

"She will get over it and realize that life is not always about her. She is a very smart, most sensitive child and is learning about life quite quickly."

Chapter Sixty-Eight

Nelson drove Alma into London early on Thursday morning for two doctor appointments and had called Tony to suggest a lunch together. He offered to pick him up, as Nelson preferred not to have Claudia and Flora along.

"Thank you, Nelson," said Alma as she stepped out of the car. "It is fortunate that my dentist and my bone doctor are side by side, so go off and enjoy yourself and I will meet you right back here in two hours. My hat shop is across the street, so if I am finished a bit early, I will be there keeping an eye out for you and do not bother to give Mr. Tony Smythe my regards," said Alma with her well-known twinkle of eye.

"Yes, Madame," said Nelson with a bit of a smile. Nelson thought that Alma was one of the most interesting people he had ever known and he was truly devoted to her.

Nelson drove to Tony's and spotted Tony in his wheelchair in front of his flat. Claudia and Flora were on either side of him. They all waved at Nelson and Nelson honked several times. The girls put Tony in the back seat and the chair in the front with Nelson and returned to the flat.

"Well, old chap, nice to see you again, and it seems my chair is taking my place."

"So where would you like to lunch, Tony?" asked Nelson.

"Right up here at the corner. They know me there and I keep a running tab. It is the only kind of running I can do these days," Tony said with a chuckle.

"You haven't lost your humor, old chap."

"Yes, I actually have. I am very depressed."

"Let's park and get you in the chair and then we will have a couple of lagers together for old time," said Nelson.

"Mike will come out and help me while you park," said Tony.

Tony knew all the chaps at the bar. "Meet my old pal, Nelson, he is the rotten chap who caused my accident," said Tony with a wicked laugh.

"Welcome to the infirmary. We all have aches and pains and bore each other to death with our woes and befores, because we have no futures," said Sam, who was legless and very slim.

"Do you all play cards, backgammon or chess?" asked Nelson. They all looked at each other.

"Mike told us no gambling in his shoppe, so we just sit and see how many lagers we can put away," said Robert, who was dressed handsomely in a white collared shirt, his school tie and the Eton school emblem on his blazer.

Tony shouted out, "Nelson is really a good chap and we are very close friends so I am going to ask him to be my best man when I marry Claudia. The rest of you can all be ushers."

"So you really are going to tie the knot again, you clever devil?" asked Mike.

Nelson simply stared at Tony, who was purposely avoiding eye contact. "Yes, I have to be a gentleman and do my duty. She has a baby arriving in January," said Tony, finally looking at Nelson.

"Maybe Flora's the daddy," said Mike, and everyone burst out in laughter except Nelson.

There was a quiet spell and another lager and lime was ordered for everyone. "Just put it on my tab," said Tony.

"Tony, would you mind if the two of us moved over to that booth so we could have a private conversation?" asked Nelson.

"Sure thing, mate, give me a shove over there and I can slip into the booth. Pardon us boys, I think I am going to get a scolding from my best man."

Nelson and Tony sat on opposite sides of the table. "This is a bit of a messy situation, my friend," said Nelson.

"Nelson, do not ever worry about me and messy situations. I can climb out of most anything, even on one leg," bragged Tony.

"What will you tell the girls?"

"Absolutely nothing, of course."

"Tony, I cannot be your best man. I cannot do that. No, I just cannot do that," Nelson said, looking Tony in the eyes.

"Well, you would have had a nice gold stick pin. That is what I am giving all the men in the wedding party," said Tony with a snicker.

"As you might say, you know what you can do with that gold stick pin," said Nelson.

"Oh, come on old boy, be a sport just for a few hours. Mike has a friend who is licensed to perform a legal marriage, so he will be here and it will be a crazy party right here at Mike's place, right here!"

"No, Tony, I cannot do this. I wish I could say yes, but I cannot," said Nelson. "I am going to have to go now, Tony. Madame will be waiting for me. I can take the wheelchair out of the car and you can stay on," said Nelson.

Tony nodded and put his head in his hands. "You are a good man, Nelson. Will you keep in touch with me?"

Nelson nodded and blew a kiss to Tony as he left. Tony's head stayed in his hands.

"Hey, man, get over here and join the party," said Mike as he came over to help Tony. "Bear up, old chap. It will all work out."

"How many lives does a cat have, Mike?" asked Tony with tears in his eyes.

Nelson met Alma, took the two hatboxes from her and said, "Some luck at the haberdashery, I see, Madame."

"Yes and all good news from the doctors, too, and how about you?"

"Not so good, thank you anyway," replied Nelson.

They were both quiet for a spell and Alma decided to break the silence. "Do you want to talk about it, Nelson?"

"I do not know what to say. It is not pleasant news, Madame."

"Nelson, most of my life has been battling bad news and more won't hurt me at all, but only if you wish to tell me."

There was another quiet spell and finally Nelson burst out: "Tony is getting married and he wanted me to be his best man, but I declined."

"Did you say that thief is getting married? Pray tell who in their right mind would marry him. Has he captured some wealthy woman he can pilfer?" asked Alma.

"No, nothing like that. He has two lady caretakers and one of them is expecting his baby."

"Oh, dear lord, what a fine how do you do he has created now," declared Alma with a raucous laugh. "Of course you cannot be a witness to such behavior," said Alma, shaking her head. "What in the world is he going to tell his girls and Louise?"

"He says he is not going to tell them. So this news must always be kept between you and me, Madame," said Nelson, looking at Alma in the driver's mirror.

"You have my word, Nelson. I shall never speak a word of it to anyone."

The ride home to Ambleside was otherwise quiet with the exception of Alma describing her two new Fall hats. When they arrived home it was dark.

"Would you care to come in and have a brandy and some biscuits? You have had an appalling day."

"Thank you, Madame, that is most thoughtful of you, and I would welcome a touch of brandy."

They both settled in on the terrace. Alma observed, "The weather is much cooler and we can really enjoy it out here with the nice clear air now. I sometimes wish I lived in London but it is so very peaceful here and the scurrying about in London is a bit frantic. Are you happy here, Nelson?"

"Yes, I can answer that thoughtful question without thinking. I am very happy and content here, Madame, and this is truly the only home I have ever known," Nelson said with a smile.

"I am honored that you feel that way and I hope you will consider this your home for as long as you wish."

"That is very reassuring, Madame, and I thank you."

Alma heard the ringing of the phone and raced to answer it but stumbled over the throw rug, landing on her elbow and, fortunately, was none the worse for it. "Nelson, that little rug has been a bother for years and I am not the first to trip over it. It was a blessing that I did not hurt myself and it is a warning to remove it. It is a lovely needlepoint rug made in France and quite old now and if you would like it in your apartment, please do me the favor of taking it for your own."

"I would be honored to have it and also think it best to remove it from here. I will be turning in now, Madame."

"Good night, Nelson. You acted very properly today and do not let that scoundrel bother you, ever again!"

"Yes, Madame, it is a most unfortunate situation." Nelson went up the stairs to his apartment and put the rug down on the floor. He decided it most certainly added a bit of class to his humble abode.

The phone rang in the morning and Alma answered. "Almama, it is me, Millicent, calling again. I called late last night but you were not home."

"Of course it is you, no one else calls me Almama. How are you today, dear child. Have you stopped pouting?"

"Yes, and my Mum says that I should stop and think before I do things that I regret later," said Millicent.

"You have a very kind and smart Mum, my dear."

"May I bring my books over for you to look at?" asked Millicent.

"Let me muse over this for a minute. Now, when do your school classes start?"

"On Monday, and I am upset about that too," whined Millicent.

"No whining now. Why are you upset about that? I thought you enjoyed learning and being with all your schoolmates," said Alma.

"They elected me to be president of my class for this year and I will let them down the very first day."

"Why in the name of heaven would that happen?"

"Because, on the first day we always have to stand up and talk about something special we did over the summer. I didn't do anything special, so I will have to just sit there and look dumb and poor," whined Millicent once again.

"Tomorrow we will take the coach train into London and I will plan a very interesting day for us. Now, no funny business with your hair all piled up and falling down. Wear your party shoes and not those sandals," ordered Alma.

"What will we do in London? I do not want to visit my Daddy."

"Neither do I," said Alma. "We will drop off one of my new Fall hats at the haberdasher's to have some of my old feathers put on it and then go to the Tate galleries. We will have a little lunch at The Ritz and then amble over to Westminster Abbey. How does all this sound to you?"

"Oh just wonderful, Almama,"

"Nelson will take us to the coach train. You must be ready by seven o' clock in the morning so that we will not miss the train."

"I will wear my party dress and bring my new red pocketbook and borrow some white gloves from Mum," said Millicent.

"Grand, we have a plan. No more whining. A girl who is president of her class never whines. Do not forget to bring a small writing tablet so you may take notes for your little story about your summer. Also, do not pile your hair all upon your head."

"What will you wear, Almama?" asked Millicent.

"Anything hanging in my closet that does not need new buttons. And I'll wear a handsome hat. London will not recognize me unless I have a feathered chapeau on my head."

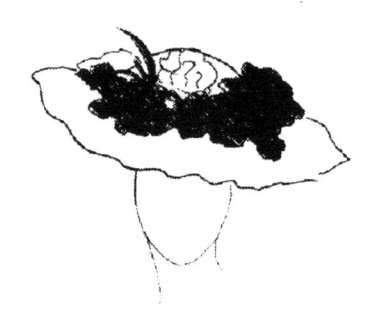

Chapter Sixty-Nine

Nelson took Alma and Millicent to the train. Alma looked stunning in a beige fitted suit, a green felt hat with large orange and brown feathers, beige gloves and a handsome alligator pocketbook. She slung a Hermes green silk scarf around her neck. Millicent wore a pretty blue dress with a white jacket, white socks and her party shoes. She was carrying her new red pocketbook. They waved good-bye to Nelson through the window.

"I have the writing tablet in my new red pocketbook," said Millicent.

"Are you ready for a wonderful, educational and enjoyable day in London?" asked Alma.

"Oh yes, I did not sleep a wink I was so excited!" exclaimed Millicent.

Millicent slept on the train and Alma had a catnap. When they arrived in London, they took a cab straight off to Alma's hat maker and then on to to the Tate.

"Almama, I have never been in a place like this. It is so big and so quiet," whispered Millicent.

"Some of the art goes back to the 1500s," said Alma. They strolled through the galleries and Alma explained everything to Millicent. "I liked the picture of the lake the best because it reminds me of our lake and second best I liked the beautiful lady with a long white dress sitting in a park, because I want to look like her," said Millicent. "Ah yes, they were painted by Monet. He was a French Impressionist painter. Everyone loves Monet's painting," said Alma. "I am going to write this all down when we are at lunch," said Millicent with a bright smile to Alma. Alma went over to the little shop and purchased a booklet about Monet and they strolled to The Ritz for lunch.

Millicent ordered an avocado stuffed with chicken salad for lunch and a large strawberry sundae for her dessert. Alma decided just to have coffee and a croque monsieur sandwich.

"I am stuffed," announced Millicent.

"You must not say you are stuffed. Say you are sufficiently sufficed," said Alma.

"Is that what proper ladies say?" asked Millicent.

"Yes, if they are truly proper," Alma bragged with a wink.

"This is a fancy hotel, isn't it, Almama?"

"Yes, it is a lovely spot." Alma looked at her watch and said, "We will come back another day and go to Westminster Abbey. We took a long time at the Tate and we do not want to miss the coach train. We will hail a cab and go straight on to the station." She took Millicent's hand. Millicent looked up at Alma with a big smile and squeezed her hand. Alma squeezed her hand back.

"This is the best day of my whole life," said Millicent.

"We shall have many days like this discovering all sorts of interesting places and things. I hope to take you to Paris before I become too decrepit to bounce around traveling. I have not been to Paris in quite a few years," said Alma.

"Oh, Almama, I will be a perfect little lady and will not behave badly ever again," said Millicent.

"For the sake of heaven, my dear child, no one can keep a promise like that."

"Mum is right, I should think before I speak. Sometimes I get carried away with myself. My teacher from last year told me that in front of the whole class," said Millicent meekly.

"Well, it stuck like plaster with you, didn't it?" asked Alma with a wink. "We are first in the queue now and here comes a cab. Take my hand as I do not want to lose you."

They arrived at the station and boarded the train. Alma had done this so many times, but usually alone. "We had a most interesting day, did we not?" Alma asked.

"It is the best day of my life. Even better than my birthday party," exclaimed Millicent and gave Alma a big hug before they sat down in the coach.

Alma removed her hat and put it on the overhead shelf, being very careful not to bend the feathers. She sat by the window opposite Millicent, who immediately started to write in her tablet.

"Almama, remember the journal you gave me?"

"Yes, what about it?"

"It is my best friend. But you are really my best friend too. I tell the journal things that I cannot say out loud."

"The train does not seem too crowded and perhaps we will have the compartment all to ourselves," said Alma. Millicent did not answer, as she was very busy writing in the tablet about her day. The conductor called "All aboard who are coming aboard" several times and the engines started.

"How pleasant to have our own compartment, isn't it?" said Alma, looking out the window at those waiting for the local train.

Alma heard a deep voice say, "I am sorry that I must disappoint you, as I have a ticket for this compartment also." Alma looked up and saw a distinguished-looking gentleman with a striped suit and vest. His shoes had just been polished and his walking stick was a fine one with gold initials on the handle. The gentleman looked at Alma and bowed, thinking to himself that he had never seen such beautiful blue eyes. He put out his hand, having removed his grey suede glove. "How do you do, Madame, I am Sir Robert Wentworth from Oxford."

"I am Alma Boeld from Ambleside," Alma said shaking his hand.

"And this lovely young lady must be your granddaughter, n'estce pas?"

"Yes, she is a lovely young lady, however we are not related by blood." Millicent looked quickly at Alma. "I am Millicent Smythe and Madame Boeld is my best friend. We have been to the Tate and we lunched at The Ritz," said Millicent with glee.

"Boeld, did you say?" Sir Robert said he had recently discovered that at least one member of the Boeld family lived in Ambleside but had not been able to secure much information about them. Could this chance encounter have brought him to the very family he sought?

"Yes," answered Alma. "I am originally from Bavaria, Oberammergau to be exact."

"My, this is a most extraordinary coincidence," exclaimed Sir Robert. "I have been doing research on the war and I knew an Alfred Boeld in my regiment. He actually saved my life by dragging me, after I was hit, to a safe Allied zone. We were both forced to fight for the Nazis, but most of us were supporting the British, though in Nazi uniforms. Life was very tenuous and it was not until December of 1941, when the USA joined forces, that we had hopes of stamping out the Nazis. You cannot imagine what bedlam went on in those years."

"Alfred Boeld is my brother," said Alma, turning away to look out the window.

"Do you live in England and return to Bavaria from time to time?" inquired Sir Robert.

"Alfred and I live in Ambleside and we hardly ever discuss the war. Alfred was badly wounded and has never fully recovered. I worked with the Allies in Munich and Berlin. We lost our younger brother, William, during the early part of the war. My brother Alfred is very fragile. What exactly do you want from him?"

"I would like to thank him and thought he might have some information I could use for my book."

"As I said, we do not discuss the war and I truly doubt that it would be healthy for my brother to bring up his memories of the war. So that is that, Sir Robert Wentworth," said Alma, turning to look out the window once again.

Alma did not have a good feeling about this gentleman. Millicent was so busy writing in her tablet that she appeared unaware of the conversation. Sir Robert's eyes met Alma's from time to time during the ride, but not another word was spoken. He was fascinated by Alma and her beautiful blue eyes and her obvious protection of her brother.

Nelson met the train and Alma and Millicent immediately went to the car. "Shall we say goodbye to the nice man, Almama?"

"It is not necessary," said Alma. Sir Robert came running toward the car. He was holding up Alma's new hat. "Almama, he has your new hat. You left it on the train." Nelson stopped the car and retrieved the hat.

"Shouldn't we say thank-you to him, Almama?"

"Yes, we probably should, but one 'how do you do' to him is quite sufficient. Nelson, please drive me straight home after delivering Millicent to her mother. I want to have a quiet dinner with Freddie this evening," said Alma.

Millicent hugged Alma and jumped out of the car when she arrived home. She turned and blew a kiss to Alma and ran in the house. She was so anxious to tell her Mum and Suzanne all about her day and she would finish writing in the tablet about the Tate and The Ritz.

Alma went straight to Alfred and told him about Sir Robert Wentworth and not to speak with him, as all he was after was some war gossip and Alfred must not take his phone calls should he call. She told Bessie and Bertha the happenings and they understood the situation.

Alma did some thinking and decided that this would be a grand time to go to visit Oberammergau. She knew she must protect Freddie from people like Sir Robert, and since most of the summer tourists would have cleared out, the roads would be quite clear and it would be a fine time to go.

Alfred was excited about the trip, but disappointed that Alma would not let him take Angel. Bessie assured him that Angel would be fine at home. Alma called Elizabeth and Millicent about the little trip, saying she and Alfred would be away perhaps for a week. Fortunately, their passports were up to date and they left for Bavaria the next morning.

They booked a flight from London and rented a sedan in Munich, and Alfred drove to Oberammergau. Alfred began to cry when they reached the Bavarian Alps and kept clapping his hands. Alma continually asked him to keep his hands on the wheel. He could not wait to get out of the car when they reached their old home.

They spent five days in Oberammergau and stayed at a pensione that used to belong to Alma's aunt. Alfred was so happy eating in the square with all the accordion polka music. Most often he danced all by himself but occasionally with Alma. They visited with old friends and heard many war stories. Some of the same people who had spat at her when she returned home after the war ended were now pleased to see her again. Many friends did not survive and Alma cried when hearing some of the stories. No one mentioned or asked about her own war years. When Alfred and Alma departed, the townspeople gathered in the square and brought sandwiches, beer and flowers. Alma and Alfred waved to the crowds in the square as they drove away and Alma promised to return soon.

Alfred drove to the airport, whistling most of the time, but Alma did not tell him to stop even though it was giving her a headache. "Alma, how come there are no flowers in the window boxes anymore? We always had flowers," asked Alfred.

"Things change, as you know, Freddie, and nothing stays the same," said Alma.

"No, nothing stays the same except you."

"Oh, for the sake of heaven, Freddie, I am not young anymore, years pass by and time goes on and so does life and things change all the time," said Alma with a glance and a smile toward her brother.

"I know," said Alfred. "And Margaret is not really here anymore. She is alive with me though and she talks to me all the time and tells me to put my vest on or reminds me to brush my teeth," said Alfred very proudly.

"Freddie, life is only what you can make of it and we all do our best and you are most fortunate to have Margaret so close to you," Alma said reassuringly. "Now, I am looking at the map and we should be in Munich very soon. And then we get on the airplane and then Nelson will meet us.

"I wonder if he will bring Angel to greet us," said Alfred.

"We will have to wait and see."

"Life is a wait and see game, isn't it, Alma?"

"Yes, Freddie it is at times."

"Alma, I am so glad we went home. I feel much better and maybe I should get a job and help out around our gardens," said Alfred.

"Freddie, you could take on the responsibility of choosing the vegetables and fruit every morning and bringing them back to the kitchen. Eric used to do that, remember?"

"Yes, Angel and I will do that. I would like to put up some window boxes with flowers."

"Such a fine idea, Freddie!" said Alma, smiling at her brother.

Nelson met them at Heathrow and drove them home. Both Alma and Alfred slept until they pulled into the driveway. Bessie and Bertha had waited up for them and had soup and biscuits ready. "Do tell us about Oberammergau, Alfred," asked Bertha. "I lived there as a boy and I would like more soup," said Alfred. He drank more soup, picked up Angel, gave Alma a kiss on the cheek and went off to bed.

"He actually enjoyed the little sojourn and laughed and danced and seemed like a boy again," said Alma to Bessie and Bertha.

"The trip was grand for you both and to be just the two of you was very nice, wasn't it Madame?"

"Yes, it was, I am glad we went. Now tell me of any news here," said Alma.

Bertha and Bessie looked at one another and finally Bertha said, "That Sir Robert Wentworth you told us about kept calling and asking for you."

Alma's back straightened up. "What did he have to say? I did not fancy him the minute he entered our coach car," she said with defiance.

"We told Nelson about it," said Bertha, "and he was upset and said that it all seemed very suspicious, so he called the police. The police said that if he calls again to have him come to the house for tea. He did call again shortly and Bessie told him he was invited for tea at four and then I called the police to tell them. When he came to the front door we both went to let him in. He was very elegant and had a handsome walking stick. The two policemen had come earlier, in regular clothes, and were sitting on the terrace with their teacups waiting for his arrival. Nelson kept out of sight in the kitchen and Bessie and I hid in the dining room and we could hear everything. The police brought pictures of him taken in St. Tropez and Baden-Baden and said he had three passports with all different names. They took him away in handcuffs and that is all we know."

"Oh, my dear Bessie and Bertha, what a fine how do you do I left for you and no one was here but Nelson," said Alma.

"Little Angel came out of the kitchen and barked her head off at him when the police took him away. She knew he was not a proper person," said Bessie. Alma began to laugh hysterically. Bessie and Bertha clapped their hands. Nelson came in and said, "I would have told you all about it in the car, Madame, but you both were asleep."

"I seem to have missed quite a mysterious happening, straight from Mr. Alfred Hitchcock!" said Alma with a deep laugh. "We will not be hearing from him again," said Nelson reassuringly.

Chapter Seventy

"Oh hello, Elizabeth dear, how nice of you to call. Yes, we had a lovely time in Oberammergau. Freddie thoroughly enjoyed it. By the by, I am planning a small 'end of summer' luncheon just for the family, so to speak, and you are of course family to me. It must be on Saturday, as I want Louise and the girls to come. Sunday is the formal get-together at church and everyone will be there, so I must attend," said Alma.

Elizabeth accepted and said she was looking forward to hearing about the trip. Alma summoned Bertha and Bessie and told them her plans for the luncheon. They were pleased to be included as family and would make a grand soufflé for the occasion and serve all the remaining summer wine. Alfred offered to pick blackberries and make sure that the hedges were cut evenly around the terrace. He had purchased a pair of lederhosen pants in Oberammergau and was anxious to wear them to the luncheon. Louise offered to bake some cookies and Millicent and Suzanne would make the place cards.

Alma called Louise to see if she would allow the girls to start dancing classes, commencing in October, on Tuesday afternoons at the Yacht Club. Louise was so delighted and had thought about the classes but she knew a personal invitation from the committee was necessary. Alma assured Louise that all would be in order and she should expect the invitations next week and not to worry about the expense. Alma suggested Louise take the girls to Fancy This and buy them proper dresses for the dance classes. Alma had already called the shop and all the charges were to be put on Alma's account. Alma was determined to make sure the two girls had every social advantage available. She knew what a wretched cad their father had turned out to be and Louise was in no position to handle these things. After all, she was their Almama!

Saturday was beautiful and warm enough at noon for all to gather on the terrace for cocktails before luncheon. Alfred wore his Bavarian lederhosen and Angel had a beautiful scarf around her neck. Alma immediately recognized the scarf as one of hers, but said nothing as she watched Angel chewing on the ends of it. Elizabeth arrived in a new silk dress and shawl perfectly suited for Autumn. She wore a brown felt beret with orange and yellow ribbons and her long hair flopped around her hips. Alfred made a joke and said that he was going to take the garden shears to her hair and trim it as he had the hedges. Elizabeth gave Alfred her evil eye and Alfred knew to be quiet.

Louise wore the very attractive suit she had purchased for a luncheon with the librarians and the straw hat given to her by Alma. The girls were dressed in the party dresses given to them by Alma. Millicent had flowers in her hair. Suzanne did not want flowers in her hair, as she was afraid that a bee might be in the flower. "Have you ever been stung by a bee?" Alfred asked. "Yes, once when Daddy was living here."

Nelson arrived looking very handsome in the clothes Tony had purchased for him when they went to Paris. He sat down next to Suzanne and she smiled up at him. Everyone had a glass of summer wine and Alma was about to make a toast when Bessie came running in with a hatbox, saying, "Madame, I just tripped over this box in the back pantry. I do not know where it came from nor when it was delivered."

"Oh, Madame, my apologies please," said Nelson. "It was delivered the day you and Mr. Alfred left for Germany and I put it in the back pantry and promptly forgot all about it what with all the troubles with that Wentworth."

"Well, let's not just sit here. Bessie, get some scissors and we will open this mystery package." Alma took off the outer wrapping and recognized the box was from the shop in London where she had all her hats designed by Mary. "This is very odd, as I did not order any more hats for the Fall season," said Alma with great interest as she opened the box. Alma pulled out a black felt hat with a black veil and enormous sapphire blue peacock feathers curling all around.

"My, Alma, what an original hat. You shall be the belle of the ball this season," exclaimed Elizabeth.

"Yes, at all the funerals," said Alma as she sat trying to figure it all out. "I am calling Mary immediately, as there has been a huge mistake. This is a very expensive hat with these peacock feathers and I have never seen it before. She must have put the wrong address on the package."

"Madame, should I hold the soufflé for a bit?" asked Bessie.

"No, Bessie, it will just collapse and we do not want that," said Alma. Nelson called Alma from the hall and said, "Madame, I have Miss Mary on the phone and have told her what has happened and she wishes to speak with you."

"Mary, for the sake of heaven, what in the world is going on?" Alma was quiet on the phone and slumped down in the chair while she listened to Mary: "A very attractive gentleman came into my store and said he had been sent by you to pick out a hat, have it charged to your account and delivered to your home. I was very impressed with his choice, as that hat was one of my specialties I constructed for the Fall show. He insisted that I part with it and I felt sure you would be pleased with the hat. Is there a problem with the hat, Madame Boeld?"

"Mary, did he have a walking stick with initials engraved in the gold handle?"

"Why yes, he did, and I admired it and he said it had been in his family for years. I'm telling you, Madame Boeld, he can put his slippers under my bed anytime he wants," Mary said with a boisterous laugh.

"Mary, he is an imposter and is in jail as we speak. Were the charges put on my account?" Alma asked.

Mary went to look up the charges, and when she told Alma what they were, Alma screamed and hung up the phone. "Nelson, call that detective and tell him to come over here immediately!"

Everyone sat still and just looked at one another. Suzanne whispered to her mother that she was hungry, so Louise went into the kitchen and asked Bessie if Suzanne could come into the kitchen and sit with her. Bessie came out to the terrace and whispered to Suzanne to come to the kitchen for some goodies. Suzanne took Bessie's hand and stuck her tongue out at Millicent. Millicent rolled her eyes and went over to get a closer look at the mysterious hat. "There is a card in the box, Almama, there is a card in the box!" Alma came quickly and took the envelope from Millicent. The card read "sapphire feathers for sapphire eyes."

Nelson returned to the terrace and told Alma that he had spoken with the chief of police and that Detective Stone would be here shortly. "Nelson, is he the same detective who came when I was away?" Alma asked. "Yes, Madame, he was here previously with his partner but he will be coming alone today."

"Alma, put the hat on and let us see how you look," said Alfred. Alma put on the hat and everyone started to clap and Alfred whistled. Alma went to the hall mirror and started to arrange the feathers around the brim. One of the larger feathers curled itself around her ear and tickled her nose. Everyone began to giggle and Angel barked as she ran to the door. Nelson opened the door and shook hands with Detective Stone.

"We meet again, Mr. Nelson. What has happened now? I just received a message to come directly to the house. Is anyone hurt?"

"No, no physical damage. Madame Boeld will speak with you." Detective Stone went out to the terrace and everyone introduced themselves. Alma explained about the hat and that she had not ordered it and was positive it was sent by this Sir Robert Wentworth. Detective Stone examined the hatbox thoroughly, read the card and scrutinized the hat.

"My oh my, Madame Boeld, this hat must be made of real sapphires!"

"He charged the hat to my account, Detective Stone," said Alma very angrily.

"What do you wish to do about this hat, Madame Boeld?"

"I do not know what to do. That is why we summoned you," Alma replied.

"I am a very good judge of ladies hats," said Detective Stone. "It just so happens that my grandmother was a hat maker and as a small boy she would make me sit on a stool and wear the hat she was designing." Everyone giggled. "Oh, I did not mind it, as she told me wonderful stories as she was working on the hat. Would you be so good as to model the hat, Madame?"

Alma said nothing and looked at him as if he were crazy. "Oh, be a sport, Alma, and put on the hat again," said Alfred.

Alma put the hat on and then adjusted it perfectly in the hall mirror. She put the peacock feathers all around the brim and some falling off to the sides. "It certainly is a beauty and suits you perfectly, what with the feathers and your sapphire eyes, Madame," said Detective Stone.

"Detective, you are here to advise me what to do about the hat and the charges and I have not heard any advice as yet!" Alma declared.

"Madame, you have two choices. One is to return the hat and take a credit to your account. We will record the incident and add it the other charges against Mr. Wentworth, who by the way has no more right to be called 'sir' than that dog over there. He is awaiting a trial in Geneva. He has multiple passports with false identifications and, from the reports, apparently has invaded bank accounts of more than ten women we know of when they were visiting Baden-Baden. Also in St. Tropez. This fellow makes tracks and gets in and out of countries at the drop of a hat, so to speak," said the detective.

"That is a clever and timely little joke, but get on with my second choice, if you please, Detective Stone," said Alma.

"If you like the hat and wish to keep it and pay for it, we will not be able to press charges, as keeping the hat would imply acceptance. We will simply make note of the incident on his record," explained Detective Stone.

Elizabeth raised her hand and started waving it, attracting attention. "What is it, Elizabeth dear?" asked Alma.

"Maybe you could wear the hat to the formal party after church on Sunday and then return it to Mary at the shop on Monday."

"Oh, for the sake of heaven, Elizabeth, do not be such a ninny" said Alma, rolling her eyes.

"No, Madame Boeld," Detective Stone explained, "that would not be an option. However, I will share with you that about ten days ago a lady from London called a detective in her district and reported the same sort of incident as you are experiencing."

"I see," said Alma, crossing her legs and looking out upon her garden, "and what may I ask did she do about it all and in which district does she live?"

"I believe she resides in Belgravia," answered Detective Stone.

"My, our Mr. Wentworth certainly knew what he was doing, did he not?" declared Alma while clearing her throat and raising her eyebrows.

"He apparently charms the ladies and he did manage to get away with it for quite a while, but his tricks are over," said Detective Stone.

"I would like to discuss this with my family," said Alma, "and I will call you on Monday. However, may I suggest that you join us for luncheon? I will have another place set at the table. Our cook is making a grand soufflé and you know how they flop if not served immediately."

"How kind of you, Madame Boeld, but I have work to do at the precinct and should be on my way. Think it over thoroughly and we will chat on Monday. I do hope your soufflé has not flopped." Millicent and Suzanne both burst out laughing. Detective Stone winked at the girls as Nelson ushered him out.

"Oh my, he came in a police car," said Alfred. "I wish he had turned the sirens on!" exclaimed Alfred as he raced out the door to catch a glimpse of the departing vehicle. Bessie came out of the kitchen wiping her hands on her apron and asking "Is everyone ready for soufflé?"

Millicent jumped up and ran into the dining room, as she had not put the place cards around the table. She had made a drawing of where she wanted each person to sit. Each place card had a different color paper flower attached to it and she wrote the names in script. Alma was at the head of the table. Millicent put herself to the left of Alma with Nelson next to her and then Bessie on the other side of Nelson. Alfred was placed at the other end of the table with Bertha to his left. Louise was seated to Alma's right with Suzanne next to her and Elizabeth squeezed in between Suzanne and Bessie. Alfred remarked how clever she was to place Bessie and Bertha near the kitchen. Millicent stood up and curtsied.

Bessie and Bertha brought out two soufflés and everyone clapped. "How in the world did you both manage to have these come out so beautifully with all the to-do about the hat going on?" asked Alma. Everyone clapped and Suzanne began to sweep Elizabeth's hair away from her chair. "Mum, this lady's hair is in my way." whispered Suzanne to her mother. "Shhhh, grin and bear it," said Louise. Alma overheard the remark and smiled at Louise.

Alfred stood up and remarked that he and his sister had been to Oberammergau and had a wonderful time but this was his home and he wanted to toast everyone: "You are our family and we love you all."

Alma stood and said, "Here's to family and being together."

Millicent thought for a moment and then stood. "I have never made a toast before," she said nervously. "But I learned that family does not mean that you have to be related by blood. Isn't that right, Almama? On the train Mr. Wentworth thought you were my real grandmother and you said we were not related by blood. Isn't that right, Almama?"

"Yes, that is correct," said Alma.

Nelson stood up and said, "I never had a real family and I consider myself most fortunate to be a part of this family. Madame, you have been most kind to me and I shall be at your service as long as you need me."

Bertha stood up and Bessie followed. "Madame took us in after the war when we had no home at all," said Bertha. "This is the only real home we know and we plan to stay until our toes curl up." They both began to cry and excused themselves, went into the kitchen and came back smiling, carrying the two remaining carafes of the summer wine.

Angel managed to get through the swinging door and jumped onto Alfred's lap. Alfred did not say anything. He just looked down at Angel and softly patted her head.

Louise looked at Millicent and smiled, stood up and began to cry. "I am so sorry. I did not mean to cry because I am really so happy to be here with you all. You all have been so kind to us and I want to thank you for your many kindnesses. And here's to Eric also." Louise raised her glass and then sat down. She took Suzanne's hand, squeezed it and cried into her napkin. Suzanne looked over to Millicent, who motioned for her to stand up.

Suzanne stood up and smiled at everyone and said "thank you" and sat down. Louise hugged Suzanne and continued to sob.

Alma stood up and said how glad she was that Louise remembered to toast Eric as he certainly was a family member for the summer and the good news is that he and his family will be visiting next summer with their daughter and grandchildren. Louise looked up and smiled.

"Well, that is the end of the summer wine," said Alma. "Let's all return to the terrace and have the cookies baked by Louise." Angel heard the word cookie and ran around the table sniffing the floor.

The hat and hatbox were in the middle of the floor on the terrace. Nelson told Alma he had noticed Detective Stone putting the card in his pocket. Alma shrugged and said, "It's all business with Stone." Bessie and Bertha brought in the cookies and sat down. Alfred picked up the hat, put it on his head and jokingly said, "How much am I offered for this smashing hat? It is a one of a kind and priceless. The highest bidder gets the hat!"

Everyone laughed and looked at Alma. Alma stood and put on the hat. Everyone clapped and Alfred whistled. "We shall take a vote and see what this family thinks about the hat. All those in favor of keeping the hat raise your hands," ordered Alma.

Everyone was quiet for a moment and then all raised their hands and shouted "keep the hat, keep the hat!"

Alma adjusted the hat to different angles and paraded around the terrace several times, stopping at the mirror in the hall to admire it once more. Returning to the terrace, she said, "Very well, the hat seems to fit quite nicely and the feathers sway and dance just slightly enough to make it interesting."

"It is, without a doubt, the most handsome hat I have ever seen on your head," said Alfred.

"It would be a shame to return such a distinguished and villainous hat," said Alma with one of her deep laughs.

"It quite suits you to a T, Madame," added Nelson.

"I shall keep it and pay the price. Imagine wearing this hat, selected and sent by a notorious swindler, to the formal gathering at church on Sunday. What a way to commence the Fall social season!" said Alma with laughter, twirling around in circles by herself.

Alfred put on a Strauss waltz record and soon everyone was dancing around the terrace. Elizabeth danced with Alfred, who had Angel on his shoulder. Angel batted her hair about, but Elizabeth did not seem concerned. Louise and Suzanne danced together and laughed at Bessie and Bertha, who had removed their aprons and were doing an Irish jig to the waltz music. Nelson waltzed smoothly with Millicent, who was trying to follow his dancing steps.

"Look Almama, over there by the steps. Little Lucy is back and she has something in her mouth," exclaimed Millicent, jumping up and down. Everyone stopped dancing and quietly watched little Lucy go to the middle of the terrace and carefully place her two baby kittens on the tissue paper inside the hatbox.

The End

Born in Boston, Mass., Patty Dickson spent her childhood in Brooklyn Heights, N.Y. She attended Packer Collegiate Institute until the seventh grade, when she became a boarder at High Mowing School in Wilton, N.H., a total antithesis to her city life. At the time she did not own a pair of blue jeans and had never lived in farming country. The three years she spent at High Mowing turned out to be a positive experience, as she learned to survive and respect totally new surroundings. She then transferred to and graduated from The Knox School in Cooperstown, N.Y., where she formed what were to be lifelong friendships. She attended Wheelock College in Boston and then taught school for many years. Patty has been blessed by living in many interesting places in the United States and Europe. In 2012, she left Princeton, N.J., and retired to Hilton Head Island, S.C., where she lives with her rescue dog, Sophie, and her cat, Peaches. All are enjoying the island life. *A Fine How Do You Do* is her first novel.

The author blowing out her 80th birthday candle.

"Sing like no one is listening
Love like you've never been hurt
Dance like nobody is watching
And live like it's heaven on earth."
-Mark Twain-

Printed in the United States
By Bookmasters